PRAISE FOR BARBARA TAYLOR SISSEL

"*Faultlines* is an in-depth portrayal of how one moment—and one mystery—can crack a family open. These compelling characters will stay with you long after the final reveal. Sissel's fans will not be disappointed."

—Catherine McKenzie, bestselling author of *Hidden* and *Fractured*

"This is that rare sort of book that grabs you from the very first line and refuses to let go. Beautifully written, intricately plotted, and perfectly executed, *Faultlines* is an intimate look at the unraveling of a family after a tragic accident. Sissel weaves a clever web of emotional fallout as she alternates seamlessly between two storylines that converge in a devastating way. An atmospheric, emotional, suspenseful journey that will stay with you for a long time after you've finished the last page."

—Kristin Harmel, international bestselling author of *The Sweetness of Forgetting*

"In *Faultlines*, Barbara Taylor Sissel brilliantly weaves a compelling, suspenseful, and emotional family drama. Through a multitude of twists and turns, each character is faced with difficult decisions that fracture family bonds while wondering who they can trust, let alone whether or not they can recover from the tragedy. As the parent of a teenager, I immediately connected with the story and the characters, and was hooked from page one. Ms. Sissel is a masterful storyteller when it comes to suspense and an exceptional writer. It's a definite page-turner!"

—Kerry Lonsdale, bestselling author of *Everything We Keep*

D1398615

THE
TRUTH
WE
BURY

THE
TRUTH
WE
BURY

BARBARA
TAYLOR SISSEL

LAKE UNION
PUBLISHING

Published by Lake Union Publishing, Seattle

www.apub.com

Amazon, the Amazon logo, and Lake Union Publishing are trademarks of Amazon.com, Inc., or its affiliates.

ISBN-13: 9781477823989
ISBN-10: 1477823980

Cover design by Rex Bonomelli

Printed in the United States of America

For B2, Barbara Poelle, agent extraordinaire, in celebration of five books and five great years.

1

Lily saw the gray sedan the moment she turned the corner. It was parked across the street from her condo, but instinct warned her that the occupants, a couple of beefy-looking men, were cops, and they were waiting for her. Lily drove past them as if she lived elsewhere, in a different life. As if the street she lived on didn't loop through a series of lush, artfully planned medians that would eventually lead straight back to her own driveway near the entrance to her gated community, where the men—detectives, if her experience was any teacher—waited. She backed her foot off the accelerator, glancing in the rearview mirror. Would they follow her, force her to the curb, demand she exit her vehicle? She remembered, although it was long ago now, how the road grit bit into her knees. Eyes front, she circled the cul-de-sac. She needed a moment to gather her composure.

She wouldn't tell them anything, she decided. Whatever they asked, she'd play dumb. They'd fall for it, in all likelihood. She was blonde after all. Steeling herself, she headed back in the direction she'd come from, hitting the remote for the garage door, watching it rise, knowing the men saw it, too. They exited their car on cue, as if a trigger had been pulled, waiting in her driveway while she parked in the garage. She thought of lowering the door, barricading herself in the house. But such tactics would only delay the inevitable. She got out of her BMW and joined them in the driveway.

"Can I help you?" she asked, sounding far more certain than she felt.

"Lily Isley?" The taller of the two men addressed her.

She was in the process of confirming her identity, but he talked over her.

"I'm Detective Hatchett, and this is my partner, Detective Lawlor. We're from the Dallas Police Department."

The two produced their identification, their movements efficient and precise.

Lily caught a glimpse of their shoulder-holstered weapons. Her pulse tapped lightly in her ears.

"Axel Jebediah Isley—that's your son, right?" Hatchett asked. "Goes by AJ?"

There it was. AJ's name, his full legal name. She had anticipated hearing it, but still her knees weakened, and a dark, long-held sense of the inevitable collapsed inside her. This was it, the other shoe. Dropping with the weight of a stone, an anvil, cleaving her chest.

"Yes," she said. "AJ is my son. What is this about?"

"Is he here?" asked Lawlor. He was shorter than Lily, and round, with a belligerent jut to his chin.

"No." *Don't answer more than the question,* instructed a voice in her brain. Was it Edward's advice she was remembering, his caution from before?

"When was the last time you saw him?"

"Last week. He came for dinner. What is this about?" Lily asked again.

"Have you talked to him recently?" Hatchett asked.

"Do I have to answer your questions? Don't you have to have a warrant—" Lily broke off. What if AJ was already sitting in a cell, and these men—these cops—were playing mind games with her? "I'm not saying another word until you tell me what this is about."

Glancing around, Hatchett said maybe she wanted to go inside. "You could sit down," he suggested.

Was the news that bad? Lily turned without asking and led the detectives through the condo's front door rather than through the garage. These men were not casual visitors. They wouldn't be settling themselves on the bar stools at her granite-topped island while indulging in lattes and idle chatter. She ushered them across the vaulted foyer and into her formal living room, where a pair of white leather–upholstered sofas with a matching ottoman flanked a marble fireplace. Her white baby-grand piano, a gift from her husband, Paul, on their twenty-fifth wedding anniversary three years ago, sat in front of tall bay windows, overlooking a carefully manicured landscape.

This time of year, ahead of the baking Texas heat, the lawn was as lush as velvet and meandered through an arrangement of perennial beds filled with globe-shaped boxwoods, the freer forms of azaleas, and clumps of agapanthus, irises, and daylilies. A crew came twice a week to tend the grounds. It was one in the package of perks that came with living in a condominium development. Paul had neither the time nor the inclination to do his own yard work. Besides, as he would point out, he owned the place. How would it look if he were to be seen out there in his shirtsleeves pushing a mower? It was a joke. His joke. Lily smiled for every new audience to whom he posed the question. She always smiled.

But not now. Not for these cops. She saw how they looked around. The one named Lawlor had his petulant rosebud of a mouth quirked into a kind of sneer. It was the sort of expression people wore when they were envious and didn't want it to show. She set her purse, a tiny pocket of finely stitched blue, yellow, and hot-pink suede, on the ottoman. The bohemian pop of color looked somehow wrong against the white leather upholstery. Who had chosen it—the white leather, the creamy linen accent pillows, the silk drapery, the lovely impressionistic art on the walls, all of it done in such good taste? The room might have been found in a magazine spread from *Southern Living*. Who lived here? Lately, she was unable to imagine the couple, the family—

"Mrs. Isley? Can you tell us where your son is?" Lawlor was studying her and not his surroundings now.

"He's twenty-five, for God's sake, and he lives across town. I can't possibly know where he is every minute." Alarm made her shrill. If Paul could hear her . . . Lily caught her torso in her arms. "Have you contacted my husband?"

"Do you think he knows where your son is?" Lawlor asked.

"What is this about?"

"When did you last speak to AJ?" Hatchett's voice, sounding more reasonable, drew Lily's attention.

"Yesterday afternoon. He wanted me to remind his father they were to meet this morning for the final fittings of their tuxedos. AJ's getting married on the twenty-first." Lily named the date two and a half weeks away.

"Where were they meeting?"

"Manheim's in the Village." It was an upscale gentleman's boutique near Turtle Creek.

"Not AJ's apartment?"

"No, they were going to have lunch after—where is Paul?"

"Mrs. Isley, according to your husband, he waited for AJ at Manheim's for half an hour this morning, and when your son didn't show up, he went to his apartment. After no one answered the door, your husband let himself in. He has a key?"

"Yes." Frightened now, Lily lowered herself to the sofa's edge, feeling the air-conditioned chill from the leather bleed through her slacks.

"Your husband found a young woman in your son's apartment, Mrs. Isley. She was dead. Apparently, she was strangled and stabbed numerous times."

Lily stared at Detective Lawlor, head empty and silent.

"AJ wasn't there," Lawlor went on. "He's not answering his cell phone, and when we called his boss at Café Blue, he said AJ didn't show for his shift last night."

"What are you saying?"

Lawlor started to answer.

She cut him off. "Where is Paul?"

"At AJ's apartment with the police, unless they've already taken him downtown. He called 911 when he found her body."

Lily dropped her gaze. Paul had called 911, but he hadn't called her. He'd let her be blindsided. But it was possible he hadn't thought how it might affect her, being accosted by law enforcement with such horrible news. In fact, he might not have thought of her at all.

"Do you know who the woman is? It's not Shea Gallagher, is it? She's AJ's fiancée." Lily wondered how she would bear it. But AJ adored Shea; he wouldn't hurt her.

"Becca Westin is the victim's name." Detective Hatchett looked up from his notepad. "Do you know her?"

"No." Lily heard herself answer through the watery rush of her relief. "I mean, I don't know her personally."

"But you recognize the name," Hatchett said.

"Yes. She's one of Shea's bridesmaids." Lily thought for a moment. "I met her at Shea's bridal shower—"

"But your son, Axel—AJ—was a friend of Becca's? Were they close?" Hatchett asked.

"No, I don't think so." Lily looked away, pained anew at how little she knew of her son's life. It wasn't deliberate, nor was it out of anger or resentment. She could blame Paul, and sometimes she did, but he couldn't have assigned her to a back room in AJ's life if she hadn't allowed it.

"Would you know of a grudge between them? Could they have had a fight?" Hatchett asked.

"I don't remember AJ ever mentioning her." Lily pulled her cell phone from her purse. "I want to call him now." She switched her gaze between the detectives, and when neither of them objected, she dialed AJ's number and waited, heart clamoring. The detectives watched her; she felt unnerved by their stares. She felt under suspicion. She willed AJ to answer, but he didn't, and she was forced to leave a message. "Please call me when you get this," she said, and no more.

Ending the connection, she glanced at Hatchett. "He's not answering."

"Yeah, like I said, we've been trying him, too." Hatchett's glance on Lily's lingered, becoming pointed, intent.

She felt dazed. "You can't think he's—" She paused, holding the word *involved* in her mouth. Of course he was involved. A young woman was dead in his apartment.

"Can you think of anyplace he might be, Mrs. Isley?" Detective Lawlor asked, not unkindly.

The ranch, Lily thought, the xL. It was the one place AJ might go if he felt threatened. She debated whether to tell them. *Anything you say may be used against you.* The warning surfaced from some half-forgotten history in her mind along with brief impressions—metal bracelets cinched around her wrists, a sheriff's hand on her head ducking her through the squad-car door. Inside, the reek of sweat and old vomit mixed with an underscore of fear had made her gag.

"Your father has a ranch south of here in the Hill Country, doesn't he? The xL? Outside Wyatt?" Lawlor's voice got Lily's attention.

Of course they would already know, she thought. She didn't bother answering. Lawlor allowed no time anyway.

"We've been trying to get in touch with your dad, Jeb Axel, down there. He's not picking up, either."

"Well, if you're asking me where he is, again, he's a grown man—"

"What about his housekeeper, Winona Ayala? Or her son, Erik? Erik Ayala is a close friend of AJ's, isn't he?"

"Yes, but what do either Winona or Erik have to do—"

Lawlor didn't let her finish. "What do you know about Erik Ayala, Mrs. Isley?"

"What do you mean, what do I know about him?" *Everything. I changed his diapers right along with AJ's,* she might have said. Erik was older; his diapers had been toddler size to AJ's infant size. She and Winona had mothered both boys. And before that, Winona had mothered Lily from the time Lily's own mother was diagnosed with end-stage ovarian cancer when Lily was ten. Win was home to Lily; Winona was her safe place, although they hadn't been as close in recent years.

Hatchett took over, peppering her with more questions. "Would Erik know where AJ is?"

"You'd have to ask him."

"His mother has her own house down there, on xL property, doesn't she? Erik lived there with her until recently, but now he's moved into Wyatt, isn't that right?"

"Why are you asking when it's so obvious you have the answers?"

"We're just trying to gather as much information as we can, Mrs. Isley, to help us find your son."

Hatchett said, "AJ and Shea Gallagher met at the Art Institute, the culinary school, here in Dallas, where they're both enrolled."

"Yes," Lily agreed, when truthfully she wasn't sure where they'd met. "They finished up their last semester a week ago."

"Is Shea still in town?"

"No, she's gone home to her mother's in Wyatt to get things ready for the wedding. Shea and AJ are being married in her mother's garden there."

"Lady we spoke to at the school said they're going into the restaurant business?" Hatchett looked interested, but for all Lily knew, it was an act.

"It's more than that, really. They want to open a farm-to-fork here in the city."

Hatchett turned to Lawlor. "That's where everything is locally grown and cooked fresh."

Lawlor said he knew that.

AJ's ambition to become a chef bewildered Paul. He characterized it as "playing around," as in, "You can quit playing around now and do something real, something that'll earn a decent living." Lily might not have chosen that path for AJ, either, but it was a safer road than the one he'd been headed down before he enlisted.

Lawlor read from his notepad. "Axel and Erik joined the marines back in 2011. Erik couldn't hack basic and washed out, but your son went on to serve in Afghanistan." He looked up at Lily. "That cause any problems between Ayala and your son that you know of?"

"Hardly. It must be there in your notes, Detective. Erik is AJ's best man. Does that sound as if there's a problem?"

Hatchett fired another question. "Your son's had some legal trouble in the past, hasn't he?"

"I'm sure you already know the answers to both questions—to every question you're asking me." Lily's bravado was a fraud.

"He was arrested on a murder charge—let's see—" Hatchett consulted his notepad.

"Six years ago, in 2010," Lily said. "He was cleared then, too."

"Yeah," Hatchett interrupted. "We know about the insufficient evidence—"

Lily talked over him. "He served his country, took his life in his hands, came home wounded—" The threat of tears stopped her. She wouldn't let these men see her cry.

Lawlor said, "Wounded mentally, right? We heard he's had emotional issues, problems with anger management, depression. There have been calls in the past. Folks at his apartment complex have complained about him yelling, fighting—"

"He has nightmares—"

"Your son was jailed last year, wasn't he, Mrs. Isley, and again a few months ago, for assault?" Lawlor's eyes were hard.

"He didn't start either fight—"

"But he finished both, didn't he? Landed one guy in the hospital. He's lucky his victim dropped the charges." Lawlor smirked.

Lily didn't answer.

Detective Hatchett handed her a business card. "If you hear from your son, ask him to give us a call, will you?"

"He's a person of interest in the matter of Ms. Westin's murder. We've issued a BOLO, a be on the lookout." Lawlor explained these things as Lily was showing the detectives out. She closed the door and, returning to the living room, picked up her cell phone, hunting through her directory for Erik's contact information. Her phone went off before she found it.

"Paul?" His name was a question, a plea. "The police have just left—"

"Listen to me, Lily. I don't have much time." He talked over her. "If you hear from AJ, tell him to keep his mouth shut. I've got a call in to Jerry."

Paul's attorney, Lily thought. His corporate attorney. Not Edward Dana, AJ's former criminal attorney. It was three years since she'd seen Edward. She wondered if he remembered, if he thought of her at all anymore.

"Lily?"

She straightened. "Is it true, Paul? Did you go into AJ's apartment and find—find Becca Westin—"

"My God, Lily, it was the worst—I've never seen anything—even when I was in Nam, Cambodia—she was stabbed. The cops couldn't say how many times, but there's blood everywhere in AJ's apartment, the bed, the floor. She—somebody had pulled down her pants. She was just a kid—just a kid, Lily—"

"AJ couldn't have done that, Paul."

"What if she did something that set him off? You know how he can—"

"He couldn't, Paul," Lily repeated, tight-jawed.

Paul changed direction. "The detective here, Sergeant Bushnell, says AJ and Becca dated. Do you remember meeting her?"

"Not with him, no." AJ had seldom brought his girlfriends home. Shea was the exception, the one who, since he'd been back from Afghanistan, had broken through his defenses. "I did meet Becca, though, last month in Wyatt, at Shea's bridal shower."

"You think AJ's been in touch with Erik? Have you heard from him? I tried getting hold of him, but he's not picking up."

"The detectives who were here asked a lot of questions about him. I have a feeling they think he's involved, maybe hiding AJ. But you know, AJ might be with Shea at her mother's."

"Bushnell asked me for her contact information."

"You gave it to them?"

"Hell, yes, I gave it to them. I want them to find our son, Lily, even if he—especially if he—before something worse happens. Something none of us can live with."

Like what? Lily wondered. A shootout with the police? Or himself? Would AJ kill himself if he had done this thing? Dread fisted in her stomach.

"You know the cops won't let him go so easily this time."

Lily went to stand at the bank of windows that overlooked the garden. "I don't know anything at this point, Paul."

"He's not nineteen, not a kid this time, mixed up with the wrong crowd. The cops are going to look hard at him for this. They're going to think he got away with murder once; now he's done it again."

"That was a whole different—"

"I'm just telling you, Lily. He made fools out of them the last time. They won't stand by and let it happen again, especially now he's been diagnosed with all the PTSD bullshit. You can bet they'll use it to burn him. Mentally unstable war vet and all that crap."

Paul made it sound like a joke, as if the trauma AJ had endured, going to war, had had no effect, and to speak of it in terms of mental and emotional harm was shameful, unmanly. But Lily couldn't tell Paul anything about war; he'd seen his share of action. He knew about the damage—enough to keep it to himself. The only wounds that were real were the ones he could see, the missing arm or leg, the gaping abdominal wound. AJ had come home in pristine condition. *"Not a scratch on him,"* Paul had said, and somehow he made it sound like an insult. There was little mention of how, while under siege from enemy fire, AJ had carried a man with half his face shot off to safety, slung over his back like a sack of rocks.

"You think he did it." Lily's anger was tinged with disbelief. "You think he stabbed that girl to death."

She heard Paul's breath go, and the despair in his voice when he said he didn't know what to think. "He's different, Lily."

"He's better now. Since Shea," she added.

"He's been jailed twice in six months for assault. Have you forgotten? And last month at the restaurant in front of Shea—"

"I'm not forgetting anything, Paul." She wasn't going to think about the restaurant incident where AJ had made a scene, shouting at the waiter, even raising his fist to him, when the poor man confused their orders. AJ had been red in the face. *"Mad enough to kill,"* Paul had said at the time. Shea was the one who had calmed him, who had brought

AJ back to himself. He'd apologized then, profusely, to everyone present, including the waiter.

"I think you need to be prepared." Paul suggested it softly.

Prepared? Lily puzzled over the word. How did one *prepare* for the eventuality that their son might have strangled and stabbed someone to death?

"I've got to go," Paul said. "Bushnell wants me downtown. You'll wait there in case AJ comes home?"

"I doubt he'll come here," Lily said, looking around. Paul was one of the most successful real estate developers in the Dallas/Fort Worth metroplex. His specialty was commercial property, but he built residential projects, too. They'd lived in several of them. Finished only last year, the condo development was his latest venture. AJ had never really moved in; he'd never called it home. He had told Lily once that while he was overseas, he'd dreamed of the old clapboard house at the ranch almost nightly.

"What do you mean? Lily, what are you going to do?"

"I'm going to try and find AJ, Paul, before the police do."

• • •

It took only minutes to change into jeans, a fitted tee, and her old western boots. She brushed her hair into a ponytail at the back of her neck, and once it was done, she felt marginally better, more like herself. She packed an overnight bag with an extra pair of jeans, a couple more tees, and a flannel shirt. It was early May, but the nights could still be chilly in the Hill Country. She added underthings and her toiletries. She traded purses, exchanging the frivolous suede poof for a worn, hand-tooled leather pouch that more closely resembled a saddlebag than a handbag, and then, before going downstairs, she sat on the side of the bed and called Winona, anxious for her to answer. But she didn't.

"Winona," Lily said when the voice mail picked up, and she couldn't help the quaver in her voice. "Something's happened—" *Bad.* She started to add that but didn't. "I'm on my way there, to the ranch, but when you get this, will you call me? If you see AJ, tell him—tell him I need to speak to him right away. Okay?" Lily blinked at the ceiling, thinking of how much she felt like the child she'd once been, sorely troubled, first by her mother's untimely death, then as a very young woman when there'd been all that terrible business in Arizona. Winona had been there for her then, too, holding Lily close, murmuring comfort . . . *"Vas a estar bien, querida . . . Ahora estoy aquí."*

Lily brought her glance down. "I should be there around four," she said. Ending the call, she thought about calling her dad. But no. She wouldn't tell him she was coming. He'd know something was up, and she didn't want to be trapped into giving him the news over the phone. Hearing AJ was in trouble—again—might just break him.

• • •

Downstairs, Lily got into the car, and after setting her tote on the passenger seat, she got her phone out of her purse and tried AJ's number, willing him to answer. But there was only a sequence of rings, one . . . two . . . six, and this time not even his voice mail picked up.

2

Dru's cell phone played through a range of notes as she was pulling the second pan of lemon bars from the oven. She could let the call roll to voice mail, or she could shout for Shea to come take it. But no. Some snaky sense of dread had her setting the pan on the counter and reaching for her phone. Her heart eased when she saw Amy's name in the caller ID window.

"We're running out of time to change the menu," Dru teased.

"Oh, Dru, I'm not calling about the luncheon." Amy sounded upset. "I just heard some news from Ken—it's not good."

Ken Carter was Amy's brother and a patrol sergeant on the police force in Wyatt.

"What's happened?" Dru's dread returned.

"I don't even know how to tell you, and when I think of Shea—"

Dru liked Amy; she really did. They'd met while Dru was still teaching sixth grade full-time at Wyatt Elementary, and even then, Amy, a kindergarten teacher, could take forever to get to the point. "Just say it, okay?" Dru suggested.

"The police in Dallas found Becca Westin dead this morning in an apartment there. Ken said she was murdered."

There was a moment of utter, blind incredulity, then Dru's startled "What?" And on its heels, "Are you sure? What was she doing there? She's in town here. Shea told me just the other day Becca was staying in Wyatt for the summer with her folks."

"They found her car and her purse and identified her from her driver's license, Ken said. It's going to kill Shea, isn't it? Becca being her bridesmaid and all."

"Yes, but my God, I'm thinking of Joy and Gene." Dru named Becca's parents.

"I think someone, one of the deputies here in Wyatt who knows them, is on his way to tell them."

"But who would do such a thing? Do they know? Becca was—was so sweet and quiet, a little—"

"Angel," Amy supplied.

"Yes," Dru said, although she'd been thinking *mouse*, that Becca had always been as quiet as a mouse. "She was over here a day or two ago, helping us with wedding things—"

"Mom?"

Dru met Shea's anxious gaze. "Amy, I've got to go. Thank you for calling. The luncheon Friday, it's still on, right?" She wasn't really asking so much as she was delaying the moment when she'd have to face Shea. Dru knew the annual year-end event to honor Wyatt Elementary's teachers would take place. As heartless as it seemed, it was the nature of life for those who were outside an immediate zone of calamity to go on with their business, their routines.

Amy confirmed Dru's expectation and the date of the occasion.

"What happened?" Shea asked when Dru ended the call.

"That was Amy." Dru paused, searching for words, as if there might be some that were better. Finally, she just got it over as quickly as possible. "Honey, there's no easy way to tell you. Amy heard from Ken—her brother in town who's a patrol sergeant?—that police in Dallas found Becca dead this morning in an apartment there. Someone—she was murdered."

Dru held Shea's stare, and when she said nothing, when the color had drained from her face, Dru guided her to a chair in the breakfast nook, brought her a glass of water, and sat across from her, taking her hands. They were trembling, and Dru chafed them.

"I don't understand," Shea said.

"Well, I don't, either. Wasn't she home with her folks for summer break?"

"She was home for good," Shea said. "She wasn't going back to Dallas."

"Really? You didn't tell me that."

"Culinary school was only an experiment for her, a way to get out of Wyatt. She never liked to cook. You saw her. She'd come over, and I'd be all up to my elbows helping you with some job, but she never got into it with us."

Dru thought about it. "You're right. It never occurred to me before."

"Mama, are they sure it was Becca?"

"They found her car there. Her purse with her driver's license was in the apartment."

"But she was sick yesterday, in bed at her parents'. She didn't even go with us when we went to pick up the jars."

The mason jars. Shea had been searching for them for weeks. She was being married in the backyard, wearing her grandma's—Dru's mother's—bridal gown. Rather than a formal affair, Shea wanted a simple garden ceremony near sundown with dancing afterward that would begin at twilight. Dru wasn't a constant gardener, but the mostly messy riot of flowers and vine-covered cedar arbors had cottage charm. The roses, irises, and clematis were just coming into their first flush of blooms, enough to fill any number of mason jars. Shea wanted sunflowers, too, which they didn't have on hand and so far hadn't found a source for. But they had finally located an antiques shop near Fredericksburg that had a supply of old mason jars, and the girls—Shea and her bridal attendants, Kate Kincaid, who was her best friend and her maid of honor, and bridesmaids, Leigh Martindale and Vanessa Lacy—had gone to pick them up yesterday; they'd had lunch at one of the local wineries, made an occasion out of it.

This was the first Dru had heard that Becca hadn't gone along.

"She told us she'd been up vomiting all night long," Shea said. "We all talked about how we hoped we wouldn't get whatever bug she had." Her voice broke now and grief came, crumpling her features. Tears slid down her cheeks.

Dru found a tissue. "You were over there, then? You saw her?"

"No, she called. I was on my way there. I'd already picked up everyone else." Shea blew her nose. "Do the police know who did it? Did Amy say?"

"No," Dru answered.

Shea left the kitchen to call AJ.

Dru cut the lemon bars, wrapped them, and stowed them in the freezer. She was slicing red cabbage for the Asian pasta salad for the teachers' luncheon when Shea reappeared. Dru looked questioningly over her shoulder.

"He didn't answer. He's probably still with his dad. They were getting their final tux fittings this morning."

Dru rinsed the cutting board. She wondered if there might be enough of the pasta salad to take to the Westins. She could roast a chicken, make another pan of lemon bars. For a moment, thinking of them—Joy and Gene—her throat closed. What would she do if she were to lose Shea, especially this way, through an act of wanton violence?

"I tried calling Erik; he didn't pick up, either."

"Well, he must be with AJ, right?" Dru said. Erik was AJ's best man. He'd need his tux fitted, too.

"I don't think so. He just started his new job and couldn't get off. He's going up later this week, I think."

"Where's he working again?"

"Greeley." Shea named the Madrone County seat north of Wyatt. "He's a salesman at the Ford dealership there."

"As charming as he is, he should be good at that," Dru said. She thought Erik Ayala, with his dark Latino good looks and his white, white teeth, could probably sell glasses to a blind man. She liked Erik better than AJ, really. His heart was lighter, and he kept it in plain view.

But he was dating Kate. In fact, they'd recently become engaged, and Kate's mother, Charla, couldn't shut up about how much it thrilled her.

"Should we postpone the wedding?" Shea asked.

Dru turned off the tap, dried her hands. "It's only two and a half weeks away."

"How can we cancel it?" Shea turned up her hands.

"How can we go ahead when Becca's—there'll be a funeral in a few days."

"Oh, Mama." Shea's troubled gaze locked with Dru's.

"It's possible your uncle Kevin is already on his way." Dru's younger brother, the only family she had left, was coming from North Dakota, where he lived with his wife, Mary, and their two daughters, twelve-year-old Kara and fourteen-year-old Lacey.

"They're driving their RV, right? Making a vacation out of it?"

Dru nodded. "We're going to need to make a decision quickly."

"AJ's parents have way more people coming than we do."

"The bigwigs," Dru said. The politicos and socialites, Paul Isley's wheeler-dealer business associates. There was no telling what those ritzy, yacht-owning folks would make of the outdoor vintage-style wedding Shea and AJ planned. Not that she or Shea, or even AJ, cared. But Dru had wondered if she ought to say something to Lily about the meadow where the reception would be held, that it could be the ruin of the oh-so-fashionable stiletto heels some of those women seemed to favor wearing.

"I talked to Kate," Shea said. "Leigh and Vanessa, too. None of them knew Becca had gone to Dallas. They're as shocked as we are. They're coming over when they get off work." Kate was an ER nurse at Wyatt Regional. Dru thought Leigh and Vanessa worked for local businesses as administrative assistants.

Shea sat at the breakfast table.

"How about a latte?" Dru asked.

"I'll have one if you're making one for yourself."

Dru whipped milk by hand, and while it heated in the microwave, she poured the last of the breakfast coffee into each of two mugs, then capped them with the white froth. They weren't lattes, exactly; they were knockoffs. The poor man's latte. She and Shea loved them.

Dru brought the mugs to the table and sat down.

"We weren't really close anymore, you know?" Shea said. "I mean, I loved Becca like a sister; she's a big part of my past."

"You were friends from seventh grade; you, Becca, and Kate were like the Three Musketeers."

"I know, but I've told you, she changed in high school. We didn't have anything in common anymore."

Dru sipped her latte. *You and Kate changed.* That's what she could have said, but she wouldn't stir that pot again. Shea, and Kate, too, had finally outgrown that unsettled time. They weren't the *rebelle fleurs* now that they'd been when they'd run off from Kate's church camp in Abilene at age fifteen and, after lying about their ages, gotten the French phrase tattooed in lovely but alarming script on their necks à la Rihanna, their latest idol at the time. The tattoo artist had embellished his work, adding a long-stemmed pink rose beneath the words—a rose with thorns. Of course there were thorns.

And, of course, when the girls returned, camp officials had been forced to expel them. Dru and Charla had gone together to pick them up, both of them furious but for different reasons. While Charla had fretted over nonsense like what her church friends would think, Dru had worried about regret. Until then, there had only been face paint, dyed hair, and body piercings to contend with, damage that could be easily repaired. Neither Kate nor Shea had ever said whether they regretted their tattoos, but their hair nowadays was untreated. Kate was a streaky blonde like her mom, but Shea took after her dad. She had Rob's brown hair, a shade so dark it was almost black. Her body piercings were limited to her ears and navel and the tiny fleck of a diamond she wore on one side of her nose. Dru didn't mind it. She didn't even mind the tattoo so much anymore.

Shea said, "This is going to sound awful, but I only asked Becca to be a bridesmaid because she introduced me to AJ. I knew who he was at school, but she's how we actually met. Asking her to be a bridesmaid was a way to thank her."

"Well, I think you felt some loyalty to her, too. I remember you saying—to me, anyway—that it was as much for old times' sake."

"Yes, there was that," Shea admitted. "I feel bad, though, and so does Kate. We really wanted to be close with her, the way we were as kids. But Becca's—Becca was so quiet." Shea sat forward, nudging her untasted latte to one side. "I just don't get it. What was she doing in Dallas? Why did she go? Who was she with? She didn't have friends there, really, and it's not like she was putting herself out there, taking chances, hanging with losers."

"She wasn't dating anyone?"

"Not that I know of, and she would have said. Everyone liked Becca—" Shea stopped, and Dru heard it, too, the ethereal chime of Shea's cell phone, coming from her bedroom. "I bet that's AJ," she said, dashing from the kitchen.

Dru was loading their mugs into the dishwasher when Shea returned.

"It was Mrs. Gordon," she said, "my adviser from school. The police came to her office. They want to talk to me."

"Why?" Dru felt a jolt of alarm.

"She didn't know. I'm supposed to call this detective, Sergeant Troy Bushnell." Shea read the name from a scrap of paper. "They want to talk to AJ, too."

"AJ." Dru, unhappily, repeated her future son-in-law's name.

"He's still not answering his phone. I'm worried now. I think I should talk to him before I call this detective, don't you? I mean, what do they want with us? What could we possibly know? I wasn't in Dallas last night."

"AJ was."

"Yes, but he was working at Café Blue. He was supposed to work till midnight, but they weren't busy, so he took off early."

Dru turned. "Maybe they only want to question you about what sort of girl Becca was, whether you know anyone who might want to harm her, that sort of thing." Dru had no idea if she was right. She could only say what she'd heard watching shows like *Dateline* and the like. She was upset, though, as disturbed as Shea. What could the police possibly want with her?

"What should I do, Mom?"

Call and get it over with. That's what Dru was going to say when her cell phone went off. She picked it up, glancing at the ID window. "It's AJ's mom," she said.

"Answer it. She might know where AJ is."

Dru did so, reluctantly, formal in her greeting—she and Lily Isley would never be friends. By contrast, Lily's voice was sharply urgent.

"Have you seen AJ?" she asked. "Has Shea? Is he there?"

Dru straightened. "Why are you looking for him?"

A moment passed as if Lily needed time to compose an answer.

"Mom?" Shea took a step toward Dru. "What's the matter?"

Dru met her daughter's gaze, shaking her head slightly.

Lily apologized. "I'm sorry," she said. "I don't mean to—to frighten you or Shea, but it's—have you seen AJ, either of you? Or spoken to him?"

"No. Shea tried calling him. You've heard about Becca Westin?" Dru was guessing.

"She was murdered last night. I know. It's awful."

"Yes," Dru said. She felt wary now and somehow suspicious of Lily. She met Shea's alarmed stare, and although she tried, she couldn't hold it. She wouldn't realize it until later, that it wasn't Shea's fear she was avoiding as much as it was some inner recognition that once again their lives were taking a sudden detour down a dark and twisted road she hadn't even known was there.

Lily spoke. "The police said AJ and Becca dated."

Dru could have confirmed that was true, but in her preoccupation with her sense of things falling apart, she didn't.

"I'm on my way to Wyatt," Lily said. "I'm going to the ranch. I should be there in a half hour or so."

Dru's heart, as if it knew there was more to come that was worse, fell against her ribs. "Why? What is going on, Lily?"

"Becca was killed in AJ's apartment." Lily rushed the words. "The police think he had something to do with it."

No, Dru thought. *They think he did it.* She turned her back to Shea, teeth clenched, fighting for breath, sense, calm. But her mind was on fire. She'd known, hadn't she, that AJ was trouble from nearly the moment Shea brought him to meet her? The guy was a time bomb, one of those IEDs, looking for a place to explode. She didn't give a rat's ass about his medal or his bravery in battle. She'd seen in his eyes the mess all that had made of his sanity, and she was sorry for him. Sorry for all the boys, the fine young men, who got their bodies and minds twisted up in the name of service to their country. But compassion for their damage didn't alter its toxicity. She'd seen what it could do—seen that same unbalanced turmoil in her ex-husband's eyes twelve years ago, the night he ran her and Shea out of their house in Houston at the business end of a loaded shotgun.

AJ had that same wild, haunted look. Not in every moment, but Dru had seen it, nonetheless. He tried to keep it masked, but the disconnect was there. Oh, yes, it was. Dru didn't want AJ having her daughter. She'd forbid the match if she could. But no, Shea loved him like she loved her daddy. And now look. Just look.

"Mom?"

Dru turned and went to Shea, pulling her in close.

Lily said, "The police are looking for AJ, Dru. I think he's at the ranch."

"Have you called?"

"I don't want to worry Dad, and Winona's not answering her cell phone."

Winona Ayala was Erik's mother and the Axels' housekeeper. Dru knew her. Not personally, but Wyatt was a small town. Everyone talked about everyone else. Over time, Dru had learned Winona's story: that she was from Oaxaca, a small town called Loma Bonita near the border with Veracruz. She'd come to the United States when she was seventeen on a visa, and a cousin had gotten her the job with the Axels—Jeb and his late wife, Roseanne, when Roseanne was diagnosed with ovarian cancer. Winona had been required to earn her citizenship, but Erik had been born in Wyatt. Dru didn't know where his father was—back in Oaxaca, if what she'd heard was true.

He was a good kid. She'd hired him once when, in junior high, Shea talked her into adopting two orphaned donkeys. Dru had housed them in the old barn on her property. Not knowing a thing about caring for them, she'd stopped in at the feed store in town, where Erik had been working part-time. He'd offered to deliver their weekly allotment of feed and bedding straw, even though it wasn't in his job description. Shea, and Kate, too, had nearly swooned every time he came over. They had acted so silly that Dru had despaired. Erik was older, eighteen to the girls' thirteen, so she'd thought he would surely get enough of them and quit. But somehow the three had become friends. They laughed at themselves and those memories now and marveled how it was that Shea had needed to go all the way to Dallas to culinary school to meet AJ when he'd spent almost every summer here, at his granddad's ranch, hanging out with Erik.

Lily was talking about the poor cell reception at the xL. She said, "Winona's probably there, but I'm worried the police are, too. You haven't heard anything, have you, on the news about the police being out there?"

"No, but Shea heard from someone at the school in Dallas that the police want to talk to her and to AJ. Shea's got nothing to do with this, Lily. I don't want her involved." *Not with the police and not with your son.* The rest of Dru's thought carved a bitter path through her brain.

"Involved in what?" Shea asked. Alert to every nuance of hostility on Dru's part, she pulled free of Dru's embrace.

Dru had never tried to conceal her misgiving when it came to AJ. But her concerns weren't personal; it wasn't, as Shea insisted, that Dru disliked AJ so much, as it was a matter of intuiting he was the wrong choice for her. No matter how Dru tried to shake it, she had a bad feeling about him.

Shutting Shea from her view, Dru addressed Lily. "Now you get hold of Paul and have him call some of his high-toned politician friends, or whoever, and you tell them to leave my daughter—" She broke off, uncertain what had stopped her. Some sound of distress, whether from Shea or Lily, she didn't know. But God knew none of them needed more distress.

Dru swept the countertop's edge with her fingertips. She had a temper; it was true. She'd be the first to admit anger was her default, her go-to place when she was scared.

And, damn, she was scared—plenty.

"I'm sorry," Lily said. "I don't know what else I can say." Her voice bumped and slid.

Dru felt her jaw loosen, her shoulders relax. It wasn't as if Lily was responsible. She hadn't killed Becca, nor had she sent AJ off to war. If what Shea had told Dru was right, that had been his father's doing. Evidently Paul Isley had been looking for a way to make a man out of his son. Dru said, "I need to tell my daughter what's going on, Lily."

"AJ didn't do it, Dru," Lily said. "I promise you he did not. He doesn't have it in him."

Really? So he shot and killed no one while he was in Afghanistan, fighting for his country, not even while he was defending the buddy whose life he supposedly saved from certain death, for which he was awarded a medal? "I hope when the police find him that he can explain." Dru didn't know what else to say.

"I hope he's at the ranch. He loves it there, you know? Ever since he was little," Lily added, and her voice caught again.

Dru's throat closed.

"Will you, or Shea, call me if you hear from him?" Lily asked.

Dru said she would, and Lily agreed when Dru asked that she do the same.

"Why did you say that to her? About Paul calling all his politician friends?" Shea spoke even as Dru bid Lily good-bye. "I can't believe you talked to her like that, Mom."

"I don't want you involved, Shea."

"But I already am. The police want to interview me."

"They are probably going to question you about AJ—when you last saw him, spoke to him—"

"Why?"

"Because, honey, they found Becca's body in his apartment."

3

Lily didn't leave the shoulder of I-35 right away after speaking to Dru. She felt light-headed and closed her eyes, waiting for the sensation to pass. Her BMW was rocked slightly by the wind of other passing cars. Looking out, she caught sight of a woman driver, one hand flung up as if in emphasis. Her passenger, a man, was laughing. It was only an instant, yet Lily felt the impact of their happiness, their pleasure in each other like a blow, and she bowed her head, willing herself not to cry. Her phone went off, and she jumped. *AJ!*

Instead, it was Paul. "Where are you?" he asked when Lily answered.

"North of Greeley. I just got off the phone with Dru. She and Shea haven't seen AJ or spoken to him." Lily allowed no sign of her offense at how Dru had spoken to her come through her voice. It would only rile Paul, who liked AJ's future mother-in-law even less than Lily did. "The police want to talk to Shea, though. They probably think she knows where AJ is."

"Does she? Did you ask her?"

"No," Lily admitted. "But Dru would have told me." *Would she have?* Dru's whole focus was on protecting Shea, not her daughter's fiancé. Lily understood that; she felt the same about AJ, but she doubted he'd look for it—her protection. The gulf between them had existed for so long that he assumed it was her choice and not her heartbreak.

"You need to ask Shea directly, Lily. Don't rely on her mother. We need to keep ahead of this thing."

"Now you get hold of Paul and have him call some of his high-toned politician friends . . ." Dru's command drummed through Lily's mind. Dru had such an inflated idea of the Isleys' importance. If there were any such *friends*, Lily thought, Paul wouldn't call them on Shea's behalf.

"I don't have long," he said. "I'm at the police station, in the men's room. I didn't want to call from the interrogation room in case it's bugged."

Lily wondered how Paul could be so sure the restroom wasn't.

"They asked me back at the apartment what AJ drove, if he had a computer, owned a gun. Did he have a phone."

"He has all of that."

"Yeah, and it's all missing. They found his wallet. That was it."

"That doesn't make sense. Why would he leave his wallet?"

"How the hell do I know?"

Lily bit her teeth together, refusing to engage. Paul was afraid; they both were, and it made them hostile. They'd been hard on each other before, the last time they'd gone down this road with AJ. "There was a cop in a patrol car outside, watching the house when I left," she said in an attempt to get them through the moment.

"Bastards," Paul muttered. "Look, from now on, if anyone from law enforcement—I don't care who it is—asks you anything, you tell them to get in touch with Jerry Dix. Do you understand?"

"You've spoken to him, then?"

"Yeah, he's on his way here."

"To the police station? Why?"

"Jesus, Lily. He's an attorney, for Christ's sake."

Corporate, Lily thought. She wouldn't say it. She wouldn't bring up Edward, the possibility that they—that AJ would need his services as a criminal attorney again. Her mind shied away from the complications that could present, so much unfinished business.

"Jerry has connections; he knows his way around the DA's office. He can get information we can't."

"Paul?" Lily was hesitant. "What if the person who killed Becca, what if they took AJ, abducted him, along with his truck, the gun, his laptop and phone? He could be a victim, too."

"Bushnell claims they aren't ruling that out. I should have told you," Paul conceded. He was exhausted. Horrified. He had said to Lily earlier that every time he closed his eyes, he saw Becca—*"pants down, stabbed, blood everywhere"*—his words rattled across Lily's brain. As a consequence, she saw it, too, but the reality would have been much worse, and coupled with the fact that their son's apartment was a crime scene, and their son was implicated—

"Bushnell says they only want AJ for questioning so far, but I feel like he's working me, Lily. Trying to be my buddy, you know? We can't forget there's history here."

He was repeating himself, and Lily wasn't going to listen to it. She switched on the ignition. "I need to go, Paul."

"You'll call when you get to the ranch?"

"I'm worried about Dad, how he'll handle this. He's so forgetful lately . . ." It was more than that. Winona had said he was sleeping late in the morning, something he'd never done. She'd said she'd had to remind him to change his shirt, eat a meal. *"He's just not himself, not right,"* Win had said.

"Oh, come on, Lily. You act as if you want Jeb to be losing his mind. That old bastard is as sharp as he ever was."

Old bastard. It was how Paul and her dad addressed each other nowadays. The two had been friends for almost thirty years. That was how Lily had first known Paul, as her dad's friend, the one who'd bring her gifts on occasion, once a stuffed bunny when she was thirteen. And when he'd realized she was too old for toys, he'd brought her jewelry, opal earrings, a necklace with a dainty gold horseshoe pendant. Neither man, her dad nor Paul, could be considered young anymore. Not that she would ever say that to Paul, and while she was well aware of the talk, the twenty-three-year difference in their ages was something that was never discussed, either. It was the elephant in the living room of their marriage. "I've got to go," Lily repeated. She checked the flow of traffic in her rearview mirror.

"You know what I thought when AJ didn't show up this morning?" Lily waited.

"I figured he was ducking out," Paul said.

"Of the wedding, you mean?" Lily dropped her glance.

"Yeah. Until I went into his apartment, I thought maybe he got cold feet."

No, Lily thought. As much as she and Paul might deplore the union, as much as they might have hoped for more for their son than a degree from culinary school and marriage to the pierced and tattooed daughter of a single mom who ran a catering business out of her kitchen, she knew AJ's heart had found its home. Lily had seen the way AJ would draw Shea's hand through the loop of his elbow when they walked together. And when Shea spoke, he tipped his head toward her as if he couldn't bear to miss a single word. Shea made him laugh; they made each other laugh. At the restaurant, where AJ had made that awful scene, it was Shea's touch, her soothing voice, that had brought AJ back to himself. Lily couldn't imagine he would ever leave Shea, not willingly, not by choice. But she said none of this to Paul. Instead, she asked about AJ's passport. "Have the police found it?"

"I don't know," Paul answered. "But he could find ways to get into Mexico without a passport."

Other countries. Lily was thinking AJ could as easily find his way to other, more distant countries. It wasn't as if he was unfamiliar with overseas travel, not since his stint with the marines, the one Paul had insisted AJ undertake once he'd gotten clear of the charge of murder six years ago. Paul had said military training would straighten him out, make a man out of him. Lily had felt he was wrong in her bones, but nothing she said made any difference. AJ went, as if even *he* felt it was his only option.

"I'll call you from the ranch," she said.

. . .

She was back on the interstate, flipping through radio stations, looking for a distraction, when she heard Becca Westin's name. Her heart stalled. She wanted to turn it off—the radio, the car, the terrible looming future. Instead, she made herself listen while the commentator ran through facts she already knew, the how, what, when, and where. It was the mention of AJ's name—the who—that jolted her. Suppose her dad was tuned in, listening to this same station? Suppose he had a stroke or a heart attack and no one was there? Lily drove faster, weaving in and out of traffic. Reckless, thoughtless now, and when she reached the ranch, she let herself through the arched iron gate using the keypad.

It clanged shut behind her with the finality of a cell door, and she stopped, keeping her hands gripped to the wheel. If there was any way not to do it, not to tell her dad that his beloved grandson . . . but there wasn't. She set her foot back on the accelerator and went up the three-quarter-mile drive to the house, slowly. Her great-grandfather, who had founded the cattle ranch and created the brand, xL, after the family's surname, Axel, had built the road more than one hundred years ago, clearing an avenue through the live oaks wide enough for horse-drawn wagons or carriages to pass. In those days, the road's surface had been layered in crushed granite and caliche. Since then, asphalt had been added to the mix, and the trees had grown, becoming thicker trunked and more twisted. They bent over the macadam, old men grasping one another's shoulders, wheezing in the freshened breeze. Sunlight through their tangled canopies dimpled the uneven pavement. Native grasses spiked with new green and patches of white-and-yellow daisies and bluebonnets past their prime verged on the crumbling edges. Every so often, there were clearings that gave sun-drenched views of juniper-clad limestone outcroppings. The cattle pens, a couple of barns, and the workshop were farther on.

AJ could be in one of those buildings, Lily thought, or inside any of a number of other outbuildings that dotted the acreage. She crossed the one-lane bridge that arched over Copper Creek, and thought, He could be hiding underneath it. There was more than enough room to conceal a man.

When the white two-story clapboard farmhouse appeared in her view, the knot in her stomach tightened. The deep L-shaped front porch was empty, the six black-trimmed windows across the front blank. She drove around back, fearful of seeing AJ's truck, but it wasn't there. Only the tailgate of her dad's pickup and the back of the old Jeep he kept for use on the property were visible through the open garage door. Even Winona's Subaru SUV was absent from its usual spot, and the hope that Lily had been harboring since leaving Dallas—of finding her here—fell to pieces on the floor of her stomach.

Leaving her car, she went quickly up the steps onto the covered back porch, careful not to slam the screen door behind her, relaxing slightly on registering the scent of cinnamon. Long sticks of the spice, uncut and raw, that Win had relatives ship to her from her native Oaxaca hung from an exposed porch rafter. She used it in everything from hot chocolate to enchilada sauce. Even though Win's car was missing, Lily half expected to find her in the kitchen, but it was dark and empty, without a whiff of what might have been served at breakfast or lunch. Mystified, pulse tapping, Lily crossed the room, trailing her fingertips along the edge of the marble-topped island as she passed it, briefly aware of the stickiness there and under her shoes. The huge, old porcelain sink was full of dirty dishes; the kitchen towel hanging askew over the oven door handle was grimy. None of this was right.

The television was on low volume in the living room, tuned to an afternoon game show. But her father's big leather recliner was as empty as the kitchen. The messy stack of newspapers beside it was topped with his coffee mug and an ashtray that held a half-smoked cigar.

"Dad?" she called, crossing the room toward his office that overlooked the front porch. "It's me. Lily."

"Huh? What?" He turned from the window to blink at her, and it was there, the bewilderment in his eyes as if he didn't know her. It had happened a few times before on the occasions when he saw her. There would be seconds of doubt, of outright panic, while he searched his mind, because there was a part of him that realized he should know her. It pained him; she could see evidence of that, too, in his expression. She knew he must hate it, feeling so vulnerable. She was no less disconcerted. It was as if the ground, or perhaps it was something more like the seat of power, was shifting between them. But she couldn't pause now to sort out all the ways in which they might be affected if he was losing his mental grip.

"It's Lily, Dad," she said gently.

"I know that," he answered. "What are you doing here? You didn't call," he accused.

"I have some—news and wanted to tell you in person. Where is Winona?"

"Gone to Oaxaca."

"What? When?"

"Last Thursday. Her mother died."

"Why didn't she call me?" Lily sat down hard in the club chair across from her father's desk, nonplussed. She and Win had once talked almost daily about everything and nothing—a book they'd read, a recipe, what Erik and AJ were doing. Lately, though, on the rare occasions when they spoke on the phone, it was only about Lily's dad. "I didn't think Win was in touch with her mom, not for years. Since before Erik was born."

"She wasn't."

"Did he go with her?" It seemed logical that Erik would accompany his mother, and it would explain why he wasn't picking up his calls.

But her dad said, "No. He doesn't know her people. Win wouldn't have gone herself if she wasn't such a good Catholic daughter."

Lily held still, feeling the prick of annoyance. She wanted to know how Win could leave without a word when she was the one reminding Lily's dad to change his shirt. But Lily couldn't exactly ask her dad that, could she?

"Before you go off getting your knickers in a knot," he said, seeming to read her mind, "I made her go. She tried convincing me it would be fine if she didn't, but I know better. She wanted to make her peace. I wasn't going to stand in the way of that."

"Dad?" Lily said after a moment, and then she stopped and looked at her hands, clenched in her lap.

"What's the matter? I'm getting the idea you didn't come here just to check up on your old man." He sat at his desk, holding her gaze.

"I wish you didn't have to know," she said.

"Is it AJ? Has something happened to him?"

"Yes," she said, and she went on, keeping it brief, fighting to be matter-of-fact.

At first he was visibly pale and seemed shaken, but a moment before she might have gone to him, he slapped his desktop with his open hand and said, "What the hell?" as if she'd left out the vital part, the one that would explain it.

Lily said, "I was certain he would be here. You haven't seen him?"

"No. But you know it's a lot of horseshit, right?"

"Paul's worried they won't let him off so easily this time."

"He wasn't let off last time, Lily. He was cleared. By the Dallas district attorney's office. Because they had no evidence. You know as well as I do he tried to stop that guy, tried getting the gun from him. A witness testified to it," her dad added.

"When did you last talk to him?"

"Last weekend. He and Erik came by, scouting a place to roast the pig for the rehearsal dinner."

The Hawaiian theme had been AJ's idea, conceived when he and Shea had decided to forgo a honeymoon in Kailua in favor of saving their money. If they were going to make their shared dream of opening a restaurant serving food they'd grown themselves come true, they would need every cent. The luau was going to be held in the north pasture nearest the house; they could move it into the barn if the weather was bad. Shea and AJ, along with Dru and Winona—and Lily had offered to help out, too—were cooking most of the food themselves. It seemed like an enormous undertaking to Lily. Paul called it total stupidity. The wedding was a lot of do-it-yourself crap, and their woo-woo restaurant plan was an amateur effort that would yield amateur results. They'll be belly-up inside a year, he'd said. Lily knew he was miffed, even hurt, that AJ hadn't asked his advice, hadn't sought out his help. The prediction of AJ's failure was a salve, a means to feed Paul's need for vindication. He didn't tolerate failure, not his own or his son's.

"I guess you've tried calling AJ." Her dad eyed Lily from under his brow.

"Dozens of times."

"Did he know the dead girl?"

"She was a friend of Shea's, a bridesmaid."

"Not the little gal Erik's engaged to—Kate, isn't it?"

"No. Kate is Shea's maid of honor. This girl—Becca was her name, Becca Westin. The police are saying she and AJ dated—" Lily's phone sounded, and she bent over the chair's arm, scrabbling for it inside her purse. But it wasn't AJ, and straightening, she shook her head at her dad, mouthing, "Shea."

"Mrs. Isley?"

"Yes, Shea, have you heard—"

"No, I was wondering if you—"

"—left message after message—can't believe—"

"No, I can't, either."

They talked over each other, creating a disjointed hash of unfinished sentences that ended abruptly in an uneasy pause.

Lily broke it, saying she was at the xL. "I thought he might come here." *To be near Dad and Erik and you.* The implication was plain if only to Lily—that AJ would choose the company of his grandfather, his best friend, and his fiancée over that of his mother. She ducked her glance to keep her father from seeing the hurt she knew was in her eyes.

"AJ didn't do it, Mrs. Isley."

Shea's voice trembled, but it was the underlying note of her conviction that struck Lily, and she felt a rush of gratitude and relief—and a warm affection that surprised and disconcerted her. "No," she agreed. "He didn't."

Shea said, "I'm supposed to call the police in Dallas, Sergeant Bushnell. I don't know why he wants to talk to me, what to say. I don't know anything."

"He told—Sergeant Bushnell told Paul . . ." Lily hesitated, wondering if she should repeat it. What if Shea didn't know? But this was no time for secrets. They would all come out now, she thought. Even her own might. "The sergeant told Paul that Becca and AJ dated."

"Yes, but they broke up over a year ago. Becca introduced me to AJ. She was always taking credit for it, that she hooked us up."

"AJ never mentioned—"

"Oh my God!" Shea interrupted. "Does Sergeant Bushnell suspect me? Is that it? He thinks *I* killed Becca because I was jealous?"

Lily considered it, the possibility that Shea could have a motive. Was it so far-fetched to presume Becca's death was the result of some love triangle gone bad? Were the police investigating that idea?

"It's ridiculous," Shea said, unhappily.

She ought to agree, Lily thought, but her mind wouldn't obey. Her tongue sat heavy and unmoving in her mouth.

"Becca and I were friends—since junior high," Shea added.

"Do you know where AJ is?" Lily was wary now, remembering Paul's admonition to question Shea herself. "When did you last see him or speak to him?"

"I saw him last Sunday before I left Dallas to come here to my mom's," Shea said. "We talked last night. He called me when he left work."

"Are you sure he was at work? Because Detective Bushnell told Paul he missed his shift."

"AJ wouldn't lie to me, Mrs. Isley. Sergeant Bushnell better check again."

Lily. Call me Lily, she thought but didn't say, although she had said it before, a number of times.

Another small silence teetered on a tight wire.

"What if he's—" Shea began.

"No." Lily cut her off. She didn't want a thing to do with it, the idea that AJ might be hurt, a victim himself, even though it was clearly conceivable, and she'd brought it up to Paul. She'd know if something terrible had happened to him, wouldn't she? She would feel it. She was AJ's mother, and regardless of her mistakes, that tie was implicit, with its own infallible means of communication. Hadn't she always heard that?

"I've been calling everyone I know from school," Shea said. "No one's seen him or heard from him. I don't know what to do. I think we should make flyers and post them in Dallas, around AJ's apartment. We need to get the word out here, too, around town, in case—"

"Tomorrow," Lily said. "Let's not do anything until tomorrow." She was thinking if AJ was close by, if he saw the police, it would drive him away. He would be remembering last time; he would know what he was in for, how it could play out. Even in his innocence, he wouldn't risk his freedom. Ending the call, Lily stowed her phone in her purse.

"She know anything?" her dad asked.

"I'm not sure. She seems nervous that the police suspect her. If AJ was seeing Becca, and Shea knew . . ." Lily paused when her dad raised his hand in a dismissive gesture.

"AJ isn't the cheating kind. You know that as well as me."

She would like to, Lily thought. But how well did anyone know another person? In her own lifetime, she had acted in ways and made decisions that in retrospect completely amazed her for their spectacular and blind stupidity. How could she judge what someone else would do, even her own son?

"Leaving AJ out of it," her dad went on, "Shea is awfully small. She doesn't look like much of a fighter. Does she weigh a hundred pounds?"

"Maybe just," Lily said.

"You realize AJ could be in trouble himself." Her dad repeated the ongoing concern, the only realistic alternative that would support AJ's innocence, the very scenario Lily hadn't wanted to discuss with Shea.

Should she pray for that? Lily wondered. Pray her son was endangered?

"Whoever did kill the girl—they could have him," her dad continued. "Or he could be running scared, thinking because of all that other business back in the day—" He got up. "Let's go."

"Where?" Lily stood up, too.

"You've got your boots on. Let's take a ride. If AJ's around here, we need to find him before the police do."

He echoed Lily's plan; her intention in coming here had been to hunt for her son, but outside, when her father headed for the garage, pulling his truck keys from his pocket, she stopped, watching him. "Dad?"

He turned to her, eyes sharp, impatient.

"I thought you said you wanted to ride."

His expression went totally blank, the way it had when she'd first arrived. It filled the space of one heartbeat, perhaps two, before his eyes cleared, but as he repocketed his keys, the pain the lapse caused him showed in the angle of his bowed head, the low, defeated curve of his shoulders.

"I'll get the horses from the pasture and bring them to the barn," Lily said, and her voice was so bright, he flinched.

• • •

Lily had sat on a horse before she could crawl. When she was a girl, her dad had liked to tell people that. He'd liked to say that when she rode, she was poetry in motion. It had embarrassed her even as it thrilled her, seeing his face take on the sheen of pride. He had glowed like the shiny half-dollars he'd handed her sometimes when she was a little girl and she'd done a chore to his liking. He, Lily, and Winona had taught Erik and AJ to ride, too, and for a while, until the boys graduated high school, if the five of them were together at the ranch, they'd saddle up before dawn and ride out to the east ridge to watch the sunrise. The boys had learned to rope and brand livestock and cut hay. They could mend a fence. Summers they'd entered rodeo competitions to show off. It had always made Lily and Winona smile, seeing the way they'd swagger, watching from under their hat brims to see what girl was looking. Both Lily and Win had drawn the line, though, at tobacco chewing, and been glad for it when Lily's dad backed them up.

Lily was remembering all this as she walked her dad's palomino, Sharkey, and her own dainty paint mare, Butternut, back to the barn. They said you could tell a lot about a person by the sort of horse they rode. She'd never questioned her dad's choice of a stallion. He and Sharkey were a lot alike, both of them hardheaded, irascible, and determined to be in control. Sharkey was old now, nearly as old as her dad in horse years, but he still stepped sharply, and she was still wary of him.

In the barn, she handed Sharkey off to her dad, and they set about saddling the horses in silence.

Her dad broke it. "I know you're scared, Sissy."

She had her hands on the front cinch of her saddle, testing that it wasn't too snug, when he said it, and she bowed her head to Butternut's neck, listening to her blow gently through her nostrils. How long had it been since her dad had called her Sissy? Not since she'd gotten into all the trouble in Arizona. She'd been scared then, too, and in sore need of his comfort.

"You ready?" he asked.

"Yes," she said, and, mounting, they rode out into the late-afternoon light that was the color of hammered gold. The wind, an unseen hand, ruffled the long grass. The air smelled of dust and verdant spring.

Her dad said they'd ride up to the old deer stand at the far end of the north pasture. "You remember how those boys used to hide out there when they were trying to duck chores?"

Lily smiled.

Her dad broke the silence that had fallen between them. "What you told me was done to that girl—that's the work of a maniac. Only somebody whacked-out would do a thing like that. That's not AJ."

"He's not himself sometimes, Dad." Lily bent forward and stroked Butternut's neck, and she tossed her pretty head, as if in appreciation.

"Who would be, after the shit he went through over in Afghanistan?"

"If you could have seen him that night at the restaurant—"

"He told me about that. It shook him up. But it only happened once."

"There have been fights."

"A couple. So what?"

"He went to jail. It looks bad now."

"Yeah. Okay. But from what AJ said, those assholes asked for it both times. Some people can't learn any other way not to mess with a guy's honor, his reputation."

"Does he talk to you?"

"About Afghanistan? What went down there? Some."

"Paul is horrible about it." Lily was a little shocked, hearing herself. She was almost never critical of her husband, especially in her father's presence, but what she'd said was the truth, and as she got older, she was finding it harder not to speak up for it. "If AJ talks about the difficulty, the—the horrors he encountered, Paul shuts him down. He tells AJ to be a man and quit his whining. It makes me so angry."

"He wants his son to be strong, that's all. If a guy isn't strong, life will take him down. It will put him on his knees. Paul doesn't want that for AJ. No father wants his kid to be weak."

"Since when is it weak to be sickened by the atrocities of war? It's madness." Butternut's ears twitched as if at Lily's vehemence.

Her dad said, "It's how the world is—how society is," and after that, they were quiet.

The farther they rode, the more Lily's sense of dread wove itself into the sound of the wind, the creaking of their saddles. The sun began its descent, falling behind a low-hanging crenellation of clouds, infusing them with lilac-tinged light. In ordinary time, Lily might have let herself revel in it, riding with her dad, the beauty of her surroundings. But even in ordinary time, she had worried about AJ. She had felt, especially since his return from Afghanistan, that he was at risk, that anything might happen. This—as unreasoning as it was, she'd been expecting something like this, a disaster of major proportions.

"Did he tell you he stopped going to counseling?" Lily asked her dad. "All of it, the group therapy, the one-on-one sessions—"

"He said it wasn't helping." Her dad was unperturbed. "Too much dwelling on the past, and he wants to move on. He's talked to me about getting involved with the Wounded Warrior Project, which would be a good thing for him, I think. But he's got to find his own way, Lily."

"I wish—"

Her dad turned to her, brows raised.

She shook her head. The list of what she wished was too long, too hard to name. But to have AJ's love and his trust, to have him feel he could talk to her, seek her help in times of trouble—those things were at the top of it. If only she knew how to reach him, how to close the distance between them. But she didn't, and it made her heart ache.

"I never talked to my mom, either," her dad said. "I didn't want to upset her."

Lily had never known her father's parents. His mother had died when Lily was two, and his dad had died before she was born. She said, "I've done some research, and men who have been in combat can have flashbacks; they're hypervigilant, paranoid. They can think they're in danger, that they have to defend themselves. They do things—"

"Not AJ." Her dad cut her off. "Not like what was done to that girl."

• • •

There was no sign of AJ at the deer blind, nor any sign that anyone had been there recently. But they did find fresh tire tracks near one of the service gates.

"Are they from your truck?" Lily looked up at her dad from the tire-treaded ground.

"Nah." He pushed his hat back on his head. "But they could belong to Wylie's truck, I guess."

"Wylie Evers? What would he be doing on our land?" Wylie owned the neighboring ranch, the Triple Oak, and the last Lily knew, he and her dad were still feuding over Wylie's refusal to pay for the repairs when his lightning-spooked cattle damaged a section of the xL's fencing a few years back. "I thought you two weren't speaking."

"I may lease the land to him," her dad said, "or I may sell it to him. Haven't decided."

"You're joking, right?" But Lily could see he wasn't. There was weariness in his eyes, the pained shadow of resignation.

"I'm tired of the responsibility. If I go through with the sale, I'll keep the house and barn and maybe a dozen or so acres, enough for AJ to run a few head if he and Shea want it."

"What about Winona's house? You wouldn't let that go?"

"I built that place for Win after your mom died. It's hers until she doesn't want it anymore."

"Okay, but I thought when you sold the herd last year, that was to relieve the stress, give you free time."

"Turns out I'm not too good at free time. I'm an old man now, seventy-four, and I don't know what to do with myself. Ain't that a kick in the pants."

"But there's Erik. If he comes on as ranch foreman—"

"He turned me down. Third time. I'm not asking him again."

"Oh." Lily was hurt on her dad's behalf. She didn't understand any better than he did why Erik chose to work a string of menial jobs over being the xL's foreman, in charge of the entire cattle operation. The first time he'd declined the offer, though, her dad had sold the herd. Now it was the land that was in jeopardy. She wondered if Erik knew what her dad was planning, if it would cause him to reconsider.

"He's never liked hard work," her dad said. "Basic training kicked his ass, too. Remember?"

"That's not really fair, Dad. His asthma flared up. He was in the ER half the time, trying to breathe. I don't know why you always harp on that." She was lying; she did know it was out of humiliation at being turned down, which was equal to, if not greater than, Erik's humiliation at having washed out of basic. "I hope Winona never hears you."

"She knows," he said, in a way that made Lily think there had been some discussion, possibly heated, between Win and her dad. "She'd change his mind if she could, but she's got no influence over him. He's his own man. He'll suffer the consequences of his dumb-ass mistakes like everyone else."

"That's what Paul says about AJ becoming a chef."

"AJ's got a focus; he's not afraid to work and work hard for what he wants. I might wish he would take over here, but I'm happy enough he's got a dream, the will to pursue it."

"He's talked to you about farming the land here?"

"Yeah, but he damn sure doesn't need six hundred and thirty-seven acres to raise a few hundred pounds of organic livestock. He talked about running a few head of that fancy brand cattle—Akaushi, it's called—and maybe some free-range chickens, a few rows of vegetables. Whatever he needs to support the restaurant. I'm happy if I can help him."

"Me, too," Lily said.

"Hell, maybe I can go to work for him. Give me something to do."

"From rancher to farmer." Somehow Lily couldn't quite picture it—her dad in overalls with a pitchfork in his hand.

He lifted his hat and resettled it. "C'mon," he said, giving Sharkey's flanks a nudge. "We're burning daylight."

It was long after dark by the time they got back to the house, and they were tired and hungry. Lily called Paul, but there was nothing new. Only fear and waiting.

She got the old cast-iron frying pan out of the sink and washed it, then made scrambled eggs. Her dad made toast, but when they sat down at the table, neither of them could eat much, and afterward, without much discussion, they tackled the pile of dirty dishes, Lily washing, her dad drying. She glanced at him as she mopped the kitchen countertops one final time. "Go to bed, Dad. You look whipped."

"Yeah," he said, pinching the bridge of his nose. "I am. Don't know that I'll sleep, though."

"Try, okay?"

"You good? You know where your old room is, right?" His eyes were soft and held a teasing light.

She smiled. "I think I can find my way."

She got her purse and tote from her dad's office and followed in his wake up the stairs.

His bedroom was at the front of the house, overlooking the drive and giving a view of a sweep of hills, while her bedroom at the back of the house overlooked the barn and the corral. A small bathroom was across the hall. Neither room had been used in a while, and the air smelled musty, but Lily didn't mind. She switched on the bedside lamp, a frilly pink-shaded confection she and her mother had bought to match her equally frilly pink-canopied bed. Lily could have had other, more grown-up furnishings. Her dad had offered them, and Winona would have helped her pick them out, but Lily had said no. She'd wanted her room to remain as it had been when her mother was alive. They'd decorated it together when Lily was ten. It had been their last project before her mom's cancer was diagnosed.

Lily opened a window, and, shucking her boots, she lay down on the bed, thinking she should take a bath, brush her teeth, but after a moment, she reached to turn off the light. Moonlit shadows flickered over the walls. The wind had picked up, and she heard it singing around the house corners, rattling through the live oaks. Crickets hummed in the greening grass. She didn't think she would sleep, but when she first heard the telephone ring down the hall, she was convinced she was dreaming. The ring was old-fashioned, the one the landline made. Lily couldn't remember the last time she'd heard it. Everyone used cell phones now.

She waited to wake up, waited for the ringing to stop. It didn't. Swinging her sock-clad feet over the side of the bed, she went out into the hallway, where the old residential phone still sat on a red lacquered table halfway between her bedroom and her dad's. Sepia-edged shadows loomed, old ghosts clinging to the walls, and the sense of dreaming persisted even as she reached for the heavy black receiver. Lifting it, she felt its weight in her hand, the coolness against her ear.

"Hello?" she said softly.

"Mom?" rasped a voice.

Lily straightened. "AJ! Where are you? Are you all right?"

"Mom? Can you bring me my passport?" he asked, and his voice was low and hoarse. He sounded hurt.

"Oh, AJ, where are you? You need to go home to Dad, or come here, to the ranch. The police—"

The hall light came on, making Lily blink.

"Let me talk to him," her dad said. But when he got the phone from her, when he said, "Son, you need to come here and let us help you," there wasn't an answer.

AJ was gone. He'd hung up.

4

"Neither AJ nor I could kill anyone, Detective," Shea said, and Dru flinched.

It flat-out pissed her off, the very idea that Shea felt the need to defend herself. Dru wanted to yank Shea's cell phone out of her hand and speak to the idiot detective herself. *Leave my daughter alone. She's got nothing to do with this nightmare.* Dru plunked the lemon bars she'd baked—was that just this morning?—into the handled grocery sack with the foil-wrapped chicken she'd roasted to take to the Westins.

Behind her, Shea paced a short path between the kitchen, where Dru was, and the table in the breakfast nook, where Kate, Leigh, and Vanessa were sitting, their eyes glued to Shea. Scared out of their minds, Dru thought. They were frightened, and so was Dru. That was the stripped-down bottom line. Her blood hammered in her temples. The very idea that her daughter was being questioned—implicated, for God's sake. What was next? Would they haul her off in handcuffs?

It was ludicrous.

Dru turned to Shea. "Give me the phone," she said. "I'll tell him you were here with me last night."

Shea waved her off. She didn't need her mother to run interference. She was perfectly capable of standing her ground on her own. She could defend herself, thank you very much. And AJ, too.

She was grown up now, twenty-three. An adult. That's what she'd say.

But the thing Shea refused to understand, even though she'd lived it, too, was how quickly the person you loved, the soul mate you trusted with your life, could turn on you. The way Rob, Shea's dad, had turned on Dru.

They'd been married thirteen years when it happened. They'd been lovers and best friends, done everything together. And when Shea came, their family circle was complete until the day a couple of thugs jumped Rob in a parking lot in downtown Houston. They'd beaten him to the ground even after he gave them his wallet, his watch, and his wedding band. And when he was down, they'd kicked him, breaking his ribs and rupturing his spleen. They'd left him there, alone, bleeding internally—dying. A passerby had found him. Until Dru got the call from the police, she'd had no concept of crime other than what she picked up from the news, which was mainly that it was awful, and it happened to someone else.

At first she'd imagined Rob's injuries, while severe, were only physical, a matter of surgical repair and eventual healing. She hadn't been prepared for the mental anguish, his nightmares and anxiety, his constant suspicion. He'd flinched if she or Shea appeared in his peripheral vision, and they'd learned to announce their presence or risk bodily harm. At Dru's insistence, they'd gone for counseling, but Rob had ultimately quit attending the sessions, arguing there was nothing wrong with him, that he was getting better, getting himself under control. She'd made the mistake of believing him until the night he'd threatened her with a loaded shotgun.

Shea had been terrified, screaming, *"Don't shoot my mama, Daddy. Please don't shoot her!"* Dru could still hear her voice, ragged with hysteria. Even all these years later, the memory of that night, what Shea had witnessed, her fear, and Dru's over what could have happened, had the power to make her chest pound. It had been the final straw. She'd taken Shea and left Rob before the police, whom neighbors had summoned, arrived to arrest him. Months later, she'd gone alone to a psychologist, who had explained that Rob was likely suffering from post-traumatic stress as a result of the assault. There was no guarantee he wouldn't do it again even if he got counseling and, if necessary, medication. Dru had filed for divorce then. It had nearly killed her, ending her marriage, but she couldn't risk taking Shea back into that situation.

Now Shea was grown, and she'd fallen in love with a man who, for different reasons, had received the same diagnosis. A man whose dark side was evident, at least to Dru. And that man might be a murderer. Damn straight, she was scared. She looked through the bank of windows above the kitchen counter. It was late in the afternoon, and the sun had dropped, making the light uncertain. Shadows crept like thieves toward the house.

Behind her, Shea was telling the detective that she'd last spoken to AJ the night before. "At around ten thirty," she said, "when he was leaving work. He usually doesn't get off till midnight, but they weren't busy. We always talk last thing before bed."

Pause.

"No, he wasn't lying to me about being at work. We don't lie to each other."

Pause.

"Who did you talk to at Café Blue? It can be crazy—" Shea stopped, listening to the sergeant.

"What neighbor saw him? What's their name?"

Pause.

"No, Detective, he wasn't seeing Becca or anyone else. I already told you, he'd never do that to me."

Dru's heart contracted. Shea's certainty—that kind of certainty could be so horribly misplaced.

"Well, of course I know a person using a cell phone can be any-where." Shea caught Dru's glance and rolled her eyes. "Yeah," she said, "if I hear from him, I'll let you know," and her response was shaded with sarcasm. "Jerk," she muttered, ending the call.

"Will we be questioned?" Vanessa asked.

"I'm wondering, too," said Leigh. "It's scary. I mean, we don't really know what this is about. Why Becca was killed. What if it's some kind of vendetta? Someone who's angry about the wedding? We could all be in danger."

"What are you getting at, Leigh? Who would be angry? AJ?" Shea huffed a disgusted breath. "Not even the cops are suggesting anything like that."

"You really don't know where he is?" Vanessa was staring at Shea. She wasn't buying it, but then Dru knew her to be a natural skeptic.

"Do you think I'd be standing here if I knew?" Shea asked, and her eyes skipped from Vanessa to Leigh to Kate, but none of the girls returned her glance, and in that telling moment, Dru realized that with the possible exception of Kate, Shea didn't have the support of her friends. But neither did she have Dru's support in her belief that AJ was innocent, as much as Dru might wish it were otherwise.

"You think he did it." Shea set her phone down on the table harder than necessary, making Vanessa jump, making Kate and Leigh flinch. Even Dru flinched.

"He dated her!" Vanessa stood up, voice rising, a challenge. "Before you."

"That was more than a year ago. And it lasted how long? Six weeks? Does that even qualify as serious?"

"It did in Becca's mind," Vanessa answered. "She never wanted you to know it, but she still had feelings for AJ."

Shea kept Vanessa's gaze. "But she introduced us. She told me it was over between them."

"Maybe for AJ," Vanessa said.

Shea glanced at Dru, hunting for reassurance, but Dru had none to offer, because quite possibly there could be some element of truth to what Vanessa was suggesting. It wasn't an unreasonable stretch. Joy had commented on occasion, ruefully, about Becca's fickleness, her tendency to create drama.

Leigh said, "I didn't know, either—that Becca still had feelings for AJ."

"I'm not making it up," Van said, looking to Shea and then Kate for support.

Kate shifted her glance.

Keeping her opinion to herself, Dru thought.

"Well, I'm sorry if she was still carrying a torch," Shea said. "But it doesn't mean anything."

The girls exchanged glances, and Dru saw their reactions, how they might have protested. *Becca was in AJ's apartment. He left work early and was seen there. Now he's disappeared.*

But no one spoke.

Leigh doodled a line along the table's edge with the tip of her finger. She'd been the first of the five of them to marry. Right out of high school, the boy she'd loved since sixth grade. She'd told Dru once it was all she wanted, a husband and children and a home to take care of. At the wedding, Terri, Leigh's mom, had tipsily told Dru she and Leigh's dad had wanted more for their daughter. But once a kid turned eighteen, it didn't matter what the parents wanted, she'd said. Remembering Shea at fifteen, the tattoo on her neck that every morning before school had to be covered if she wanted to avoid suffering a range of consequences from her peers, from school authorities, Dru had thought that as far as stubborn went, age had nothing to do with it.

"I know how it looks, trust me," Shea said. "But how things look isn't always how they are."

"The last couple of times I talked to Becca, she seemed pretty stressed out." Kate looked around the table. "Did y'all notice?"

"Yeah," Van said, "it was like she had something on her mind, but when I asked, she blew me off."

"That whole deal about her being sick yesterday when we went to pick up the jars?" Leigh said. "I didn't believe it."

"No, me, either," Vanessa agreed.

"Something was going on with her," Kate said.

"Well, she seemed fine to me," Shea said, "but maybe I'm just in wedding la-la land." A beat passed, and the furrow in Shea's brow deepened. "She'd decided not to go back to school." She went on, thoughtfully. "Did you guys know? She seemed relieved, too. Happy." Shea looked around, but no one offered a response. "She had a plan." Shea was insistent now. "She was going to take the summer, stay with her folks, and enroll at GCC in the fall."

GCC was the community college in Greeley. Dru knew a lot of the local kids went there after graduating from Wyatt High before moving on to four-year universities.

"She thought she might like to teach elementary school, like her mom," Shea said.

"Well, she never said anything about that to me," Kate said. Her phone rang. "It's Erik." She looked stricken.

"Oh," Shea said, "I've been trying to get hold of him. Answer it. Maybe he knows where AJ is."

But it was clear, listening to Kate's side of the conversation, that while Erik had heard about Becca's death and the gruesome circumstances, he hadn't heard from AJ and had no idea where he was.

Ending the call, Kate said, "He thinks maybe he's here somewhere, hiding out at the ranch or something."

"That's what AJ's mom thinks," Shea said.

"Why would he hide?" Dru asked the most obvious question—at least to her, it was.

"He isn't hiding, Mom." Shea was impatient.

"Erik is coming by here later when he gets off work." Kate didn't sound especially happy about it.

"Are you guys ever going to pick out a ring?" Van asked.

Dru had heard Vanessa calling herself the old maid of the bunch. She had never dated anyone seriously that Dru knew of. Shea said Van was too opinionated. She had a tongue like a lash. Not many guys wanted to contend with Van's cynical view of them, herself, the world.

"I don't know," Kate said. "I'm not in a rush. Especially now after what's happened. It's the last thing on my mind."

"Did Erik say when he last talked to AJ?" Shea was pleading with Kate.

Dru's heart turned over. She wanted to go to Shea, to wrap her daughter in her arms, but she knew better, knew Shea wouldn't have it.

"Yesterday, at lunch," Kate answered. "AJ called him to find out when he was planning to get his tux fitted. But you talked to AJ after that. You must be the last one who did."

"That we know of," Shea said. "Something terrible has happened to him." She paced to the breakfast-nook window. "I can feel it." She turned to face them, her mother, her friends. "I'm going to get people searching for him. I don't care what anyone says. We need to get flyers up, get the word out."

"Where?" Dru asked.

"In Dallas, around the apartment complex and the neighborhood where the school is. Here, in town, too. There are places up and down 1620 between here and the turnoff for the xL." FM 1620 was the main road, running east and west through Wyatt. There were a few small businesses scattered along the section Shea had mentioned, a convenience store, one or two gas stations.

Kate said, "He could be anywhere, though."

Shea said that was her point. "He could be hurt. Someone could have him locked up somewhere; I don't know. But somebody does. That's why we need to get photos of him out there. Someone might recognize him. If only we could get news coverage—"

"If someone has him, they could be dangerous," Vanessa said. "Maybe you should leave it to the police to do the looking."

"But they aren't looking for him; they're hunting him down like he's a criminal."

Van ducked her gaze.

Shea looked back at Kate. "Will you help me make flyers? We can do them on the computer."

Dru, stepping through the archway that separated the kitchen from the breakfast room, said, "Maybe you want to come with me to the Westins'. I'm going to drop off this meal and give them my condolences."

"What?" Shea stared at her. "Are you crazy, Mom? What if they're like the police and think AJ is responsible?"

Vanessa said, "I heard the police in Dallas called her parents to come and ID her body."

"Oh my God, that's awful," Kate said.

Dru got the sack with the food inside it from the kitchen. "I'll leave this with the neighbors if they aren't home."

"You're really going?" Shea was in disbelief.

"Yes, because no matter how it occurred, Joy and Gene have lost their daughter. Taking them a meal is the least I can do."

"Okay, but don't be surprised if they slam the door in your face." Shea sounded more forlorn than bitter.

"You'll be here when I get back?" Dru asked her. She looked around at the other girls. "I could pick up a pizza."

Her query was met with a chorus of maybes. Shea said flat-out she couldn't eat.

Letting it go at that, Dru walked outside to her car. A SUV she didn't recognize pulled up the driveway, a Lexus so new the dealer tags were still on it. She recognized Erik Ayala at the wheel. She clicked open the garage door, a signal to him that she was leaving and he should park on the apron.

"Hey, Mrs. Gallagher," he said, coming toward her.

"You have a new car," she said.

He glanced at the SUV. "Nah. It's off the lot where I'm working. One of the perks of the job, driving the cars. Pretty sweet ride, though, huh?" He didn't wait for Dru's answer. "God, I can't believe this is happening, can you? Poor Becca." His dark eyes were somber, worry filled.

"I know. It's terrible. Shea, Kate, Leigh, and Vanessa are inside. You haven't heard from AJ at all?"

"I wish to God I had." Erik shifted his glance. "I know how it looks, too, what everyone's saying."

"Shea had to talk to a detective in Dallas. The police there seem to think she knows where AJ is, that she's involved in some way."

"Yeah, I talked to them. They think the same thing about me." Erik brought his gaze back to Dru. "Because we're close to him, you know? How's Shea holding up?"

"She wants to put up missing-person flyers. Lily's got her half-convinced he's at the ranch, hiding. But I don't know why he'd hide. Do you?"

"I hope he *is* at the ranch, because like I told Kate, the alternative— what scares me is that AJ was the target. They took him, and they're holding him for ransom."

"God, I hadn't thought of that." It sounded so dramatic, like something from the movies or television. Dru held Erik's troubled gaze. "You said *they* just now. You think if he was taken, there was more than one person?"

"AJ's a big guy."

Dru saw Erik's point. AJ was over six feet and strong. It would have taken a lot to subdue him. "There hasn't been a ransom demand, has there?" she asked.

"Not that I've heard, but the cops may not publicize it."

Erik was right, Dru thought. They might insist that even Lily maintain secrecy.

"Becca was such a good person," Erik said. "Really sweet and kind. She never hurt anyone. It's fucked-up. Sorry."

For the language, he meant. Dru said it was fine, and after a beat, she said, "Vanessa thinks Becca still had feelings for AJ."

Erik frowned. "Really? I guess—I set them up. New Year's Eve, a year ago. They split a few weeks later."

"They weren't serious then?"

"AJ wasn't. He's the one who broke it off."

"Becca was unhappy about it?"

"Yeah, but she knew AJ wasn't coming back."

"She introduced Shea to AJ, though, right?"

Erik chuffed a wry breath. "She did, but it wasn't like she could have known she was bringing together the couple of the century."

"She regretted it?"

"Becca could be a bit of a drama queen, but she was a good sport. She was happy for them. She bragged about what a great matchmaker she was."

"So what was she doing at AJ's apartment?"

"I don't know. Maybe she did think she could change his mind." Erik shrugged.

"He let her in and they argued—" Dru was thinking out loud.

"She could have let herself in," Erik said. "AJ kept a key outside, in one of the gas lamps. We all knew about it."

Dru shifted the weight of the grocery sack to her other arm.

"What's Van trying to say, anyway? That Becca was stalking AJ, so he killed her? That's total bullshit. Sorry, my mouth gets away with me."

"It's all right." Dru asked Erik about his mother. "I heard she went home to Oaxaca, that her mother died. I'm so sorry."

"Yeah," Erik said. "They weren't really close, but Mom felt obligated. You know Catholics, big on guilt." He grinned briefly. "My grandmother never forgave Mom for leaving there, for wanting a better life. She always said Mom turned her back on her heritage."

"Well, it must have been hard for your grandmother, having her daughter and her grandson so far away—in another country."

"That's not my heritage, though, and Oaxaca isn't my country. I was born here. I'm an American. I barely speak Spanish."

He sounded annoyed, even defensive. But maybe that was how he dealt with it, the hard fact that his dad was there, in Oaxaca, instead of here, where he could be part of his son's life. Dru had wondered about him— whether it had been Erik's father's choice, or Winona's, that he stay away. If the tongues in town had an answer to that mystery, they'd kept still about it.

"I'm taking the Westins a meal," she said, indicating the bag. "I told the girls I'd pick up a pizza on my way back. I hope you'll stay."

Erik thanked her and started toward the house.

"Congratulations, by the way," Dru said after him.

He turned, brows raised.

"I don't think I've seen you since you got your new job, and I heard Kate said yes."

"She did. Last week. Her mom loves me," he added.

"Charla, yes, I know." Dru made an effort not to roll her eyes at the idea of Charla's devotion. "It pays to have your fiancée's mother in your corner."

Erik's grin was quick, spontaneous, a reflection of his total joy, and lasted only moments before he seemed to remember AJ, the terrible circumstances, and the uncertainty of the outcome. The memory of his engagement to Kate, this happy time in their lives, would forever be marred by this, Dru thought, no matter how it turned out.

• • •

The Westins lived on the east side of Wyatt in the Mustang Hill subdivision, an older neighborhood of winding streets, lined with a mix of Craftsman bungalows, small stone-faced Tudors, and Queen Anne cottages. The overall effect was charming, a throwback to another era, one that might have been pictured in a Norman Rockwell illustration for the *Saturday Evening Post*. When Dru and Shea had first moved out here from Houston, after Dru accepted the teaching position at the middle school, she had looked at houses in this neighborhood, but the yards were too small. Although most of them were beautifully landscaped, they were the size of postage stamps.

It had been a stretch financially, buying the three acres of land and the farmhouse on the outskirts of town. The house, built in 1910, needed constant attention, but Dru loved it. And over time she'd gotten pretty handy at plumbing and wiring. Last summer, with Shea's help, she'd gutted the laundry room, exposing the oak beams and longleaf-pine flooring. She'd learned enough that she was ready to tackle the kitchen. She wanted to enlarge it and take down the walls that separated it from the breakfast nook and dining room. Her catering business was growing; she could use the space.

Dru pulled to the curb in front of the Westins' tidy bungalow. Evening shadows encroached on it, softening the porch corners, erasing the eaves. The windows were dark, the driveway empty. No one was home. Dru's relief felt wrong when she thought of where the Westins were, the terrible task confronting them.

She was on the front porch with the sack of food when she heard a car approach, and turning to look, her heart faltered on recognizing Joy's Suburban. Gene was at the wheel, looking grim. Joy was staring in Dru's direction but not with any kind of recognition, or even animation. Gene parked in front of the garage, and as he and Joy were getting out, the next-door neighbor's front door opened, and TC, the Westins' eight-year-old son, shot across the yard, flinging himself at

Gene, throwing his arms around his dad's hips. Gene tousled his hair, saying something that sounded like "Hey, little buddy."

TC tilted back his head, looking up at Gene. "Did you find Becca, Dad? Did you bring her home?"

Gene knelt in front of TC on the sidewalk. "We did find her," he said, "but we didn't get to bring her home. Not yet. We couldn't."

"Why not?"

Gene looked at Joy, but she was mute, her face knotted with grief.

Dru's throat closed. She met the neighbor's eyes. Sharon Jefferson shook her head. *How awful.* She might have spoken the words aloud.

Gene took TC's hand. "Let's go inside, okay?"

He gave no indication he knew Dru was there until he reached the porch steps when she—not knowing what else to do—stepped forward and said how sorry she was. He stopped and thanked her then—thanked her! He looked hollow eyed and haggard, as if he'd aged twenty years. She felt terrible for him. She felt like running with the bag of food to her car. What use was a meal? She shouldn't have come. But here was Joy—and as Gene unlocked the front door, TC clinging to his free hand—Dru reached for her, enveloping her in a one-armed hug, murmuring her regret, her useless apology.

Joy tolerated Dru's attention without reciprocating it.

"I brought a meal, some chicken, a pasta salad," Dru said, releasing Joy.

"It was kind of you," Joy said, "but you shouldn't have gone to the trouble."

"It was no trouble," Dru protested. Joy was dry-eyed, and Dru wondered if she was in shock, if there was someone she should call. Was there family close by? She and Joy had been out of touch long enough that Dru couldn't remember.

"I've got food prepared, too," Sharon said. "I'll just go and get it."

Dru would never be certain if the Westins invited her into their home, or if she took it upon herself to follow them inside. She'd once known them better, Joy more than Gene, but that had been back when Shea, Kate, and Becca had been inseparable. Although it had been a while—a few years, in fact—Dru remembered the layout of the house, and while Joy, Gene, and TC went into the great room, she went to the kitchen and unloaded the food, stowing the dishes in the refrigerator. The shelves weren't entirely empty, but looking at them, Dru would have bet Joy planned to grocery shop in the next day or two. She could do it, Dru thought, if Joy would let her.

Closing the refrigerator door, she looked around, feeling helpless, wondering what else she could do. There must be family to notify, funeral arrangements to make. But the house was so quiet. The phone wasn't ringing; no one else was here. Where was Pastor Ingalls, or any of the folks from United Methodist, where the Westins attended church? Dru was a member there, too, although she hadn't been in a while. She didn't go as often as she had when Shea had lived at home. She didn't like attending alone.

She walked back through the house to the great room, thinking she would offer to call Pastor Ingalls before she left. Joy was sitting on an ottoman, and Gene was sitting on the sofa, holding TC between his knees, telling him that Becca was in heaven.

"She's an angel now?" TC asked.

"Yes," Joy said. "She's your angel, and she'll always be with you."

TC doodled a pattern with the tip of his index finger on Gene's jeans-clad thigh. "When can she come home?"

Dru's heart broke a little more, hearing that. How could a child understand a thing like this when even the parents couldn't accept it— that their own child had predeceased them?

"Well," Gene said, "she can't. That's just how it works. When you go to heaven and you're an angel, you have to stay there."

"We'll have a funeral for her in a few days," Joy said, smoothing TC's hair.

"Like we did for Molly?"

"Yes," Gene said.

Joy must have been aware of Dru after all, because she looked up. "Our Westie," she explained.

"I remember," Dru said. "Can I do anything for you? Call Pastor Ingalls or anyone?"

"He knows. He's coming by later."

"Would you like me to make a pot of coffee, then?" Dru wanted to do something, anything, almost as much as she wanted to leave.

"Oh, that would be nice," Joy said, and while her response seemed normal, her face and voice were devoid of expression. Her gestures were rote. It was eerie and horrible.

Dru turned away, retreating to the kitchen. She found the makings for coffee, and once it had brewed, the Westins joined her, sitting at the island. They'd put on a movie for TC.

"*Toy Story*," Gene said.

"It's his favorite movie to watch with Becca," Joy said. She had her eye on Dru as she filled the mugs. "I should make him something to eat." She sounded fretful now.

"He said he wasn't hungry. Remember, honey?" Gene said.

"Yes, but still . . ."

Dru brought the mugs to the island. "What about a PB and J?" she asked. "Would TC eat that, do you think?"

"I don't know what to tell Pastor Ingalls about the funeral." Joy spoke as if Dru hadn't. "No one at the morgue could say when we can bring Becca home. It might not be until next week."

Gene glanced at Dru. "They're doing an autopsy."

"I can't stand the thought of it." Joy curled her shoulders, holding her elbows in the cups of her hands. "All those people, the police and medical examiners, all of them looking at her, touching her. Becca would hate it. She never liked being the center of attention, and she was so modest. She would barely let me see her in her bra and panties."

A sound broke from Gene, something between a cough and a sob.

Dru put her hand on his shoulder, and he looked at it, and then up at her, and his eyes filled with something bitter like hatred, even loathing. Dru took her hand away.

"We know that punk your daughter's marrying did this. He hurt our girl." Gene stared at Dru. "The cops know it, too."

"I don't think they know that for sure." Dru backed away a step, shocked by Gene's accusation despite Shea's warning.

"Becca was murdered in his apartment." Gene's voice rose. "He's missing. Add it up."

Dru had added it up, and AJ's lack of a motive aside, her conclusion was the same as Gene's, but she couldn't tell him how sick it made her. Not without betraying Shea, and that was the one thing she simply would not, could not, do—not for anyone. Not even the Westins, who were in such terrible pain.

"I never liked that kid. I went to school with his mother. Lily Axel." Gene made the name sound like a joke. "Rich bitch. Thought she was better than everyone else. At least until she stepped in all that shit with the cops over in Phoenix. Like mother, like son."

What shit? Dru wanted to ask, but of course she didn't. She couldn't.

"What I heard, the old guy she married, Paul Isley? It was his influence and her daddy's money got her out of that, but I will be goddamned if it gets AJ out of this. I'll see Jeb Axel and his fucking punk grandson in hell first, if I have to take us there myself." Gene got up, fast enough that the bar stool went over, slamming to the floor. Dru jumped, and she jumped again when Gene went out the back door, slamming it so hard the glass rattled.

Dru looked at Joy, but she was staring into her untouched mug of coffee, gone cold now. Her nose was red and running; tears smeared her face. Somehow Dru was relieved to see them. She found a box of tissues in the powder room off the kitchen and brought several back to Joy, handing them to her.

"Becca was pregnant."

Dru was righting the stool when Joy said it. "Pregnant?" she repeated. *As in having a baby?* The words ran stupidly through her mind.

"The medical examiner said she was about five weeks along." Joy looked up at Dru.

"I didn't know she was seeing anyone."

"She wasn't—I mean, not since AJ broke it off with her. I told her she should go out more, find another boyfriend, that it was the fastest way to mend a broken heart, but she wouldn't hear of it. She said AJ was the one for her, and he knew she was the one for him, too."

Dru stared, speechless.

"I wasn't happy to hear it, either, trust me. They evidently ran into each other at Starbucks, in March, I think. One thing led to another. Becca only told me about it a couple of weeks ago." Joy paused. "I'm sorry for the pain this causes you or Shea."

"The baby was AJ's?"

"Well, yes. Who else? The ME's doing a DNA test to determine paternity for sure, but I told him he didn't have to for my sake."

"Was the murdering son of a bitch going to tell Shea?" Dru gripped the seat back of the bar stool she'd righted. Her mind flashed to Erik, his assertion that there was no way AJ had been interested in Becca. AJ had fooled him, too.

"Becca said they were waiting for the right time. That's why she went to Dallas Tuesday. She said they were going to figure it out, and I let her go." Abruptly, Joy's head fell back. "I let her go," she wailed, and the sound was like nothing Dru had ever heard. After a moment, leveling her gaze, she said, "I will never forgive myself."

There was no point in arguing, Dru thought. She would blame herself if she were Joy. Dru shifted her glance, jaw knotted, struggling for composure. She thought if AJ were to appear in front of her, she would strangle him with her bare hands. How could he have done this to Becca, to Shea? Betrayed them in such a horrible way? It made sense now, though, that he was on the run, because that's what rat bastards did—they ran.

"Gene thinks Becca was fooling herself. AJ didn't want the baby," Joy said. She was back to speaking in her eerily flat voice. "Gene thinks if it had been born, it would have kept AJ from what he did want, which was to keep screwing—to keep fucking—Gene said fucking—Becca behind Shea's back."

"What do you think, Joy?"

"I don't know. Becca seemed convinced AJ loved her." Joy fiddled with her coffee mug. "Maybe it wasn't AJ but someone else who was there in his apartment."

"Like who? Who else would have a reason to—"

"Someone who hated her." Joy looked at Dru now, locking her gaze, and there was some awful disturbance in her eyes, a sort of challenge.

She seemed to be waiting for Dru to catch on, and when Dru did, her stomach lurched. "You think it was Shea! You talked to that detective, Bushnell. He put the idea in your head."

"He asked me about her—"

"Joy, for God's sake, Shea's been at home, with me, since Sunday. The girls were all together on Tuesday, getting the mason jars in Fredericksburg, having lunch. Becca was sick—"

"I told the police that, but Shea could've gone to Dallas later."

"No. She was here on Tuesday night, all night. We had dinner. We worked on the wedding favors." Dru said what came into her head. She and Shea might have done something else, or nothing. What mattered, though, what she was sure of, was that Shea hadn't driven to Dallas or anywhere else since she'd been back in Wyatt.

Joy didn't confirm or deny Dru's defense of Shea, and the air between them was thick with foreboding, a darker shadow of doubt.

"The wedding is two weeks from Saturday." Dru didn't know why she said it.

"I'll have buried my girl by then," Joy said.

5

Lily called Paul in the hour or so before dawn, and when he answered, his voice, like hers, was gravelly with lack of sleep.

"I heard from AJ just now," she said. "He asked me to bring him his passport."

"So he's not out of the country," Paul said after a moment. "But the cops haven't found his passport."

"Does he have a safe-deposit box?" Should she know? Did other parents know such things about their grown children?

Paul ignored her question. "Did he say where he is? How did he sound?"

"I don't know. Tired?" Lily thought about it. Her dad had gone downstairs to make coffee, but she was still in the upstairs hallway near the ancient landline, afraid to leave it in case AJ called again. "He didn't talk much above a whisper."

"I wish he'd called me," Paul said with obvious disappointment.

Lily agreed. "Yes, I'm sure you would have handled it better." She meant it; she wished AJ had called Paul, too. Then when he came away with no more information than she had, he'd have only himself to blame.

AJ had a safe-deposit box, Paul said. He'd seen to it when AJ went overseas. If Lily didn't know, it was because she'd forgotten, not because Paul had failed to tell her. "Bushnell can get a warrant," he said, "if they won't let me open it. He's getting one now for AJ's cell phone. It's just a long damn process."

Lily said, "Don't you think it's time to contact Edward and let him know what's going on?" It occurred to her if he'd listened to the news, he might know already. It was even possible, she thought, that he would reach out to her. The realization made her heart pound irrationally. The possibility of talking to him again, of seeing him, thrilled her even as she was panicked by it.

Paul said, "I think getting a criminal attorney involved at this point is premature, but should the time come, I'm not calling on Dana. I'll get someone else."

Lily was taken aback. What did he mean? She was afraid to ask. Afraid a discussion would lead to an argument. Paul would see that she cared, that it mattered. It wasn't a risk she could take.

A silence closed around them, an empty room without an exit.

Paul broke it. "I asked Bushnell if he was still thinking this could be a kidnapping and Becca somehow got mixed up in it. Got in the way."

Lily couldn't speak. Her mouth was dry, as dry as sticks.

"I could see by the look on his face that he doesn't. I almost wish for it, you know? A ransom demand? At least then we'd know what the hell it is we're dealing with. The cops would get the FBI involved, get somebody on this that's got a fucking brain."

Paul didn't ordinarily use foul language. He claimed those who did were only showing their ignorance and lack of civility. But he was at the end of his rope now, and he had no control. The police weren't his employees; they didn't take orders from him. Inside, he must be seething, Lily thought. He must be ready to explode.

"If Bushnell or any of those assholes call you, don't tell them you spoke to AJ," he said. "I don't want to help them find AJ, not until we know more about the kind of trouble he's in. Tell them to call Jerry—let him deal with them."

"But I don't understand." Lily went to the top of the staircase and looked down it, seeing nothing. "Suppose AJ *has* been kidnapped, or someone *is* keeping him against his will. We need the police to get him back. Not telling them could get AJ killed." *I will never forgive you, never speak to you again if that happens.* The threat burned through her mind. It was the same one she'd shouted at Paul after he'd forced AJ to enlist.

"You want him arrested and charged with murder? Fine, talk to them, then. I can't stop you."

"No, Paul. I didn't mean—" Lily stopped. "Paul?" she said, but she knew he'd hung up on her, that she was talking to dead air.

She was annoyed when her father agreed with Paul.

"If AJ's trying to get away, get somewhere he feels safe, we don't want to go tipping off the cops," her dad said. "If they were to corner him and things got heated, it could go bad in a hurry."

They were sitting in the pair of old rockers on the front porch now, drinking the coffee her dad had made.

"Paul said it's likely they're watching the airports."

"Because they haven't found the passport."

"Yes." Lily set down her mug, feeling too shaky to hold it. Before coming outside, she'd put on an old sweater she'd found hanging in the coat closet, and she wrapped it more tightly around her.

"I just don't think the kid would go on the run without telling someone. If not you, me, or Paul, then Shea. He'd want her with him."

"She hasn't talked to him, though."

"So she says."

Lily looked over at her dad. "You think she's protecting him?"

66

"I don't know her well enough to answer that. But we both know people lie. For any number of reasons," he added, and when he shifted his gaze from hers, it gave Lily an odd feeling.

"Paul said they're getting AJ's cell-phone records. Won't they find out who he's called and where he is?"

"Yeah, they have to get a subpoena, and that can take a while if a judge will even grant the request. The cops have got to establish probable cause."

It seemed to Lily there was plenty of that. While they sat around talking about the alternatives—maybe AJ was a fugitive, maybe AJ was a hostage—the evidence was pointing to something far worse, a possibility that none of them wanted to look at, much less discuss. "Paul wants me to call Jerry Dix if the police try to question me again."

"Dix? He's a corporate attorney, for Christ's sake. Who was the attorney you worked with before when AJ was arrested? Edward something."

"Edward Dana. I think we should call him, but Paul wants to hire someone else."

"But if it hadn't been for Dana back when AJ got into all that trouble before, he would have seen prison time. Paul knows that. What's his objection?"

"I don't know." Lily was lying, and possibly her dad knew it. She could feel his gaze, but she couldn't meet it. She was afraid he would see, as Paul must have, the warmth of her feelings for Edward, the telltale signs of her attraction for him that wouldn't go away. It was three years since they'd last met at their place—one of them—the little roadside café with the terrible food and worse coffee north of Greeley. It had been raining that day, hard enough that she'd felt the wet seeping through the thin soles of her flats, splattering her ankles. Standing beneath the awning with Edward, waiting for a break in the storm to make a run for it, he had brushed the side of her hand; he had linked his little finger with her own. Even the memory of that—his slightest touch—heated her longing for him. And it was wrong. It could never be.

Sudden birdsong shattered the silence, and she shied from it. *See me, see me, see me,* it seemed to cry. Lily hunted for the singer and spotted him, the bright-red flash of a cardinal flitting through the bony spread of an old live oak near the drive.

Her dad said, "You realize whoever murdered Becca could have AJ's credit cards and driver's license, his bank-account numbers."

"But his wallet was found in his apartment."

"Was everything in it?"

"I don't know."

"Well, we know they've got his truck, unless they've ditched it by now."

An image darkened Lily's mind of AJ, driving God knew where, with a gun to his temple. She slammed a mental door on it. "If he's picked up in another state, it might be days before we hear," she said, and it didn't surprise her when her dad locked her gaze.

He knew the reference Lily was making. When she'd gone off with Jesse Kerman after graduating from high school, her father hadn't known where she was until she was arrested and jailed a week later in Phoenix for being an accessory to armed robbery and murder when Jesse held up a mini-mart. The police there had kept her almost seventy-two hours before allowing her to call her dad. He'd been out of his mind with worry by then. Lily had always thought fear was the reason he hadn't killed her when he got to Phoenix with Paul.

She'd been eighteen, only months younger than AJ had been when he'd been arrested. The charge had been similar, too—accessory to murder. Even the circumstances were similar. AJ had been out with a rough gang of friends he'd taken up with, like the crew of guys Jesse had ridden with, guys who were into mostly petty crime. They were an older crowd, the way Jesse's crowd had been, and seemed dangerous in a way that AJ had thought he wanted to be. Who knew why. Lily hadn't understood the compulsion in herself. But it had taken AJ to the same wrong time, wrong place as it had Lily. In AJ's case, at a party, a fight over a girl had ended in gunfire. Two people had died, three had been injured. AJ had tried to stop it; evidence had ultimately proved that, the same as evidence in Lily's situation had proved her innocence. But it had taken months of expensive legal wrangling, and once AJ's ordeal was over, Paul was finished. That's when he'd delivered his ultimatum: AJ could enlist or get out. Either way, Paul was done supporting him. AJ needed discipline; he needed to grow up, find a direction. Be a man.

Lily had been torn.

Her dad had had a similar response when he'd brought her home from Phoenix. Get a job, go back to school, or get married, he'd said. He and Paul had gone out on a limb for her, and she'd been given a second chance. He wasn't about to let her piss it away. *"I never thought I'd say this,"* he'd told her, *"but I'm glad your mother's dead, that she didn't live to see what you've done to yourself."*

It had nearly crushed her, hearing him say that. Lily had always thought she would be a better person if her mother had lived. She wouldn't have made so many terrible and irrevocable mistakes.

She looked over at her dad now. "Did AJ ever tell you that he dreamed of this house while he was in Afghanistan?"

"Yeah." Her dad scrubbed his hands down the tops of his legs to his knees. He looked at Lily, looked away.

"What?"

"You know," he began, "this—what's happening now—you know it's not got shit to do with that gang crap he got into before he joined the marines. He was responsible for that, and he knew it—not for the violence, those people getting killed, but for getting involved with those losers to begin with. This deal, the murder of this girl—it's different."

She knew, Lily said.

Her dad went to the porch rail, tossed the last of his coffee into the yard, and he was turning back when both he and Lily were distracted by the noise of car engines. Within a couple of minutes, two SUVs, one shiny black, the other a sun-faded red, came into view and parked in the driveway, near the front of the house.

"What's he doing here?" her dad said when Erik got out of the new SUV, a Lexus, Lily thought.

"Let it go, Dad," Lily said. "He's as worried about AJ as we are." Then, watching Dru and Shea get out of the older-model SUV, she felt a sinking sense of regret and added, "We need to pull together for AJ's sake," and she was admonishing herself now as much as anyone.

"I'm so glad to see you," Lily told Erik, hugging him tightly as he came up the porch steps. He was as tall, broad shouldered, and strongly built as AJ, and she was loath to let him go. "When you didn't call me back, I started to worry you'd disappeared, too." She thought of the times when the boys had been younger and they'd gone off somewhere on the ranch, promising to be home by dinner, how she and Winona had looked at each other when it got to be dark thirty and there wasn't a sign of them or the sound of hoofbeats. A few times either she, Win, or her dad had saddled up and gone to hunt for them. But that worry paled in comparison, and Erik must have sensed it, because he apologized.

"New job," he said. "It's crazy."

"Ha!" Her dad snorted. "I heard about that. You're a car salesman, right? Up in Greeley? That where you got the Lexus? Is that why you went to work there? So you could drive a fancy car without having to pay for it?"

"Dad . . ." But even as Lily was provoked by his attack on Erik, she understood it. She wondered if it could be true, that Erik had chosen to be a car salesman over xL's ranch foreman so he could drive an expensive car, act like a big shot. Although she'd heard him deny it, maybe he preferred living in town, wearing a coat and tie to work, having clean fingernails. Maybe the job of car salesman was perfect for him. Unlike his mom, who was quiet and reserved, Erik was easygoing and sociable to the point of being boisterous. He was perfect for a career in sales.

Lily touched his arm. "I'm glad you're here now," she said, meaning it.

Dru had come up behind Erik and regarded Lily now over his shoulder. She hadn't missed it, Lily realized—the crackle of antagonism that existed between her dad and Erik.

Shea said, "I hope it's okay that we came. I couldn't stand sitting at home, waiting around one more second."

Lily embraced her; it seemed the thing to do, and after a moment's hesitation, she and Dru shared a hug, too. It was awkward, and it struck Lily it would never have happened under ordinary circumstances.

"AJ called here last night," Lily said as soon as Dru stepped away from her.

Shea was speechless. A thousand questions haunted her eyes.

Lily quickly related the specifics, and during her recital, all of them, with the exception of her dad, sat down, Dru and Shea in the pair of rockers, Erik and Lily on the swing.

Her dad leaned against the porch rail.

They talked about AJ's request for his passport, the possibility that he'd been kidnapped. Lily's dad reiterated his opinion that AJ was still in the area.

Shea said, "We put up missing-person flyers around town early this morning, but we need to get the media involved, too. There's been almost nothing on television about it."

"Some councilman and his girlfriend up in Dallas are missing, along with a bunch of money. They're all over that," Erik said.

"Well," Dru said, "I'm listening to all this, what y'all are saying, and my question is if AJ's around here, if he's not being held against his will, why doesn't he just go to the police? I mean, you've said he's innocent, right?" She looked around at each of them.

But Lily saw that no one was looking back. No one was answering. And then it hit her. Dru didn't know about AJ's past arrest, the prior history that made him such an attractive suspect now. Shea's glance collided with Lily's and seemed filled with pleading. *Don't tell,* she seemed to say.

Lily got out of the swing. "I'm going to get the Jeep and drive around. Maybe it's crazy, but if AJ is nearby—"

Erik got up, too. "It's why we came over, because we thought—well, we have to do something, right? Even if it's stupid. AJ's always loved this place."

Lily put her hand on Erik's shoulder.

He met her gaze. "We'll find him," he said, and the conviction in his voice heartened her. He wouldn't give up until AJ was found, and neither would she.

Her dad said he would saddle Sharkey and ride west toward Little Bottom Creek. "It'll be easier searching that area on horseback."

Lily was surprised to hear Erik say he'd ride out with him.

"Sure you can take time from your job?" her dad asked, and Lily was irked anew.

"Yeah. I told my boss the situation. He understood." If Erik was offended, he didn't let on. "I've only been there a short time, but so far this month I'm lead salesman."

Lily looked at her dad, willing him to say something supportive, but he didn't, and it was left to her and Shea and Dru to cover his silence with their offers of congratulations.

"I'd like to ride with you and Erik," Shea said to Lily's dad. "AJ talked once about a fort y'all built out that way—on past the creek, right? He was going to show it to me, but it got dark too fast."

Lily's dad smiled, and glancing at Erik, he said, "How old were you when we built that thing? Twelve, is that right? AJ was nine. It was some work rigging it up in those trees."

"Yeah," Erik said, "but it was so cool. We were like the pioneers. We built a raft using cedar logs and ferried all the building materials across the Little Bottom on horseback."

"You remember when we lost that load of cedar logs?"

Lily's dad's eyes on Erik now were warm with affection.

Erik laughed. "Water was high after the rain that spring. AJ and I had to swim like hell to catch the raft. If you hadn't jumped in, we would have lost it."

"I've still got the plans we drew up someplace." Her dad's gaze was loose.

"We should check it out," Shea said.

"Yeah," Erik said. "But last time I was out there, it was mostly fallen in. I doubt you could even get up in there now."

Lily's dad straightened. "Well, there's a hell of a lot of ground to cover between here and there. We should get a move on, if we're going."

Shea turned to her mother. "You don't have to stay. Erik can bring me home."

"No," Dru said. "If you're staying, I'm staying. I won't ride, though. Horses and I don't get along."

"You can go with me in the Jeep, if you want to," Lily heard herself say.

Dru wanted to decline; Lily hoped she would, but after a moment, Dru shrugged and said, "Fine." It took her another longer moment to act, to come to her feet, shoulder her purse.

Lily addressed her dad. "We'll go south to the old well site. We'll check out the cabin, too, and the railroad trestle."

"All right," he said, and then he gripped her upper arm a moment, steadying her, telling her through his touch—the best way he knew—that he wouldn't give up, not on his faith in AJ's innocence, not on finding him.

Lily searched his gaze, hunting for a sign of yesterday's mental fumbling, finding none, and grateful that she didn't. She had heard that in the early stages, the symptoms of Alzheimer's, or senility—that sort of brain ailment—could come and go. Her dad seemed strong now, his usual take-charge self. Maybe his lapses were from stress. He hadn't really known what to do with himself since he'd quit ranching and sold off the herd. She didn't want to think what would happen if he were to sell off the land, too. Where would he go to live? Town? She couldn't imagine it. The Texas coast? She'd heard him say he wouldn't mind settling down where he could hear the ocean. But moving away would kill him, she thought. The xL was part of him.

She followed him around back, Shea, Dru, and Erik in her wake, and before they split up, they exchanged cell numbers and agreed they'd meet back at the house in three hours, earlier if they found something.

Dru waited in the driveway for Lily to back out the Jeep, then climbed into the passenger seat. She fumbled with the seat belt.

"It doesn't work," Lily said. "Neither does the AC."

Dru shot her a look, some mix of scorn and disbelief.

Lily's jaw hardened. "Don't worry, you're safe with me," she said. "I'm not a maniac."

6

Unlike your son, Dru thought, shifting her glance from Lily's. She set her purse on the floor at her feet. It was heavy with the weight of a .38 Special revolver. It belonged to her; she was licensed to carry it. Her instructor in Houston had called her a natural, a crack shot. She'd never repeated his praise; she wasn't proud of it. She wasn't into guns, had never imagined owning one, but when the man who professed to love you, the one you snuggled up to in the night, the one who had made you laugh and made you feel safe for thirteen years, could suddenly and with little provocation back you out of your house at gunpoint, you have to rethink things. You can't go on in the same way, trusting the world, or the people in it, who in the end will only break your heart and try to kill you.

Shea didn't know she had the .38 with her, and she wouldn't like it, but Shea was still young enough to have faith in people, especially those she loved. She believed her father when he said he'd dealt with his issues and was no longer subject to violence. She thought she knew people and what went on in their heads. Dru couldn't afford to be so naive. Not when it might be her daughter's life on the line. Unlike Shea and Jeb Axel, Dru didn't believe AJ was close by. He wasn't that dumb. He'd have left the area, even the state, by now. If Dru thought he was anywhere near here, she'd have found a way to keep Shea home.

The Jeep bounced over a cattle guard, and Dru put her hand on the dash, bracing herself. It surprised her that the Axels owned a vehicle that was so old. Circa 1980 was Dru's guess. It was an even greater surprise to see Lily Isley at the wheel, much less dressed in worn jeans and faded brown western boots. Old Gringos, from the look of them. Her hair was caught in a messy ponytail. Her shirt was creased. She looked disheveled, half-panicked and exhausted, but even so, she was an attractive woman. *Queenly* was the word, Dru thought, along with regal and cold.

"Dad taught me to drive in this Jeep," Lily said. "AJ, too."

Dru propped her elbow on the window ledge.

"I know you don't like my son, but you're wrong if you think he had anything to do with Becca's death."

You don't like my daughter. Dru thought of tossing that bit into the mix. She thought of saying how it made her feel, knowing Lily didn't think Shea—who was as beautiful on the inside as she was on the outside, and who was filled with a zest for life and possessed of an uncommon faith in it—was good enough for AJ. But Dru sensed Lily was struggling to keep her composure, and it bothered her, enough that she kept still.

"There's no motive." Lily's voice was firmer than before.

"I took a meal over to Becca's family yesterday evening," Dru said. "They'd just come back from the morgue in Dallas. They were called there by the police to identify Becca's body."

Lily glanced at Dru, shock and horror mingling in her expression, and Dru knew she hadn't thought of it before, the terrible necessity for Becca's parents to make a firm identification of their child's body. "While they were there, the medical examiner—" Dru stopped to consider. Had Joy told her in confidence? But even if she had, the media wouldn't respect the Westins' privacy.

Dru felt the weight of Lily's gaze.

"Becca was pregnant," she said.

Silence. Quick impressions of Lily's eyes pouring disbelief, the white of her knuckles as they gripped the Jeep's steering wheel.

"It's true," Dru said. "The ME told Joy—Becca's mom—she was five weeks along."

"It isn't—? You aren't suggesting it was AJ's?" Lily's eyes darted to Dru's, back to the road. "My God, you must know how much he loves Shea. He would never betray her."

"But he did. Becca told Joy she and AJ were seeing each another again, starting back in March."

"No," Lily said.

"She was happy about it." Dru went on. "I guess AJ was, too, until Becca told him she was pregnant." Gene's theory that a baby would have interfered with AJ having his cake and eating it, too, passed through Dru's mind. She wouldn't repeat it; she wouldn't add to Lily's anguish.

"It's not possible." Lily was tight-jawed, grim.

Denial, Dru thought. The last refuge. She thought of her own denial when Joy had insinuated Shea might have played a role in Becca's murder. Dru had forced herself to consider the possibility, but it simply wasn't logical. She had seen Shea go to bed around eleven on Tuesday night, and when Dru passed by Shea's bedroom near seven on Wednesday morning, she'd been curled on her side, facing the open doorway, her hair a dark fan on her pillow. Dru had lingered for several moments, thinking how few mornings were left for her to have her daughter home, to watch her unaware as she slept. But sentimentality aside, if the cops had even the whiff of a suspicion Shea was involved in Becca's death, wouldn't they have questioned her personally? Wasn't it likely they'd have brought her to Dallas and interviewed her there, rather than over the phone? Dru didn't know. Maybe she only wanted to believe that was how law enforcement operated.

The Jeep slowed, making a right turn onto a narrow, winding lane. Morning sunlight glinted off the caliche surface, heated the air blowing through the car's open windows. Coming around a broad curve, Dru saw the cabin in the distance. Made of cedar logs with a rusted tin cap for a roof, it slumped, incongruously, in the shadow of a magnificent and towering red oak.

Lily broke the silence. "If you're so convinced AJ has done all these horrible things, if you think he's a liar, a cheater, and a murderer, why are you here? Even more to the point, why is Shea? You must hate him. You must wish him dead."

Moments passed in an awful, sinking silence. Shea didn't know about AJ's betrayal of her, or the baby that had been the result. It hadn't been Dru's intention to hide the truth, but arriving home last night with the pizza, she'd found Shea sitting with Erik and Kate in the great room, and the atmosphere had been so charged with tension and anxiety— Shea's fear had been palpable—that Dru had lied when Shea questioned her about her visit with the Westins. They were coping, Dru had said. They hadn't mentioned AJ or Shea, she had said.

Lily pulled up to the cabin, near what was left of the front stoop, and turned off the Jeep's ignition.

"Shea doesn't know about Becca's pregnancy." Dru didn't look at Lily when she said it, but at the sad, broken face of the small house. The front door hung askew from a single hinge, and the glass was missing from the windows on either side. They seemed to stare like shattered eyes.

"No one really knows who built this place," Lily said. "It was here when my great-grandfather bought the land. Dad has always thought it was the home the original settlers built. They were German people who came west. There's a rock out back, part of the foundation for the original barn, we think, that's got the year 1862 carved in it."

Dru glanced at Lily, wondering what to make of her impromptu history lesson. Maybe it was a distraction, or a way to keep her emotions in check. Dru felt almost sick with her own stew of feelings.

"I'm going to look inside. You can wait out here if you want to." Lily got out of the Jeep, tucking the keys into her jeans pocket.

"No, I'm coming, too." Dru looked at her purse, thinking of the .38. But in the end she left it and followed Lily. Somehow toting the gun didn't seem justified.

The air inside the cabin smelled musty. They had only crossed the threshold when something swooped by them, a black blur that shot through the open doorway. Dru didn't know how she kept the frightened cry she felt scrape her throat from coming out.

"Bat," Lily said, pushing her sunglasses onto the top of her head.

Dru did the same, waiting for her eyes to adjust to the gloom.

Neither of them moved for several moments.

Light through the broken-paned windows shafted the worn pine floor, turned the dust they'd disturbed into glittering swirls. Across the room, a carved cane-bottom rocker, surprising in its delicate stature, sat before the yawning, blackened maw of a rough-hewn limestone fireplace. The chair looked out of place. Dru would bet there was a story in it, one that would intrigue her. She would have asked about it under other circumstances, if she and Lily were friends, say. If they were here for any other reason than to hunt for Lily's son, who might be a danger or endangered. Which of the scenarios was the correct one was the million-dollar question.

There were two bedrooms on either side of the front room, and Dru and Lily looked in both of them. In the second one, a pretty, old four-poster bed, missing a foot post and its mattress, was pushed against the far wall. Along with the rocker, the bed was the only other furniture in the house. There was no sign of AJ. No indication he had been here, or that anyone had, not in a long time. Walking out, Dru noted that her footprints and Lily's were the only ones tracking the dust on the floor. And outside, only the tread from the Jeep's tires, and their own shoes, matted the scruffy apron of grass that led to the cabin's door. She glanced at Lily and was startled to find her looking back.

"Are you going to tell her?"

Dru looked into the field across the road. The wind bent the hip-high grass, roughing it into dry waves. "I wish I could protect her." Dru brought her gaze back to Lily.

They considered each other, and the understanding of how alike they were as mothers in their desire to shield their children—for they are always your children, regardless of age—arced between them.

Lily said, "You know she could hear it elsewhere—on the news, if they get around to it."

"I'm going to tell her," Dru said. "I wanted to do this for her, though, come with her here—to give her support, let her see for herself—" She looked off again, not saying the rest—that her fear was that once Shea knew of the pregnancy, she'd be angry at Dru. Shea would assume it made Dru happy having her low opinion of AJ confirmed when nothing could be further from the truth.

"Have they done a DNA test? They know for certain AJ is the father?"

"Not yet. Joy said it could be days, even weeks, before the test results are in."

If Lily was relieved, she didn't say. Instead, she mentioned the old railroad trestle. "It's close by. Erik and AJ used to go there when they were kids." She lowered her sunglasses, covering her eyes, and pulled the car keys from her pocket. "I'll take you back to the house first. You can wait for Shea there. I think we'd both be more comfortable."

Lily's clipped tone as good as said she didn't want Dru's company any longer, and it rankled. "It's not personal, you know." Dru addressed Lily over the Jeep's roof.

"What isn't? Your dislike of my son, or your wish that he's dead, as dead as Becca."

"Oh my God! I never said—you can't deny AJ has—" Dru hesitated. "Issues. He's not the only one to come back from Afghanistan, from war, damaged, and it concerns me. Yes, it does, for my daughter, her well-being, her safety and happiness. It's not AJ's fault this happened to him. We're not—the United States should do more to help our veterans."

"Our veterans? What do you know about them, Dru? Shea didn't enlist. She's never risked her life to save others the way AJ did. Does that sound like the action of a murderer to you? Would someone who put his life on the line the way AJ did, time and again, come home only to kill someone, a pregnant woman?" Lily huffed a breath, agitated by disgust, the huskier undernote of withheld tears.

"I know you don't want to believe it, but he could have suffered a break, a psychotic break. It happens."

"AJ isn't capable—"

"My ex-husband, Rob, Shea's father, suffers from PTSD," Dru said. She didn't want to bring it up, not any part of her personal life, but she felt pushed to do it. "His experience wasn't the result of going to war. He was assaulted and robbed. The thugs who attacked him beat him to within an inch of his life. As horrible as his physical injuries were, they were the least of it. He had night terrors. He was paranoid. He thought everyone was out to get him, even me. He bought several guns, one for every room of the house. He slept—when he did sleep, it was with a .357 under his pillow, one eye open, one foot—"

"I'm sorry, but I don't have time—"

"One night he heard me in the kitchen." Dru kept talking. "I'd gotten up because Shea wasn't feeling good, and I'd been in to check on her, then came downstairs to make myself some warm milk and honey. My ex claimed he thought I was an intruder, that I'd broken into the house to rob him. He had a shotgun and threatened me with it. Shea heard us, and when she came downstairs, Rob didn't know who she was, either. He could have killed us, he was that out of it. To this day I'm not sure why he didn't."

"My son is missing, Dru, possibly injured or worse." Lily's eyes on Dru's were hard. "I need to keep looking for him."

"I never would have believed Rob was capable of violence, if I hadn't been there, seen it with my own eyes." Dru paused, fighting a dirty wash of emotion. "I loved my husband with my whole heart," she said softly. "I still do. He was the one for me. Our marriage wasn't perfect; he wasn't perfect, but up until the assault, he was—was a great guy. Maybe if after the assault he'd talked to me—to someone, but he didn't. He withdrew, went into himself. When he looked at me, I couldn't tell what he was thinking." Dru sought Lily's glance. "If one act of violence can so irrevocably change someone, I can't begin to imagine the emotional effect of multiple acts of violence such as what soldiers experience during war."

Lily averted her glance. It had gotten to her, though, Dru's story. She could sense that Lily knew her point exactly. Lily wouldn't admit it, though. She wasn't going to come out and say AJ had PTSD, and that he may have, like Rob, lost touch with reality and become a danger to others and maybe to himself.

Dru got into the Jeep. "It's not that I don't feel compassion," she said, "because I do."

Lily keyed the ignition, not acknowledging if she'd even heard Dru.

"I'll ride with you to the railroad trestle," Dru said.

"All right, then," Lily said. "The old well house is a few miles farther on. I'm going there, too."

There were other buildings, Lily said, additional well houses, sheds, and the like; it would take days to search them, and Dru sensed that by talking, Lily was determined to ignore the rancor between them. Or possibly she was intent on drowning it out.

"AJ knows the ranch as well as my dad does," Lily said. "He could be any number of places."

"If he's hiding, you mean."

Lily didn't respond.

Dru said, "You don't like the idea of your son and my daughter marrying any better than I do—even before all this happened."

"No, but like you, it's not personal. Anyway, Shea is his choice."

"So you'll make the best of it."

"I'll do what I have to in support of my son."

"Does he know how you feel?"

"No, and even if he did, my opinion isn't that important to him."

Dru looked at Lily, surprised by her admission, touched by it.

"We aren't close." Lily pushed her hand over her hair.

"I'm sorry," Dru said, and she was, and when Lily asked about the wedding, whether there was a way to avoid canceling it, Dru said she didn't think so.

"It's going to be awful," Lily said. "There are more than a hundred people invited between us, aren't there?"

"It's nothing in comparison to planning your child's funeral," Dru said.

"No."

"Shea's bridal attendants will help with sending regrets."

"I can take care of our guest list and cancel the rehearsal dinner. Or if there's some other way you'd like me to handle it . . ." Lily glanced at Dru.

"I was thinking we could each contact the guests we've invited."

"And the vendors we've hired?"

"Yes. It feels horrible, doesn't it? Impossible—like stopping a train."

Lily started to answer, but her phone went off, and she pulled to the road's edge, slamming on the brake, grabbing her purse.

Dru watched her, heart racing.

"It's Paul." Lily looked up from the caller ID.

"I'll just stretch my legs," Dru said, getting out of the car. She closed the Jeep's door quietly and headed across the road, where a section of old cedar fencing supported the thick growth of a morning-glory vine, smothering it in cascades of sky-blue flowers. Still, she heard Lily's voice, the ring of her anxiety: "But did anyone actually see him?" A beat. "It makes no sense that he would . . ." The wind took away the next bit. Then, "He might not have . . ." Dru lost the rest.

She didn't turn around, though, until Lily called out, "Dru! We need to go now. I have to get back to Dallas."

"What happened?" Dru got into the Jeep.

"The police found AJ's cell phone and his laptop." Lily made a U-turn. "At the bus station in downtown Dallas, abandoned in the seat of a chair."

"Did anyone see him?"

"A janitor said he saw AJ coming out of the men's room at around three in the morning. He remembered him because he was wearing dark glasses, and it struck him as odd, given that it was the middle of the night."

"So he got on a bus? He's on the run?" Accusation cut through Dru's voice, but her mind was on Shea, how terribly she was going to be hurt. She didn't know Becca had been pregnant. Now this? "Do the police know where he was going?"

"I know how it looks, but no one they interviewed actually saw him get on a bus." Lily glanced at Dru.

She shifted her glance. She was tired of hearing everyone say that—as if how it looked wasn't the way it was. As if there could still be an explanation other than the obvious one for AJ's actions.

Lily called her dad and arranged to meet him back at the house. After that, neither she nor Dru spoke for several miles, but then Lily said, "He's my son, no matter what."

Guilty or innocent, it didn't matter.

Dru understood. She would feel the same if it were Shea. Your children are your children, and you love them regardless. But Dru understood something else as well: Lily wasn't as certain about AJ as she sounded.

Lily had doubts.

· · ·

The others weren't back when they arrived at the house. Lily went inside to pack her things while Dru waited on the porch. A moment later she heard the screen door open, Shea's voice.

"Mom?"

"Oh, Shea." Dru took a step toward her daughter but stopped when Shea threw up her hands.

"I'm fine." *Stop.* She might as well have shouted it. Her jaw was set, her eyes stubborn. She didn't believe it, that AJ was on the run. How could she not believe it? But her faith in him would end. Once she knew about the baby.

Dru met Erik's glance when he joined them on the porch.

"Hey," he said, and that was all.

He seemed heartsick—a reaction more in keeping with what Dru had expected from Shea on hearing her betrothed, a wanted man, had hopped a bus and skipped town. Erik looked as if he'd begun to accept that his best buddy had done something pretty terrible, monstrous even.

Lily came out, a tote over her shoulder, followed by her dad. She didn't look at Dru, but Jeb Axel did. His eyes, a shade of blue that had been faded by time and weather, were caught in a net of fine lines, but his gaze was piercing nevertheless. It was unapologetic. Talk around town was that back in the day, all the girls had crushes on him—Lily Axel's daddy. They had compared him to Clint Eastwood. He was still a looker for an older man—age hadn't thickened him. If anything, the years had pared away whatever softness he might have once had the way the wind chiseled the soil from the face of a rock. Dru hated it, but Jeb Axel intimidated her.

"Are you ready?" she asked Shea.

"No one saw AJ get on the bus, Mom." It was a challenge. Shea, thinking she possessed all the facts, was throwing down the gauntlet.

Knowing what was ahead, the terrible hurt that lay in wait, Dru left it there. She wasn't about to get into it here, not in front of Jeb and Lily, or even Erik, as good a friend as he was to Shea. No one needed to watch while Shea's world was taken apart.

"He wouldn't leave like that." Shea was adamant. "He wouldn't do that to me. Or to you." Shea looked at Lily and then at Jeb.

Lily was searching in her purse—for her car keys, Dru guessed, but she paused now, and her eyes widened as if she found Shea's pronouncement of AJ's regard for her startling.

Erik said, "I wish I knew what to believe."

Jeb, who'd been pacing, stopped and, thumping his palm with his fist, said Shea was right. "There's no goddamn way in hell AJ got on a bus," he declared.

And then he collapsed.

Dru watched it happen, the inharmonious dance of steps that first had him staggering, then dropping to his knees, then toppling sideways onto the porch floor. Because he was tall, well over six feet, rangy and hard boned, he made a lot of noise going down, but then he lay still, and there was only the sweet sound of a spring breeze through the live oaks and the full-throated call of a tiny wren that perched in that instant on the porch rail.

7

Lily was frozen in place, watching her dad fall. It was like watching a tree coming down in sections, one that had stood for an eon until it didn't. Shrugging off her tote, she went to her knees beside him, cupped his cheek with her hand, smoothed scraps of white hair from his brow. He was cool but not cold to the touch, and damp with sweat. She could see his pulse beating, a tiny piston, hammering inside his temple. His chest rose and fell, a series of shallow dips. "Dad?" she whispered, and his eyelids fluttered.

Behind her, she heard Erik talking; he had his phone out, trying to call 911. When he couldn't get a signal, Dru and Shea said they'd try.

"In the house," Lily said. "Upstairs. Use the landline."

"No."

Lily looked down at her dad.

"I don't need an ambulance." Rolling onto his back, he groaned softly, and the breath he took in was deep enough to make him shudder.

"Are you sure?" She touched his face again, his shoulder.

"I'm all right, Lily. Help me up."

She braced his elbow while he levered himself into a sitting position, pushed his back against the porch railing.

Lily looked him over. He was as pale as skim milk, and his hands shook as he ran them over his face. They were long fingered, thick knuckled, and strong. She'd seen him wrestle a calf to the ground with those hands, wield an ax, bandage her knees. They were an old man's hands now, the skin across the backs mottled and so thinned by time that the veins were as visible as lines on a road map. When had he aged so much?

"What happened?" she asked softly.

"Got light-headed." He bent his head back against the railing, closing his eyes again as if to shut her—shut all of them—from his sight.

He was embarrassed, Lily thought, and it made her heart ache.

"Y'all go on now. I'm good. Lily, you call me when you get back to Dallas."

"I'm not going," she said.

He argued, but he knew that when she made up her mind she could be as stubborn as he was. She and Erik got him into the house. Dru held the door. Shea picked up a stray coffee mug and followed them into the kitchen.

"What can we do?" Dru asked.

"Nothing," Lily said, easing her dad into a chair at the table. "Thanks," she added, "but it's fine. We're fine." She was looking at her dad.

He nodded.

"All right, then," Dru said. "Well, you'll call us if you need anything?"

Lily met her glance, but only briefly. "Yes, thanks," she repeated.

Dru and Shea left, and while Erik stayed with her dad in the kitchen, Lily went out onto the front porch to call Paul, steeling herself, unsure how he'd react when she said she wasn't coming back to Dallas after all. He would in all likelihood be angry with her, but beneath the icier currents of her panic and concern for AJ and her dad, she felt relieved. She wasn't glad for her father's collapse, but she didn't regret that it kept her here.

Paul was leaving the police station when she caught him, via a back entrance, he said. "The press is out front. Not looking for me," he added hastily when Lily voiced her dismay. "It's that councilman, Hawkes. I don't wish trouble on anyone, but whatever mess he's in, it takes the spotlight off us. Hawkes is a bigger fish."

Lily perched uneasily on the swing's edge. "Why are you at the police station at all? I thought they were through questioning you."

Paul's laugh was truncated. "I don't know," he said. "It's like they suspect me."

"Why?"

"They're making a big deal out of the fact that there was no forced entry, that I found the body."

"AJ kept a key outside."

"What?"

"AJ kept a key to his apartment in the gaslight outside his front door. He told us about it, and you said it wasn't a good idea. Becca, or anyone who knew, could have used it to get in. You need to see if it's missing."

"I'll tell Bushnell, but since I already told him I have a key, I doubt it'll make a difference. He's pissed anyway because I had Jerry meet me here this morning. I've lawyered up, as they say, but damned if I'm going to deal with them and not have legal counsel—the way those bastards twist everything."

"Jerry is your corporate attorney, Paul. We need Edward on this." Saying his name out loud caused her heartbeat to slow and thicken, but it wasn't as if she was inventing an excuse to mention it. This situation was real, not some dire-straits charade she'd invented in the hope that once Edward heard about it, he would feel compelled to meet with her again.

"I still think getting a criminal attorney involved is premature at this point, Lily. Trust me. I know what's best."

"All right." Lily forced herself to agree, to seem amicable, even as mutiny hardened her jaw. It was wrong to delay; she could feel to her core that it was. She wanted to shout it at Paul, to say, *This is not about you and what you want. This is about our son—his life—*

Paul was talking, something about surveillance cameras.

Lily apologized. "I'm sorry, can you say that again?"

"The cops have got the tapes, video off the cameras around AJ's apartment. If the film's any good, they'll be able to see who, besides me, AJ, and the girl, went into his apartment. It'll take time for them to review it, though."

"More waiting," Lily said, and she regretted it, because it set Paul off.

He was sick of waiting, he said. He'd told Bushnell to get off his ass. "While he's wasting time looking at me, the real killer is out there, footloose, and he's got our son."

Lily stood up, abruptly enough to set the swing on a crooked path. "There's something you should know, Paul." *Maybe he'd heard it by now.*

"What?"

"Becca was pregnant."

Silence. Shocked and disbelieving. Lily had lost her power of speech, too, when Dru told her. "Paul?"

"Who says?"

Lily went through it, repeating what she'd heard from Dru, who'd heard it from Becca's mother, who'd heard it from the coroner. "They'll do a DNA test to determine paternity, of course, but it might be weeks before they get a result."

More silence.

Lily said his name again. "Paul?"

"I don't know what to say, what the hell to think or believe anymore. What if he just wanted to get rid of the problem—"

"No!" Lily wasn't having it, Paul's doubt. She had no room for it, no antidote of faith held in reserve to counteract it. "We don't know anything at this point," she told him. "We have to wait for the DNA."

"The cops are hoping they get something useful off his phone and computer."

What they found could as easily damn AJ as clear him. It scared her. She wanted an advocate, someone to represent them, shield them. She wanted Edward. He was the logical choice. But even the memory of him, of his touch, burned her.

Paul said, "I'm not sure I'll be home when you get back. I've got to get some work done."

"I'm not coming back, Paul, so don't worry about it," Lily said, and she explained about her dad's collapse. "I want to get him in to see a doctor if I can talk him into it."

She was glad when Paul didn't argue. "I should go," she said. "I've left Erik with Dad, and he probably needs to get back to work."

"The cops seem to think Erik is covering for AJ. You get any sense of that?" Paul asked.

"No," Lily said. "He's as clueless and worried sick as we are."

Erik had made sandwiches while she was talking to Paul, ham and swiss on rye. He was setting the plates on the table when Lily returned to the kitchen. She poured glasses of iced tea, brought them to the table and sat down.

"I don't need all this fussing," her dad said.

"Becca was pregnant," Lily said.

"The hell?" Her dad stared at her.

"No way." Erik sat back, wide-eyed, stunned. "It was AJ's?"

Lily went through it again, all that Dru had told her.

"You realize that makes it a double homicide," her dad said.

She set down the sandwich half she'd picked up. She hadn't thought of that. What kind of monster would murder the woman who was carrying his child? *Scott Peterson.* His name surfaced in Lily's mind.

Thanks to the extreme media focus following his arrest and trial for the murder of his wife and unborn child, even all these years later, she could recall his face, the eerie look of bland unconcern he'd turned to the cameras. Casey Anthony had had the same empty-eyed look after being charged with murdering her small daughter. They were psychopaths, according to the experts. Narcissists. While they could be quite charming, dangerously so, they had no real capacity to feel—anything. Compassion. Remorse. Real love. Not even true anger. And the numbers of such people—the ones who lacked humanity—were growing. Reaching epidemic proportions. If you believed the experts, one in twenty-five children born today was a socio- or psychopath. Was it true? Or merely media hype?

Hadn't Casey Anthony's mother turned her in?

Would she turn AJ in if she knew—knew, irrevocably—he was a murderer? Lily's heart faltered.

"Does Shea know?"

She looked at Erik. "Dru said she was planning to tell her."

"It'll kill her." Erik took his plate to the sink.

"I've seen how he looks at her."

Lily met her dad's glance. His color had improved; he seemed steadier since he'd eaten, and his hands were no longer shaking.

"AJ adores that girl," he said. "He wouldn't do anything to hurt her." Her dad wiped his mouth with his napkin. "The DNA—whoever it belongs to, the father of that baby—that's your killer, and it's not AJ."

Erik came back to the table, standing behind his chair, leaning on the top rail.

Her dad looked up at him. "He say anything to you about taking up with Becca again?"

Erik shook his head. "But, you know, he's different since he got back."

"Different how?" Lily's dad was testy.

"He's closed up, moody. If I ask too many questions, he chews my head off. It's like he's wound too tight."

"Dru thinks he's had a breakdown."

The men looked at Lily.

"I get the impression she doesn't like him," her dad said.

"She doesn't," Lily said. "If she could, she'd stop him from marrying Shea." Lily turned to Erik. "You know Dru. Has she ever talked about AJ to you?"

"She knows better."

Lily tucked her napkin beside her plate. "I don't think she's aware AJ was arrested before. If she's thinking badly of him now, wait until she finds out about that."

"That was a long time ago," Erik said. "The guy got a medal since then for his service in the war. He's a hero."

"I don't think she cares about his military service."

"She's an idiot," Lily's dad muttered.

"I don't think so." Lily shrugged when her dad shot her a look. It had cost Dru, telling Lily about her experience with her ex-husband. As much as Lily might want to believe otherwise, Dru hadn't confided in her out of meanness, or a wish to cause more anguish. Although Lily was more afraid for AJ after hearing about Dru's ordeal with her ex-husband. When she'd described how he'd looked and acted, his empty eyes, his lack of recognition of Dru or his surroundings—it was too eerily similar to the way AJ had looked in the restaurant. And now Erik was saying AJ was different since he'd come home from Afghanistan— Lily didn't want to, but she knew what he meant. It raised the fine hairs on her head.

She knew AJ was struggling. She knew, too, how quickly you could lose yourself. How in a matter of seconds, you could act in ways—horrible ways—you'd never imagined. Lily found her dad's glance. Did he not remember how it had been with her in the wake of her mother's death, the sudden eruptions of temper, the chaos of her emotions? Could her state of mind have been what put her on the back of Jesse's motorcycle that long-ago night?

Her dad went to lie down, and Lily walked Erik to his car. "I'm worried about Dad."

"Yeah, that was scary, when he went down. Big, tough man like that. I never thought—" He looked off. "Guys like Jeb Axel—they're invincible. Superheroes, you know?"

Lily said it was true.

"He's pissed at me, but I'm not too happy with him right now, either."

"He's just disappointed, Erik. It's been hard on him, selling off the herd, shutting down the xL. I understand why you didn't want to come on as foreman," she said, although she didn't. "You need to be your own man, do your own thing. But I think Dad was kind of counting on one of you—AJ or you—"

"But he never offered the foreman job to AJ, did he?"

The question caught Lily off guard, and she was trying to sort it out—*had* her dad asked AJ?—when Erik, tipping back his head, groaned.

And apologized. "God! What is wrong with me? You're worried sick—we all are—and I'm bitching about nothing."

She put her hand on his arm. "It's all right."

"I'm going to see if I can get time off. I'll come back. We'll search every square inch of this ranch, all of Madrone County—all of fucking Texas if that's what it takes. Sorry . . ."

"Don't jeopardize your job, Erik."

"AJ is my best friend; he's my brother. You're like a second mom to me. You guys are like family."

"We *are* family, Erik. You know that."

"Yeah." Erik looked off. "I just wish AJ had talked to me."

"Me, too," Lily said.

"I know he didn't do this. I know it." Erik brought his gaze to Lily's.

"No," she agreed.

"I keep thinking he's going to show up, you know? He'll be at my apartment; he'll call me—"

Lily's throat closed at the hitch in Erik's voice. "Tell me," she said, quickly scooting them past the emotion, "how is Kate? You're engaged, I heard."

"Yeah, she finally said yes, last week."

"Have you set a date for the wedding?"

"Not yet. I can't even get the girl to go ring shopping. But it'll be soon. Real soon. AJ's going to be my best man, just like I'm his."

"It's wonderful."

"I think I might be the happiest man on the planet." He sobered. "You know, I didn't mean—"

"You have every right to be happy." Lily touched his arm. "Don't let this ruin it, okay? Try not to."

"When we get AJ back, get this mess straightened out, we'll have the biggest damn celebration Madrone County ever saw. We'll roast a half dozen pigs—"

Lily laughed. "Have leis flown in from Hawaii."

"Wear hula skirts." Erik got into the Lexus.

"Have you told your mom about AJ?" Lily asked when he powered down the window.

"Not yet."

"I can't believe she didn't call and let me know about her mother's death, that she was going down for the funeral."

"Well, she wasn't going to go, but then Jeb got on her. He knew she'd feel terrible if she didn't."

"Have you talked to her?"

"Once. Cell service down there can be pretty bad. I don't want to tell her over the phone, anyway. It's hard enough on her, being there, and I know she's set on getting everything wrapped up so she doesn't have to go back."

"She is coming back? Here, I mean, to the xL?" Lily was suddenly seized with the fear that she wouldn't.

"Sunday or Monday," Erik answered.

Lily nodded. She couldn't trust her voice; her relief made her want to cry.

"She's going to be pissed at me for keeping her in the dark." Erik looked through the windshield, thinking about it. "Not just about AJ, but Jeb, too. If Mom knew he collapsed, she'd be on the next flight."

"It's all right, though. I'd stay even if she were here."

Erik nodded and keyed the ignition. "I'll be back," he said. "Call me if you need anything."

Lily checked on her father when she returned to the house and found him sleeping soundly on the sofa in his office. A lightweight throw was folded over the back, and she covered him with it. He looked defenseless, not at all like the tough guy Erik had described. She laid her hand softly on the ledge of his brow, his lean, furrowed cheek. She smoothed his silvery-white hair that floated from his head like dandelion fluff. He could be hard; he had a temper. She knew that, but she also knew his heart could be as soft as melted marshmallow.

Leaving him, she went upstairs to shower and wash her hair. He was still napping when she came back down. She wandered into the kitchen, thinking she could saddle Butternut and ride out again, maybe head east, check on Winona's house. But it was likely Erik had already done that. Lily leaned on the counter. It was fruitless searching on her own, anyway, when she had no solid direction to go. Grabbing her cell phone, she went outside, onto the front porch, and sat in the swing. The afternoon air was thick and sultry, more like midsummer than spring, and it hung as heavy as the passing time. She was up, pacing, within seconds.

She'd seen news stories about families who had a loved one missing. They all said the same thing, that the waiting and the not knowing were hell. They described jumping every time the phone rang, at every knock on the door. They spoke of their feelings of helplessness and dread. Lily had never imagined she would be one of them.

Taking her phone from her pocket, she scrolled through her directory, and when she found the number she hadn't intended to hunt for, she tapped it on the screen.

He picked up on the second ring. "Edward Dana," he said.

Her knees weakened at the sound of his voice, and returning to the swing, she perched on its edge.

"It's me," she said.

8

Shea claimed she wasn't hungry after they left the xL, but Dru stopped at Crickets, the café on the square in Wyatt, anyway, and bought a chicken salad sandwich. Getting back in the car, she handed the sack to Shea. "I only got one," she said. "We can share it."

"Fine," Shea said.

Ha! Dru thought.

Nothing was fine, but Shea had informed her mother on leaving the xL that she wasn't going to participate in "a bunch of speculation" about AJ and why his laptop and phone had been found at the bus station. *It isn't speculation.* Dru had clenched her teeth to keep from saying it. It was an irrefutable fact from which only one conclusion could be drawn—that AJ had been at the bus station, and now he was gone, on the run. Dru wheeled into the flow of traffic.

Becca was pregnant! The words bit at her mind like flies. Why couldn't she say them and have done with it? But neither she nor Shea spoke. Even after they were parked in back of the house and Dru had turned off the ignition, they sat in silence, staring straight ahead. The windshield framed a view of the deck that was furnished with two wicker chaise longues, a vintage iron table, and three iron chairs, all different styles. Dru hadn't found a fourth chair with the right character. She looked at Shea.

"What?" The syllable was wary. Shea was poised to run defense, an end game around whatever Dru said.

"I've got to tell you something," Dru began.

Musical notes chimed from inside Shea's purse, and she fumbled inside it for her phone.

Dru's heart began to pound. It was becoming routine every time a phone rang.

"Dad?" Shea said. Opening the car door, she stepped out, glancing at Dru, shrugging slightly.

Dru watched her walk onto the deck, settle on the edge of a chaise longue. Picking up the lunch sack, she went into the house. She wondered if Rob had heard what was going on, if that was what had prompted his call. But it was doubtful. The Houston media had a surfeit of its own crime stories to cover.

She had divided the sandwich and set the halves on each of two plates when Shea came inside.

"Want a glass of iced tea?" Dru asked. "It's raspberry."

"Did you talk to Dad?"

"Not in several days. Why?"

"Because he's just like you. He thinks AJ killed Becca, and he's a fugitive now."

"He said that? I didn't think he would have—"

"This is like the first thing in years I've ever heard you and Dad agree on. Go figure."

Dru brought the plates to the table, then fetched the glasses of tea. "Come and eat," she said.

"Becca was pregnant," Shea said, sitting down.

Dru stared at her.

"Dad was at a sports bar at lunch. It was on the noon news. You know it, though, don't you? Becca's mom told you."

"Oh, honey." Dru sat across from Shea. "I should have told you. I just couldn't—"

"It's not AJ's."

"Well, the DNA—"

"I don't need DNA to tell me the baby wasn't AJ's. Just the same as I don't need hard evidence to know he isn't a killer. He's in trouble, Mom. Either that, or he's—" Shea broke off, crossing her arms tightly over her midsection.

Dead.

The word resonated, seeming more horrible for being unspoken.

"Does his mom know—about the pregnancy, I mean?" Shea asked.

"I told her," Dru admitted. She thought how alike in their denial Shea and Lily sounded.

"Becca's mom—What did she say? She doesn't think it's AJ's, does she?"

Shea locked Dru's gaze, leaving her nowhere to go, but she couldn't bring herself to say it, that Joy believed AJ and Becca had been a couple again, that they had linked up behind Shea's back.

"It isn't true," Shea said, but her faith was shaken. Dru could see the wall crumbling in her eyes, and it broke her heart.

"Dad said if AJ contacts me, I should get him to turn himself in. He said it may be hard right now for AJ to know the right thing to do. He said AJ's mind is probably in a million pieces."

"Well," Dru said, "of all people, I think your dad would know."

"Because he got diagnosed with PTSD, too." Shea made it sound like a prison sentence.

"They do have that in common. It's why I've been concerned. I don't want you threatened the way I was—"

"AJ's situation is nothing like Dad's, Mom. Dad wasn't a trained soldier. He never even owned a gun until after he was attacked."

"So because AJ was trained in combat, because he handled weapons, he's better equipped, mentally and emotionally, to cope with the violence he was subjected to? Is that what you're saying?"

Shea doodled a line on the table with the tip of her finger. "I might as well tell you before Dad does."

"Tell me what?"

"AJ was arrested before—for being an accessory to murder."

"What? When?"

"It was before he joined the marines. He was at a party, and some guys got into a fight. One of them, someone AJ knew, who he thought was a friend, had a gun. A couple of people were shot."

"By AJ?" Dru felt light-headed.

"No, by his friend. AJ tried to stop the guy, but he got arrested anyway, even though he didn't know that the 'friend'"—Shea tweaked air quotes—"had brought a gun to the party."

"Well, I'm sorry, but it sounds to me as if AJ must have known."

"Call the police, Mom. Ask them. The charges against AJ were dropped because there wasn't any evidence against him."

Dru pushed her plate away. She didn't know what to say. AJ was dangerous, that was all. He'd been dangerous even before his military service. The violence he harbored wasn't an aberration. It was part of his nature.

"I can't believe the media raked up all that stuff. AJ is going to hate it, everyone knowing. People get the wrong idea." Shea caught Dru's gaze. "He's not a criminal, Mom."

Shea wanted Dru's agreement, but Dru couldn't offer her that.

"He is the last person—" Shea stopped to press a single knuckle to her mouth, taking a moment. "After everything he went through in the war," she began again, "all the horror he saw over there, the things he had to do—for his country"—she set the phrase apart, and it was steeped in sarcasm—"he is the very last person who could do harm to another human being. Can't you see that?"

Dru bent forward, touching Shea's cheek, thumbing away her tears; she tucked strands of Shea's hair behind her ear. "I want to believe in him, I do, but my major concern is for you, for your safety. Your dad was a wonderful and kind man, too, who wouldn't hurt a fly."

"God, Mom!" Shea jumped up. "What's it going to take? AJ isn't Dad! And, anyway, Dad got help. He was in therapy. For years! You know that. You know he'd never point a gun at anyone now. He doesn't even own a gun anymore." Her voice rose. "*You*—you own a gun, because you still think Dad's a psycho, that he's going to come after us. You still hold a grudge against him, and now you hold the same grudge against AJ. I'm sick of it, Mom. Sick. Of. It." She stared down at Dru, trembling, chest heaving. Hurt laced the fury in her gaze. "You know what your problem is?" she asked before Dru could say anything. "You don't trust—not me, not anyone."

Dru stared at Shea, feeling she'd lost the power of speech. Even thought wasn't possible in the moment, and she watched Shea push her chair under the table. She tracked Shea's rapid retreat across the kitchen floor.

"You know we're going to have to work on canceling the wedding." Dru found her voice. "Today," she added. "It can't—"

"What am I going to say?" Shea whirled to face Dru. "'Oh, I'm so sorry, the wedding's off. One of my bridesmaids is dead, and my fiancé is on the run, because everyone, including my wonderful, open-minded parents, thinks he murdered her'?"

"You won't need to talk to anyone, honey."

"No, of course not. What am I thinking? It's all over the news."

"We still need to write notes to the guests, saying that we're canceling due to unforeseen circumstances, or something to that effect. We'll get the word out as quickly as we can via e-mail, if we have an address. Otherwise we'll have to go the snail-mail route."

"What about Uncle Kevin and Aunt Mary? Aren't they on the road?"

"Maybe they haven't left yet. I'll call them."

Shea pressed her fingertips to her temples, letting out a soft moan. "This is so horrible, like a nightmare. I keep thinking I'm going to wake up."

"We'll get through it," Dru said, having no clue how. "Kate, Vanessa, and Leigh are coming by later to help with the notes, and Lily will take care of her guest list and everything related to the rehearsal dinner."

"She thinks we should cancel, too?"

Shea seemed suddenly so small and bewildered. How had it come to this, all her beautiful wedding plans? The question was written into the furrow of her brow, the tight purse of her mouth, her wobbling chin. Dru got up, throat pinched with the effort not to cry, and went to her daughter, wrapping her in an embrace. It was all she had, all she knew to do.

"I love him so much, Mama," Shea said, broken-voiced. "I don't care about the wedding. I just want him to be safe. I want him to come home."

Dru felt Shea's tears bleed through her cotton shirt. "I know, honey," she murmured. "I know you do."

• • •

"I don't know what to hope for," Dru told Rob later. She'd come outside to the deck to call him, not wanting to risk Shea overhearing them, even though she was in her bedroom, having agreed to at least try to nap until Kate, Leigh, and Vanessa arrived. Dru perched on the end of a chaise longue. "I don't know whether it's best if AJ's guilty or innocent, or if he comes back or gets arrested."

"As terrible as it is, she's going to have to face—we're all going to have to look at the fact that he might be dead, either by his own hand or someone else's."

"You didn't say that to her?"

"Of course not. Shea's not even close to being ready to hear it."

"What worries me is how little she's willing to consider AJ's role in this—if he fathered Becca's baby and if, because of that, he killed her. It'll do more than just break Shea's heart, Rob."

"It worries me, too," Rob said. "But she's tough, Dru, like her mama," he added.

Dru crossed her ankles. She was barefoot, and her glance was drawn to the sight of her toenails; the Chinese-red polish was chipped and peeling. It reminded her of times she had painted Shea's nails when her daughter was a little girl. Red, always red, and the polish had always chipped within hours of application. Dru could see that little hand, spread like a starfish, the tiny nails flecked with red. "I don't think she'll give up on him. Even if he's guilty."

"Don't take this wrong, I'm not excusing him, okay? I agree with you. I think AJ probably did it; he probably murdered that girl. But I just don't buy that he's a cold-blooded killer. He's not a psycho or a sociopath. He's got issues, sure, but something's got to have happened for him to—"

"Are you saying you want him to marry our daughter? I mean, assuming he's found and gets out of this somehow," Dru broke in, unable to bear Rob's attempt at placating her. "You're happy about it? Because Shea doesn't seem to think—she was amazed we shared the same negative—"

"Who Shea marries isn't my call, Dru."

"You aren't concerned for her safety, then. Is that right? But why should that surprise me, when you so obviously didn't care about it when we lived with you." Dru got up. She was shaking now and tucked her arm around herself.

"Jesus, Dru, I have tried every way I know to make amends for the harm I caused you and Shea."

"This isn't a twelve-step issue, Rob. It's not a question of you having one too many toddies and passing out on the sofa night after night. You would have only hurt yourself, then."

"I don't know that I agree. What's the difference between chronic drinking and chronic fear? Either one can be deadly. The only difference is when someone quits drinking, you can see the evidence. With fear, you'd have to take my word I'm not that scared, paranoid guy anymore. I've got ways to handle it now. But you'd have to trust me on that, and I guess that's never going to happen, is it?"

She didn't answer, and she hated it—her silence and the way she felt trapped by it.

"You know," Rob began carefully, "I never figured you for someone who would hold a grudge. And it's a hell of a thing to me, because I still love you, and I don't know why."

• • •

"Am I supposed to feel bad for Rob?" Dru asked Amy.

They were in Dru's driveway, packing the food for the teachers' luncheon into Amy's car. Dru had been so grateful when Amy had offered to take over delivery and setup, not only for this meal, but next week's engagements as well. There was the handful of regular clients for whom she delivered daily meals, plus a dessert selection for a women's bridge club and a twenty-fifth wedding anniversary dinner for ten. Dru didn't have the attention span of a gnat at this point, and even if she did, who could predict if she'd have the time to do the preparation, to get the job done right? Catastrophes had a schedule all their own.

"Has he told you before that he loves you? I mean, since you divorced?" Amy asked.

"Not in so many words." Dru settled a sack packed with linen napkins and flatware behind the passenger seat.

Amy closed the door. She found Dru's glance. "You know, everything you've ever told me about Rob, it seems to me what he wants—all he wants is another chance."

Dru looked into the street.

"What if he's truly okay now? I mean, if you could know that, be certain he was stable, back to the guy you married, what would you want? Would you take him back?"

Dru met Amy's gaze. "If he came with a guarantee, you mean?"

Amy made a face, and Dru laughed.

"We both know when it comes to men, there are no guarantees," Amy said.

"Honestly?" Dru sobered. "I can't think about what I want or what Rob needs right now. Shea is in such jeopardy."

Amy touched her arm. "I'm so sorry this is happening to her, to both of you."

"I guess you heard Becca was pregnant."

"I can't believe it. When Ken told me she'd been stabbed there—in her abdomen—"

Dru gave her head a slight shake. She hadn't known that.

"It's true," Amy said. "Seven times in her stomach and four times in her chest. Ken said a buddy of his on the force in Dallas told him they think she was sexually assaulted, too. Her underpants were down around her ankles, and there was a note on her back that said, 'Fixed you.' They think it was written in lip liner."

"How in God's name am I going to tell Shea?"

Amy rubbed Dru's arm.

"Is it weird that I wish she could sleep forever?"

"Or do a Rip van Winkle and wake up in a hundred years. Maybe the world would be less insane then." Amy went around to the driver's side of her car and got behind the wheel.

Dru followed her.

"I can come back later if you want, and help with the wedding cancellation."

"Thanks," Dru said, "but I think between us, Kate, and the others, we can get it done. Besides, you're already doing so much. I don't know how I'll ever repay you."

"You know I don't come cheap, right?" Amy winked. "Seriously, though, I'm happy to help out. If there's anything else, I'm here, okay? Just call me."

Dru looked away. "Don't be nice to me or I'll lose it."

"Oh, honey. Should I stay?"

Dru sniffed, wiped her eyes, got a grip on herself, and said, "No, I'm fine. But you're a godsend, you know it?"

"Will you call my husband and tell him that?" Amy said, deadpan.

Her joke worked. Dru smiled.

The girls arrived a little later. Dru woke Shea, and she joined them, sitting at the table in the breakfast room. Her eyes were thick-lidded and reddened, not from sleep, or the lack of it, Dru thought, but from crying. Kate, sitting adjacent to Shea, took her hand. Vanessa and Leigh, too, reached out to her. Dru was glad for them, for their support. Shea needed it. Dru brought glasses of ice and a pitcher of tea to the table.

"I know Becca was pregnant," Shea said. "I just want to get that out right now. I know what everyone thinks, too, that it was AJ's, but you're wrong, and you'll see it when the DNA test comes back."

Vanessa said, "You heard, didn't you, where Becca was stabbed?"

Dru set her hand on Shea's shoulder. "We don't need to go into detail."

Shea looked up at Dru. "Did you forget I have a laptop? I can get the news."

Dru didn't answer.

"It's horrible, and I'm sick about it. Just as sick as any of you, but it's got nothing to do with me or AJ."

Dru felt a jolt of anguish so strong, she backed away, turned, and went into the kitchen, where she leaned against the countertop.

"So, how do we do this?" Dru heard Shea ask. "How do we cancel my wedding?"

Van was opening her laptop when Dru returned to the breakfast room.

"When in doubt, Google," she said.

"Really?" Kate asked.

"Yeah. Unlike Siri, Google knows everything. It's all here. Even how to word the note."

"You looked already?" Leigh asked.

"It's best to get it done quick—like ripping off a Band-Aid."

"Great," Shea said.

Kate rolled her eyes.

"I'm just sayin'." Vanessa looked around the table. "There's a standard note so nobody has to think what to write. You don't have to go into detail." Van was addressing Shea now, looking earnestly at her.

She meant well, Dru thought.

Shea extended her arms across the table. "What if he comes back, though? What if he can explain?"

"Then you get married. I'll dance at your wedding." Kate smiled.

Shea smiled, too, and Dru's heart eased a bit. She got her laptop and sat beside Van, and they worked on the note. Shea, Leigh, and Kate broke the list into categories, separating out AJ's guests, cross-checking addresses.

Dru had called her brother earlier and left a message when he didn't answer. She'd spoken to a handful of friends, too, the folks who were close enough to her and to Shea that Dru felt they should be contacted personally. Responses had been sympathetic, shocked, and/or horrified, depending on how much they'd heard. Thankfully, no one had asked many questions.

She began to feel the blunt edge of a headache bearing down on her brain. Exhaustion crawled behind her eyes. Excusing herself, she went into the kitchen to find aspirin. She was at the sink when Kate touched her elbow. "Are you okay?"

"Yes," Dru said, because lying was best. "Just tired. You doing all right? Erik is looking very happy since you said yes."

"He is—happy, I mean."

"You aren't?" Something in Kate's tone, her demeanor, made Dru ask.

"I guess. I mean, I care about him. He makes me laugh. Mother and Daddy love him. Mother, especially."

"I know. He's all your mom can talk about. But, honey"—Dru lifted Kate's chin—"you're the one who's marrying him, and it's for life—or it should be. You, more than your mom, should be sure he's the one, right?"

Kate shifted her glance.

"Are you?"

"He treats me like a queen."

"Yes," Dru said, but she was thinking worship wasn't love.

"I feel so heartbroken for Shea. She's supposed to be my matron of honor. We dreamed of this our whole lives, that we would be in each other's weddings, live in the same neighborhood, raise our kids together." Kate looked at Dru through the film of tears. "We were besties, marrying besties. It was so perfect, you know?"

Dru wrapped Kate in an embrace, murmuring the rote nonsense that in time everything would work out. She wasn't sure when she was first aware there was a disturbance in the breakfast nook. She heard the sound of the back door closing—not quite a slam but close, then a voice—Dru thought it was Leigh's—raised in consternation.

Dru followed Kate through the archway.

"Look what Leigh found under the windshield wiper of her car just now." Shea held up what looked like a three-by-five notecard, marked up with something—pink.

"Is that lipstick? Let me see it," Dru said.

"Lip liner. It's an apology, written in lip liner." Shea handed the card to Dru.

"It says he can't help himself." Leigh was loud, almost shouting. "Why did he put it on *my* car? Why not *your* car?" She was addressing Shea.

"'I'm sorry for hurting you,'" Dru read. "'I'm in trouble and I don't think I can stop.'" Written in lip liner on paper like the note that was left on Becca's body. Dru looked up at Shea.

"Anyone could have left it," she said.

"You don't recognize the writing?" Leigh asked.

"No," Shea answered. "It's printed. Any kindergartner could have written it."

Standing at Dru's elbow, Kate said, "We have to call the police."

"Nooo." Shea drew out the syllable so that it was almost a moan.

Kate went to her, wrapping an arm around Shea's waist.

"I'm scared," Leigh said.

"God, I am, too." Van sounded as if she couldn't believe it, that she, of all people, could be afraid.

But she had every reason to be, Dru thought, going back into the kitchen to retrieve her phone, because whoever had authored the note—and who else could it be but AJ—had given fair warning they were going to kill again.

9

"I didn't know who else to call," Lily said, because the level of her fear, the space it took up in her brain, left no room for an exchange of pleasantries.

"What's happened?" Edward's tone was neutral to such a degree that she couldn't guess what he might be thinking.

"Could you—would you be willing to meet me?" Her breath stopped. She hadn't known she was going to ask for that.

"Where? When?"

She couldn't think.

"I've had a cancellation this afternoon." He filled in the silence. "I could be in Greeley and meet you at Bo Dean's at four. Would that work?"

"Yes," she said. "Thank you."

A pause came, and it was a little awed, as if neither of them believed in what they'd arranged. They had said they wouldn't meet again, that it would be wrong on too many levels. She considered taking it back, telling him to never mind, but then he said her name—"Lily?"—and she knew she wouldn't.

"I'm glad you called," he told her, and then he was gone.

When her dad woke a while later, she was in the kitchen. "I was writing you a note," she said.

"I can't believe I fell asleep." He went to the sink and, turning on the tap, splashed his face with cold water. "Any news?"

"No." She handed him a kitchen towel.

"What are you leaving a note about?" He dabbed his eyes and cheeks, wiped along his jaw.

"I thought I'd run up to Greeley, do some grocery shopping. The HEB store there is better than the one in Wyatt."

Her dad didn't say anything.

"Is it okay? Will you be all right?" she asked.

"I'll be fine. You don't have to hover. Don't we have food here? It's not like we're eating a whole lot."

"Truth?" She held his gaze, not knowing how she managed it. "I need the distraction." The moment she said it, she wished it back. Suppose he needed a distraction, too? Suppose he asked to come with her?

But what he said was that he didn't blame her. "You should call Mary Nell." He named her best friend from high school, who lived in Greeley now. "Every time I run into her, she wants to know why you haven't been in touch."

Lily picked up her purse, thinking if Mary Nell asked after her, it was likely out of deference to her dad. He was remembering when she and Mary Nell were girls, when they loved horses and barrel racing, experimenting with the latest eye shadow, or hanging out at the Sonic in town, flirting with boys. Girl stuff. What he'd forgotten was how different she was after he'd brought her home from Phoenix, how little she'd resembled the flighty, silly girl who'd been Mary Nell's best friend. She'd done things, been in places so awful that she couldn't talk about them, certainly not to Mary Nell, who would have been horrified. There'd been gossip. It was unavoidable in a town the size of Wyatt. Lily had hidden from it, isolating herself. She'd seen almost no one back then, with the exception of her dad, Winona, and Paul. She still kept to herself. What did she have in common with Mary Nell, especially after almost thirty years, given all the unaddressed history that sat between them? It wasn't a question she wanted to ask her dad.

"Maybe I'll call Mary Nell," she said instead, and she was happy when it brought a brief light of relief to his eyes. "You sure you'll be all right?" she asked him. "I should be back by six or so. I'll make dinner."

He shooed her away with his hands. He might saddle up Sharkey, he said, do a little more exploring. He'd keep his phone on. "You've got yours?"

She pulled it out of her purse along with her car keys, showing it to him.

• • •

Lily arrived in Greeley an hour later with no clear recollection of having driven there. Bo Dean's, the roadside diner where she was meeting Edward, was ten miles farther north on the outskirts of town. It was one of their chosen places from the past. The coffee was bitter, the food marginal, and there were few regulars. Any crowd was mostly made up of truckers and other highway drivers, families with kids, salesmen. The fact that there was almost no chance of recognition was what made the place ideal.

She was early, but Edward was there before her. In a booth at the back. And when his gaze found hers, there was a moment when his happiness at seeing her seemed to infuse him with light. The world receded, and over the odors of bitter coffee and rancid grease, Lily instead caught the scent of the starch that she knew from memory permeated Edward's crisp oxford shirt. She could smell the fading note of his aftershave, some mix of citrus and pine. There was more silver threading his dark hair than when she'd last seen him, but it was still rumpled and unruly, appealing, like a careless boy's hair. But his gaze had sobered now, and his dark-brown eyes were grave, and a little wary, in their regard of her.

"Ma'am?" A waitress appeared at Lily's elbow and spoke.

"It's fine," she said to the woman. "I see him."

The waitress nodded and walked away, but Lily felt rooted to the floor, her stomach knotted with the thrill of his proximity even as a voice in her brain lectured that their meeting was a mistake. She hadn't changed from her jeans and boots, or put on lipstick for him, but the lack of preparation didn't alter the fact that her intent, at least in part, was to woo this man. It was still there, her lovely and terrifying desire for him. It hadn't lessened, hadn't changed.

And she had no right to it.

Edward might be unencumbered by a spouse, but she was not.

His marital status could have changed, though, couldn't it? In three years he could have acquired a wife and even children, for all she knew. Her heart grew cold at the thought.

Still, she walked toward him and, sliding into the booth across from him, thanked him for coming.

The intensity of his gaze caused her face to warm. *What is this about? What are we doing here?* The questions weren't less overt without the shape of his voice.

"It's AJ," she said.

"That's what I figured." He leaned back. "I heard something about it, driving down from Dallas just now."

"He didn't kill that girl, Edward."

"You don't know where he is?"

"No. He called last night and asked me to bring him his passport, but I told him he needed to come to the ranch or go home to Paul."

"Was he upset when you refused?"

"I don't know. Dad took the phone, but before he could say anything, AJ hung up, or the call was disconnected."

"You realize he might have been forced to make the call."

"Yes, but I could kick myself. If only I'd agreed, he'd have had to tell me where he is."

"You're sure it was AJ?"

Lily took a moment. "I'm sure," she said. "As sure as I can be."

"On the news, they said his laptop and cell phone were found at the bus station in Dallas."

"But no one saw him get on a bus."

The waitress came to their table. They ordered cups of the terrible coffee and sat in silence once she left. Edward looked out the window. Lily wanted to put her fingertip on the delicate netting of lines that fanned from the corner of his eye. She wanted to trace a path to the dimple that appeared when he smiled. She didn't dare do either.

Other than the last time they'd been together here, sheltering beneath the diner's awning from the rain, when their fingers had briefly linked, or when Edward had cupped her elbow in his palm while accompanying her to her car, they had never touched each other, not deliberately. And yet those encounters were seared into her memory and made her ache.

"Is it my advice as a criminal attorney that you want? Is that why you wanted to meet?" Edward brought his attention back to her.

She didn't know if the edge in his voice was from anger or disappointment. Once, in an unguarded moment, he had told her he hadn't ever known a woman like her, one to whom he felt he could say anything without risking judgment. It had been after he'd admitted his darkest secret—that he had a gambling addiction. The day he'd realized it, he had said, was the day he'd put another man down on his knees and aimed a gun at his head with the intention of robbing him to get money to go to a casino. That incident was the one that had finally penetrated the fog he'd been operating in. He had been on a rural road somewhere in Louisiana when he woke to himself—that was how he'd worded it, the end of his acting on his compulsion—and he'd run, leaving the man on his knees, leaving his car, the driver's-side door hanging open. The police had caught him eventually. He'd received probation and a court-mandated order to enter a twelve-step program, which he'd done. He hadn't placed a bet or gone into a gambling establishment in eighteen years at the time he'd described his experience to her. Twenty-one years now. If he was still keeping his promise.

Lily remembered Edward telling her the promises you made to other people weren't as important as the ones you made to yourself. What mattered, he had said, was what you did out of the sight of others. She kept his glance. "If—when AJ is found, if he needs a criminal attorney, then, yes, I want you to represent him. He'll want that, too."

"And Paul? What will Paul want?"

Now it was Lily's turn to stare out the window. Her gaze drifted to the highway beyond the café parking lot, where a stream of traffic flowed, constant, monotonous, indifferent. When Paul had contacted Edward Dana after AJ's first arrest for murder, it had been at the recommendation of a friend who was a business associate. Edward had gotten the friend's son cleared of a felony assault charge. He'd said Edward was a bulldog in the courtroom, that if he couldn't get AJ off, no attorney could.

Paul had discouraged Lily's participation in the legal discussion concerning AJ's defense. He'd said it was men's business. But Lily had attended the initial consultation anyway, arriving at Edward's office unannounced, ahead of Paul and AJ, determined to inform Edward of her intention to be included. *AJ is my son, too*—that phrase had repeated in her mind. *I have a right to be here,* she had planned to say. But when Edward appeared in the reception area, the moment became uniquely charged. Lily lost her power of speech. A few minutes, or an eternity passed—she was never sure which—and when Paul arrived and found her already there, standing with Edward, he'd stopped, his glance switching between them as if he were trying to sort out what he'd walked into.

"You may not believe me," Lily said now, bringing her gaze back to Edward, "but before this happened, I was only waiting for AJ's wedding to be over."

"To do what? Nothing has changed, has it? You're still married."

"No. Yes. I don't know." Her answers came in quick succession. She realized with a jolt that she didn't know which of them was the correct one.

The waitress came and set mugs of coffee in front of them. "Cream?"

Lily nodded, taking the small silver pitcher from her, upending the contents into her cup, knowing it wouldn't make the bitter brew more palatable.

"What does AJ's wedding being over have to do with anything?" Edward spoke as soon as the waitress was out of earshot. "I haven't heard from you in three years. I have tried, tried my damnedest to—" He broke off, turned his mug in a circle, contemplating it.

Forget you.

She knew he had tried his damnedest to forget her. He didn't need to say it for her to know his meaning. She had tried to do the same with her memories of him.

"Six years ago"—Lily went back to the beginning—"when AJ was charged with murder, when I thought he would go to prison, I prayed. I don't know if there is such a thing as God, and if there is, whether he hears, but I begged him for AJ's life. I said to this god I'm not even sure of that if he would please keep AJ safe, I would be a better person, a better wife and mother.

"And he was saved." She raised her glance to Edward's. "Because of you, your legal expertise, my prayer was answered. But I was never a good mother. Even before that happened, there were times—I was always afraid AJ would come to harm because of me—my—my lapses of attention. When AJ was two, we . . . Paul hired a nanny. She took over AJ's care."

"Why? Did something happen?"

"I—it was—" Lily broke off. She couldn't talk about it, the first time she had bargained with her uncertain god for AJ's life. She was already mortified.

"You were so young when he was born. Only twenty, right?"

She'd been twenty-one, but her youth was no excuse. She thought of the dozens of times she and Edward had met in the past. With few exceptions, their conversation had been inconsequential. They shared a love of books. They liked being outdoors. Where Lily loved riding a horse at full gallop, Edward loved skimming a sailboat over the water. He had a second home on Lake Buchanan, and a boat he'd named the *Summer Wind* after the Sinatra song.

He would teach her to sail.

She would teach him to ride.

In some fairy-tale place.

"You know I have a son I haven't seen since he was twelve," Edward said. "Charlie's thirty-three now, and I don't know where he lives."

"Because of the gambling."

"Yes."

"Once you told me you were thinking of hiring a private investigator to locate him."

"Yeah, well, I can't seem to find the guts to make that happen. I'd have to face him, then. I'd have to explain why making a bet was more important than being his dad."

Edward kept Lily's gaze, and his love for his son and his pain at the loss of him was naked in his eyes. They were no longer dealing in fairy tales, she thought, but in the harsher edges of reality, the places in their lives where they felt they had failed. "AJ and I aren't close. He doesn't know me—the dreams I had, the life I planned."

"Before Jesse, you mean."

Edward knew the story. How Jesse had happened upon her on the highway outside Wyatt one summer day after she'd graduated high school, struggling to change a flat tire. He'd stopped and offered to do it for her. She'd been enthralled with his twentysomething bad-boy good looks, his hard, lithe body, the way he sat on his motorcycle, long hair curling over the collar of his leather jacket. He'd ridden a Harley like the one in the movie *Easy Rider*. Jesse could have passed for Peter Fonda.

He'd followed her home to the xL, somehow conned her dad into giving him a job. Jesse had wanted the job, but he had wanted Lily, too, the boss's daughter. The power she'd had over him—over both Jesse and her dad—had thrilled her. She'd driven them both crazy for different reasons. She'd been glad in a perverse way when her dad caught her and Jesse smoking pot behind the barn, when he caught them half-naked up in the loft, making out.

It wasn't long, maybe a week or ten days after she'd brought Jesse to the xL, that her dad booted him off the property, and when Jesse went, she'd gone with him. She thought she was such hot shit. She'd loved it when he'd showed her off to his biker buddies, holding her out to them as if she were a trophy, a notch on his belt. During the month she rode with him, if any other men had so much as sniffed around her, Jesse had challenged them. He'd beaten them down if they'd wanted to carry it that far. But he'd turned that temper on her, too, in the weeks they'd spent together, using his fists on her, punching her low, where no one would see the damage. During sex, he'd put his lips to her ear and call her *cunt* and *whore*. Her stomach heaved, remembering.

"AJ doesn't know about Jesse, or that I was arrested," Lily said now. "Paul forbade my talking about it. I thought it didn't matter, that it was best to pretend it never happened."

The waitress came, and left when both Lily and Edward declined refills.

"You think it was a mistake, not telling AJ." Edward wasn't asking.

"Yes, but I don't mean to compare our experiences. It's just that I understand your fear that if you found Charlie, you would have to explain why you weren't in his life—" She broke off, shrugging slightly.

"But unlike me, you aren't to blame, Lily. You rode up to the convenience store on the back of Jesse's bike, thinking he was going to buy beer and cigarettes. You didn't know he was armed when he went into the store."

It was true. She'd had no idea when Jesse warned her not to follow him that he had the .357 he carried in his saddlebag shoved in the waistband of his jeans. It had been concealed by his jacket. She hadn't been paying attention, anyway. She'd been too excited. He'd taught her to drive the Harley, and he'd promised she could drive it when he got back. She'd scooched up on the seat, fingered the keys, used her hands to twist the handlebars, pretending to gun the engine. When she'd heard the cracking noises and looked around, she'd thought a car on the highway backfired. She ought to have known better. She'd grown up on a ranch and shot plenty of guns. "The kid Jesse killed was younger than me," she said softly. "Only seventeen."

The remembrance of that day was vivid now, making Lily shake. She could smell the tarred surface of the parking lot, warmed by the sun. She heard the shots, three in quick succession—*bam, bam, bam.* Jesse's sudden weight on the seat of the Harley behind her had almost unbalanced her. *"Go! Go! Go!"* He had shouted it in her ear.

"It's all right," Edward said.

She felt him scoot in beside her, felt his breath stir her hair. When his arm came around her and he pulled her close, she went still. The whole length of his leg—hip, thigh, calf—pressed against hers. She felt the swell of his breath. She wanted to look at him, to see what was in his eyes, but she was afraid if she did, she wouldn't be able to stop herself from kissing him, from crushing herself against him.

As if he read her mind, Edward turned her face to his. He locked her gaze, and she felt his thumb trace the contour of her lower lip. His fingertips brushed a slow path down the length of her neck, coming to rest in the hollow of her throat, where her pulse was beating as rapidly as the heart of a small bird. The moment held, shimmering, electric.

He looked away first, and she felt almost sick with disappointment. A sound broke softly from his chest. "I'm sorry," he said. "That crossed a line."

"No," she murmured. "You have nothing to be sorry for."

"I wish things were different."

"Yes. I do, too." *He's leaving.* The thought surfaced in her brain. Lily wondered how she would stand it. She wondered how she could be so consumed with longing for Edward when her son was missing. "I think, sometimes, if the police hadn't caught us, I might have become a criminal. Maybe I have that kind of mind." She revealed another of her secrets, one that haunted her.

Edward looked sidelong at her.

"I was so scared, going to jail. But I deserved it. I did what they said. I was there when Jesse robbed that store and shot that boy. The fact that I didn't know what he planned is no excuse."

"You're assuming too much responsibility, and that's my legal opinion. If you're guilty of anything, it's bad judgment, like ninety-nine percent of the rest of the population."

She toyed with her spoon.

"I know the charges against you were dropped, but you never said how."

"When Dad came to Phoenix, he brought Paul with him. They'd done business together, been friends a number of years. He knew Paul was from Arizona and had connections there. Favors were called in, and I was released." Lily felt a wave of old bitterness. She hadn't wanted anyone's favors. "I was back home in Texas within a month. Jesse died in prison a year and a half later in a knife fight with another inmate."

"And you married Paul."

"That was the price of my freedom," Lily said.

"Are you saying you felt obligated to marry him?" Incomprehension lightened Edward's voice.

"Dad and I both felt we owed him, but the way the marriage came about was more subtle than that."

Edward bent his elbow on the table and leaned his head on his hand, looking at her, still incredulous.

"Do you remember when you got the charges dropped against AJ, and Paul gave him the ultimatum about joining the military?"

"Your dad told you to marry Paul? Or what? He'd kick you out?"

"Not in so many words, no. I could have enrolled at A&M. But the idea of being on a college campus with all those kids—I didn't feel like a kid anymore. I didn't feel much of anything, really. I was depressed, I guess. Angry at myself and Dad. Paul came around a lot then. We'd go riding. He didn't enjoy it; he wasn't good at it, but he went as a favor to me, because it was the one place I felt safe, on the back of a horse. After a while, he asked Dad if it would be all right if he pursued a romantic relationship with me."

"That sounds so—old-school. You were okay with it? What was he, forty when you married?"

"Almost forty-two. I was nineteen." Lily extended her arms, picking absently at her thumbnail. "I was really scared of what I'd done. I didn't trust myself. Paul was settled. He had a good life, one I could walk into." *Hide out in.* She had wanted that, too. She had wanted to be different, to become someone else. Better, smarter. Instead, she had become more afraid. She was subject to anxiety. She kept to herself, to her home. Her gynecologist had once suggested she might be mildly agoraphobic.

"So your dad okayed it." Edward's voice still carried an echo of disbelief. "I mean, it sounds as if, like AJ, you were given an ultimatum."

"Dad would be angry to hear it called that." Lily remembered waking in a panic on the morning of her wedding. She remembered sitting on her bed, rocking herself, terrified of the promise she'd made to marry Paul, knowing she didn't love him, wondering if the gratitude she did feel toward him was enough. Winona had sat beside her, and while Lily's tears had speckled her bare thighs, Win had taken her hand and smoothed her hair. When Win had found out about the marriage, she'd argued with Lily's dad, declaring Lily too young to make such a commitment, but he had been unmoved.

"I didn't think—I mean, happiness—" Lily stammered in her attempt to capture it, the state of her mind at the time. "It wasn't something—being happy wasn't a consideration. Paul needed a wife, one he could—" *Groom.* She almost said it, and while she believed that had been Paul's intention—part of it, anyway—she couldn't go that far with her disloyalty. "He was kind to me in the beginning," she finished lamely.

Edward said nothing, and they sat for several moments, not looking at each other. What were they doing here? What did she want to happen? Lily imagined Edward wondered, too.

"We're all fallible," he said. "But the price for our mistakes shouldn't be our happiness."

"I regret not being honest with my son. What if it could have made a difference?"

"It's parenthood, Lily, not perfecthood. At least that's what I tell myself. You still have a chance with AJ. He's still in your life."

"If I do, so do you. You can find Charlie, talk to him."

Edward turned to her, and she wasn't sure what was in his eyes.

"I'm sorry," she said. "I shouldn't give out advice I'm unwilling to take."

"You're unwilling because it's a risk. You don't know how AJ will react."

"No."

"Having some connection with your son, or in my case, no connection, is better than confessing the truth and risking his hatred. Then it would be real, not something we only imagined."

Although Edward had described how she felt, Lily didn't answer.

"I've always thought life was a gamble. Maybe that's my downfall, my Achilles' heel, but to me, you either play and take your chances or sit on the sidelines, watching everyone else. That isn't living, really."

When Lily looked at him now, he smiled slightly, and an understanding that there would be risk involved in any undertaking to repair the damage they'd done as parents seemed to flare between them. There was an acknowledgment, too, of their frailty as human beings that was searing in its honesty and so visceral that Lily felt it as surely as if Edward had taken her hand. But it was clenched in her lap.

Time passed, a space of heartbeats she could feel in her ears.

The waitress came, and Edward asked for the check. When it was paid, he walked Lily out to her car.

"Would you like me to see what I can find out about the investigation?" he asked.

They'd reached her BMW, and turning to him, she said, "Would you?"

"Yes, but you realize it may not be good news. You know Becca Westin was pregnant."

"Yes, and that her mother claims AJ and Becca were involved behind Shea's back. If it's true, and if AJ didn't want the baby, it means he would have had a motive."

"What Becca's mother says is considered hearsay by the court. They'll need DNA to prove paternity. Other than AJ's laptop and cell phone that were found at the bus station, was anything else missing from his apartment?"

"His truck and his handgun, a .45."

Edward looked out into the middle distance. "There was no sign of forced entry, I heard."

"No. Paul thinks he's a suspect because he has a key to the apartment, which is ridiculous."

"Yeah, but it's standard procedure, looking at family members. The way the girl was killed—" Edward paused. *Do you know?* The question was implicit in his eyes.

"She was stabbed," Lily said.

"Eleven times, and she was choked, but there was no sign of ligature. Someone used their bare hands. They suspect she may have been sexually assaulted, too."

"My God." Lily felt light-headed. She felt her vision darken at its periphery, and she leaned against the car. Edward put his hand on her arm, and his touch steadied her.

"Whoever did it left a note."

"A note?" This was a new detail to Lily.

"It was written—not in lipstick, the other stuff, the liner. It said, 'Fixed you.'"

Lily took a moment, processing the words, *Fixed you*, running them through her mind. "They did fix her, didn't they?"

"I want to help you and AJ," Edward said after a moment, "but I don't want to get too deeply involved, not unless Paul agrees."

Lily nodded. She understood the risk. If Paul found out she'd met with Edward today, he might suspect there had been other occasions, if he didn't already. But what was there to know? Lily wondered. Today was the first time Edward had touched her intimately. She still felt it, the weight of his fingertips resting in the hollow of her throat.

• • •

She was almost to the ranch when her phone rang. She pulled off the highway, digging it out of her purse, heart tapping with anticipation that possibly it was Edward. But then, seeing it was her dad, she was seized with anxiety. *He's found something,* she thought.

"Dad?"

"Ah, thank God, Lily."

"What is it? Did you find AJ? Is he all right?"

"No, no, I'm sorry. Nothing like that. The safe, here at the house—it was robbed."

"What? Did someone break in?"

"Not exactly. I didn't lock up before I left. Sometimes I don't, you know, if I'm not going to be gone long.

You forgot. Lily didn't say it. She rested her head on the seat back.

"They got your mom's jewelry and about five thousand in cash I kept in there."

"Did you call the police?"

"Yeah. They think because the safe wasn't damaged, whoever got into it knew the combination. They think it was AJ."

10

After Dru made the 911 call, she and the girls went into the great room to wait for the Wyatt police. Dru sat with Shea and Kate on the sofa, but Leigh and Vanessa paced. They were angry. Dru sensed they blamed Shea. She must have felt it, too, because she told them to go. "Mom and Kate and I can handle it," she said, and while she was shaky and pale, there was a stubborn set to her jaw that Dru recognized.

"I'd like nothing better, trust me, but what if *he's* out there?" Leigh asked.

"He?" Shea asked. "AJ? Do you mean AJ?"

"Your fiancé is off the ledge." Leigh hurled the allegation at Shea, a small bomb.

"Shut up, Leigh," Kate said.

"It's not helping," Dru said, keeping her voice low. *You*, she wanted to say to Leigh, you *aren't helping*. She could slap the girl, she thought.

"Leigh's right, though." Vanessa—Ms. Big Mouth—spoke up. "He said he couldn't stop, so who's next? One of us?"

"My husband is worried sick," Leigh said. "Connor wants me out of here. When I called him, he told me to make the cops bring me home. He said it's not safe any other way."

"I thought we were friends." Shea's glance darted between Vanessa and Leigh.

"We are." Their protest was rendered in harmony.

"It's just AJ—there's something off about him." Leigh softened her tone. Did she assume Shea would agree with her now? Dru wondered.

"You don't see it," Vanessa said, "and I get that. I mean, love is blind, right?"

Oh, they were so magnanimous in their judgment of Shea and her choices. Dru's jaw tightened. That she, too, judged AJ wasn't lost on her, but she wouldn't club Shea over the head with it.

Thankfully, now, the far wall opposite the sofa was washed in a faint-hued rainbow of red-and-blue light, announcing the arrival of a squad car. Dru went to the front door, opening it. The sun was down, the light clear and mellow, and she was relieved to recognize Ken Carter exiting the driver's side of the Wyatt patrol car. Amy's brother. Someone familiar. Another officer, shorter than Ken, and heavier set, came with him.

"Patrol Sergeant Daryl Henley." He introduced himself when Dru greeted him.

Turning to Ken, she said, "I'm sorry we're meeting again under such circumstances."

"I was real sorry to hear from Amy about the wedding," he said.

"Thank you," Dru said. "Coming from Houston, I thought maybe living in Wyatt, I was leaving this kind of crime behind. Especially having it hit this close to home," she added.

"I hear you," Ken said. "You know Amy and I were raised here, and I joined the force here, figuring to keep it on the quiet side, but this is shaping up to be as big an investigation as the one we dealt with last year. The car accident—?"

"I remember," Dru said. "I had both those boys, Jordy Cline and Travis Simmons, in my sixth-grade math class. It was so awful what their families went through—what the whole town went through."

"It's been a difficult time, that's for sure. The WPD is still dealing with the impact, still shorthanded."

Dru wasn't surprised. The accident itself had been horrible enough, but then there had been all the ensuing legal fallout, radiating damage along a network of unforeseen fault lines. Dru imagined similar consequences would rattle even a big-city police department. "I guess this sort of thing goes on everywhere," she said.

"Yes, ma'am, especially in towns like Wyatt, where the population is growing," Ken said.

Dru liked it, his easy courtesy and friendly manner. It reassured her. "We're in here," she said, leading the way into the great room.

"Hey, y'all." Ken looked around at each of the girls.

Of course he knew them, Dru thought. Even though he was several years older, Dru imagined through his work as a police officer he probably knew almost everyone.

"Could I see the note?" Ken got down to business.

Dru picked it up from the coffee table. "We've all touched it," she said. It occurred to her they shouldn't have passed it around.

Ken took it at the corner between his thumb and forefinger and studied it.

Daryl left to get an evidence bag.

Ken said, "Looks like it's written in lipstick."

"It's lip liner," Shea said. "You use it to outline your lips, then fill them in with lipstick. Well, not you—"

"I get it." Ken half smiled.

Daryl came back, and Ken slotted the note carefully into a clear plastic wrapper. He asked Leigh a series of questions: What time and why did she go to her car? Did she see anything out of the ordinary there other than the note? Her answers sounded unremarkable to Dru, and Ken didn't appear overly concerned, either.

"What will you do with the note?" Kate asked.

"We'll get it over to the lab, get it checked for fingerprints, see if we can run down the source of the lip liner. None of y'all recognize it, do you? The color, maybe?"

Leigh and Vanessa said no. Shea, looking at Kate, said, "It kind of looks like that Revlon pencil we bought right before finals. We each got one, remember?"

"Not really, no," Kate said.

"You have a receipt?" Ken asked.

"I doubt it. It was three or four weeks ago. I don't even remember the name of the shade. Something pink." Shea looked at Kate. "Are you sure—?"

"No." Kate cut Shea off. "I don't remember, okay?"

"Okay." Shea let it go.

They were all jittery, even short-tempered.

Ken pocketed his notepad.

Daryl said, "We'll talk to your neighbors. Maybe one of them saw something."

When Leigh asked if Ken and Daryl would take her home, Daryl suggested he and Ken would follow her and Vanessa. "We'll set up a patrol, too," he said. "We'll monitor your neighborhoods, as often as we can, as often as the manpower we have will allow."

Ken said, "Don't hesitate to call if you see anything suspicious, or if anything makes you worry. Dispatch'll send somebody. The same goes if you remember anything else, whether it's about this note or some other aspect of this investigation. Let me know, no matter how insignificant you think it is. Sometimes it's the smallest piece that can complete the puzzle." His glance logged them each in turn as if he sensed that one of them was withholding something, but when no one spoke, he turned to go, Daryl behind him, Dru in their wake.

"I got a text from Becca."

Dru recognized Kate's voice.

Ken made a sound, "Ah," as if to say, *There it is.*

He turned. Dru and Daryl did, too.

Shea, Vanessa, and Leigh were all staring at Kate in astonishment.

"Before she was killed?" Ken asked. "It's pertinent to the investigation?"

"Yes. At least it might be." Kate rubbed her crossed arms briskly.

A pause that seemed breathless to Dru held for a moment.

"She wanted me to meet her on Tuesday," Kate said.

"Where?" Ken asked. "In Dallas?"

"No. She was here in Wyatt. She asked if I'd could come to her house."

"We picked up the jars on Tuesday," Shea said. "When did you go to her house? Why didn't you tell me?"

"I didn't go—she texted later and canceled."

"Wait a minute," Ken said. "Back up. Tell me about Tuesday, everything that happened, in order."

Kate explained their mission to pick up the mason jars, that Becca had begged off, supposedly sick to her stomach.

"You *knew* she was faking." Shea was upset.

"Maybe she wasn't," Vanessa said. "Maybe she had morning sickness."

Kate said, "I didn't say anything because Becca made me promise not to."

"But you didn't go to Becca Westin's house, is that right?" Ken's brow was creased; the effect was almost comical. He was confused in the way men could be by women's conversations.

Kate said, "No. I texted her when Shea dropped me off at home after we got back from Fredericksburg and told her I was on my way to her house, but she texted back and said she had to go to Dallas."

"Did she indicate where in Dallas she was going, or who she was going to see?" Daryl asked.

"No. She just said she was sorry and hoped no one would hate her."

"What did that mean?" Shea asked.

"I don't know. It was weird."

"Did you know Becca was pregnant, that it was morning sickness that kept her home on Tuesday?" Ken asked.

"You know I would have told you if I had known anything like that." Kate addressed her answer to Shea.

"Are you saying you had knowledge from Becca that there was something else bothering her? Something other than her being pregnant?" Ken was persistent.

"No, only what everyone else has said. She seemed really stressed lately."

"So, on Tuesday, when you texted back and forth—that was the last time you heard from her," Ken said.

"Yes," Kate said.

"Is there a reason you withheld this information?" Ken's eyes were locked on Kate.

She stared at the floor.

"Can you give me a reason, Kate?" Ken repeated the question.

"I didn't think it was important?" Her voice rose as if she were asking him.

"What changed your mind?" Ken wasn't letting her off.

"It was what you said before, that you wanted to know about anything we remembered, no matter how insignificant."

Kate's response was reasonable. She was looking at Ken, maintaining eye contact with him, but something was off.

Dru remembered the Christmas a few years ago when Rob had bought Shea an iPad. It had gone missing the following New Year's Day after Shea hosted a holiday sleepover for several girlfriends, including, of course, her best friend, Kate. Shea had thought at first she'd lost it. She'd been reluctant to tell Dru, or Rob, for fear she'd be blamed, so she'd waited a couple of days to confess it was gone, and then she'd insisted someone must have broken into the house, that none of her friends would steal from her.

When Charla had found it a week later at the bottom of Kate's overnight tote that had been stuffed under her bed since the night of the sleepover, Kate had looked Dru right in the eye and claimed she'd picked it up by accident, without realizing it, and she'd apologized profusely. Dru knew if she thought about it, she'd remember other incidents when she'd felt Kate wasn't telling the truth. She'd assumed Kate had outgrown the tendency to lie, but maybe not.

Ken said, "The Dallas police might want to interview you. They might want to check out your phone." He seemed suspicious, too.

"Why?" Kate was visibly alarmed. "I've told you everything Becca said, everything that went on. I don't know anything else."

"We'll be in touch," Ken said. He switched his glance to Dru. "A word?" he asked, and it was clear that he meant for her to follow him, that his intention was to speak to her alone.

She walked with him and Daryl onto the front porch, her stomach in a fist.

The sun was down, the light uncertain. Dru couldn't read Ken's expression, but when he spoke, his voice was grave.

"I didn't want to say this in front of the girls—they're spooked enough—but there was a break-in out at the xL late this afternoon."

"Oh, no. Is everyone okay?" Dru thought of Jeb, the way he had collapsed earlier.

"Yeah. Neither Jeb nor Lily was there." Ken looked off into the street at a car that passed.

"You think it was AJ?" Dru asked.

"Whoever it was knew where the safe was and the combination. No muss, no fuss. In and out." Ken swiped one hand with the palm of the other.

"Along with the cash Jeb Axel kept in there, they took his late wife's jewelry," Daryl said.

"We think they were probably staked out close by and saw Lily and Jeb leave," Ken said. "They knew the house was empty, that it would be for a while."

"They knew the family hardly ever locks the doors," Daryl added.

"I bet they will now," Dru said.

Down the way, someone shouted for Angie. Dru recognized Angie's mom's voice. It was that time, dark thirty. Mothers wanted their kids home. It passed so quickly, Dru thought, the years when you exerted a measure of control over your children's lives. One day you were changing their diapers, and the next, with those same hands, you were giving them the keys to the car.

"We can't be sure it was AJ," Ken said.

"But it could have been," Dru said.

"If it was, he's got the resources now to leave the area, leave the country, if he chooses. He knows his way around international travel. He could even have connections—"

Dru interrupted, "You're—the police are watching the airports, I guess."

Ken nodded.

Daryl said, "They're stretched pretty thin in Dallas, like our department here in Wyatt. They're handling a big case involving a councilman up there, but there's a BOLO out on AJ. Law enforcement across the state is on the alert for him."

"That's not to say we're looking only at AJ," Ken said.

"So I heard," Dru said, and when Ken raised his brows, she said, "The detective from Dallas who questioned Shea made it seem as if they suspect her. I heard it from Joy Westin, too, that the Dallas police asked her about Shea, but she was here, Ken, with me, all night on Tuesday. She had nothing to do with what happened to Becca, no knowledge of it whatsoever."

"It's procedure," he said, "questioning those closest to the victim."

"But you know Shea's not involved, right?" Dru wanted Ken's affirmation, his support. He didn't give it to her.

"It's not my call," he said, and then, perhaps relenting, he said, "Look, it's too early in the investigation to rule out anyone at this point, but AJ Isley is the main focus, okay? You should keep an eye out."

"You think AJ may come here for Shea." Dru felt a renewed jolt of alarm.

"It's possible," Ken said. "You and Shea should be vigilant, which is good advice in any case. Keep your doors locked. Be aware."

"The note Leigh found, it's written in the same lip liner as the note that was on Becca's body, isn't it?" Dru hadn't wanted to mention it in front of the girls. "Joy told me."

Ken looked annoyed. "It'll take the proper testing to determine if the two were written with the same material, and only an expert can say if they're the work of the same person. You just need to take care of yourself and your daughter—"

The front door opened. "Sergeant Carter?" It was Leigh's voice. "Van and I didn't want you to leave without us."

"No," he said. "If you're ready, we can follow you home now."

Once they were gone, Kate and Shea went with Dru into the kitchen. She wished she could keep going, out the back door, into the oncoming night. But she stopped and turned to face them, leaning against the kitchen counter, waiting for the question that was inevitable.

Why did Ken want to talk to you?

Shea was the one who asked.

"Y'all were out there a long time." Kate's observation was oh-so-casual.

Or was Dru imagining that? Her mind scrambled for clarity, direction. What could she say but the truth? But did she want to repeat what she'd been told by Ken in confidence in front of Kate, whom she was unsure she could trust?

"Mom?" Shea mixed an element of warning into her query.

"There was a break-in at the Axels' this afternoon. Someone took a lot of cash and jewelry."

Shea's eyes widened. It was a moment before she took it in, before surprise hardened into accusation. "By someone you mean AJ, right?" Her voice shook. "Did his granddad or his mom see him?"

"No. They were out. Ken said they don't have enough information yet to say who it was."

Shea put her fingertips to her temples, dragging her hair behind her ears.

Kate put an arm around her waist, pulling her close. "It could have been anyone."

"If it was AJ," Dru said, "he's got what he needs now—the funds to leave here, the state—the US, if he wants to. It's possible he'll try to contact you, Shea, that he'll try to talk you into leaving with him."

"Well, he hasn't, if you're asking," Shea said, "and you can tell that to Ken for me."

"AJ may not be himself, honey. The man you remember, that you fell in love with—"

"Stop." Shea held up her palms at Dru. "There isn't going to be a wedding. I've given up on that, but I am not giving up on AJ. He. Didn't. Do. This. None of it. I don't know who did, but it wasn't him."

"All right, fine," Dru said. She went to the table in the breakfast nook and picked up the tea glasses. Kate helped her carry them to the sink. Shea loaded them into the dishwasher. She walked Kate to the back door.

"You sure you don't want to spend the night?" Shea asked. "You're off tomorrow, right?"

"Yeah, and I would," she said, "but I promised Erik I'd meet him at Bella Vista in the morning at six thirty. He wants to get a hike in before work." Kate glanced over at Dru. "'Bye, Mama Dru," she said.

Dru smiled. "See you later, Katie gator."

In the predawn hours while walking, sleepless, through the house, keeping a vigil, Dru couldn't get Kate's secrecy about the texts she'd shared with Becca out of her mind. Why, if they meant nothing, hadn't she mentioned them to Shea, at least? Dru knew Kate; she knew when Kate was afraid, and she would bet money the girl was afraid now. But of what or whom?

11

Lily was almost back to the ranch when her phone chimed again. This time she saw Paul's name in the ID window, and instantly her heart was in overdrive. How much could it stand? How many more times could this happen, she wondered, before it would simply pound out of her chest?

He was breathless when she answered and didn't bother with a greeting. "Have the local cops gotten in touch with you?"

Thinking he was talking about the break-in, Lily said, "No. They talked to Dad—"

"Is he gone?"

"Who? Dad?" Lily fumbled for sense.

"No, damn it. AJ. Look, some guy down there at one of the private airfields called Bushnell and said he saw AJ talking to a pilot who flies for an oil-field service company out of Lubbock."

"Here in the Hill Country? When?"

"Less than an hour ago."

"Which airfield?"

"I don't know. Bushnell said something about a lake."

"There are dozens of lakes and private airstrips all over the Hill Country." Lily thought for a moment. "It wasn't Monarch Lake, was it? That's the lake nearest the ranch. But there's no airfield there."

"Guy's name—wait a sec, I wrote it down here somewhere."

Lily heard the rustle of papers being pushed around. She imagined Paul at his desk. It was huge. Topped with a mattress, she could nap on it.

"Evers. Wylie Evers is his name. You recognize it?"

"He's a neighbor. His ranch, the Triple Oak, shares a boundary with the xL. Was Hershey the name of the lake? That's close to the Triple Oak on the far north side."

"That's it," Paul said. "Lake Hershey is the location of the airfield."

"Is Wylie sure it was AJ?"

"Not absolutely, according to Bushnell, but—"

"Did he actually see AJ get on the plane?"

"No. Where would he get that kind of money? I told Bushnell, my son works as a chef, no way could he—"

"Paul?" Lily's voice rose, tight, shrill. She couldn't help it. "There was a break-in here this afternoon. Someone got into the safe and took Dad's cash, five thousand dollars, and Mama's jewelry."

"Where were you? Where was Jeb?"

"Dad was out looking for AJ. I was at the grocery store. I'm on my way back now." The lie came quickly, sounding hollow, tasting of shame. "Dad called the police, the Wyatt police," she said when Paul didn't respond.

After several moments, she realized he was giving her an opportunity to see it, the ugly inevitability of the truth that seemed to be taking shape—that their son was the thief, and worse, he was guilty of murder. Not a victim but a perpetrator, a fugitive, a wanted man.

• • •

"Dad?" Lily called, entering the back door, setting her purse and keys on the island.

"Office," he answered.

He was sitting at his desk, writing, and he looked up when she appeared. "They want an inventory," he said.

Lily sat down. "The police? Of everything that's missing," she surmised.

He nodded.

"I don't think I can remember all the jewelry. Your mom had a wad of it."

"Because you kept buying it for her."

"She loved it," he said. "Remember how she used to say nothing went better with denim and western boots than diamonds? She was partial to turquoise, too."

"I remember a ring with turquoise, big and shaped like a triangle."

"I bought that for her, our tenth wedding anniversary. She'd seen some work by that Navajo artist—"

"Lee Yazzie." Lily supplied the name. Her mom had loved his work.

"Yeah. I had him make a bracelet for her, too. A cuff, your mother called it."

"What did the police say?"

"They think AJ was hanging around, waiting for the house to be empty."

Although it was what she had expected to hear, Lily felt her air go as if she'd been punched.

"I had to tell them AJ knew about the safe, knew the combination."

Lily held her dad's gaze. "Do you think it was him?"

He tossed down his pen. *Maybe.*

The word—the doubt was there in his eyes. It would tear him up if AJ had done this. *How could he?* The question rang through Lily's mind, heated, angry. How could AJ put them in this position of having to speculate, wonder—was he capable? Could he have hurt that girl? Lily thought if it was true, if she had to face the fact, it would crush her. It would crush them all.

"I can't stomach it," he said, echoing Lily's thinking. "The cash, yeah. He's on the run, scared. He needs money to get away. But his grandma's jewelry? What's he going to do with it? It's not as if he can sell it, or even pawn it without the cops finding out. If he knew a fence—but AJ's not—he's never run with—"

"It's not even that, Dad." Lily's pulse ticked in her ears. "If he's taken the money and jewelry, if he's on the run, it means—it means he—" She stopped, unable to finish.

Her dad stared at her, and when his eyes reddened, she realized he was seeing her through the glaze of tears. It astonished her. In her entire life she hadn't ever seen her father cry, not even when her mother died. Winona had said that he did cry then, just not in front of Lily.

She went to him, wrapping his shoulders in her embrace from behind, setting her cheek against his, which was damp now. He closed his hands over her forearms, and they held on to each other.

"I love that boy either way," he said in a rough voice.

"Yes," Lily said. "I do, too."

"We'll find him, find a way to help him—forgive him if he did all these terrible things."

"Yes," Lily said, although she wondered, *How?* How did you—how *could* you forgive a person who wantonly took the life of another? People had done it; she had read about them. Even Holocaust survivors had forgiven those who had tortured them. But those monsters hadn't been their own children. The very idea that this was the awful possibility shaping her future vacuumed her breath from her lungs. She felt she might collapse, burdening her father with her dead weight, and from somewhere she summoned the effort to straighten, to back away. She found tissues in the half bath and brought him one, keeping one for herself.

He used it, wiping his eyes, blowing his nose, his movements somehow suggesting disgust, resentment.

It was only going to get worse, Lily thought, resuming her seat across from him. "I talked to Paul," she said, and recapping the conversation as quickly as she could, she told her dad that AJ had been spotted at the Lake Hershey airfield.

"Why didn't Evers call me?" Her dad didn't wait for Lily's answer. "The son of a bitch is ten years older than I am and half-blind. He wouldn't know shit from Shinola." He pawed through the papers on his desk. "Where the hell is my phone?"

They spent a half hour hunting for it, finally finding it outside in the seat of an Adirondack chair, one of two that sat in a grassy meadow halfway between the house and the barn. Lily didn't know what led her to look there. The chairs were out of the way, a detour to nowhere. Her dad was vague as to how his cell phone could have ended up there. Maybe he'd stopped there going to or from the barn.

"Why?" Lily asked.

"To watch the grass blow," her dad answered.

That might have been a reasonable response for someone other than her father.

. . .

She was in the kitchen, breaking eggs into a bowl to make an omelet for their dinner, when her dad came to tell her he'd talked to Wylie. In addition to the eggs, she'd found a box of frozen spinach, a can of mushrooms, and a chunk of Gruyère cheese. Not that either she or her dad had an appetite. But there was something soothing about going through the motions of preparing a meal.

"The way Wylie described him, it could have been AJ." Her dad went to the refrigerator, pulled out a beer, twisted off the cap, and drank deeply.

Lily watched him, shaking her head no when he asked if she wanted one. She turned her attention back to whipping the eggs. It relieved her that he hadn't seemed to notice that the refrigerator shelves were still fairly empty.

"I figured it had to be years since Evers saw AJ. How can he remember what he looks like?"

"Dad, you know how it is around here. You can't go a month without running into everyone you know."

"Yeah. Wylie said he saw AJ and Shea in town a couple of weeks ago, shook AJ's hand. He knows it was him at the airfield. Like Wylie said, there's a lot of air traffic goes in and out of there—tourists, nature freaks, the bunch of damn fools that buy land and a few head and think they're in the cattle business." He took another swallow of beer.

Lily didn't reply.

Her dad spoke into the silence. "Five thousand dollars would get you somewhere. Mexico. Canada. And from there, you could go anywhere." Her dad pitched his empty bottle in the trash and got another. "Wylie wondered if the wedding was off."

"I hope you told him yes."

"I did. I guess all the folks who are coming are going to have to be contacted."

He had only just now thought of it, what calling off the wedding would entail. "Dru and I talked about it earlier," she said.

Lily and Paul hadn't discussed the wedding once since this happened. How would they word their regrets? *As parents of the groom, we're sorry to inform you of the cancellation of our son's wedding due to the fact that not only may he have murdered a bridesmaid, but he might very well be a fugitive on the FBI's Ten Most Wanted list.* Would that be socially acceptable as an explanation? She could have the notes printed, she thought, on her monogrammed, beveled, and gilt-edged notecards. The jolt of her laughter came unaware, butting against her ribs, finally wedging itself in her throat beneath the fist of her sorrow. Maybe she could add a caveat: *If any of you happen to see AJ, please inform the police.*

"Lily?"

She glanced at her dad. "Did I ever tell you what Millie Kramer said to me once? She's married to Harvey Kramer, the bank president who does most of Paul's financing?"

"I've met him a time or two, but not his wife."

"It was during the first year Paul and I were married. We were out to dinner—some fancy restaurant—with several other couples, and in front of all of them, she said—and she thought it was funny, a cute joke—she said when Paul told her and Harvey he was planning to marry me, their advice was that he should just get a red Corvette."

"What's that supposed to mean?"

"A sports car would be cheaper, less maintenance—you know, than a gold digger like me. That's how they saw me. They still do. They think I married Paul for his money."

"I never liked Harvey. The guy's a know-it-all, arrogant as hell."

"I've never fit in with those people, Dad. In all this time, I haven't made a single friend. They're so much older, but it isn't even that. There's no common ground." Lily stopped, hating the way she sounded.

"Is this about canceling the wedding?"

She shrugged. "They've criticized me behind my back for years. I shouldn't care at all what they're thinking of me—saying about me and AJ now."

"He's Paul's son, too."

"Yes, but if he's turned out badly, it must be my influence. He couldn't get into Rice University or SMU or Yale, or wherever it is those people sent their kids."

"He didn't have the grades, but he could have gone somewhere else—a community college—"

"He got arrested, Dad, the same way I did, but that's never been discussed—the fact that we have this terrible thing in common."

Her dad looked perplexed.

"AJ doesn't know about Jesse, or that I was jailed once, too, as an accessory to murder the same way he was when he was nineteen. Paul didn't want him to know; he's never wanted anyone to know that about me, and yet I'm never allowed to forget it." Making a fist, Lily pressed it to her mouth.

Her dad came to her, wrapping her into his embrace. The gust of his sigh stirred her hair.

"Maybe it would have helped him if I'd been honest." She spoke in a hot whisper against his chest. "He would have known when he was arrested that first time that he could talk to me, that I would understand. Maybe, together, we could have kept Paul from forcing him to enlist, and the PTSD—it wouldn't have happened."

"Oh, Sissy, don't go blaming yourself." Her dad's voice slipped and broke. She wondered if he was crying again.

Taking a breath, she pushed away from his embrace, wiped her face, and composed herself, for his sake. "We should eat," she said. She got out the cast-iron frying pan, wiped it with olive oil, and set it over a burner to heat.

• • •

Lily takes his small hand, and they wade into the warm water of Monarch Lake far enough that it laps their ankles. On the opposite shore, the sun is cresting a distant ridge of hills, a golden ball rolling along a ragged tree line. AJ dances his small, chubby feet, and when she smiles, he laughs, stomping harder, showering them in a sparkling rain. Laughing, too, she scoops him up, settling him on her hip. "You ready to learn how to swim like a fish?"

He nods, but his expression is grave. His eyes look into hers, and although he is barely two, his glance seems wise. She thinks he can see into her soul. She loves him profoundly, more than she thought was possible.

"I swim?" he says.

"Yes, but I'll be with you the whole time. Okay?"

He nods again.

Paul doesn't like it, that she brings AJ to the lake, but she does it anyway, every time they visit the ranch. Before he could walk, she cradled him in her lap at the shoreline, letting the water flow around them; she had let it fall from her fingertips, anointing him. It's the way her mother introduced her to the water. Here at this very spot is where she taught Lily to swim.

She carries AJ back to the quilt she spread beneath a live oak and sets him down, and he waits while she slathers him with sunblock. Butternut has strayed a few yards to the water's edge. Lily can hear her drinking. They had ridden over here just after daybreak, AJ's warm weight tucked in front of her. He is learning to ride and sits on a horse as naturally as she did at his age, spine ramrod straight, easy in the saddle.

Fearless.

She caps the sunscreen and stows it in her tote.

"Let's go," he says, eyes alight.

Hand in hand, they head back to the water, and even as she is washed through with her joy in him, she is half-frightened by his utter trust and the knowledge that his safety and well-being are her responsibility. Paul has pointed out her tendency to be dreamy, forgetful. *"Pay attention."* His voice barks in her head, feeding her anxiety. He treats her like a child, everywhere except in the bedroom. What he does to her there, the way he talks to her, thick voiced and panting in his frenzy to have her, to have his mouth everywhere on her—she is no child to him then. It is distressing; she is uncertain of her role as his wife. Standing at the water's edge, she thinks of the day she will bring Paul here and show him how she has taught their son to swim. She imagines his look of amazement, perhaps even of respect.

It is a weekday; the lake is deserted, the surface a dimpled reflection of a flawless sky. She has chosen the time for AJ's first swimming lesson deliberately. Contrary to what Paul thinks, she isn't so young that she has no sense, nor is she into taking stupid risks.

AJ tugs her hand, saying, "Let's go, Mommy," impatient and imperious in his rush to get on with the adventure. He leads the way, marching strongly through the lucent green water until it passes his knees, then he stops, tilting his gaze questioningly to hers. They have never gone farther out, because of Paul, his oft-repeated warning that she isn't qualified as a swim instructor. While his lack of trust feeds her doubt, she knows she is a good swimmer, that she wouldn't attempt to teach AJ if she weren't.

Swinging him onto her hip, she carries him some twenty-five yards farther from the shore until the water laps at her waist. "Okay?" she asks him, holding his gaze.

AJ nods, and his eyes on hers are intent, as if to register every tiny detail, every sensation.

"I'm bending my knees." She sinks slowly, watching his face for signs of alarm as the water rises, covering his torso. His eyes widen now, and there it is, that glimmer of dawning delight. It comes every time he experiences something new, and it thrills her. She finds herself waiting for it. Her grin mirrors his. She carries him out another ten feet, stopping when the water is at his waist level. "Can you blow bubbles? Like this?" Bending her head, she demonstrates.

He follows her example, comes up, laughing, and does it again. And again. She loses count of the repetitions. He is a natural, taking to the water with the same ease as when she and her dad first sat him on Butternut. "Want to float on your back?"

He nods vigorously, and bracing him, she lays him on the water, letting it hold him, weightless. His feet dangle. He fans his arms, spreading his fingers, making plump starfish. She swishes him gently, to and fro, humming some nameless tune. Sunlight sequins the water. She feels its warmth on her shoulders. Happiness swells from inside her, seeming to expand around her. Sleek as an otter, AJ bumps against the raft of her arms. She feels the knobs of his shoulder blades, the swell of his small calves. The fine strands of his hair float around his head, a halo of the palest seaweed. She looks into his eyes wide with wonder and thinks of the blessing he has brought to her life.

The sound of the boat is there in the background. It registers, but at a level too deep in her brain to command her attention. Her focus, her whole heart and mind, are lost in the sensation of AJ's small body floating in her loose embrace, so that when the boat's engine noise explodes around them, she flinches. It is a moment before it hurtles into view. And then she is horrified to see that it is coming straight at her and AJ, bearing down on them from the right, boat bottom cracking hard against the water's surface. It's close enough that she recognizes it as a cigarette boat; she sees the name, *Slap Shot*, on its side. Adrenaline-fueled panic ices her veins. Tightening her grasp on AJ, she wheels and runs for the shore. The water is like sludge, hampering her movement. But she has AJ. He is a snug, warm, wet bundle against her—and then he is gone.

Gone!

Lily stops, looking around wildly.

"AJ!" she shouts, and then she dives. The water is only four or four and a half feet deep. The boat has turned sharply away, but its wake and her frantic movement have churned up a sand of debris. She can't see her hand in front of her face. Her lungs are bursting when she breaks the water's surface. Dragging in air, she shouts his name again, "AJ!" But it is futile. Does she suppose he can hear her?

She dives over and over, choking on water, her own breath, her sobs of terror. It is on the sixth dive that her hand encounters his forearm, and pulling him up, she stumbles with him to the shore, where she lays him down, dropping to her knees beside him. He is cold to her touch, inert and deathly white except for his eyes, which are sunken and blue, like ghost eyes. His lips are blue, too, and his belly is distended. Gorge rises in her throat. It isn't conscious on her part when she turns him on his side and thumps his back, hard, between his shoulder blades. The spasm is immediate, a full-body shudder, and the gout of water that spurts from his nose and mouth is shocking. She waits, terrified, and she prays, *Give him back, please, God, and I will never ask another thing. Please, please just give him back . . .*

It is a matter of seconds only, but in her mind what passes is a hellish eternity before AJ coughs. He lets out a wail. Color, miraculous color, suffuses his cheeks. She lifts him into her embrace, rocking him, humming. She tastes the salt of their mingled tears.

"*Oh God,*" she whispers. "*Oh, thankyouthankyouthankyou . . . never ask another thing . . .*"

• • •

Lily woke choking, heart hammering. Images from the dream reeled through her mind, a disjointed film played in double time. The lake, the sun on her shoulders, AJ in her arms . . . the horrifying absence of weight when he'd slipped from her grasp. The strain she'd felt, diving for him, the promise she'd made God, her first useless bargain . . .

Swinging her feet over the side of the bed, she almost expected to lower them into water. She could smell it, smell the odors of water, damp earth, and fish. She saw it, the small, protected cove where she had first gone to swim with her mother, where she had taken AJ and almost let him drown.

She stood up. She hadn't bothered taking off anything other than her jeans and boots when she'd come up to her bedroom after dinner last night, and she pulled the jeans back on now, shoved her feet into her boots. She wasn't that girl, and AJ wasn't a baby, either. But she knew where he was. After the dream . . . so vivid . . . she knew where to find him.

Downstairs, she took the keys to the Jeep from the hook by the back door. She and AJ had ridden Butternut over to Monarch Lake on that long-ago morning, but she couldn't spare the time to saddle Butternut now. Nor did she leave a note for her dad.

12

Fixed you . . .

I'm sorry for hurting you. I'm in trouble, and I don't think I can stop . . .

The contents of the notes, their implicit threat, haunted Dru. She'd been restless all of Thursday night, finally falling asleep near dawn, only to waken with a jolt a bare half hour later when light from the rising sun cracked the window blinds. She checked Shea's bedroom and, finding it empty, went through the house on bare feet, quickly and silently.

The smell of fresh-brewed coffee permeated the air, but the kitchen was empty. She turned in an anxious circle, then heard Shea's voice coming from outside. Walking to the back door, Dru felt on the offense; she had one thought in mind: wherever AJ was running to, he was not taking Shea. Dru would get the .38 if she had to; she would make him understand.

Fully expecting to see him, she was perplexed for a moment after she edged aside the mini blind and didn't find him there. She darted her glance over the wedge of lawn she could see, the side of the garage, part of the concrete apron. It looked as if it had rained during the short time she'd slept, but there was no sign of AJ. Shea was alone, in one of the chaise longues, her cell phone to her ear, and as Dru watched, she lowered it to her upraised knees. Whomever she'd been talking to, the conversation was over now.

Dru opened the door, making a show of it, calling out, "Good morning, honey," as if it were any one of the hundreds of ordinary mornings they'd shared.

"Bring a towel," Shea said, "if you're going to sit. It rained earlier."

Dru retraced her steps into the kitchen and grabbed the dish towel from the oven-door handle. Outside, she mopped the chair. "I never heard it," she said.

"It came down hard, but it didn't last very long," Shea said.

Dru hung the towel over the deck railing and settled into the chaise, stretching her legs, crossing her ankles.

"Uncle Kevin called," Shea said. "He got your message about the wedding."

"Is that who you were talking to?" Dru was only a tiny bit ashamed of her prior suspicion.

"Kara's in the hospital in Topeka. She's the youngest daughter, isn't she?"

"Yes," Dru said. "But Topeka? What happened? Is she all right?"

"She's fine. She had to have an emergency appendectomy. Uncle Kevin said he was glad they weren't in the middle of nowhere when she got sick."

"Still, what an awful thing to have happen so far from home. Did Kev want me to call him back?"

"No. Not unless he could help some way with our issues." Shea's voice took on a note of irony.

"They wouldn't have made it to the wedding after all," Dru said.

"No," Shea answered.

They shared a silence.

"I tried calling AJ's mom earlier."

"Why?" Dru was annoyed.

"I wanted to ask about the break-in, what was taken. I wanted to know if she's like the cops, if she thinks it was AJ."

"Did she tell you?"

"She didn't answer, and she hasn't called back. It seems weird. Where could she be?"

"I have no idea," Dru said. *Out hiring a dream team to defend her son.* That was the thought that seared a path through her brain. They'd get AJ off, the Axels, with all their money. He'd be like OJ, declared innocent in the face of overwhelming evidence to the contrary. If that trial had proved anything, it was that justice in the United States could be bought and sold like any other marketable commodity. It flat-out pissed Dru off. She stood up. "I'm going to get some coffee. Do you want a refill?" Dru nodded at the mug sitting empty on the table at Shea's elbow.

Shea said no, and she turned down Dru's offer of toast, too. She wasn't hungry.

You should eat anyway . . . You're going to make yourself ill . . . The guy isn't worth it . . . You'll find someone else . . . The plethora of useless and unwanted advice trailed through Dru's mind. She stood, looking down at Shea. "If AJ came here and asked, would you go with him?"

"Are you kidding me? You're really worried about that?"

"Is it so far-fetched? You love him, right?"

"My God, Mom! How many times do I have to say it?" Shea got out of the chaise, grabbing her mug. "Something has happened to him, something terrible, or he'd have been here, or called, long before now." She paused in front of Dru, fear mingling with disgust in her expression.

Dru raised her hand, intending to tuck fallen strands of Shea's hair behind her ear, intending to say she hadn't meant to start anything, but Shea evaded her touch, brushing by her. She turned at the back door. "You made up your mind not to like AJ in the first five minutes after you met him. Who knows why? Because he's related to Jeb Axel? Because his family has money? Because as soon as you found out he'd fought in Afghanistan, you decided he had mental issues—that he was Dad?"

"Wait, no—" Dru tried to interrupt.

Shea wasn't having it. "You're so judgmental."

"No," Dru said. Was she?

"All my life you've told me how I should feel about stuff—people, situations—Dad, Kate, even poor Becca. It's just how you are. I should be used to it by now."

"What is so wrong with *me* wanting *you* to be safe?" Dru shouted it toward the back door, flinching when it slammed. Her knees weakened, suddenly, inexplicably. She felt light-headed, and bending over, she braced her hands on her thighs.

An hour later she was sitting at the table, trying to merge the address list for the wedding guests into a label document when Shea appeared in the doorway. Dru kept her eyes on the computer screen. It was safer.

"Erik just called," Shea said.

Dru glanced at her.

"He wanted to know if we'd heard from Kate."

"I thought they were going hiking this morning."

"Yeah, he was out at Bella Vista at the trailhead at six thirty, where they were supposed to meet, but she never showed."

"Maybe she decided to sleep in. Did you call her?"

"No answer. I left a message." Shea came and sat down. "Are you working on the notes?"

Dru nodded. "I can't get the docs to merge. The addresses aren't showing up on the label template."

"Let me see," Shea said, and Dru turned the laptop so it faced her.

She studied the screen, tapping a few keys. "There." Shea scooted Dru's laptop over to her.

"How did you do it? I worked for an hour."

"I'm brilliant." Shea smiled.

Dru smiled, too. Reaching out, she patted Shea's arm. They weren't finished with the hurt feelings or the hard words, but for the moment, they'd declared a truce.

"Maybe I'll try some toast." Shea stood up. "Do you want a slice?"

"Are you making it?"

"Yep." Shea pulled the toaster out of its cabinet cubby and plugged it in. "After I eat, I'm going to get dressed and go out to the ranch." She got the butter out of the refrigerator.

"I don't think you should go on your own. It's not safe."

Shea started to argue, but when her cell phone chimed, she handed the butter knife to Dru. "Can you finish?"

She was setting their plates on the table when Shea came back, clutching her phone, white-faced.

"What's the matter?" Dru asked.

As if Shea hadn't heard, she went to the small television Dru kept in the breakfast nook and flipped it on. Alarm shot up Dru's spine. "Who called? What's wrong?" she demanded.

"It was Vanessa." Shea got the remote, raised the volume. "Someone found a body—"

"Recapping," the commentator was saying, "the body of a young woman hiker was found by two other hikers early this morning at Cedar Ridge Canyon Park, a half mile from Monarch Lake. Police so far haven't officially declared the death suspicious, but an officer at the scene, Patrol Sergeant Ken Carter, indicated there would be a thorough investigation. The young woman is described as being in her mid- to late twenties, petite build, with blonde hair. Her identity is being withheld until her family can be notified."

Shea locked Dru's gaze. "It couldn't be—"

"No," Dru said. "Of course it isn't Kate. She went hiking at Bella Vista."

"But Erik said—"

"They missed each other," Dru said, but the sick feeling in her stomach belied her reassurance.

The cordless phone on the kitchen counter rang, and she and Shea stared at it. Few people called the landline anymore. Telemarketers, people looking for donations. Dru crossed the floor to answer it, blood pounding in her ears. She didn't recognize the number on the caller ID screen. She answered anyway. "Hello?"

"Dru, it's Ken Carter with the Wyatt PD."

"Yes, Ken," she said, and she stiffened, preparing herself to hear it, the awful confirmation. Shea knew it, too. It was as if the sense of it was borne on the air, absorbed through some horrible process of osmosis. She came to Dru, and she wrapped her arm around Shea's waist.

Ken went on talking, as Dru had known he would, about the body that was found at Cedar Ridge Canyon Park. He was terribly sorry to inform her and Shea it was Kate Kincaid.

"Are you sure?" Dru asked fruitlessly, as if asking could alter reality. Ken confirmed that he was.

Shea pulled away, stricken. "It's Katie?"

Dru said, "Yes," gently. It struck her that, unlike Joy, Charla didn't have another child to live for, and the wave of her grief for Charla's loss cut more deeply, knotting her throat, burning the lids of her eyes. "Does her mother know?" she asked Ken.

"Kate's fiancé—Erik Ayala?—is on his way there. He asked if he could be the one to tell her parents. It's a real help to us. We need our officers at the scene."

"Well, it's a blessing. Charla, Kate's mom—she likes him so much."

"Yes, ma'am. I've heard."

Shea's hands, tented at her mouth, were outlined in her tears.

"Erik is telling her folks," Dru said to her.

"Was he with her when she fell?" Shea asked, and Dru relayed the question to Ken.

"He arrived shortly after my partner and I did. Evidently there was some mix-up about where they were meeting, and when she didn't show at Bella Vista, he went to Cedar Ridge Canyon, figuring she was there. I don't know much more than that. He's agreed to come to the police station here in Wyatt and give a more in-depth statement once he's spoken to Mr. and Mrs. Kincaid. Here's the thing, though, Dru, why I'm calling." Ken's voice sharpened. "We're investigating this thing; we've got eyes on it, you know, because of everything else that's happened."

"You think Kate's death is related to Becca's murder?" Dru's voice thinned. She was aware of Shea, backing up, shocked, disbelieving.

"I'm not saying that, not yet. But we did find something, a charm on a silver chain. When we showed it to Erik, he recognized it. He identified the charm as a lotus blossom and said it belonged to AJ, that your daughter gave it to him before they got engaged. Seeing that necklace shook Erik up, I can tell you."

Dru looked at Shea, and the knowing was cold inside her that if she asked, Shea could produce the exact same charm on the exact same silver chain. Shea had hunted for the charms after learning that the lotus blossom was the symbol of rebirth. It was her and AJ's shared amulet, their juju, Shea had said when she'd shown the charms to Dru. She could see them in her mind's eye, two finely made flowers, wrought of silver, no bigger than her thumbnail.

What could it mean if one of the pair of charms had been found at Cedar Ridge Canyon this morning other than that AJ had been there, that he had something—if not everything—to do with Kate's death?

"I know this is rough," Ken was saying, "but you add it up—you know, there was the break-in at the xL yesterday and the note that was left on Leigh's car last night. The two deceased young women were members of the same wedding party. They evidently exchanged texts prior to Becca's death, a fact Kate wasn't exactly forthcoming about."

"I thought that was odd, too," Dru said.

"We can't ignore the possibility of a connection among these events, and while we don't know Isley's exact whereabouts, finding the necklace makes it pretty obvious he was following Kate, possibly stalking her."

"Is my daughter in danger?" Dru didn't wait for Ken's answer. "You need to find him." Fury heated her voice. "You people need to have every officer in this state looking—" She broke off, darting a glance at Shea, inwardly wincing on meeting her daughter's anguished gaze.

"Trust me," Ken said, "we're closing in on his location. In fact, his truck was found today, around daybreak. About the same time those hikers found Kate's body. Close to the same location, too."

"Where?" Dru asked.

"Monarch Lake. Do you know it? It's maybe a half to three-quarters of a mile southwest of Cedar Ridge Canyon."

Dru said she was familiar with the lake. "Who found it?"

"AJ's mother," Ken said. "Lily Isley."

13

Thunder cracked overhead as Lily left the house, and the sky opened as she slid into the Jeep. The rain broke over the windshield, sounding like birdshot, sheeting the glass. She was glad for the noise. She had worried her dad would hear the car, that he'd catch her, question her, try to stop her, and there wasn't a way to explain where she was going without sounding insane.

She could have driven down to the front gate and taken the highway as far as the turnoff to Monarch Lake, and she considered it. It made sense, given the stormy weather. But, instead, once she got the Jeep started and dropped it into gear, she turned right onto the old service road that led around the back of the barn. It wound first in a southeasterly direction, passing Winona's house, before looping north and then west. Few people knew about it; even fewer used it. The twisted, meandering route, what remained of a long-ago state highway, was barely passable even in good weather, but it would shave minutes off the drive.

The Jeep's tires bumped and slid over the uneven pavement, dropping into caliche-choked potholes, jerking over muddy ruts. Passing

Winona's house, Lily was surprised to see a shaft of light cracking the front curtains. Had she come home? Lily hoped so; she prayed for it. But she couldn't stop to find out. The dream, the sense that AJ was at Monarch Lake, that he was in trouble and needed her, was too strong. The old service road ended at CR 440, and turning left, she accelerated, feeling the Jeep's tires grab the county road's firmer surface. Water rose on either side of her; the white froth churned in her wake. Her hands gripped the wheel, sweaty and slick in her anticipation and fear.

Scenes from her dream flashed before her eyes, vivid and terrifying. It felt as if it was only days ago she'd almost let AJ drown. She'd had nightmares for weeks after it happened. AJ had wakened in the night, crying, too, but only for a little while, and then he'd seemed to forget. There had been no lasting effects. Not even a fear of the water. Before that awful summer was over, he'd learned to swim from a certified Red Cross instructor in a proper pool. Paul had insisted; he had forbidden Lily to take AJ to Monarch Lake again. But that hadn't been the worst of it. No. One morning not long after the incident, she had wakened at home in Dallas and gone to AJ's bedroom, as was her habit, but he hadn't been in his crib. She'd found him downstairs in the kitchen with the nanny Paul had hired. Behind her back without consulting her. Whatever confidence had remained to her, whatever pride, was all but destroyed.

She hadn't fought Paul on it, and that had cost her—so dearly—thousands of treasured moments she would have shared with her small son, whispering nonsense into his ear, waking to his tiny hands patting her cheeks, his astonished joy at new discoveries. She'd given all those precious memories away, given *him* away, God help her, to the nanny, because she had felt incompetent and frightened that she couldn't keep AJ safe. She had retreated from his life, left him on a separate shore. But she couldn't think of that now, the terrible wrong she had done him and herself.

The rain had eased, and cresting a hill, she caught a glimpse of the eastern shore of the lake, and beyond it, the bright glint of water. She found the turnoff and followed it past an assortment of picnic tables, deserted at this early hour just as they had been the last time she'd been here. The rain stopped, and the sky began to clear. Water puddled the road, fell from the trees. The windshield fogged. She bent forward, straining to see.

She was almost past the clearing, where she'd come with AJ before, when she recognized the live oak where she'd spread the quilt, and beyond it, the graveled shoreline where Butternut had gone to drink. Heart tapping, she pulled into the weed-choked verge and got out of the Jeep. The growth of juniper trees was more pervasive than she remembered, and so dense that only the tops were green, like paint-filled brushes, while nearer the ground their branches were desiccated and viciously tangled. They tore at her clothing as she made her way to the water's edge.

It was while she was standing there that the cloud cover broke widely, making her blink in the sudden glare. But as the moment lingered, shimmering, she became aware of the deep silence, the utter sense of desertion. Was AJ here? Hiding? A shout rang out from the water; someone was crying. She looked and saw nothing. *Dream,* said her mind. More dream images came, pulling her back, but this wasn't the past. AJ was here now. She felt his presence. He would have heard her, cracking a path through the underbrush that was dry despite the rain. He'd come out now, seeing her. He would know he was safe with her, the way he'd known it as a very little boy.

"AJ?" she called softly, sidestepping a bit along the shoreline. "AJ?" Louder now. She turned in a circle.

That was when she caught sight of it. Some fifty yards beyond where she'd parked the Jeep, a pickup truck was nosed partway into the juniper thicket. There was something not right about it. Or was she misled by the vestiges of her dream? They hung about her like a shroud, obscuring her sight line. Closing her eyes briefly, she became aware of a peculiar smell; it permeated the air, acrid, nose burning. Her brain labeled the odors: smoke, gasoline, chemical, plastic. It was the sort of foul smell that hung around after a fire, the kind of evil stench that said, *Get away.* But she took a few steps toward the vehicle, then stopped to study it. It was a white double-cab pickup. A Dodge. AJ drove a white double-cab Dodge pickup.

Now she was running as she had before, twenty-three years ago, but instead of water, she was tearing through a wicked maze of juniper. Dead branches as bony and sharp as witches' fingers ripped her cotton shirt, tore her skin, drawing blood. Breaking through the last of the needled scruff, she stopped abruptly, several feet from the driver's side of the double cab, panting, brain ticking, registering the relatively undamaged exterior, stark in comparison with the interior, which looked as black as the inside of a closed coffin. The windows were up. She was perhaps ten or twelve feet away; the light glancing off the glass made seeing inside impossible. But fearing what she'd find, she didn't want to go closer. Latent terror uncoiled from the floor of her mind, begging her—warning her—to leave. If she didn't look, advised a voice in her brain, AJ couldn't be in there. It was in spite of herself that she took a step toward the truck, then a series of steps before stopping again. How could she do it?

But it was AJ's truck. If he *was* in there . . . injured . . . worse . . .

Quickly now, she covered the remaining distance, and when she was within reach, she touched the front door handle tentatively. It was cool under her fingertips. Still, Lily drew back her hand. Glanced off to her left, where the surface of the lake was visible through the trees, sparkling, serene. She could hear it laving the shore. She saw herself out there, water lapping her torso beneath her breasts. She held baby AJ on his back, balanced in the cradle of her arms. She saw his small face, the soft curves of his cheeks, the rosebud of his mouth, his belly button, that tiny adorable part of his anatomy that had once connected them.

A noise—a sob? a scream?—rose in her throat. She clamped her jaw, and turning back to the truck, she grabbed the front-door handle hard, yanking it toward her. Nothing happened. She tried the back-door handle. Neither door would budge. *"Nooooo . . ."* Her protest broke through her teeth. She looked around for something to shatter the glass. The ground was strewn with rocks, but none were big enough. Impulsively, before she could think about it, she put her face to the glass, cupping her hands at her temples, making herself look carefully. Although the window was cloudy from the smoke, she could see that the instrument panel was blistered, and the seat upholstery was burned through to the padding in some places. She shifted to the back window. The bench seat was damaged but not as badly.

There was something on the floor.

Blankets? A tarp? A rug? Her heart faltered.

Her gaze was drawn to the passenger side. Juniper branches were smashed against the window, but it was the hook hanging over the door that caught her attention. It supported a number of paper-wrapped hangers, like those used by dry cleaners. Whatever was suspended from them now—AJ's dress shirts? His chef's jackets?—was singed and filthy and coated in melted plastic.

But what was that bulky thing on the floor?

She fought looking again.

Backed away from the truck, casting a glance over the roof. Panic rooted her feet to the ground. But she had to do it; she had to see if she could somehow get to the passenger-side doors and open them. But there wasn't a way. As soon as she rounded the truck bed, she realized it was wedged too tightly into the thicket to allow access.

Returning to the Jeep, she opened the hatch, hunting in the cargo area for a crowbar, any kind of tool that would work to pry open the truck doors or break the glass. But there was nothing of any use. Her hands pattered over the contents—a single, cracked rubber boot, a fishing tackle box. Rags. A pair of sunglasses with a missing lens.

Going to the driver's seat, she got her phone, dialed the landline at the ranch. The call wouldn't go through. She looked at the screen. No bars. She tried 911. Wasn't it supposed to work regardless of reception? She put the phone to her ear. Nothing. Only the frightened huff of her breath. She felt on the verge of hysteria and, closing her eyes, willed herself to calm down, to order her thoughts. A sound came from out on the highway, high and thin, a siren, she thought, coming from the east, from Wyatt. She straightened, but the jolt of her relief was momentary. It couldn't be coming here. No one knew what she'd found. She hadn't even left a note for her dad. The siren went by her location, unseen, heading west, hell-bent.

Car accident, maybe. But Cedar Ridge Canyon was *that* way. Lots of hikers there. Maybe someone had fallen. A boy in her eighth-grade class had died there from the injuries he'd sustained in a fall.

Lily looked back at her phone. She would never get service here. If she wanted help, she'd have to leave. Leave the lake, leave AJ's truck and whatever was inside it.

It took her half an hour to get back to the ranch road. She pushed the Jeep to the maximum speed, losing traction around curves, bouncing over the ruts, jaw tight. Her dad came to the back door when she drove up.

"Where have you been?" He opened the porch screen. "I was worried as hell."

"I found AJ's truck." She stopped at the foot of the steps. "We need a crowbar, but first, I want to call the police so they can meet us there."

"Lily, slow down. Meet where? Where is AJ's truck?" He ducked back onto the porch and got his hat off the hook.

"Monarch Lake." She flattened her palm on her breastbone, willing herself to do as he suggested and slow down. "It was set on fire," she said, and she relayed the rest, pulling her cell phone from her jeans pocket. "I tried calling 911 from out there but couldn't get service."

"I don't think you will here, either. The storm knocked out service, phone and electric. Who knows when they'll get crews out." Her dad came down the steps, striding past her, heading for the barn, where he kept his tools.

"It wasn't that bad when I left here." Lily followed him.

"It got worse. Wind blew like hell. Woke me up, and I went looking for you. I couldn't believe you went out in it."

"I'm sorry if I scared you. I had a dream—" She broke off. There was no way to explain that part.

"Maybe we don't want the cops involved," her dad said.

"Didn't you hear me? There's something, a rug, a tarp—I couldn't tell, but AJ could be in there, hurt or—" *Dead.* The word *dead* stood up in her mind. She bit her teeth against it.

"Sissy." Her dad faced her. "Think about it. If AJ took the money and your mama's jewelry out of the safe, if he then went to the airfield and hired himself a pilot to fly him out of here, it's entirely possible he stashed his truck first. The location's good. Hardly anybody knows about Monarch Lake, much less goes there."

"But it's not really hidden. Somebody would be bound to see it." Lily followed him into the barn. "If he really meant to get rid of it, wouldn't he have made sure the fire burned it up?"

Her dad disappeared into the tool room without answering.

Lily paused in the doorway of the tack room, thinking about it. There would have been smoke, but at night, it wasn't likely anyone would have noticed. She was thinking that, and trying to sort out the timing, when the fire might have been set, when she noticed the bundles of cash. They were lying on the old worktable. Five rubber-banded stacks, sitting there as if they belonged among the rest of the litter, a jar of saddle soap, a couple of brushes, some kind of antibiotic ointment in a tube.

Lily crossed the room to the table to be sure that's what she was seeing. The windows above it needed washing; the light wasn't the best, but she knew money when she saw it, and she knew this money was from the safe in the house. The very cash her dad had reported stolen—that the local cops were certain AJ had taken. But if he had, why had he left it here? In plain view? It made no sense—unless AJ wasn't the one who had opened the safe. She'd never believed it, or at the very least, she hadn't wanted to believe it. But even as her heart buoyed with relief, it fell in consternation. She picked up two of the bundles, holding one in each hand, studying them.

"Dad?" she called.

He came to the doorway. "C'mon. I've got the crowbar and a mallet if we have to bust the glass."

Lily held up the two bundles of cash.

His eyes flared. "What the hell?"

"It's the money from the safe, Dad. All five thousand."

"Why would AJ leave it here?"

"He didn't take it."

"Then who did?"

Lily didn't answer.

It was possibly a full minute before he took her meaning, but she saw it happen—the flash of pained comprehension in his eyes, followed by the darker shadow of his shame. Almost instantly, though, his mouth twisted; his expression hardened, a stubborn knot of denial. "C'mon, we don't have time to talk about it now."

Lily followed him from the barn, wordless, needing him to be all right, praying that he was, that his mental clarity of the moment would hold.

They took the Jeep. She drove, retracing the same route she'd driven before dawn. If she hadn't seen the rain earlier, she wouldn't have believed any had fallen. The road was dry; the sky soared overhead, high and blue, almost laughably innocent of any blemish. Coming up to Winona's house, she said, "There was a light on earlier."

Her dad looked past her, through the driver's-side window. "There's not now," he answered.

Once they got to the clearing and made their way to the truck, it took him several minutes, working the pry bar, to get the truck door open, and then he did what she couldn't have—he leaned into the cab, through both doors, front and back, shoving the charred debris around, hunting for evidence of the horror neither one had put into words.

"There's nothing here." He straightened. He was black to his forearms. Even his face, sheened with sweat, looked dusted with charcoal.

He should have worn gloves. They should have brought water. Lily's thoughts distracted her from the plague of her anxiety that even now was shot through with a bone-lightening sense of reprieve. "What is it, rolled up back there?"

"A tarp. I found this under it." He held the knife, an eight-inch chef's knife, by the silver endcap, between his thumb and index finger.

Lily's heart bucked against her ribs. It was one of a set, a Shun chef's starter set she had bought for AJ a year ago. She'd had his initials, AJI, engraved on the bolster.

"You recognize it?" her dad asked.

"It's AJ's," she said.

Her dad locked her gaze. "That girl was stabbed."

"Yes," Lily answered.

"Last I heard, they hadn't found the murder weapon."

"No."

Her dad bent at the waist and laid the knife carefully on the ground between them.

"What should we do?" Lily asked when he straightened.

"I don't know," he said.

"Should we call the police?"

"Is that what you want to do?"

"I want to know AJ is safe."

Her dad shifted his gaze. "When they hear we found his truck, the condition it's in, burned up with a knife inside it, you know it'll just confirm what they already suspect."

Lily hugged her arms around herself, looking through the trees at the lake. "Do you want to wash up? There are some rags in the Jeep." Not waiting for his answer, she went to get them. When she came back, her dad was standing at the water's edge.

He said, "You know that day when AJ almost drowned—you know that wasn't your fault."

"I shouldn't have panicked." Squatting, she dampened a rag, wrung it out, and handed it to him. He wiped his face and neck. Taking it from him when he was done, she rinsed it, wrung it out, and handed it back to him again. They repeated the routine two more times until he'd gotten all the grime he could wiped away. Still, they didn't leave the shore but stood together, watching the water. That was when she told him about the dream and how when she'd wakened from it, she'd known to come here.

"This was the spot? Where you and AJ were when it happened?"

"Yes," she said. "The boat came from over there." She pointed to her right, east, she thought.

"Well, maybe you did panic," her dad said, "but you recovered. You did what you had to do. You got hold of your boy and got him to land. You saved him. Anybody looking at it any other way is a fool."

Did he mean Paul had been a fool to take AJ's care out of her hands all those years ago?

"I didn't speak up then," he said, "but I should have. I should have," he repeated, and his voice caught.

"Oh, Dad," Lily said, and she set her hand on his back.

. . .

"Are you sure you want to go to the police station with me?" Lily looked at her dad over the roof of the Jeep.

He kept her glance.

She thought he knew the direction she was going in. "They assume the safe was broken into," she said, "that it's AJ who took the money. We can't let them—"

"You think it was me, that I opened the safe and don't remember. You think my mind is slipping." He sounded resigned, and it was almost worse, hearing that, than the angry reaction Lily had been anticipating.

"I think you should see a doctor," she said.

He lifted his hat and ran his hand over his head, before resettling it. "Yeah," he said. "We can talk about it, I guess."

"There are drugs nowadays, Dad, that can help. There are things you can do with diet and exercise."

"I'm not losing my goddamn mind." He glared at her, but he was trembling, vulnerable in a way Lily had never seen him. Her heart broke for him even as she was seized with a fierce need to protect him.

They got into the Jeep.

"I'll drop you at the ranch, then go into town to the police station. I want to get my car, anyway."

"What will you tell them?"

"About the cash? I'll say I did it, that I got out the money and forgot to tell you."

"What about your mother's jewelry? I've got no damn recollection where I—"

"We'll find it. I'll help you look when I get back."

He drummed his fingers on his knees. He was sorry, he said. "For the whole damn mess." His voice was thick.

She patted his hand. "Me, too," she said.

He asked again if she was sure about going to the cops. "You know how it'll look, finding that knife in AJ's truck."

"I can't help how it looks. I have to know where he is, if he's all right. That's the only thing that matters now."

"It's possible he won't thank you."

She jerked her glance to her dad's. If AJ had done it, if he was guilty of murder, her dad meant. "I'll worry about that later."

"Okay, then, if you're dead set on finding him, you need police help to do it."

• • •

Lily saw the sun-faded red SUV when she pulled into the WPD parking lot, and her heartbeat slowed. It looked much like the one Dru had been driving when she and Shea had come to the xL on Thursday. *Something's happened,* she thought. She went quickly up the walkway, but stepping through the door, she was hit by a blast of air so cold it took what was left of her breath. She paused, getting her bearings. Across from her, the counter that served as the duty desk was unmanned, which was no surprise. The Wyatt PD was perennially shorthanded.

"Mrs. Isley?"

She looked up. Shea was coming through a swinging door behind the counter, Dru in her wake. Both women were red-eyed. From crying? Exhaustion? "What's happened?" Lily asked, but then, suddenly she knew. "The police have found AJ."

"No," Shea said.

"What is it, then?" Lily asked, and her voice was sharp, but in her distress, she couldn't help it.

"Kate, Kate Kincaid." Shea lifted her hand to touch her face, or perhaps her hair, but then it faltered midway, as if she'd forgotten it was there.

"Kate is—was—Shea's maid of honor," Dru said.

"Yes?" Lily knew that.

"She's dead." Shea lowered her hand.

"What?" Lily was incredulous. "When?"

"This morning. She was hiking at Cedar Ridge Canyon. She was supposed to meet Erik at Bella Vista, but they got their wires crossed, and when she didn't show up, Erik figured she must have gone to Cedar Ridge by mistake. He went there to check. The police were already there. A couple of other hikers had found Kate and called 911."

"He was just telling me about their engagement." Lily felt winded. "He must be devastated. All of you must be. I'm so sorry."

Shea said, "I can't get my mind around it. She was my best friend, like a sister."

"Is Erik here with you?" Lily asked.

"He's at her mom and dad's," Shea answered. "He didn't want them hearing what had happened from a stranger, or on the news. That's how Mom and I found out. It was awful."

"The police don't think it was an accident," Dru said in a manner that seemed pointed, ominous.

Shea pulled a delicate chain from inside her shirt. "You know I bought these lotus-blossom charms, one for me and one for AJ—they found one on the trail, above where Kate fell."

Lily felt her blood cool.

"There were signs of a struggle." Dru said. "The police think it was AJ, that he attacked her, that he was stalking her."

"I heard the sirens," Lily said. "I was at Monarch Lake. I—I found AJ's truck—"

"Lily?"

She glanced up. "Oh, Clint." She knew Clint Mackie, the Wyatt police department captain, in another, friendlier capacity, as a hunting buddy of her dad's. "Shea and Dru were just telling me about Kate."

"Jeb called a while ago and said you were on your way in."

Clint's look was trenchant, probing, as if Lily and her father, and their actions, were somehow suspect, and she realized she'd be foolish to consider he was anything other than her adversary. "Dad told you I found the truck?"

"Why don't you come on back and we'll talk in my office."

"We can talk right here," Lily said, because Shea and even Dru had a right to hear of her discovery. They'd know soon enough anyway.

"All right." Mackie leaned against the duty counter. "Jeb said the truck was burned?"

Shea inhaled so sharply that Lily turned to her immediately, reassuring her. "No, no, AJ wasn't there."

"It was his truck for sure, though?" Shea asked.

"Yes." Lily paused. She didn't want to tell the rest, but she had to. "We found a knife, a chef's knife under a tarp. A Shun, from the set I gave AJ last year."

"Oh my God," Dru said. "What more proof—"

"All that means," Shea said, "is that whoever killed Becca took the knife and AJ's truck from his apartment, and AJ, too. Can't you see that, Mom?" Shea looked at Captain Mackie.

He said, "Sergeant Carter is on his way there now to retrieve the vehicle. It'll likely go to Dallas, along with the knife and any other evidence they find."

"So that's it?" Lily flung out her hands. "You've made up your minds; you and your counterparts in Dallas have decided my son killed these girls? You know AJ, Clint. You know he isn't capable."

"There's quite a lot involved here that you may not be aware of, Lily. For instance, did you know a note, written in lip liner, was found on Ms. Westin's body?"

"He just told me about it," Shea said, indicating Clint.

"I heard about it, too," Lily said, not citing Edward as her source. *Fixed you* . . . The note's message hovered in her mind.

"Another note was found yesterday evening under the windshield wiper of Leigh Martindale's car," Clint said. "Someone left it while she was parked outside the Gallaghers'. It was also written in lip liner."

"It said, 'I'm sorry for hurting you. I'm in trouble and I don't think I can stop.'" Dru sounded accusatory, as if Lily had been the author.

"In addition to the notes," Clint went on smoothly, "there's evidence that Ms. Kincaid and Ms. Westin exchanged several texts on the day Becca was murdered."

"Is that suspicious?" Lily asked.

"Not in and of itself, but taken along with everything else—"

"What's suspicious," Dru said, "is that Kate didn't mention she and Becca had texted until last night, when the police came about the note Leigh found. Kate hadn't even told Shea about the texts, and they told each other everything."

"Are you saying she knew something about Becca's murder, Mom?"

"No!" Dru seemed horrified by the idea, but maybe it was only pretense.

"Sticking to the facts," Clint said, and he ticked them off on his fingers as he named them. "A piece of jewelry, a vehicle, and the possible weapon used in Becca Westin's murder—all items belonging to AJ—were found in the same vicinity where Ms. Kincaid was hiking."

"Why would AJ follow Kate, Captain Mackie? Why would he stalk her? What's his motive? Can you answer that? No, I didn't think so." Shea was derisive.

"Are you going to keep patrolling our neighborhood, and Vanessa's and Leigh's neighborhoods?" Dru asked. "None of us is safe until this maniac"—she paused to glance sidelong at Lily, and Lily saw the accusation, the clear conviction in Dru's eyes that AJ was the maniac—"the person," Dru amended, out of pity, perhaps, "is caught."

Mackie said he'd run a car by as often as he could spare an officer. "We're pretty shorthanded. You know how it is."

"What I know," Dru said, "is that there's a murderer running loose, and it appears my daughter and the members of her bridal party are targets. You need to get off your ass and catch this guy before another one of these girls comes to harm. Catching bad guys, it's what you're paid to do, isn't it?"

Clint reddened and looked to Lily as if she might defend him. Dru glanced at Lily, too, but she looked at the floor, tense, fuming. How either of them—Mackie or Dru—could expect support from her was a mystery. She was grateful for it, though, when Shea took a step toward her. It was tiny, almost imperceptible, but a sign of support all the same.

Mackie mentioned the break-in. "I guess from what Jeb said, it's no longer an issue?"

Lily gave her head a small shake, hoping that would be the end of it. It wasn't.

"I heard about that," Dru said.

Lily could feel her gaze. *It's not your business.* She was on the verge of telling Dru, of making it clear, when Clint said, "I understand," in a way that let her know her dad had been honest. She couldn't imagine what it had cost him, admitting to his mental lapse, something so humiliating. He would have been thinking of AJ, though, wanting to get him clear of that suspicion at least.

Clint said, "Okay, ladies, if we're done here—"

"No," Shea said. "We're not done." She looked at Lily now, brow knotted, jaw set in a stubborn line. "I know who murdered Kate and Becca. I told him"—she jerked her thumb at the captain—"but he's refusing to investigate."

"If you can bring me something concrete—" Clint began.

Shea kept Lily's glance. "Becca and Kate both dated this guy— Becca only went out with him a couple of times, but he and Kate got kind of serious until he abused her."

"As I explained before, Shea, if you can bring me evidence, a police report. Proof of injury. I need something more than your word before I can question the guy."

"Fine," Shea said. "I'll do it myself, then." She headed out the door.

"I don't advise it," Clint called after her.

"Shea!" Dru followed her daughter.

"You're sure about this guy, that he's the one who hurt the girls? Does he have AJ? Do you know?" Lily asked, catching up with Shea and Dru outside.

"Probably, yes," Shea answered. "But no one believes me. Not even my own mother."

"I didn't say I didn't believe you," Dru protested. "You need to let the police handle it, that's all. If it's true, we are not talking some minor act of delinquency; the man is dangerous. He could be a killer, for God's sake. You can't go there. I won't have you getting hurt, too."

"Two of my friends are dead." Shea addressed Lily, nearly shouting. "One of them was my best friend in all the world. And my fiancé, the man I love more than anything, is gone, lost somewhere, in trouble, terrible trouble, and Mom wants me to go home and lock the doors."

"I want you to be safe."

I know. Lily's understanding of Dru was automatic and visceral and had nothing to do with her dislike of Dru. It was something universal to mothers, the instinct to protect her child. "Who is the man?" Lily asked.

"Harlan Cate," Shea answered, and on hearing the quick intake of Lily's breath, she asked, "Do you know him?"

"I do," Lily said. "I certainly do."

14

Harlan worked for my dad," Lily said.

Dru and Shea had gotten into the car to escape the midday heat. It had been at Shea's invitation that Lily joined them. Left up to Dru, they wouldn't be having this conversation.

"Really?" Shea was animated. "Was he—did he have a temper that you saw?"

"I remember he got into a couple of fights. He was a hard worker, though, and Dad kept him on until he sold the herd last year." Lily took a moment.

"What?" Shea asked.

Looking at Lily in the rearview mirror, Dru saw it, too—the flash of misgiving that crossed Lily's expression.

"Harlan didn't take the news well. He said something to my dad to the effect that the richer a man was, the harder he could fall."

"That sounds like a threat," Shea said.

"You said he was abusive to Kate. Did he hurt Becca, too?" Lily asked.

"Not that I know of, but he did hit Kate one time in the arm. That was all it took. She broke it off."

This was news to Dru. But like most best friends, the girls had always kept secrets.

"Did it happen recently?" Lily asked.

"Around six months ago, right before Kate and Erik started going out. Harlan stalked her, too, and Erik wanted her to get a restraining order, but Harlan stopped, or so they thought. Now I'm not so sure."

Dru said, "You do realize that finding who did this to Becca or Kate, getting justice for them—it won't bring them back."

"I can't just go home, Mom."

"Well, I can't ignore the risk for you, Vanessa, or Leigh. Their parents are upset, and I am, too." Dru found Lily's glance in the rearview. "The break-in at the ranch—I heard money and jewelry were taken. It was AJ, wasn't it?"

"That's what the police thought, but the truth is that Dad—" Lily looked off, uncomfortable. Dru thought she might not explain after all, but then she looked back. "The truth is Dad is having some issues with his memory."

"You're saying *he* got the money out of the safe?" An unexpected flush of sympathy warmed Dru's tone.

"Yes," Lily said. "There have been a few incidents lately. I want—I hope to get him to see a doctor."

"Well, that's awful—a man like Jeb Axel—"

"Does AJ know? He must be heartbroken." Shea sounded stricken. "He loves his granddad so much."

"I haven't talked to him about it," Lily said, "but I plan to. I will . . ."

She couldn't be sure anymore that she would, Dru thought. She caught Lily's glance again. "How did you know to look for AJ's truck at the lake?"

"I had a dream. It was the oddest thing—so vivid. We were swimming—"

Dru interrupted her. "He called you again, didn't he? I bet you know where he is."

"No. No, I don't," Lily insisted.

But the way she dodged Dru's glance, the evasive shift of her shoulders, made her look guilty. She knew—*something.* Dru was convinced of it, and it pissed her off. She rounded her seat back. "Would you even tell the police if you knew where he was?"

"I keep asking myself that." Lily's gaze was unflinching now. "Do you know what you would do if you were in my place? Would you turn Shea in?"

Dru didn't know what she'd do. Protect her child, but how far? At what cost?

"I feel like Harlan Cate's involved." Shea broke the silence. "He's the one who knows where AJ is."

"He's a big man," Lily said.

"The same size as AJ," Shea said. "It would have taken someone big to take AJ out of his apartment."

Lily bent forward. "Maybe if I go with you . . ."

"You can't be serious." Dru met her gaze in the mirror. "Do you even know where he lives?"

"The Little Grove RV Park," Shea answered. "On 1620, past Decker's Auto Salvage."

"I know where it is," Dru said, "and I know the folks who live there aren't the sort you want to mess with."

"I don't think Harlan will try anything if I'm there," Lily said. "When he threatened Dad, Clint—Captain Mackie—paid him a visit. Harlan will know if anything happens to me, the police will come looking for him."

"If that's true"—Dru eyed Lily in the rearview—"why isn't the captain showing an interest in questioning Harlan now concerning the whereabouts of Jeb's grandson?"

"Mom, please, if you don't want to go, then I'll go with Mrs.—with Lily."

Dru glanced at Shea. She'd done it, called Lily by her first name. Dru had grappled with it, the idea that once Shea married AJ, Lily would be a mother to her of sorts, the dreaded mother-in-law. Their relationship to date had been cool. Shea had remarked on it, how awkward she felt around Lily. *I don't know what to say to her. I don't think she likes me.* Dru had advised Shea to give Lily time even as she'd fumed over Lily's treatment of Shea. But that aloofness was nowhere in sight now.

It was the side effect of calamity, Dru thought. It forged bonds among the unlikeliest of people. "I don't know what either of you expects," she said, but she was already shifting the car into reverse. "It's not as if Harlan Cate is going to invite us in for tea and confess."

• • •

The turnoff into the RV park was so choked with underbrush that Dru would have missed it if she hadn't known its location. The road itself, narrow and crudely surfaced, cut through a towering forest of oaks. Gradually, as Dru drove more deeply into the neighborhood, the light dimmed, the air cooled. Other roads leading off the main access road disappeared around curves, dipped into shadowy hollows. Wheeled homes were strung along the various routes in a haphazard pattern. Some rested flat on the ground like they'd gone their last mile. They all looked rough, beat-up and done. Dru wouldn't have lived in one of them. She caught Shea's eyes and then Lily's, seeing her own apprehension mirrored in their expressions. She waited for one of them to say it, that they had no business here, that they should go and let the cops handle Harlan Cate, but no one spoke.

They found Harlan's place by accident at the end of a cul-de-sac. Shea spotted his motorcycle, black with silver trim that sparkled in the light, and at her instruction, when Dru pulled over, it was against her better judgment. The man who lived here, in this busted tin can of a home, with his shiny new motorcycle parked beside it like a guard dog, would be some kind of renegade, a society dropout, a tough guy. No one she cared to tangle with. "We should leave this to the police," she said, and she raised her hand, cutting off Shea's protest. "We can go to the sheriff in Greeley. Questioning this man ourselves is just plain foolish."

Lily leaned forward. "Harlan knows me. Let me talk to him. You and Shea can wait here."

Dru looked at her, considering. "I'll go with you," she said after a moment. "I've got my .38 in my purse. We'll leave Shea here."

"Mom, for God's sake, I'm not a child." Shea opened the SUV's door, jaw clamped in a stubborn line.

Heaving a sigh, Dru and Lily followed her out of the car.

The wind had picked up. It caught at the car doors, and at Dru's hair. It plucked at her shirt, buffeted the legs of her cropped jeans. She grabbed her purse and wedged it beneath her arm. Her mouth was dry, her breath shallow. She had never pointed a gun at anything but a target before. Her instructor had talked about it, the cool detachment required should you encounter the need to defend yourself, if the target were to become human. Dru had questioned whether she'd have that kind of nerve. But she knew now that if anyone were to endanger Shea, she would do what had to be done. She would shoot them down without hesitation.

Lily led the way, but before she reached the step to the front door, it opened. The man who appeared was big, as Shea had described him, well over six feet, long-haired, tattooed, and barefoot. Older than Dru had thought. Thirtysomething, at least. And astonished to see them on the rock-strewn patch of earth that aproned his front door.

"What the hell?" he said. "You ladies come to sell me something, I don't want any."

"Harlan? I'm Lily Isley. Do you remember me? Jeb Axel's daughter."

"You come to offer me my job back?"

"Um, no—"

"Then I got nothing to say except you can tell your old man to shove it." He backed up, started to close the door.

"Wait," Lily called out.

Dru was surprised when he did.

"We—I was wondering—have you seen AJ? Maybe in the Cedar Ridge Canyon Park or Monarch Lake area?"

"You're asking because you, what, think your son and I are buddies? What in the hell are you up to, lady?"

"You know he's missing, the circumstances." Lily took a step.

Dru shifted her purse from her side to her front. A pulse tapped in her ears.

Shea said, "What about Kate Kincaid or Becca Westin? When was the last time you saw them?"

Dru wanted to clap her hand over Shea's mouth; she wanted to grab Shea and run. Instead, she inched her hand into her purse, closed her fingers around the butt of the revolver. It startled her when, looking up, her eyes collided with Harlan's. She knew he'd seen her, knew she was out of her depth. What fools they'd been, coming here.

"I think someone took AJ, that they're holding him." Lily's voice was stretched thin like a wire on the point of breaking.

"You think I've got him here? Are you shitting me?"

Lily didn't answer. There was only the sound of the wind. Dru's pulse hammered in her ears. *What had Kate or Becca ever seen in this guy?* The question hung in her mind.

"Jesus Christ." Harlan laughed a little, looking bemused. "You're serious. You think I took the kid for revenge against your old man for firing me? Or, hell, maybe I'm holding him hostage, for ransom." He paused as if to consider. "Not a bad idea. Wish I'd thought of it."

"What about Kate?" Shea asked again. "When did you last see her?"

"Shea." Dru breathed her name softly. "Let's go."

"No, Mom. He needs to answer. You were in a relationship with both of my friends, Harlan." Shea wasn't backing down. Dru tightened her grip on the gun.

"So?" he said. "That bitch Kate ditched me for fucking Pedro fucking greaser. I heard she's engaged—"

"She's dead. They're both dead, asshole." Shea said it flatly, baldly.

Harlan's eyes widened; he looked freaked out, but the moment was gone so fast, Dru thought she might have imagined it.

"You need to git on out of here," he said.

"I told the cops in town about you," Shea said. "I told Captain Mackie you hurt Kate. That's why she broke it off with you. I told him you stalked her."

"Git! Now! Or am I gonna have to run you off?"

"I'm not afraid of you, Harlan Cate," Shea said.

"Is that AJ's toolbox?" Lily spoke so quietly Dru thought she was the only one who heard her. The gray metal box that had caught her attention was sitting on a concrete block next to the RV. She started toward it.

"Goddamn it," Harlan muttered. "You women are out of your fucking minds." Grabbing the box, he retreated into the RV, slamming the door behind him. But suddenly he was back, holding a shotgun, pointing it at them. Dru would never remember it, pulling out her .38, but there it was in plain view. She dropped her purse, assuming the stance she'd learned from her instructor, gun butt clenched in both hands. "Shea, Lily, go to the car. Now!" she shouted when neither one of them moved.

"It's AJ's toolbox," Lily said. "I recognize it."

"You're crazy," Harlan said. "Now, git!" He brandished the gun.

Dru cocked the revolver's hammer. That move got Harlan's attention.

He said, "You're probably just lunatic enough to fire that damn thing, ain't you?"

"Please go to the car," Dru said, addressing Lily and Shea. Grabbing her purse in her free hand, she backed toward her SUV, feeling gratified when they did the same, moving slowly, keeping pace.

Harlan stepped down out of the RV.

Dru kept the gun aimed at him; she didn't turn her back, none of them did, until they reached the car. It was as if by prearrangement that while Dru stood guard, Lily ran around to the driver's seat, yanking open the door. Shea took Dru's purse and found the car keys, passing them to Lily. Dru was barely inside before Lily gunned the SUV into a U-turn, flooring it up the hill. Spewing gravel, she turned right onto the main access road. Dru looked out the back window past the pale oval of Shea's face, hunting in their wake for a sign of Harlan, chasing them on his motorcycle. But he didn't appear. They reached the highway, and Lily made a second right turn, tires squealing, barely checking for oncoming traffic.

They were halfway to town before Dru asked, "Is everyone all right?" She turned to Shea.

"He's such a jerk," she said, and her voice was sharp, furious.

Dru was relieved.

Lily said, "I know that was AJ's toolbox."

"Are you sure?" Dru asked, glancing at her. "I have one like it. They sell them everywhere, Home Depot, Lowe's. I think I got mine at Walmart."

Lily didn't answer for a moment, then she said softly, "Maybe I only wanted it to be AJ's toolbox."

She looked exhausted. Beaten, Dru thought. She would have wanted Harlan to be the guilty one. She might have prayed for it to be true. But in her heart she knew better. In her heart, she would, at some point, have to come to grips with the fact that her son wasn't a hostage but a murderer. And Shea—Shea was going to have to face it, too, that AJ was not the man, the hero, she'd believed him to be, but a monster who, until recently, had been hiding in plain sight.

15

Back at the police station in Wyatt, Lily parked Dru's SUV next to her BMW.

"I'm going to the sheriff in Greeley about Harlan," Shea said to her when Dru got out to come around to the driver's side. "Do you want to come with me?"

"There's so much evidence now against AJ." It made Lily sick, thinking about it.

"You don't believe it?"

It was an accusation, or that was how Lily perceived Shea's astonishment. "I don't know what to believe." Lily felt like a traitor. "I'm sorry. I don't mean to let you down."

"It's not me you're letting down, Mrs. Isley. It's AJ."

The words, the way Shea was back to addressing her as Mrs. Isley, were like a slap across Lily's face, one she probably deserved. She sounded as if she'd given up—on her own son.

Had she?

"That was some kind of driving you did," Dru said when Lily got out.

"Thanks," Lily said. "I was glad you had your gun. I don't know that Harlan isn't involved somehow. I don't trust him." She looked into the middle distance. "I used to know someone like him once. He was dangerous, the way a snake is, in ways you never see coming." Lily didn't know why she was bringing up Jesse, but the memory was there, clear in her mind. Jesse and Harlan were the same sort—men on the margins. Bikers, outlaws.

Dru got into her car. "If you hear anything . . ."

Lily nodded. "You, too."

Her dad called as she was getting into her BMW.

"Where are you?" he asked. "Mackie said you left the WPD with the Gallaghers, Dru and her daughter. He said there was quite a scene."

"I wouldn't go that far, Dad. Did Clint tell you that Kate Kincaid was found dead at Cedar Ridge Canyon this morning?"

He'd heard, her dad said. He knew about the lotus-blossom charm and all the rest, too.

"There's so much evidence now, Dad, and all of it points to AJ. The police are refusing to consider anyone else."

"Yeah, but they're dead wrong. Mackie's saying as soon as I can bring him proof it's someone different, he'll consider them."

"Shea gave him someone else, and he's refusing to follow up."

"Who?"

"Remember Harlan Cate?"

"The guy who worked for me? He's got a mean streak, sure enough, but what's his connection to the girls?"

"They both dated him."

"He doesn't seem like their type."

Lily ran her fingertip along the arc of the steering wheel. Jesse hadn't seemed like her type, either. "We went to see him—Dru, Shea, and I."

"You went to see Harlan? Lily, for God's sake, the guy's a powder keg."

"Yes, but that's exactly it. He's got the temperament, the reputation. He was abusive to Kate, and later, once she broke it off, he stalked her. He threatened you. He could have done this, Dad. He could have driven AJ's truck to the lake after he killed Becca. He could have left the knife inside it and set it on fire. He could have pushed Kate off the ridge and left the lotus-blossom charm there. He's framing AJ, making it look as if AJ is the murderer when it's *him*." Lily stared through the windshield. Was it true? Was it even plausible?

"Did you ask him?"

"He denied it." Lily decided not to mention the guns, Dru's .38, Harlan's shotgun. "Maybe Shea's right and we should go to the sheriff in Greeley since Clint won't do anything."

"All those guys work together, though. The blue wall. You know." Her dad didn't sound encouraging.

"I'm coming home now," she said. "I'll fix lunch. We can figure out what to do."

Her dad agreed. The call ended, and Lily checked her messages.

There were two, one from Paul: "Where in the hell are you? I just got a call from Bushnell. You found AJ's truck? The goddamn knife out of his kitchen? And I have to hear about it from a cop? Jesus. Call me."

A second message was from Edward. He had information, he said. The sound of his voice conjured up his face, the smallest details. She loved his smile, the intent way he looked at her when she spoke, as if he cared about her words, as if it mattered to him what she had to say. She had told him her story, and he had heard her out without a sign of censure or judgment. He had offered her comfort, instead. Comfort. Of all things.

Paul wasn't a comforter, nor did he welcome it. He would scoff at the idea.

She tapped Edward's number on her screen.

"I've got some news," he said when he answered. "Maybe good. I'm not sure yet."

"I could use it if it's good," she said.

"I heard you found AJ's truck and possibly the murder weapon." Edward spoke gently. "How did you know to go to Monarch Lake?"

Lily told him about her dream.

"It doesn't surprise me," he said when she'd finished. "I know you don't believe it, but your connection to AJ is stronger—deeper—than I think you're aware of."

"What makes you say that?"

"Just watching you with him in my office. There was a warmth and a kind of respect between you. AJ was more formal with his dad, if that makes any sense."

"It does," Lily said. "The dream I had . . . I feel as if AJ is out here somewhere, trying to tell me something." Edward would laugh now; Lily was sure of it.

But he didn't. He said, "You might be right. I think you need to follow your instinct on this."

"The evidence, though, it's hard not to see it the way the police do—as if AJ is guilty."

"Evidence can be wrong, and it may well be in this case. Has anyone said anything to you about a traffic altercation that took place here in Dallas a few days before Becca was murdered, between Kate and Becca and a guy driving a light-gray, late-model Ford F1 pickup?"

"No," Lily said.

"Do you know anyone who drives a truck like that?"

Lily said she didn't. "Not that I can recall." She hadn't seen any vehicle at Harlan Cate's place other than the Harley.

"Well, evidently this guy was a real head case. The girls were in Becca's car, and he claims he saw her texting, that she came over into his lane and nearly clipped him. He ran them off I-35 onto the service road and pulled a gun on them. He had both girls on their knees when a highway patrol officer, setting up radar, happened to catch sight of them and went to investigate."

"My God."

"If it hadn't been for the cop, the guy might have killed both girls right there."

"Who told you this?"

"A connection in the DA's office, on pain of death if I should ever reveal my source. But here's the thing—the very significant thing—the guy is missing. The cops have issued a BOLO for him. Not even his wife seems to know where he is. Word is, the guy went missing the very same night that Becca was killed and AJ disappeared."

Lily felt light-headed. Breathless.

"He has a history of emotional instability, Lily. According to his wife, he's under court-mandated psychiatric care for going after the woman who drives their daughter's bus. The woman brought charges against him when he roughed her up after she disciplined the girl for not staying in her seat. Like I said, he's a head case."

Lily's relief, the thrust of her hope, felt wrong and lasted only a moment. "He has AJ," she said.

"It's possible," Edward said. "The cops are actively looking for him."

Somehow Lily didn't find it reassuring. "It's hard, waiting, doing nothing, listening for the phone to ring."

"I'm so sorry you're going through this, Lily."

Her throat closed; tears sanded the undersides of her eyelids. It was his kindness that undid her.

"Try and rest. Eat something."

"Yes," she said. "I will."

"What I said about your instinct, Lily—don't discount it, okay?"

Lily thought about Edward's advice on the drive back to the ranch. Maybe it was true. Maybe the bond she shared with AJ, the tie that had so closely connected them when he was small, before Paul took the care of him out of her hands, was still there. She thought of the dream she'd had, the nightmare of reliving AJ's near-drowning at Monarch Lake. She had perceived the dream as renewed punishment. How could she have done it, brought him into such jeopardy? She didn't deserve to be his mother. If his life was again at risk, she must be to blame. She had felt all that, as if a sickness had overtaken her, whether it made sense or not.

But maybe that wasn't the point of the dream.

Maybe, like Scrooge, she'd been given a review of the past so that she could see that although she had put AJ in danger all those years ago, she had saved him, and she might have the means to save him now. It seemed far-fetched. She could imagine Paul's reaction. He wouldn't say a word. The only sound would be the disapproving click of his tongue.

. . .

Over lunch, Lily told her dad about the traffic altercation involving Becca and Kate. She'd made sliced chicken sandwiches, and they sat at the kitchen island to eat them. "When I spoke to Paul, he said he'd talk to Detective Bushnell about following up."

"Paul still set against retaining Edward for AJ? He's going to need a lawyer when we find him, even as promising as this lead sounds."

"I'm not pushing it," she said. "I'll wait till we know more."

Her dad took their plates to the sink and rinsed them. "I'm going to ride over to Little Bottom Creek," he said over his shoulder. "The fort's over that way. I didn't get a chance to check it out yesterday. You want to come?"

She started to ask how he could still think AJ was close by, but there was something working in his eyes that stopped her, a kind of canniness, a sharp knowing that raised the fine hairs on her neck. She remembered Edward's advice to trust her intuition. "I'll come," she said, "but give me a minute, I want to call Shea and Dru and tell them about the traffic incident." Neither woman answered, though, and Lily left a brief request for a return call.

A billowing mass of thunderheads the color of ripened plums was gathering in the northwest corner of the sky as Lily and her dad rode out of the barn. They headed in a westerly direction. The wind snapped, an invisible sheet on a line whipping through the canopies of the oaks, turning up the leaves, showing their pale undersides.

"Don't reckon we'll beat the rain," her dad said. "You might want to turn back unless you don't mind getting soaked."

She gave him a look.

They didn't speak again until they'd ridden across the Little Bottom. Her dad paused on the opposite bank, lifted his hat, ran a hand over his hair.

"You remember where the fort is from here?" Lily asked, riding up beside him.

"Over that way, I think." He nodded vaguely. "It's been a while since I've been back this way." Confusion mixed with defeat in his voice. It was there, too, in the slump of his shoulders. He wouldn't meet her gaze. Whatever had brought them out here—whether intuition or impulse—it was gone now, just as Lily had begun to believe in it.

A thrust of irritation knotted her brow. *Fool's errand.* The words lifted from the floor of her mind. She said, "I think you're right about the direction." She nudged Butternut's flanks with her boot heels. She wasn't at all sure, but she couldn't face going back to the house, sitting there, waiting for the next thing and the next to happen. She didn't care how little sense it made to continue searching—at least she was moving. At least she was doing something.

She heard the clomp of Sharkey's hooves as her dad followed behind her. They skirted a cedar thicket, climbed a coarsely graveled incline. A clap of thunder rattled the air, muttered, faded. The birds fell silent. Lily waited to feel the rain, but it held off.

"Look." Her dad had stopped some distance back.

She reined Butternut and turned to follow his line of sight. Across a rocky meadow, she saw a stand of oaks, ancient, thick girthed. Looking closer, some twelve feet off the ground, she could make out the rough outline of a wall. Above that, the slant of a rusted metal roof caught a storm-shot glimmer of light. She rode back to her dad's side. "Is that it?"

"Yeah," he said. "I can't believe it's still here. C'mon." The purpose was back in his voice, his posture.

She was there before him, though, and dismounting, she circled the trees, the three oaks that provided the main support for the fort, hunting for the way up, finding a ladder half the distance around.

"Sissy, wait," her dad called. "That ladder may be rotten. It won't hold your weight."

"Well, it for sure won't hold yours," she called back, and it was in the short silence after her words died away that she heard it, a noise overhead, a light scraping followed by a knocking sound. And now—now—was that a voice? Human? Animal? Her heart hammered in her chest. She set her hand and her foot on the rungs of the ladder, and she began to climb.

"Lily! Don't do it."

She looked down at her dad, warning finger to her lips. She caught the serrated flash of lightning, and moments later thunder shook the tree limbs. The ladder shifted, and a squawk of alarm jammed her throat, thankfully stopping there. The scrabbling noises increased. She thought she heard panting, moaning, but it might have been the wind, her own blood in her ears. The fort was small, maybe ten feet square, and built of cedar logs. The walls were set inside a platform some eighteen inches deep, creating a narrow porch. Reaching it, she peered over its edge and saw that the door, and the windows on either side of it, were open. She ducked out of sight, and while the fresh crack of thunder startled her, she was glad for it and for the sound of the wind that kept her presence secret. Pulling herself onto the ledge, she looked at her dad, raising her thumb: so far, so good.

"Come down." His face, pale, uptilted, he mouthed the words.

She raised her finger at him. *In a minute.*

He shook his head, walking in a frustrated circle.

On all fours, she crawled to the wall and, flattening herself against it, leaned around the door frame. At first she could make out nothing specific, but once her eyes adjusted to the gloom, a wave of sheer panic jolted her. What seemed like an eternity but was in fact only seconds passed before she was crawling back toward the ladder, shouting, "Dad! Oh my God, Dad, get up here!"

16

Kate was your best friend, Shea." Dru looked over at her daughter. They were in Shea's white Camry, parked at the curb, a block down from the Kincaids' house. A dozen or more cars lined the street. Others were crowded into the Kincaids' driveway. Dru recognized Joy's Suburban and Terri's Explorer. She didn't know what Vanessa's mother, Connie, drove, but she was no doubt here. Terri and Connie would have brought their daughters, Vanessa and Leigh, Shea's two remaining bridal attendants.

Dru wondered if the coroner in Dallas had released Becca back to her mom and dad yet. She wondered if Kate would undergo forensic examination prior to her burial, too. It was so awful to contemplate. Who was next? Dru was scared for Shea, scared for anyone who had a connection to the wedding. The most joyous occasion, turned now into a horrible, twisted nightmare.

"I can't go in there, Mom." Shea lifted her hands from the steering wheel. That gesture, the helplessness it suggested, set Dru off.

"This isn't about you, Shea. It's about Charla and Kent, giving them our condolences, paying our respects. Joy and Gene, too—they need to hear from us."

"You go, then."

Dru looked at Shea in exasperation. "You're going to have to face everyone at some point, like it or not."

"Fine!" Shea barked the word. "But this is a mistake. They don't want my condolences, trust me." Flinging the Toyota door open, she got out of the car, marching down the sidewalk toward the Kincaids' house.

Dru clamped down on her annoyance, a hot urge to shout, "Wait!"

Shea had rung the doorbell by the time Dru reached the front porch, and the two waited for someone to answer, standing shoulder to shoulder, grim-faced, barely breathing. Dru felt panic grip her stomach. It was almost without thinking that she reached for Shea's hand. Her heart eased at Shea's answering grasp.

Dru didn't recognize the woman who answered the door. She was older, gray-haired. Grief combined with exhaustion bruised her eyes. She greeted them and introduced herself. "I'm Leona, Kent's mother," she said.

Dru offered her name, and Shea's, as they followed Leona into the foyer. She said how sorry she was they were meeting under such horrible circumstances. They had paused beneath the archway that separated the foyer from the great room when Leona turned to stare at Shea. "You're the bride." She made it sound like an accusation.

Dru's glance shot past Leona, taking in the crowd of mostly women. Some were gathered in a group near the fireplace; others were seated on a pair of nearby sofas.

"Why are you here?" Charla rose from a tufted leather ottoman.

Ignoring the frisson of unease that tapped up her spine, Dru extended her hands to Charla. "We came—Shea and I came to say how sorry—"

"Get out!" Charla batted at Dru's hands. She addressed Leona. "Why did you let them in?"

"I didn't know."

"How dare you show yourself here." Joy put her arm around Charla.

"Who do you think you are?" A woman whose name Dru couldn't recall stepped into her view.

"Did you think you'd be welcome?" another one wanted to know.

"Wait a minute," Dru began, but then she faltered, groping for words, not finding any. Her heart thumped in her chest. Beside her, Shea was mute.

"Look at you." Joy's mocking glance swept from Dru to Shea. "You're safe and sound. He won't come after you, will he? Your beloved groom, the monster you can't wait to marry. You know where he is, don't you? Don't lie. You're in this with him. Am I right? You and your saintly mother—"

"That's enough, Joy." Dru stepped in front of Shea.

"Don't you tell me what's enough, Dru Gallagher. You still have your daughter."

The deafening silence was broken within seconds by a small cry, a mewling kitten cry. Dru heard it and then the sound of steps, Shea's steps, running from her, from the women, their mean, accusing eyes. The front door opened and slammed shut with a resounding crack.

Dru followed her.

"When is it going to stop?" a voice shouted.

"When all our girls are dead?" another cried out.

Dru halted on the Kincaids' front porch, glance careening up and down the street. The sky had darkened while they were inside. The wind blew, raising ribbons of dust along the curb. She caught the sound of thunder. Where was Shea? Frantic minutes passed before Dru caught sight of her, three doors down, on her hands and knees on the front lawn of some stranger's house. The wind caught at her hair, the loose hem of her shirt. Dru cut across the two yards that separated them, and reaching Shea, knelt beside her, pulling back her hair, drawing it over Shea's heaving back and shoulders. Until Shea spoke, until she said, "I tried to tell you," through her clenched teeth, Dru thought Shea's trembling was caused by her sobbing.

But no.

Shea was furious.

At Dru.

She took her arm away, braced her hands on her thighs. A curtain twitched at the window fronting the lawn. Dru prayed that whoever was watching would mind their own business, although the witness, likely the home owner, would have every right not to.

She rubbed tentative circles between Shea's shoulder blades. "I'm really sorry," she said. "I don't understand—"

"They're just like you, Mom." Shea sat back on her heels, angrily swiping at her eyes. "They made up their minds the second they heard Becca was murdered, and where, that AJ did it. *He's* the monster responsible. For poor Katie, too. God!" Shea locked Dru's gaze. "Why would anyone do this, Mama? Kill my friends? Make it look as if AJ did it? It's got to be someone who hates him."

"Does Harlan Cate know AJ well enough to hate him?" Dru asked.

Shea thought about it. "I don't think so."

Dru tucked Shea's hair behind her ear. "I'm sorry I didn't listen to you."

"About AJ?"

Dru couldn't go that far. "About paying a condolence call on Charla. I never imagined she and Joy would—I thought they were our friends."

"They don't deserve this, Mom, losing their daughters this way. They want someone to blame. But so do I—the right person." Shea's voice took on an edge. "I want whoever did this to be caught and punished. I want justice for Becca and Kate."

"I'm really proud of you, that you're able to be so understanding of Charla and Joy."

"I feel just like them. I'm so angry inside. I feel like I could kill whoever is doing this."

"Oh, honey—"

"I'm going to miss Katie so much, Mama." Shea's voice broke, and Dru wrapped her in an embrace, grateful for the chance to hold her daughter so close she could feel the tempo of her heart. Dru rested her cheek on the crown of Shea's head and tried not to think of Joy and Charla, that neither one would ever experience this privilege again.

After a moment, Shea straightened, mopping her face, swiping under her nose.

Getting to her feet, Dru said, "Let's go before whoever lives here calls the police."

They walked back to the Toyota, and when Dru offered to drive, Shea handed over the keys. "At least you won't have to cook the Kincaids a meal," she said.

"Well, yeah, there's that, I guess."

Gallows humor. Their hallmark. They shared a grim smile.

Shea got out her phone.

Dru pulled away from the curb. It occurred to her that it was possible no one in town would hire her to cook for them again. She wondered if, given the circumstances, the teachers' appreciation luncheon today had even taken place. Perhaps they'd tossed the meal Dru had prepared. She hadn't heard from Amy. Had she been at Charla's? Dru didn't remember seeing her, but given the scrambled state of her mind, that didn't mean anything.

"Oh my God. Listen to this."

"What is it?" Dru glanced at Shea, who was reading from her phone.

"It's a text from Erik. Kate's mom flipped out on him, too. Told him to get out of her house just like she did us."

"Why? She loves him."

"She accused AJ of pushing Kate off the cliff." Shea was scrolling through the message, reading it as it revealed itself. "Erik defended him, and Charla told him to leave."

Dru briefly met Shea's disbelieving gaze. She didn't know what to say.

"He sent this over two hours ago, while we were at the RV park. I wonder why I didn't get it until now." Her head was bent; she was engrossed. "There's a phone message from Lily, too." Shea tapped, accessing her voice mail, putting it on speaker.

"Call me. I've got news," said Lily's voice.

Dru's eyes jerked to Shea's.

Shea tapped the screen again and put her phone to her ear.

The call went through as Dru crossed a quiet intersection. After going a few hundred yards farther, she turned left onto the narrow asphalt lane that wound through her subdivision, and while it did register in some part of her brain that the light-colored pickup that had been behind her for several miles turned, too, it was only on a subliminal level. She was listening to Shea, the message she was leaving for Lily.

"I wonder what she wanted. She sounded upbeat—maybe." Shea held her phone in her lap. "I'm not getting my hopes up," she added, as if she had heard the warning in Dru's mind.

Dru glanced in the rearview at the pickup truck. It was closer now, too close. Close enough for her to see the driver clearly, to see that he—or a woman with very broad shoulders—was wearing a ball cap pulled low. "Sorry, buddy, I'm not going any faster."

The truck sped up, coming within inches of Dru's bumper. "What is he doing?"

"Who?" Shea twisted, looking through the back window.

The truck accelerated again, this time tapping the Toyota's bumper.

"Holy shit, Mom! He hit us." Shea's eyes were round with alarm.

Dru punched the gas pedal, shooting the Camry forward.

The truck—she didn't recognize the model, only that it was light colored and huge—kept pace, and when it struck the Toyota again, Dru knew it was no accident.

"He's wrecking my car!" Shea cried.

Dru stomped on the gas pedal again, swerving a bit, fighting the urge to overcorrect, somehow remembering advice Rob had given her long ago.

Shea flattened her palm against the dashboard, gaze careening from the scene behind them to Dru to the windshield. "What is wrong with him?" Alarm shot her voice high. "Did you piss him off?"

"I don't see how. I didn't cut him off or turn in front of him." Dru wanted to tell Shea to tighten her seat belt, to assume the crash position. But she couldn't form the words. Ahead, the road looped into a near U shape before it straightened, and she stiffened in anticipation, praying she could safely navigate the deep curve at this speed. The truck kept pace. There couldn't be a cat whisker's width between them. If she could make it home—but what would she do there? She and Shea would be trapped. Dru glanced at her purse. She had the .38. She felt a momentary relief, stinging and cold, that vanished in the wake of her mind's observation that this maniac, whoever it was, could also be armed.

And then the truck slammed into them hard enough that her head recoiled.

Shea yelled, "Oh my God, Mama! He's going to kill us!"

"No, he's not." Dru was furious now. She slammed on her brakes, tires shrieking, Toyota skidding, mind on her gun, focused on the thought that once they stopped, she'd shoot him. Before he had a chance to get at them, she would blow out his fucking brains where he sat.

As if he could read her mind, he pulled alongside her, crushing the heavier weight of his truck against the smaller car, pushing it off the road. The noise, metal grinding on metal, the higher squeal of tires, was horrifying, deafening. Dru held the steering wheel, stiff-armed, both feet pushing down on the brake pedal as if by the sheer force of her will she could keep her car upright and on the road. The thought roared into her brain that if the Toyota turned over, Shea would take the brunt of the impact.

But she wasn't safe, either. She could feel the heat from the truck, feel the force of it crushing her door. The Camry was off the road now, skidding along the shallow ditch, sliding into a neighbor's yard, metal screaming. She jerked her gaze to the truck's driver. It must be a man. But who? Who would do this? He was staring at her, but his hat was low over his eyes, his face in shadow. She had no clue as to his identity. The sedan rocked on its axles. Dru reached for Shea, finding her hand, closing her eyes—and it stopped—the noise, the motion—so suddenly, it was a moment before Dru realized it. Opening her eyes, she saw that Shea was holding the gun, extending the .38, in her trembling grasp, looking past Dru out the driver's-side window.

"He's leaving," Shea said. "Should I shoot him?"

"What?" Dru whipped her gaze to the window and saw that Shea was right. The truck was backing off, reversing, fast, on the grassy verge, dislodging chunks of dirt, sod, and gravel as it navigated back onto the road. Then it was gone, in a heated rage of screeching tires. Dru could have sworn when it headed into the deep curve, it was balanced on only two of them.

She looked back at Shea. "Let me have it," she said, gently, taking the .38. "Hand me my phone. I'm calling the police."

But before either she or Dru could act, Shea's phone went off, and she answered it, saying it was Lily.

Their conversation was clipped, frantic, and lasted less than a minute, but Dru knew by the time Shea clicked off, before she spoke a word, that everything had changed.

17

The stench was of blood and putrefying flesh mixed with sweat. It made Lily's stomach roll, and she clenched her teeth, crawling toward the body in the far corner of the fort. The body she thought was AJ's was on its back, lying so still. Too still. *Pleasepleaseplease . . .* the word was a prayer, as much a demand as it was a plea.

When she was close enough and saw that it was her son, a sound escaped her, something between a cry and a groan. She took his hand. "AJ?"

"Is he alive?" Her dad, having come up the ladder at her shouted command, stood in the fort's doorway, his face grim.

"Yes, barely. We need an ambulance."

"I called already. I told them to go around to the old service gate."

Lily nodded, watching AJ struggle for breath. His pulse was rapid, his skin clammy to her touch. Incongruously, his chest was bare, and what looked like a very bloody shirt was wrapped around his right thigh. He was shoeless, and his right ankle was swollen and discolored, angry shades of blue and red.

"I'll ride Sharkey out to meet the EMTs and guide them in. Can you tell what happened?" Her dad knelt on AJ's other side. If he was affected by what he saw, he gave little sign of it.

"Something under that shirt has bled pretty badly," Lily said.

"Gunshot, maybe," her dad said. "Looks like his ankle's broken or sprained. Hard to tell."

"Mom?"

"I'm here, honey. So is Granddad."

"We've got help, coming, son."

"Good," AJ said, and he grinned—grinned!—"'cause lying here on this floor is starting to give me a backache."

"Oh, AJ." Laughter that felt awfully close to hysteria bumped Lily's ribs, and she clamped down on it.

"What happened?" her dad asked.

"Maybe he shouldn't talk," Lily said.

"I think I got the bleeding stopped," AJ said. "It's my ankle that's killing me. I tried getting out of here a while ago—don't know when. I lost track. I fell off the damn ladder, though. Can you believe it?"

"But what about here?" Lily's hand hovered over AJ's thigh.

"Gunshot. Bled a lot. Got my shirt off—"

"You made a tourniquet," Lily's dad finished.

"Yeah. Once a marine, always a marine."

"Semper fi," her dad said, and AJ smiled, eyes closed.

Lily's glance collided with her dad's.

"He's tough, our boy. He did good."

She nodded, knowing he was trying to reassure her, to reassure them all.

"I better get going." He got to his feet. "Hang in there, champ. Take care of your mama. You know how she gets."

"Yeah," AJ murmured.

Lily still held his hand and felt the pressure when he tightened his grasp. "Go on," she told her dad. "We'll be fine."

AJ asked for a drink. "I got some rainwater in a cup." Lily found it and held it to his lips. Afterward, he lay back, keeping his eyes closed. He felt cooler to Lily's touch than before, and his color had gone from chalky white to gray. His lips were blue. She recognized the symptoms of shock and knew his feet ought to be elevated, but she was afraid to move him, afraid it would start the blood flowing from the gunshot wound again. Where was the ambulance?

"After I fell off the ladder," AJ said, "the coyotes came. I think. Unless I dreamed . . ."

"Just rest." Lily smoothed his hair from his brow. How long had he been lying here? Since Becca was killed? Two and a half days?

"Shea?" he asked, and his eyelids fluttered; he shifted as if he might sit up.

"She's fine. Lie still."

"I know she's scared . . . everybody scared . . . worried. Sorry for that . . ."

"It's fine, honey. Just rest," Lily repeated. *What happened? Who did this to you? How did you get here?* She was desperate to ask, but no more desperate than to hear the sound of her dad returning with the ambulance.

When it finally came, she worried how the paramedics would get AJ down from the fort, but she needn't have. They'd come equipped with nylon ropes and a lightweight rescue basket. She waited with her dad near the open doors of the ambulance, watching as they lowered AJ as gently as possible to the ground. He was unconscious for the most part and only groaned when they transferred him from the basket to the gurney inside the ambulance.

"Is he going to be all right?" Lily asked one of the paramedics, the only woman among the crew of three. Jeannette, her name tag read.

"He's getting oxygen now, and we started an IV, saline. We're giving him morphine for the pain. He's shocky, so we'll be watching his vitals."

Jeannette rattled off the information. "He's lost a lot of blood. Looks like the bullet missed his femoral, though, and that's a good thing."

The three of them turned to look when a Wyatt police patrol car bumped toward them, across the meadow. Clint Mackie was driving. Lily's heart sank.

"I'll handle him," her dad said, but Mackie avoided them, going to another of the paramedics, an older guy. The way the two men greeted each other, Lily thought they must be friends. Maybe Clint Mackie was a better friend to the paramedic than he was to her dad.

"Captain Mackie is probably asking for a rundown of your son's injuries. It would be routine, given the circumstances." Jeanette spoke gently.

Lily wondered how much she knew about the circumstances. What if she, or the other medical personnel—doctors, nurses—believed AJ was a criminal, a murderer? Would they still treat him? "Could I ride in the ambulance with AJ?" she asked Jeanette.

The paramedic shook her head. "It's against policy," she said.

Who knew if that was true?

Moments after the ambulance left, Mackie appeared at Lily's elbow. "You want to ride with me, I'll run you to the hospital."

Lily looked at her dad, unsure if she wanted to ride with the police captain.

"Go on," her dad said. "I'll take the horses back and be along in two shakes."

"I'm not answering any questions." Lily addressed the captain. "I don't know anything. AJ was barely conscious."

"That's fine." Captain Mackie opened the front passenger door of the squad car for Lily. "I'll be questioning him myself as soon as he comes around. I expect a couple of detectives from Dallas will be down here pretty quick to question him, too."

· · ·

Lily called Paul from the hospital, and he was headed to his car before they hung up.

"I should be there by seven," he said. "Call me if anything changes."

Lily said she would.

"God, it's a miracle, isn't it?" There was the sound of the car door slamming, the garage door going up. "I was scared we'd never find him."

"I know," Lily said.

"Tell him not to go anywhere, okay?" Paul's voice was thick with emotion, but Lily heard the smile in it.

She smiled, too, as if he could see her. "I'll tell him," she said.

Unlike Paul, Shea went completely silent when Lily called to say AJ had been found. Lily had to prompt her. "Shea? Are you there?"

"Yes. I'm just—I didn't give up hope, you know, but—" She broke off, and Lily sensed she was fighting for composure, steeling herself. "Is he all right?"

"He's been shot, Shea, but he's receiving treatment right now." Lily spoke quickly, relating the rest of what she knew. "His ankle is injured, too. Dad and I found him at the old fort. He tried getting down the ladder and fell."

"But he's going to be okay, right? Please—"

"He's lost a lot of blood, he's dehydrated, and he's in shock, but he was able to talk to me—"

Shea interrupted. "Who shot him? Was it Harlan?"

Lily said she didn't know.

"We were on our way there the other day we came to search, your dad and me and Erik. If only we'd—but how did he get there? It doesn't make any sense."

"I know." Lily had been thinking about it, all the ways nothing added up. "It's for sure it wasn't under his own power," she said.

"At least now the police will know he wasn't anywhere near Cedar Ridge Canyon this morning. Someone is trying to frame him."

"But who? Harlan?"

Shea didn't answer. Lily heard voices, people talking in the background, wherever she was. "Shea?" she prompted.

"Mom and I had a bit of trouble a while ago. Someone—a guy in a pickup ran us off the road."

"What?" Lily stopped her pacing in front of the entrance to the ER.

"Mom thinks someone followed us from Kate's house. We'd gone there to—to pay our respects, and he followed us from there. We don't know who it was. He was wearing a hat pulled low, so we couldn't see his face. He kept inching up on us, and when we turned in to our subdivision, he rear-ended us, then he came up alongside and broadsided us. Mom was driving my car, my Camry, and he pushed it right off the road. It was scary."

"You called the police?"

"Yes, Ken Carter is here."

"Shea, did you know that a few days before Becca was killed, she and Kate were involved in a traffic altercation, and a man threatened them?"

"Here? In Wyatt?"

"No, in Dallas. But the man drove a pickup. He ran them off the road."

"Are you kidding?" Asking Lily to hold on, Shea repeated what Lily had told her to Dru.

In the rumble of conversation, Lily recognized the lower timbre of a man's voice. Ken Carter, she thought, the officer who was there; he was listening, too.

A moment later Shea was back. "You won't believe this, but Sergeant Carter is saying he saw a report about it." She sounded incredulous, alarmed and angry all at once. Lily had the sense she was struggling to hold on to her temper. "I told him AJ's at Wyatt Regional, and he knew that, too. He knew and never said a word to me. I don't think any of these cops have a clue what's going on."

"No, I agree, but Shea, none of us does. Be careful, okay?" Lily cautioned. "Whoever is behind this, they're still out there."

• • •

She was alone in the ER waiting room across from triage when the doctor, Kelvin Dermott, found her a bit later.

Lily stood up, feeling a wave of relief. "I was hoping you were here," she said. "You're taking care of AJ? How is he?"

Kelvin took her hands, looking grave. They were friends, having gone through public school together. "I'm not going to lie," he said. "AJ is not in great shape. He's on his way to surgery now to remove the bullet and repair the damage. Jim Matthews is operating. Do you know him?"

Lily shook her head.

"He's a good man—"

"Kelvin?"

Lily glanced over her shoulder at her dad as he joined them.

The men shook hands. Kelvin repeated what he'd told Lily. Her dad asked about AJ's ankle.

"It's badly sprained, but it should heal fine," Kelvin said. "The leg wound, too, should be all right, barring complications."

"Thank God," Lily said.

"It's a good thing you found him when you did," Kelvin said. "Given the blood loss, the risk of infection—he's not out of the woods, but if he'd been left out there any longer, his chances would be much worse. Or if the shooter's aim had been any better, if they'd hit the femoral—"

"Yeah. Well, maybe they missed on purpose."

"What do you mean, Dad?"

"When it comes to shooting someone—another human being—you can lose your nerve. The situation—the way this looks with AJ—I don't know." He thought about it. "It just seems off somehow."

"Clint is sure hot to question him," Kelvin said.

"Can you keep him from it?" Lily asked.

"I already told him there wasn't going to be an interrogation without clearance from me or one of the other attendings, and he told me that along with him, I can expect to get pressure from the Dallas PD. They've got a couple of detectives on the way."

"Paul is on his way from there, too," Lily said.

"What about Shea and her mom? You called them?" her dad asked.

Before she could answer, Kelvin excused himself, saying he'd keep them advised.

Lily followed Kelvin's progress until he disappeared, then, turning to her dad, she explained what Shea had told her about the incident with the pickup truck. "It's like what happened to Becca and Kate," she said.

"Yeah. Too damn similar to be a coincidence. Shea and her mom are lucky." Her dad wiped his hand over his head. "I guess the one good thing is no one can pin it on AJ."

Lily's relief felt oddly deflating.

Her dad wrapped her in his embrace. "We found him, Sissy," he said. "We got to him in time. That's all that matters, all that matters right now."

18

"Can you tell me about AJ Isley?" Shea had asked the same question of two other nurses, one in the emergency room and another on the surgical floor, without success.

Dru could feel her anxiety coming off her like sparks.

"Are you a relative?" the recovery-room nurse—Kelsey, according to her name tag—asked.

"Almost. He's my fiancé."

Kelsey's smile was sudden and warm, an unexpected gift. "Shea, right? He couldn't stop talking about you. Some people do that under anesthesia. They talk and talk. He described you to a tee." She was inspecting Shea's neck, the rose tattoo.

Dru waited to see her disapproval; instead, Kelsey said she loved it. "AJ talked about another tattoo, a lotus blossom? Here, right?" The nurse indicated an area of her abdomen between her belly button and the jut of her hip bone. "He has one, too, same place. Very pretty."

Dru was astonished. She looked at Shea. *Matching tattoos? Really?* But her dismay dissolved when Shea laughed, a small, half-strangled sound, then covered her mouth. Dru took her hand.

"He's all right, then?" Shea asked Kelsey.

"Well, you need to speak to Dr. Matthews," the nurse said, "but between you and me, your fiancé is looking real good." She winked, making Dru want to roll her eyes. "They got the slug out of his leg and stopped the bleeding. He's on IVs for pain and hydration, but overall he's hanging in there. He's one lucky guy that his mom and granddad found him when they did."

Shea thanked the nurse, squeezing her arm.

Dru thought Shea would hug Kelsey next, but instead she flung herself into Dru's embrace. "Did you hear? Oh, Mom!" Pulling away, almost staggering in her happiness, Shea addressed the nurse again. "Can I see him?"

"He'll be in recovery a bit longer, but he's been assigned a room." She looked at the chart she was carrying. "Third floor, room 302. He should be along within the hour. His mom and granddad are already up there, I think."

"Thank you, thank you so much again." Shea was trembling in her jubilation. "It's a miracle, isn't it? The one I was praying for."

Dru didn't have the heart to caution her, to say it might be too soon for celebration.

• • •

Of course room 302 was private. The Axels and the Isleys were that sort; they had that kind of money. *Must be nice.* That's what Dru was thinking as she crossed the threshold. And then she felt small. What good was her envy of them? She assumed because they were rich, their lives were easy, but their wealth hadn't protected them from fear and heartbreak, had it? Lily's son had been shot. Kate and Becca were dead. Dru and Shea had been run off the road. The threat was real.

Ongoing.

And it wasn't AJ.

Dru was still grappling with that fact. It was awful, but she'd been so sure—and even though she was relieved to be proven wrong on that score, she was still certain that AJ had issues. Maybe he wasn't the monster behind the awful violence, but she would be willing to bet that it was related to him, to something he'd done. She didn't know what, and she wouldn't say it aloud, but neither could she shake the conviction that he was involved.

Lily was telling Shea how lucky AJ was. "The bullet did some tissue damage but missed the bones and major arteries."

Dru glanced at Jeb. She'd noticed him, leaning against the wall opposite the door, but she hadn't acknowledged him. They only exchanged a frosty glance now. Her greeting of Lily was similarly cool. They didn't share an embrace the way Lily and Shea had. Dru had all but come out and accused AJ—Jeb and Lily's boy—of heinous crimes. She could defend herself, remind them of the evidence. Say she wasn't alone, that the police—in two different departments, no less—had believed AJ was responsible, too, that it had seemed reasonable, doubting his innocence. But it wouldn't be the apology they were, in all likelihood, looking for. If Lily and Jeb had accused Shea in a similar fashion, that's what Dru would want—amends, an acknowledgment of their error. She'd want them on their knees. But Dru couldn't bring herself to go there for them.

"Folks?" An orderly appeared in the doorway. "We're bringing in your guy. He's still kind of out of it, so go easy on him, okay?" He grinned.

The four of them, Dru, Jeb, Shea, and Lily, moved out of the way to the far windowed wall. The sense of anticipation was electric; a loose bolt of lightning couldn't have felt more volatile. AJ was wheeled in headfirst. Shea started toward him.

"Let us get him comfortable," the nurse said to her.

Shea nodded; she was trembling, though, and Dru sensed her agony at having to wait yet one more minute.

The nurse and the orderlies stepped around, adjusting IVs, the machine that monitored AJ's vitals. A top sheet was folded to expose his right leg, which was encased from the top of his thigh to his foot in a compression bandage. He was unshaven, and his face under the stubble was bleached of color. His cheeks were sunken. He looked gaunt, wasted, as if he'd lost weight. But he was alert. His gaze jumped around, searching the room. Until he found Shea. He teared up when he saw her, his jaw shook, and his mouth pursed in an effort to keep his composure. Dru's heart wobbled.

Shea pressed her fingertips to her mouth, holding AJ's gaze. The medical team left, and she glanced at Lily, ready to defer, but Lily made a little shooing motion toward her son.

She was more generous than Dru would have been. She crossed her arms, fighting an urge to grab Shea and run with her out of the room.

At AJ's bedside, Shea was tentative, hands fluttering about his face, his shoulders. "Are you okay? Do you hurt?"

"Not now," AJ said, and, raising his untethered arm, he grasped Shea's hand gently, as if it were a terrified bird, and, bringing it to his lips, he kissed the back and then her palm, inhaling deeply as if he might take her very essence into himself. Lily and Dru exchanged a glance, and Dru saw that Lily was wondering the same thing: whether they should leave the room, leave these two alone, but they both, along with Jeb, seemed unable to walk away.

"I was so scared I would never see you again," Shea said softly.

"There was no way I wasn't coming back to you." AJ's voice was husky with emotion—with love.

Even Dru couldn't deny that he loved Shea. But was he good for her? Would he be good to her? Was he really innocent?

"It doesn't matter what we think." Lily spoke softly at Dru's elbow.

"No," Dru agreed, readily enough. She watched as Shea cupped AJ's cheek, bent to kiss him. Her jaw tightened. She wasn't sure why. It wasn't that she didn't want Shea to be happy. She wanted that for Shea more than anything.

"AJ would never hurt Shea."

Dru glanced at Lily. She would have sworn that was true of Rob, too, before he put a shotgun in her face.

"It could have been a lot worse," AJ said, and he included everyone in his glance.

"That's what Dr. Matthews told us," Lily said, walking around the foot of the bed to the side opposite Shea. Lily touched AJ's shoulder. She laid her hand on his brow. "How are you, honey?"

"I wouldn't be here if it wasn't for you and Granddad, that's for sure." He looked from his mom to Jeb, who had joined her.

"Your granddad is the one who knew where to find you," Lily said.

"You have one of your hunches?" AJ asked, grinning.

"Ha. Yeah. At least some part of my brain still works."

Jeb Axel seemed abashed somehow. Dru felt her heart reaching out in sympathy, and it disconcerted her. She'd never liked the man, his arrogance, his egotism, his cowboy swagger.

"I'm sorry to barge in, folks."

Dru looked up as Clint Mackie walked into the room.

"I need to ask AJ some questions."

Jeb said, "No, Clint, what you need to do is get the hell out there and find whoever did this."

"I know who it is, Granddad," AJ said, and as happy as he had sounded before, there was misery evident in his voice now. "Help me sit up?" AJ asked Shea.

She adjusted the bed, the cushion under his leg, and when she was finished, he captured her hand again.

"So, tell us, son," Mackie said. "Who shot you?"

"Erik. Erik Ayala."

"What?" Shea and Lily spoke together.

Dru's breath stopped, but it was Jeb's reaction—the way he jerked upright, looking stunned, as if he'd been sucker punched—that kept Dru's attention. She heard AJ say he couldn't believe it, either, then Lily and Shea were talking. Lily saying she'd seen Erik yesterday: "He fixed lunch in my kitchen." And Shea saying Erik had called her looking for Kate: "He wanted to know if I'd heard from her when he knew, knew she was . . ."

They didn't notice it when Jeb walked around the foot of the bed, returning to stand at the window. Perhaps he felt Dru's gaze, though, because he looked at her, and he was gray-faced. He might have aged ten years in the space of ten seconds. She couldn't fathom his expression; some kind of anguish, what might have been a plea for help, haunted his eyes. Dru looked away, doubting what she saw, but the sense of her foreboding was real enough, an icy finger tapping up her spine.

"Why? Why would Erik hurt those girls?" Lily asked.

"Why would he hurt you?" Shea looked at AJ.

"Erik hates me. I mean, he really hates me, as crazy as it sounds. I'm not sure why I'm still alive."

"You want to start at the beginning?" Mackie wasn't really asking.

AJ asked for water, and Shea poured it into a cup from the pitcher of ice water the orderlies had left behind. She fed it to him, holding the cup, guiding the straw, and while the gravity of the situation was apparent, there was also an intimacy in the moment; there were notes of merriment and teasing in their attention to each other. AJ didn't need Shea's help to drink, but it was their pleasure to pretend.

They might have been alone in the room, in the world, Dru thought.

Mackie pulled out his cell phone. "You don't mind if I record this, do you? I'll want to get a formal statement later, but I'd like this on the record."

"Whatever you need," AJ answered. "Where do you want me to start?"

"You worked your shift at Café Blue on Tuesday, right?"

"Yeah. We weren't busy, so I left early."

Shea said, "The detective in Dallas tried to tell me you weren't there at all."

"They said the same thing to me." Lily was staring at Mackie.

"Well, I was there. You can check my time card."

"We did that already. Initially the DPD was misinformed." Mackie was perfunctory. "So, after you got off, what did you do?"

"I called my girl." AJ glanced at Shea, squeezing her hand. "I think it was about ten thirty, then I drove to my apartment. I was whipped, and all I wanted was a hot shower and bed. But when I walked in, I saw Erik at the kitchen sink. The water was running. I didn't really register at first what he was doing." AJ spoke slowly.

He seemed bewildered, Dru thought, as if he was trying to connect the dots. He hadn't reacted to the mention of Kate's death. Maybe he already knew, or maybe in all the turmoil, he hadn't registered the reference.

Mackie asked him what happened next.

"Erik was like, 'Oh, man, I'm glad you showed up.' He said he'd had an accident. I saw he had blood all over him and figured he'd cut himself. I was like, 'God, what did you do?' But then I saw his eyes. They were—I can't even describe the look. Cold. Empty, like nothing was there."

"Go on," Mackie prompted.

"He told me he'd done something bad and asked me to come with him to the bedroom. When we got there, I couldn't figure out what had happened. There was this body on the bed and blood splattered everywhere, and my knife, my Shun chef's knife—" AJ twisted his head, hunting his mother's glance. "The one out of the set you gave me?"

Lily nodded. "We found it, Granddad and I did, in your truck."

"You found my truck? Where?"

Lily told him. "It was burned," she said. "I guess Erik was trying to destroy evidence."

The shared moment of silence was astonished, sickened.

AJ broke it. "I saw a lot in Afghanistan, but that was war—different somehow." He thought about it. "But maybe not," he amended quietly. "We all bleed the same."

"Did you know the victim was Becca?" Mackie was staying on task.

"Not until he told me."

"Did he say why he killed her?"

"Not really. He said she was yelling, and he was scared the neighbors would hear and call the cops. It was like he blamed her. He told me we had to get rid of her body, that I had to help him, that I owed him. He said he knew stuff about us, that he could blow our family to hell."

"What did he mean?" Lily asked.

"I wish I knew," AJ said. "I told him he was talking crazy, that I was calling 911, and that's when he went off. He got my .45—he knew it was in the bedside table. He made me give him my phone, then he walked me out to my truck. He had me drive, and I thought I might get a chance to—I don't know, get away or something, but he kept the pistol on me the whole time. He had me take him to Mickey D's. We rolled through the takeout, and the son of a bitch ate two Big Macs and a double order of fries. The smell, watching him eat—I don't know how I kept from being sick."

"Sounds like y'all had quite a conversation, but you're telling me in all that time he never said why he murdered Becca?" Mackie didn't bother hiding his skepticism.

"No, Clint, he never did. He just kept shoving the burger in his mouth. He was calm by then, so I kind of pushed him some more about going to the cops. I said we could say it was an accident. I'd back him up. You know, Becca fell on the knife or something." AJ's laugh was wry, harsh. "I was grabbing at straws, trying anything. I still don't know why he didn't kill me."

"Thank God he didn't," Shea whispered.

"He couldn't," Jeb said softly.

"Why not?" AJ asked.

Jeb looked up, startled, as if he hadn't expected to be heard.

"You mean because he lost his nerve?" Lily gathered them all in her glance. "Dad said earlier that sometimes people can't bring themselves to pull the trigger."

"Yes," Jeb said. "That's what I meant."

But looking at him, Dru sensed there was more to it.

Captain Mackie directed AJ back to the night of Becca's murder, and AJ related how Erik had made him drive around Dallas, eventually ordering him to head south on I-35 to Wyatt. There had been little conversation. When they got into town, they'd driven around as aimlessly as they had in Dallas.

"We went by your mom's house," AJ said, looking at Shea.

The thought of how close Erik and AJ had been to Shea, to her home, startled Dru. A couple of madmen, she thought—because how did she know AJ wasn't part of it, involved some way? Jeb Axel, too. He was acting so odd. Dru had a bad feeling. It kept growing. She didn't know whether to trust it. Or even whom to trust.

AJ said it was after that when Erik started talking about the fort. How he wanted to see it again, how he and AJ could camp out the way they used to in the old days. "I was so tired by then," AJ said. "It was getting light outside. I just wanted to stop driving."

"He was with us," Shea said in a voice soft with disbelief. "Erik was with us when we rode out that way, looking for you."

"It couldn't have been more than a few hours since he'd left you there," Jeb said. "If I'd only known, if I'd gone on, I would have found you then."

Jeb's bleak astonishment seemed genuine. But he would do anything for AJ, Dru thought. She didn't doubt Jeb Axel would lie for his grandson. She thought of the missing contents of the safe at the xL.

Suppose Jeb was pretending senility in order to put the blame for that on himself to cover for AJ?

"You guys were close, I thought." Mackie was puzzled.

"Yeah, like brothers, but when I said that, Erik said I better think again, and then he shot me. I wasn't sure what happened until my leg buckled. I heard him leave, but after that, I passed out for a while. When I came to, it was full daylight; my mouth was as dry as dirt, and I knew I'd lost a lot of blood, that I had to get help. I used my shirt to tourniquet my leg, then crawled to the ladder, thinking I could get myself down. It didn't work out too well." AJ looked toward his ankle. "After I fell, I passed out again, and when I woke up it was night. I thought I saw coyotes. Scared me enough to get me back up the ladder."

"Erik said you were going to be his best man." Lily's voice was faint with disbelief.

"He said he loved Kate, too," Shea said, "but then he killed her."

"What?" AJ turned to stare at Shea. "What are you saying?"

"Oh no—" Shea was mortified. "I didn't think. Of course you don't know—"

When Shea didn't seem able, Lily explained what had happened to Kate.

Shea touched the hollow at the base of AJ's throat. "He took your necklace—"

"Yeah, I don't know why."

"After he pushed Kate off the ridge—"

"Allegedly."

Shea shot Mackie a look of disgust. "Erik left the charm there to make you look guilty." She addressed AJ.

"He's trying to frame me?"

"Maybe," Mackie said. "But why? Why would he do that?"

Dru got the sense that, like her, the police captain was weighing the odds that AJ was telling the truth.

Again, AJ said he didn't know. "Erik's got it in for me, for whatever reason."

"You have any idea where he is?" Mackie asked.

"Have you checked his apartment?"

"First place we went, but if he's there, he's not answering his door. He's not at work, either."

"I think AJ should rest," Lily said.

"Just a couple more questions." Mackie looked back at AJ. "How do you think Erik talked Becca into coming to your apartment? How did they get in?"

"There's a spare key. Becca knew—several people knew I kept one in the gaslight out front."

"Okay, but say Ayala was setting you up. He must have realized you'd show up before he was done. Seems odd that he'd wait till so close to your quitting time to make his move."

"I left early, remember?"

"Did you see the note he pinned on her, the one that said, 'Fixed you'?"

"No. What does it mean?"

Mackie studied AJ, not answering.

"Do you suspect me of something, Clint? Is that why you're grilling me?"

"Isn't it clear by now that AJ couldn't have been involved?" Shea was pissed. "I guess next you're going to say he was driving the truck that ran Mom and me off the road."

"What truck? What are you talking about?"

"Oh, AJ." Shea was stricken at having blindsided him again.

This time Dru explained, making less of the encounter with the truck than it had actually been. Looking at Mackie when she finished, she said, "The police are looking into it."

"Was it Erik?" AJ's gaze was locked on Mackie.

"We don't know at this point, or whether there's a connection to Erik."

"You can be damn sure there's a connection, Captain," AJ said. He struggled to sit up. "I'll find him—"

"AJ, no," Shea said. She bent close, whispering to him. Dru caught the gist of it, that Shea wanted AJ to let the police handle it. "If he hurts you," Dru heard AJ say, "I'll kill the son of a bitch." But finally he gave in and settled back, white-faced, tight-jawed.

Mackie said, "I've got to tell you, AJ, we've got a ton of evidence that suggests you have some involvement."

Shea started to protest.

Mackie ignored her. "For instance, how do you explain the phone call you made to your mother asking her to bring you your passport?"

"It wasn't me. I was in no shape to call anyone, not to mention the last I looked, there was no phone service at the fort." AJ turned to Jeb. "You put in a phone out there, Granddad?"

Mackie wasn't amused. He flicked his glance to Lily. "She swore it was you."

"I don't believe I swore it was," Lily said.

Mackie returned his attention to AJ. "We have witnesses said they saw you at the bus station in Dallas, where your laptop and cell phone were recovered. Any idea how they got there?"

"None. I told you Erik took my phone. He must have gotten my laptop, too." AJ indicated his leg. "Anyway, if I couldn't get myself down the ladder at the fort except by falling on my ass, how would I make it to Dallas?"

"We have another witness says you were talking to a pilot at the Lake Hershey airfield yesterday. You going to tell me that wasn't you, either?"

"Again, Clint, how would I get there?"

"Maybe you and Ayala are in this together."

Dru's breath caught. Her heart slid against the wall of her chest at hearing her own suspicion so baldly stated.

AJ stared at Mackie, as gape-mouthed and astonished as a fresh-caught fish. Shea and Lily were dumbfounded.

He seemed oblivious. "Maybe these girls, Kate and Becca, had something on you guys. You did know, didn't you, that Becca Westin was pregnant? Was it your kid? Ayala's kid? What was going on there?"

"Are you serious? Becca was pregnant?" AJ's eyes shot to Shea's.

"It's true," she said.

Dru wondered at the tremor in Shea's voice. Was her faith at last beginning to crumble?

"They're waiting for DNA test results to say for sure who the father is," Shea said.

"Could I have some more water?" AJ asked.

Shea poured it, handing it to him to drink this time. His hand shook, taking it from her.

"The death of the fetus makes it a double homicide," Mackie said. "So whoever is responsible is looking at three counts of murder." He pocketed his cell phone, looking satisfied, Dru thought, as if in shaking everyone up, in putting them on the defense, he'd gotten the exact result he'd wanted.

Dru said, "Charla Kincaid might know where Erik is."

"I talked to her," Mackie said. "She indicated she hadn't seen him since this morning."

"You know Erik went there, that he volunteered to give her parents the news about their daughter's death. Why would he do that if he's responsible for it?"

"What are you trying to say, Mom?"

Dru put up her hands. "Nothing. I'm not trying to say anything." But even as she spoke, she was thinking how little sense Erik's involvement made. Was she the only one who saw it?

"I think I saw lights on at Winona's house this morning," Lily said. "If she's home from Oaxaca, maybe she's spoken to Erik."

Captain Mackie said, "I'll get someone out there. We're issuing a BOLO for Ayala, too."

"You need to find him, Clint," Jeb said, startling everyone.

He'd been so quiet. Even Dru had forgotten his presence.

"The state he's in, there's no telling what he'll do." Jeb crossed the room to the door, and turning on the threshold, he addressed Dru. "I'd keep her close if I was you," he said, nodding at Shea.

19

Lily followed her dad into the hallway, taking his elbow. "What was that about? Do you know where Erik is, what he's done?"

He shook her off. "Shea needs to be careful, is all. If Erik's behind this—look, he's already killed two of the girls in her wedding party. It just makes sense—"

"Lily? Jeb?"

They turned at the sound of Paul's voice. "How's AJ? How did the surgery go?"

"Better than expected," Lily said. "He's doing really well, considering."

Paul's embrace, his kiss on Lily's cheek, were perfunctory. He shook hands with her dad.

"I'll let Lily fill you in," her dad said when Paul began asking the litany of questions that was inevitable. "I've got to tend the horses. I'll see you both later."

"I've got a couple of fires burning and may have to drive back to Dallas tonight." Paul avoided Lily's gaze.

She put her hand on her dad's arm. "What you said in there—"

"We'll talk about it later," he told her, and he left them, walking quickly. There was something agitated in his steps, in his posture.

Lily felt uneasy, watching him, but at Paul's prompt, she walked with him toward AJ's room, filling him in, giving him the gist of AJ's statement to Mackie, and the captain's seeming doubt of its credibility.

"You know, I always felt like Erik was jealous of AJ," Paul said when she'd finished.

"You're the only one." Paul's differing opinion annoyed Lily. "Even AJ is shocked, devastated, really. He thought of Erik like a brother."

"Even brothers can be jealous of one another, Lily. Maybe you're too close to the situation—to the two of them—to see what's really going on here."

"But whatever is motivating Erik—it goes a skosh beyond jealousy, don't you think?" She kept searching her mind for a cause in Erik's past, something large enough, horrible enough, to make him behave in such a monstrous way, but there was nothing. Times they'd spent together at the ranch, the boys had been treated the same. They'd been assigned chores and paid equally for them. They'd been equally praised and fairly disciplined when they broke the rules. Her dad, especially, knew about boys, knew the firm, steady hand they needed. Had Lily been asked, she would have said Erik looked up to her dad, idolized him, in fact. Now she wondered if she knew Erik at all, if she had ever known him.

"Is that Mackie?" Paul asked, nodding at the uniformed man exiting AJ's room.

"Yes," Lily said.

"I'll get a uniformed officer up here on the door," the police captain said, joining them.

"Why? Do you think AJ is going to try to escape?" Sarcasm sharpened Lily's tone.

"It's a precaution," Mackie answered. "For his protection as much as anything. And Shea's, too. She says she's staying."

"In addition to being the captain of the WPD," Lily informed Paul, "Clint is also a longtime friend of my dad's, and even though he's known AJ most of his life and knows the sort of person he is, he thinks AJ was involved in the girls' murders, that he and Erik were in collusion. Never mind that AJ was shot and left to bleed to death."

"Really." The word from Paul was caustic.

"This is my husband, Clint," Lily said. "Paul Isley."

Clint's nod was curt. "We can't rule out any possibility at this point, Mr. Isley. Both your son and Erik Ayala were involved romantically with Ms. Westin. They both had ties to Ms. Kincaid."

"So if Ayala and AJ are in it together, explain to me how my son ended up shot? Or maybe you think AJ shot himself?" Paul glanced at Lily. "Now there's an idea."

"They might have argued," Clint said reasonably. "Any number of things could have gone wrong between them. Like I said before, nothing can be ruled out."

There was a measure of silence, as if Clint was giving Paul time to consider the possibilities. But he didn't need time, did he? Lily glanced at him, waiting for him to say there wasn't a smidgen of evidence to suggest AJ had played any role in the murders of the two girls.

Instead, Paul said, "Let me tell you something, Mackie," and Lily tensed with misgiving at his arrogance. "If anything happens to my son, or his fiancée, it's on you. I'll have your job. Do you understand me? I'll see that you never work in law enforcement again."

Clint's eyes hardened, but his tone was civil when he said, "I understand you're upset."

Paul flung up a hand, dismissing the lawman's effort at goodwill, even the man himself as unworthy. "If you'll excuse me, I'm going to see AJ."

Lily was embarrassed by Paul's blustering, yet on another level she felt it, too, the need for ultimatums: *Protect my son or else.*

"I'll be in touch," Mackie said.

"The truck," Lily said, "that nearly ran Shea and Dru off the road earlier—"

"What about it?"

"Were you aware that Becca and Kate had a similar experience in Dallas right before Becca was killed?"

"We're following up with the Dallas PD on it, Lily. Trust me, we're doing our job regardless of what you, your husband, or Jeb thinks. If there's a connection to the traffic altercation or anything else, we'll find it. We'll get to the bottom of it."

"Not if you can't look farther than AJ, you won't."

"I'm not out to get him, okay? I want the truth like everyone else."

Mackie sounded sincere enough. The trouble, Lily thought, watching him walk away, was that people could say anything, and when it came to saving themselves, most of them did.

Lily was outside AJ's room and just about to step through the door when she caught the mention of Edward's name and realized AJ and Paul were discussing him. She retreated, turning to lean against the wall, aware of her heart beating, the flush that warmed her neck and face.

"He did a good job for me before, Dad," she heard AJ say. "If I need legal help, I don't see a reason to find anyone else."

Lily didn't trust herself to join AJ in his defense of Edward. She wondered if he knew that AJ was safe. Looking down the corridor, she wondered if she could steal a few minutes to call him. But then she heard Dru say, "Shea told me you were arrested before," in a sharp, accusatory voice, and she straightened. *No, you aren't doing this now.*

"That's got nothing to do with anything," Paul said, barely glancing at Lily when she crossed the threshold. "The charges were dismissed."

"She knows that," Shea said. "Mom, I told you—"

"It's unsettling." Dru came away from the window. "I mean, that he was charged with murder before, and now this."

"He was cleared—" Lily began.

"Please, Mom." Shea's eyes on her mother's were half-angry, half-pleading.

Dru fanned a hand at her. *Whatever.* "I think we should go, let AJ rest."

"I'm staying," Shea said, "but you go. I know you're tired."

"I can't leave you here, Shea. Not when we have no idea where Erik is, assuming he's the one behind all of this." Dru looked hard at AJ.

"He is, Mrs. Gallagher, as sick as it makes me. Everything I told Captain Mackie is the truth. I wish you could believe me. I wish I knew where Erik was. I want him caught as bad as you do."

"I'm sorry"—Dru didn't sound at all as if she was—"but I'm not taking chances with my daughter's life."

"Hold on—"

Paul began to speak even as Lily said, "That's unfair—"

Shea's voice overrode them both. "It's not your call to make, Mom. It's mine. Please, go home."

It was a moment before Dru conceded. Lily watched as she lowered her gaze, then her shoulders. She let go a sigh, and Lily had the sense it was a struggle for her—giving up her parental authority. But Shea was grown now. It wasn't as if Dru had a choice.

"I'm sorry." Dru repeated her apology, crossing the room, pausing at the door to look back at Shea. "I'll be the first to admit it if I'm wrong."

An awkward silence lingered in her wake.

AJ broke it. "I didn't have anything to do with any of this." He was looking at his father, and following his gaze, Lily saw it, too, the flash of Paul's doubt, the lack of faith that was very like Dru's lack of faith that mere seconds ago Paul had decried.

Lily set her hand on AJ's shoulder. "Your dad and I know that, honey." She smoothed her voice over the rough saw of her fury.

"You need legal counsel, AJ." Paul was equally cool. "The sooner the better. I'll make some calls."

"No, Dad—"

"Paul?" Lily interrupted. "Since Shea's here to keep an eye on AJ, I think we should go." She divided her glance between AJ and Shea. "Captain Mackie promised to have a uniformed officer outside the door. You'll both be safe."

"Thank you," Shea said. "Thank you for letting me stay."

"You didn't cancel the wedding, did you?" AJ asked.

Lily exchanged a look with Shea and saw she was as unprepared as Lily to respond.

"We talked about it," Shea said tentatively.

"You haven't changed your mind?" AJ sounded panicky.

"No. No!" Shea repeated. "Never, it's just—"

"Well, thank God." He kissed her hand, set it against his cheek. "Because Doc Matthews says I'll get out of here in a couple of days. I can get down the aisle on crutches. I'll crawl if I have to, but we are getting married. Two weeks from tomorrow, right? Today is Friday?"

"Yes, and I want to, AJ, more than anything, but so much has happened."

"I know, but—"

"It's just—people are—they think—"

"I don't care a damn what they think," he said.

But Lily sensed he knew feeling in town was running against him. As Clint had said, the evidence was there to support AJ's guilt. Paul thought AJ needed legal counsel. Even Lily had wavered. Only Shea had remained steadfast in her faith, and Lily loved her for it.

"Our life together—it's all I thought about while I was trapped at the fort." AJ's voice was low and rough. "You're my heart, babe."

Lily glanced at Paul, but he was intent on his phone. When he looked up, she gestured toward the door, launching into a flurry of good-byes. She walked with Paul to the elevator. He pushed the "Down" button.

She shot him a heated look.

"What?"

"How do you suppose it makes AJ feel, knowing you think he's guilty?"

"I can't be concerned about his feelings, Lily. I want to keep him out of prison. Don't you?"

She didn't answer.

He punched the elevator button again. "I guess I'll come to the ranch," he said.

"Fine," Lily said. "I'll pick up something for dinner."

20

Dru was sitting at the table in the breakfast nook early on Saturday morning, an untouched mug of coffee at her elbow, when Shea peeked in at her from the back door, looking worn-out, happy, contrite.

"Are you mad?" she asked.

"I was never mad, Shea," Dru answered. "Worried and scared, but not mad."

"There was a policeman outside AJ's door the whole night."

"Who brought you home?"

"Vanessa. I called her and Leigh last night to tell them about Erik so they'd know to be on the lookout for him."

"You haven't heard anything else?"

"No. I'm going to take a quick shower and go back to the hospital—that is, if I can borrow your car?"

"The service department is bringing over a loaner for you later this morning, if you can wait."

Shea's face fell.

"Fine," Dru said. "I'll drive the loaner."

"AJ wants to go ahead with the wedding." Shea sat down. "They had him up on crutches this morning. They'll probably discharge him on Monday."

Dru was nonplussed. "But the funerals—Becca's and Kate's funerals—will be next week, if not sooner. No one will want to come to a wedding after that."

Shea looked away, blinking, clearing her throat. "Is there coffee? Do you want a refill?" Picking up Dru's mug, she went into the kitchen.

"Maybe rather than cancel, we could postpone the wedding for a month or so." Dru waited, and when Shea didn't respond, she said, "I don't see how we can have a wedding when Erik is still out there. It's not safe."

"I don't think he's the one who ran us off the road yesterday, Mom. I think he probably left town on Thursday after he did his little acting job at the ranch." Shea brought the coffee to the table and sat down again. "The detectives from Dallas came to question AJ last night, and they said every law enforcement agency in Texas is looking for Erik. If he was around here, they'd have found him by now."

"Well, maybe he's just that good at hiding. I hope you won't let your guard down."

Shea stirred cream into her coffee. "I don't think even the Dallas detectives suspect AJ anymore, but you do, don't you?" She looked up. "You still think he's involved."

"Honey, you need to look rationally, and without emotion, at the evidence—"

"You need to stop looking at AJ through the warped lens of your experience with Daddy. That was, what, fifteen years ago?"

"It was twelve," Dru said. "Is that what you think I'm doing?"

"In your mind, every man is a gun waiting to go off. You've never moved forward, never forgiven Dad."

"So what should I have done, Shea?" Dru was tired, out of patience and angry now. "Should I have stayed, trusted your dad wouldn't threaten me with a gun again? Maybe I was wrong, leaving him, but I had a little girl to protect, and I made the only decision that I felt would ensure her safety as well as mine. Just wait until you have a child of your own." Dru stood up, pushed her chair under the table, balancing her hands on the top rail.

"I know it was scary, Mom. You did the right thing getting us out of there. If you hadn't, Dad might never have gotten help."

Dru bit her teeth together. She wasn't the only one fighting tears.

"He was scared, too, Mom, you know?" Shea said softly.

Dru didn't answer.

"He hasn't threatened anyone since then."

"He's never been in a relationship since."

"Because he loves you, Mom, only you."

Dru considered it, Rob's love, and she knew it was real, that what Shea said was true. But she couldn't give that to Shea.

At the sound of the doorbell, she and Shea looked at each. No one came to the front door—except the Jehovah's Witnesses and the police. Ken Carter and his partner had rung Dru's doorbell the night before last, when she had called 911 after Leigh found the cryptic note on her car. *I'm sorry for hurting you. I'm in trouble and I don't think I can stop.* Kate had still been alive when Leigh found the note, and now she wasn't. "I'll get it," Dru said to Shea. "You go take your shower."

But Shea didn't do as instructed. She was still in the breakfast nook when Dru brought Ken Carter into the kitchen. Shea and Ken greeted each other.

"You said you had news," Dru prompted.

"We've been looking at Kate's computer, going through her e-mail, that sort of thing. She's got a Word file she labeled 'Journal.' It's like a diary of her day-to-day activity. Did you know she kept a record like that?" Ken was asking Shea.

"No, but it doesn't surprise me," Shea said. "She was always writing something."

"Well, the most recent entries indicate she wanted to break off her relationship with Erik Ayala."

"Really? Why?" Shea asked.

"We don't have a full answer on that yet, but in her last entry, Thursday night, she wrote that she was going to confront him, possibly on Friday, on their hike. I was hoping you might know what that was about."

"I don't," Shea said. "We told each other pretty much everything, or I thought we did."

"Except for the text messages between her and Becca. She didn't tell you about those."

"No," Shea said.

"Did you know Erik took Becca out one night back in March? According to Kate's journal, she and Erik fought over his wanting to spend money on a four-wheeler."

"Kate told me about the fight and that he got together with Becca, but there wasn't anything to it. He apologized, practically crawled on his knees to Kate. He spent the four-wheeler money on a bracelet for her. She made him take it back. She was practical that way."

"Did she tell you she saw Erik and Becca arguing in the parking lot of the Starbucks near the culinary school in Dallas around three weeks ago, before the semester ended?"

"No." Shea looked at Dru, but she could only shrug. "Did Kate say what the argument was about?"

"Money. Evidently Becca had borrowed a few hundred dollars from him. When Kate asked him why he hadn't told her about the loan, he claimed it was because he didn't want her to be mad at Becca. But Kate suspected it was something else. She thought Erik was cheating on her with Becca, that they'd gone out more than the one time Kate knew about. Kate used the word *intimate* when she described the argument in her journal. She said they looked too wrapped up in each other for it to have been about money."

"Why didn't Katie tell me any of this?" Shea was distraught.

"Well, there's more. She wasn't exactly honest when she said Becca was the one asking for a meeting in those texts they exchanged. It was actually Kate who wanted to see Becca. According to the entry, Kate planned to confront her about the possibility Erik and Becca were having a—a thing, you know."

"We were besties, marrying besties. It was so perfect . . ." Kate's voice rose in Dru's mind. *Was* perfect, not *is* perfect. Why hadn't Dru noticed it that night when Kate had sought her out in the kitchen—her use of the past tense when she'd spoken of her and Erik's plans? What she had noticed was that Kate had seemed discouraged and anxious. But they'd all been anxious.

Shea said, "Kate would have broken their engagement if Erik was cheating on her."

"How do you think Ayala would have reacted if she broke it off with him?" Ken asked.

"Not good," Shea said.

Dru remembered Erik's elation when they'd spoken about Kate in Dru's driveway only days ago. "It would have devastated him," she said.

Enough to kill her? The obvious question hung in the air, unasked.

"Here's the thing," Ken said. "The ME says Becca's pregnancy was about five weeks along, which means it happened in April, around the time Kate and Erik broke up."

Shea looked stunned. "You're saying it was his baby?"

"We can't know for sure—"

"Did Kate suspect?" Shea talked over Ken. "But if she thought he killed Becca over that, why would she agree to meet him? Why didn't she tell me, or the police, or somebody?"

"She didn't have proof, like we don't. Until we get DNA, this is all speculation. Reading Kate's journal, the last entry, she had spoken to Erik, told him of her suspicion. She mentioned the lip liner. Evidently she did remember the two of you buying it, same brand, same shade.

She told Erik about that, too. From what she wrote, she felt she could reason with him, get him to turn himself in. She said he agreed to it, that if after they talked, she thought he should go to the police, then he'd do it. I don't think she realized the kind of mental instability she was dealing with. It doesn't appear from her writings that it crossed her mind she might be putting herself in danger."

Dru moved to Shea's side. "Do you have any word on where Erik is?"

"Not yet. We're working on getting a warrant to search his apartment, but y'all need to be extra careful, because we're thinking—and Dallas PD agrees—Ayala is still in the area, and he's got to be feeling pretty desperate by now. We thought he might try to beat it down to Oaxaca to his mom and her family, and we're trying to get information one way or another on that, but we've had no luck so far. We haven't been able to locate Ms. Ayala, either."

"That's not my heritage . . . Oaxaca isn't my country." Erik had said that to Dru, and he'd seemed offended now that Dru thought of it. He'd seemed to resent she would even suggest there was a connection.

"I doubt he's gone to Oaxaca," she said.

"You've cleared AJ, right?" Shea swiped at her eyes.

"That note Leigh found? We've been able to determine for sure it was written in lip liner, and we found a print on it, a partial, enough to rule out AJ, but he's not off the list entirely."

Shea started to argue.

Ken held up his hand. "It's how the law works, Shea. You just have to roll with it, okay? Let us do our job, and we'll get there."

"The print on the note, could it be Erik's?" Dru asked.

"We're checking now. His prints should be in the system through the military, but so far we've not been able to get hold of them, maybe because they cut him loose. I don't know."

"He was always so helpful and kind," Dru said. "I would never have imagined—"

"It's possible something snapped," Ken said. "People do. They go off the deep end. I can't stress enough how dangerous he is now. You need to keep alert. If you've got a gun and know how to use it, keep it loaded and handy."

"AJ's in more danger than we are," Shea said. "Erik's already tried to kill him."

"We've got an officer with him, but let's hope we get Ayala soon."

Shea's phone rang. She got it from her purse. "It's AJ," she said.

Ken and Dru waited to hear that the call was of no concern before walking to the front door. "I'd keep Shea home if you can," Ken said.

"Trust me," Dru said. "I'm not letting her out of my sight."

She ought to have known better. Shea left to go back to the hospital and AJ as soon as she'd had a shower and changed her clothes.

21

Lily picked up a pizza for dinner, sausage, cheese, and black olives, on the way back to the xL. She wasn't hungry. She didn't imagine her dad or Paul was, either, but she would provide a meal nonetheless. She expected to find both men in the kitchen, but Paul was the only one sitting at the island. He had his phone in his hand, texting, but when he saw her, he shut it off. Something about the furtive way he did it gave Lily a bad feeling.

"Where's Dad?" She set the pizza on the counter. Redolent smells of cheese and sausage made her stomach churn.

"Gone to lie down," Paul said.

"Is he all right?"

"Yeah. Just tired, I think."

She was worried it was more, possibly a whole lot more. What if her dad was losing his mind? She considered sharing her concern with Paul, but when she spoke, all she said was, "I'll make a salad."

"Don't go to the trouble on my account," Paul said.

Lily held his gaze. The air between them was thick with words that needed saying. But she was as weary as her dad. And while she was beyond relieved that AJ was safe, she was heartsick over Erik—that he could have committed such violence, murdered those girls, and injured AJ was no less fathomable or acceptable than if it had been AJ who was responsible. Lily couldn't bear thinking of Winona, of how this would affect her, the enormous devastation it would cause.

"We have to talk," Paul said.

"I want to check on Dad first," Lily said. "Did he go upstairs?"

"No. He's in his office, I think."

Lily felt Paul's eyes tracking her as she left the kitchen. Perversely, she wished he would leave. Be gone. Poof!

Opening the door to her dad's office, she peered in at him. It was dusk; the light was translucent, greenish, swimmy. She crossed the room noiselessly to the couch. He was sleeping, but his face was drawn, his brow furrowed as if in terrible consternation. His eyes twitched in a way Lily found disturbing. She noticed he was holding his cell phone, tightly enough that his knuckles were white.

Oh, Daddy . . .

She lowered her hand to touch his brow, letting it hover there. What was happening in his brain? To his mind? His strong, reliable, singular mind?

Lily drew the light throw from the back of the couch and covered him, phone and all, and left him, closing the door quietly. She couldn't work out her dad's issues now, not with Paul in the kitchen—Paul who would say there was nothing wrong with her father, that her worry was for nothing.

He was back, texting, when she returned to the kitchen, and he looked up at her. "Client," he said as if she'd asked.

Lily retrieved plates, napkins, and silver, setting them on the island.

"I've got a call in to a couple of criminal attorneys in Dallas."

"AJ's not going to need legal representation, Paul."

"Maybe you should be the one talking to Mackie and Bushnell."

"What does that mean?"

Paul held her gaze.

"They still suspect AJ, is that it? And you agree with them. God, you're incredible." Lily turned away, turned back. "Didn't I hear you warn Clint earlier that if anything happened to AJ he'd better fear for his job?"

"You did, and I meant it. What's your point?"

"You truly think AJ killed those girls, don't you?" The knot of Lily's fury pulsed in her throat, beat a tattoo at her temples.

"I don't see the harm in covering all the bases. He needs a lawyer; I'll get him one. And it won't be Edward Dana," Paul added.

"He needs his father and his father's faith."

"But I don't care if he's guilty. He's my son, and it's my job to protect him either way."

"So you'd cover for him if you knew he'd committed murder?"

"I'm not covering for him. I'm hiring legal counsel. Like I said before, I'll do whatever I have to, to keep him out of prison, keep his name, his reputation, and his record clean the way I did last time, the way I did years ago for you."

"But it isn't his name and reputation, or mine, that really matters to you, is it? It's your own. It's the Isley name."

"What do you suppose our lives would have been like if I'd let you or AJ drag our name into the dirt?"

"Your name."

"Fine. Let's play it that way. What kind of lifestyle do you think you would have had all these years if it had become public knowledge that you were an accessory to murder? If it were known that you were some thug's girlfriend, that he robbed a store and murdered a clerk, a seventeen-year-old kid, to get money for a pair of western boots you wanted?"

"What are you talking about?" Lily asked. "I had no idea what Jesse was going to do, and you know it."

"Ah, but I don't, you see. According to Jesse, it was your idea. You wanted those boots. They were handmade of crocodile skin. You remember, don't you? A vendor on the side of the highway had them for sale. Six hundred for the pair. Jesse didn't have that kind of cash, but when he pulled off the highway at the convenience store, you said all he had to do was ask the clerk for it, and he'd hand it over. Jesse told me you laughed when you explained it."

"Because I was joking." Lily's heart was beating so erratically it was difficult to breathe. "How do you know this?"

"I paid Jesse a visit before he was sent to prison. I wanted to know the real truth of what went down that day, not the legal truth. He was happy to tell me in exchange for—I don't remember—like a couple hundred in cash? Cigarette money, he called it."

"You believed him when he said I encouraged him." Lily wasn't asking. "You really think I'm capable of that."

"You do like to dress well."

Lily dropped her gaze, unable to look at Paul or speak for the shame that was thick in her throat, bitter on her tongue. She *had* admired the boots. She had teased Jesse about asking the store clerk for the cash. She'd said once they had it, they could ride back up the highway and buy the boots. She'd been a foolish, thoughtless, irresponsible eighteen-year-old girl, a feckless runaway who thought she knew everything. And a boy was dead because of her. But she'd truly never imagined Jesse would take her joke literally. She hadn't known when he went into the store that he was armed and intent on robbing the place. She'd believed the gun was in the saddlebag, where he kept it.

"You were hell-bent on destroying yourself, Lily. If it hadn't been Jesse, you would have chosen some other loser. AJ's like you in that respect. He's got no sense when it comes to the company he keeps."

"You're our savior, then, is that it?" Lily raked her hair behind her ears.

"You were going nowhere except prison. It was the same with AJ. At least you can pack a boy off to the military. I guess your dad could have done the same for you—"

"Or he could give me away in marriage. The military, even prison, would have been easier. At least it would be over by now."

Paul laughed, a short, bitter sound.

"Did you ever love me?" Lily flattened her palm to her chest. "Not your idea of me. Not the woman you have tried for years to mold me into—"

"You were beautiful, Lily, and for all your wildness, you were so innocent. Fragile and vulnerable."

"It's always been about control with you, hasn't it?" she said after a moment. "I didn't want to see it, but I played into it; I went along. It's what I always do." She was talking more to herself than to Paul. Turning from him, she went to lean stiff-armed against the counter. It was full dark now, and the kitchen window over the sink was black. There was nothing to see but her own ghostly reflection. "I've been so blind, following you, even Dad—I don't know myself who I am."

"Well, I think that might be a bit of an overstatement," Paul said, and she hated it, the condescending note in his voice, the way he patronized her.

"I think you need to go," she said, turning to him, speaking quietly. "Now?"

"There's a Motel 6 in Wyatt if you don't want to drive back to Dallas tonight."

He nudged the plates she'd brought to the island, toyed with the forks. "I was going to wait until this business with AJ was settled, but maybe I'll just get it out of the way now."

Somehow Lily knew what he was going to say, but she wasn't going to let on. She wasn't going to help him.

"I think we should separate."

"You make it sound as if you think we have a chance. Do you?"

"Truth?" He met her glance.

She waited.

"I'm seeing someone. I'm in love with her. I didn't mean for it to happen, but matters of the heart—"

"Please stop."

His mouth closed. A fed-up sort of impatience fished through his eyes. He wanted to be done with her, with their marriage. He was done. The old Groucho Marx joke ran through her mind: *"Marriage is a wonderful institution, but who wants to live in an institution?"* If that was true, Paul had turned off the lights and left the building. Closed the door on twenty-seven years of wedded bliss without warning. Or, she guessed the warnings had been there; she'd chosen to ignore them.

"Who is it?" Lily didn't know why she asked.

"Pilar Dix, if you've just got to know."

"Jerry's wife?"

"Ex. They were divorced last year."

"He doesn't mind?"

"No."

"Didn't Pilar just have twins?"

"Three years ago. They aren't mine, if that's what you're asking." He shuddered slightly.

She wondered if he really thought he could do it, be a father to toddlers. He'd hire a nanny, no doubt.

He stood up, pulling his keys from his pocket. "I'll call," he said.

She nodded. They didn't say good-bye.

· · ·

She didn't think she would sleep, but she did, falling off the ledge of consciousness into an abyss so deep that when she heard the phone ring—the landline out in the hallway—she had the sense it had been ringing for hours. It was a struggle to waken, to lever herself into a sitting position.

She ran her hands through her sleep-matted hair, registered the glowy red numbers, 6:25, on the nightstand clock. Her mind felt logy and soft. She wasn't certain of her footing and staggered a bit when she stood up, catching her hand on the mirrored vanity corner to steady herself.

She heard her dad's tread on the stair.

"I'll get it, Dad," she called out to him.

He flipped on the hallway light, and their eyes met, blinking. She saw her own worry reflected in his gaze.

Lily picked up the heavy receiver. "Hello?"

"Lily! Oh, Lily, thank God!"

"Winona?"

"Yes, yes. Can you come? It's Erik. He's here."

"Where are you?"

"Home. I got in a few hours ago. I didn't expect Erik would be here. He scared me when I came in. He was sitting on the couch, in the dark. He—Lily, he has a gun. He says he hurt AJ. Is it true?"

"Oh my God, Win! You have to get away from him. Where are you now? Where is he? Did you call the police?"

"No. I'm in the bathroom. He is still in the living room, I think. He told me—he said the girls, Becca and Kate, Shea's and AJ's friends—Erik says they're dead, that he—he—" Win's voice broke and fell into small hurt sounds.

"Win? Oh, Win—" Lily fought to keep the panic from her voice. "Hang on, okay? I'm coming. I'll call the police. Just stay away from him, okay? He's not—not stable, not right in his head."

"I know. He's talking so crazy, going to shoot me. Going to shoot himself. What is the matter with him? Do you know? He was fine when we last talked—yesterday. I think it was yesterday—"

"What's happening? Is it Erik? He's there with her?"

Lily glanced at her dad. "Yes. He has a gun. He says he's going to kill them both."

"Tell her I'll be there in five minutes."

"We need the police."

"Call them, but I'm going now. You don't wait for the cops when a dog's gone mad." He disappeared down the stairs.

"Lily? Is it true, all these terrible things Erik is saying? He's never harmed anyone in his whole life. I want someone to wake me up, to tell me—oh no—" Win's protest ended in an abrupt shriek.

"Win?" Heart beating wildly in her chest, Lily called her name. She heard a crack as if wood had been splintered. She heard angry shouts and recognized Erik's voice. She heard a clattering sound, as if Winona's phone had fallen to the tile floor, and then she heard . . . nothing.

Nothing.

"Winona?" Lily bit her teeth together, waited.

Nothing.

Dropping the receiver back into the cradle, she shouted, "Dad? Daddy, wait, I'm coming with you." Lily went into her bedroom, pulled on her boots, got her cell phone. She was dialing 911 as she ran down the stairs. There was no one in the kitchen. She flew out the back door just as her dad was wheeling the Jeep around the corner of the barn toward the old service road.

She shouted, running after him, waving her arms. She'd almost given up when he stopped. Reaching the Jeep, she yanked open the door, threw herself into the seat. "Go!" she said to him. "Hurry." And when the 911 dispatcher asked, Lily gave the woman their location and a brief summary of the facts. But it wasn't really necessary. At the mention of Erik Ayala's name, the woman indicated she knew the police were looking for him.

The operator left the line for several moments, and when she came back, it was to advise Lily that patrol cars were en route. "How far out of town are you?" the woman asked.

"Thirty minutes, at least," Lily answered.

"A lot of damn shit can go down in thirty minutes," her dad said.

Lily looked at him, and then down at his shotgun firmly wedged between the seats.

22

Winona's house looked deserted. The front porch was shadowed, the windows dark. Except for the slow, measured crunch of the Jeep's tires against the caliche, there wasn't a sound. Not even the birds were awake.

"Let's wait for the police, Dad," Lily said.

"He's not going to try anything with me." Her dad pulled off the road, some fifteen feet from the porch. "I've got the shotgun if he does."

"But Winona's in there."

"Stay in the Jeep, Sissy." He issued the order as she was getting out, and when he saw she had no intention of obeying him, he said, "I shouldn't have let you come."

She held his gaze. "Winona said he was going to kill her, Dad, and then himself."

"He's not going to hurt anyone else if I've got one goddamn thing to say about it."

The front door opened suddenly, making Lily flinch. Her dad raised the shotgun.

Erik came out onto the porch. His clothes, filthy and wrinkled, were the same he'd been dressed in on Thursday when he'd made lunch in the kitchen at the xL. *"AJ is my brother,"* he'd said that day. *"You've been like a mother to me,"* he'd told her. Incongruously, his feet were bare, and for a moment, Lily's attention was riveted there—to his feet—but then he said, "I wondered when you'd show up, old man," and her gaze rose, first snagging on the gun in his hand—she recognized AJ's .45—then going to Erik's face. His gaze was locked on her dad. Lily wondered if he even realized she was here.

"Put the gun down, Erik," her dad said.

Lily heard the sound of tires and prayed it was the police, but when she looked over her shoulder, she saw a faded red SUV, coming fast around the curve, dust swirling in the new-morning light. Dru? But no, it was Shea driving, Lily saw, and AJ was riding in the passenger seat.

"What are you doing here?" Lily asked AJ as soon as he'd maneuvered himself out of the car. "You shouldn't be out of bed. You're white as a sheet."

"Get back to the hospital."

"No, Granddad." AJ gripped the top of the SUV's door, keeping himself upright.

"He made me bring him." Shea pulled crutches from the backseat. "He was going to hijack an ambulance, or something worse."

"But how did you—?" Lily's uncertain glance wavered from Shea to AJ. He was dressed in scrubs. The right pant leg had been jaggedly scissored off at the thigh to accommodate the compression bandage.

AJ thrust his chin at Erik. "He called Shea and told her there was something he needed me to hear before he checked himself out."

Lily took a few steps toward AJ, as if to force him back into the car. "You're bleeding."

He looked at the bloom of red midway down his thigh. "It's fine."

"Hurts like a bitch, I bet," Erik said.

"Put the gun down, Erik, and we'll talk." Lily's dad's voice was quiet. It was the voice he used with the livestock when they were spooked and liable to go berserk.

"Like hell, old man. Mom and I are done listening to you, done keeping your secrets. It was all lies and bullshit anyway, wasn't it, you old fuck?"

Lily stared at Erik, not believing that this wild, foul-talking man was the same as the Erik she'd known from infancy. The change in him seemed impossible; it made her head swim.

Winona crept into the open doorway, and Lily saw her own shock mirrored in Winona's eyes. But there was some other element working in Winona's expression, too. Was it remorse? Apology? *What is this about?* Lily opened her mouth to ask, but Winona's attention had shifted, and she was looking at Lily's dad now. He was standing a few feet to Lily's right and a little closer to the porch, and while he held the shotgun easily enough, Lily knew that could change in less than a second, less than an eye blink. He was a crack shot.

AJ came to stand beside Lily, and they exchanged a glance. Her heart was hammering so loudly, she wondered if he could hear it.

"We can't talk unless you put the gun down," her dad said to Erik.

"I can talk just fine." Erik swung the .45 at AJ. "You think you're such a big fuckin' hero. Who's the hero now, huh?"

"Why don't you just say what's on your mind, Erik? We're all friends here." AJ held his ground, and Lily marveled that he could.

"Ha! We're a lot more than friends, *vato*."

"What do you mean?" AJ asked.

Winona came over the threshold onto the porch. "Erik, no—"

"I'm done, *Mamita*. We both are. Can't you see? We're not getting a fucking dime. Jeb lied to you."

Was he talking about an inheritance? Lily imagined, although she didn't really know for sure, that Erik was included in her dad's will, along with Winona. Her father wouldn't leave them out. They were family.

Family . . .

The word resonated in Lily's brain. The weight of it, its possible meaning, fell like a stone to the floor of her gut. She was cold, suddenly so cold. "Dad?" She glanced sidelong at him.

But he wouldn't look at her. His chin was lowered nearly to his chest; his eyes were closed. He looked done in, beaten—old and frail. Lily had never thought of him as frail. Not even after he'd fallen the other day.

"What kind of a game is this, Erik?" AJ hitched forward on his crutches. "You murdered Becca and then Kate. You shot me. You've twisted the evidence, trying to frame me—"

"That part was easy. It helped you'd been arrested before. You saw how the cops—everybody went for it."

"We were friends, Erik. Granddad has never been anything but kind to you and your mom. He's given you everything. He built this house—"

"You want to know why? Guilt."

Winona grasped Erik's arm. "No, *mijo*. Not like this. Not like this." She clung to him, desperate to silence him.

He shook her off. "Guilt," he repeated.

"He's crazy," AJ said softly, as if he meant only Lily to hear.

She glanced past him at Shea, standing on his other side, looking shell-shocked. They all were. Where were the police?

"Can you explain what Erik is saying, Winona?" Lily appealed to his mother.

But she only shook her head and sank to her knees as if she no longer had the strength to support herself. Her braid was unwound, and its tip dragged in the dust on the porch floor. Somehow, the sight loosened a memory in Lily's mind from a long-ago morning. She'd been maybe fifteen or sixteen when she'd gone into her dad's bathroom, the bathroom he'd once shared with her mother, and found a robe—Winona's robe—hanging on a hook on the back of the door. She'd known it was Winona's because she'd often stayed overnight with Win.

When she was angry with her dad.

When she needed a mother's touch, a friend to talk to. Another woman.

Win had been all those things.

Now, holding her eyes, a knowing came to Lily, and Winona saw that it had come and wrenched her gaze away. Her shoulders heaved, but if she was crying, she made no sound.

Lily looked at her dad. "Is Erik your son?" she asked. "Yours and Winona's?"

"You got it, Lily." Erik was excited. "That's the goddamn answer to the million-dollar question of who in the fuck I am—your half brother and AJ's uncle." Erik laughed, but it was a harsh, broken sound. "It's crazy, isn't it? But it's true; there's paperwork on it."

"Did you just find out?" Lily addressed Erik as if she believed what he was saying. She spoke as if the discussion, the situation, was rational and comprehensible, but inside she was reeling.

"I've known it nearly all my life, but *Mamita* said we could never tell anyone. She said if word ever got out, the good life we had here would end and we'd have to go back to Oaxaca to her family. No way was I going there, so I kept their secret. It was part of the deal."

"We thought it was best for him, for everyone." Lily's dad spoke for the first time.

Lily stared at him, mute. AJ, too, seemed incapable of speech.

"Bullshit! You never wanted me."

"Erik." Winona's protest was laced with sorrow.

He rounded on her. "He may care about you, but he's treated me like shit my whole life." Erik looked out at the rest of them. "How do you have a kid, watch him grow up right under your nose, and never

246

recognize him? Never call him son? He's my dad"—his voice broke—
"but I couldn't call him that. Do you know what that's like?"

"What deal are you talking about?" AJ asked.

"Maybe we could all go inside—"

"No, Granddad. Let Erik say what his problem is."

"You want to know, *vato*? He cut me out of his will. That's my
problem. All these years I keep his secret, keep my mouth shut about
who I am, figuring it's going to be worth it. I'll get my share of his
estate, something like a quarter million. That was the deal, the promise
he made Mom. If I never let on I was as much an Axel as you or Lily,
he'd cut me in for my share. Isn't that right, old man?"

"You didn't want any part of the ranch, Erik. I asked you to come
on as my foreman, but you turned me down flat. Three times. You left
me no choice. I'm not leaving the xL to somebody who doesn't give a
shit about it."

"I don't see AJ taking on the job of foreman, but you didn't cut him
out of your will, did you?" Erik swung his gaze to AJ. "Do you know
how it's been for me, bro? Hearing you call him Granddad, watching
how he treated you with respect like you mean something to him. Like
you're something more to him than the dirt under his boot heel?"

"Jesus, Erik," AJ began, "I didn't know anything about any of this."

"You were never shit to me." Erik's voice rose, shattering in the air
like so much glass. "A pain in the ass. A snot-nosed kid I had to look
out for. Another fucking responsibility Jeb piled on me."

Lily moved closer to AJ, as if she might shield him from the lash
of Erik's words. She wanted to speak, to somehow defuse the hostility,
but her tongue felt rooted to the floor of her mouth.

"So we join the marines, right?" Quieting, Erik swiped his eyes
and under his nose. "I wash out and you come home a hero, and I've
got to deal with the bullshit all over again—how you're better, stronger,
smarter. I'm sick of it. Sick of walking ten paces behind you like I'm
your damn lackey."

"But why did you kill Becca and Kate?" AJ raised his voice. "To get back at me? What?"

"You realize, don't you, that Becca was in love with you. Like, crazy obsessed."

"I doubt that, Erik," AJ said. "We dated, but it was never serious, and, anyway, what does that have to do with—"

"She was preggers, *vato*. She told me she wished it was your kid. But no, hell no, my shitty luck, it was mine, and she's all like I had to 'do the right thing.'"

"She wanted you to marry her, is that it?" AJ asked. "And what? You got pissed?"

"She was going to tell Kate about the kid. I couldn't let her do that. Kate was the best thing that ever happened to me, and after I saw how Jeb screwed me over, she was the only thing, the only good thing, I had left. I told Becca I'd pay for an abortion. Hell, I gave her the money last month."

"It wasn't just a loan," Shea said.

Erik looked at her.

"Kate kept a journal. She wrote that she knew when she saw you and Becca fighting that it was about more than a loan."

"She thought I was cheating on her with Becca. Can you believe it? It broke me, you know? She didn't believe me when I said I'd only slipped the one time. She wouldn't let it go. She texted Becca last Tuesday and said they had to meet. Becca freaked and called me, making all kinds of threats. I told her to meet me at AJ's. I knew he'd be working, and I figured I'd have time to reason with her. But no, hell no. The second I said the word *abortion*, she went all bat shit, called me a murderer. I said, 'I'll show you murder, bitch.' I was only playing when I grabbed her around her neck. I just wanted her to understand I was serious about not wanting the kid. After a minute I tried letting her up, but she screamed like a fucking hyena. I was scared the neighbors would hear." Erik paced now, a short path, toward Winona.

"Give me the gun, *mijo*," she said, reaching out her hand. Erik ignored her, walking back to the top of the porch steps.

Lily saw her dad pull the butt of the shotgun to his shoulder and thought, *No*, and as if he heard her, he lowered the weapon. Or maybe he couldn't bring himself to shoot Erik. *"When it comes to shooting someone—another human being—you can lose your nerve."* He'd said that to her at the hospital on Friday—a scant forty-eight hours ago—in reference to AJ, and it was ironic, given that he hadn't known or even suspected Erik was the shooter who'd lost his nerve. Now her dad was in the same place, pointing a gun at someone he purported to love. His son.

His son. The revelation had all the substantiality of a balloon in the wind.

"She kept fighting me." Erik walked back to the head of the steps. "I just wanted her to get the damn abortion and keep her mouth shut. I get so goddamn sick and tired of everybody screwing me over, you know?" He looked out at them in anticipation of their agreement, as if they must see his reaction was one that any of them might have, sane and justified.

Over the dull thudding of her heart, Lily listened for the sound of a siren, praying for it, but there was nothing, not even in the far distance. Maybe the police wouldn't use them, she thought. Maybe they were here already, in the trees, and they would come out, guns drawn, any second.

"Bec went limp, finally," Erik said. "I gotta say it was a relief. But then I got scared. I mean, what if she woke up? I'd seen your knife, bro, in the kitchen sink." Erik addressed AJ. "You left it out." He shrugged. "I had to be sure."

"What about Kate, Erik?" Shea stepped forward. "You just said she was the best thing that ever happened to you, but you killed her. Why?"

His expression softened; his shoulders slumped. "You and Katie— you girls were so damn cute, you know? So funny and sweet." He grinned, but his eyes were horrible, bottomless black wells of regret. He looked at AJ. "You remember, *vato*, how it was going to be, the four of us? Living on the same street, raising our kids together? You remember how they talked about it? Kate and Shea? 'Besties marrying besties,' that's what they said. Our giggle girls. Remember how we called them that?"

"I remember all of that, bro," AJ said, and his voice was thick, hurt.

Erik addressed Shea. "Thursday night when I left the note on Leigh's car—"

"The one you tried to make look as if AJ wrote?" An undercurrent of fury heated Shea's voice.

"Kate called me when she left your house. She knew—well, she didn't know for sure it was me and not AJ who killed Becca, but I knew it wasn't going to be long until she—until everyone figured it out." Erik shoved his hand over his head. "God, I was scared. I knew by then I was done, that it was over. Kate would break our engagement. Losing her, our life together—that was just the fucking cherry on top of the shit sundae that is my life."

The pause was taut, fragile.

Erik broke it. "I got her to agree to go on one last hike, give me one chance to talk it through in person. I said I could explain, and if afterward she thought I should go to the cops, I would. She went for it. You know how she was."

"The story you told, that Kate was confused about where you were meeting, you made that up, didn't you?" Shea asked.

"Yeah, it was messed up. I never figured she'd get found so fast. But I made so damn many mistakes. Like taking AJ to the fort. I should have known it would be about the first place the old man would look." Erik gestured at AJ. "I should have killed you right off, but I couldn't, *vato*, you know?"

"But you could kill Katie?" Shea was anguished, furious.

"I couldn't let her go to the cops. And I'm a shit for it. I know that."
He raised the .45 to his head.

"No, *hijo!*" Winona scrambled to her feet. "Give it to me; *por favor, te lo suplico.*"

"Don't do it, Erik."

Lily glanced at her dad as he took a step, then another, over the rough ground.

"I don't know what started this," he said, "but it's over now. Give your mother the gun."

Winona said, "You left your will out on your desk, and he saw it, Jeb. That's what started this, that's when he knew you had broken your promise—"

"No. I would never do that."

"I didn't want to believe it, either, but Erik wouldn't lie. You meant him to see, didn't you? You couldn't tell him or me to our face how you have lied to us all these years, could you? He's nothing to you, isn't that right? Your own son—"

"My father, and his father before him, poured their sweat and blood into this land. They built the xL brand and made it count for something. I carried on the tradition, worked my ass off, because that's what it takes. But Erik's not into hard work. He doesn't like getting his hands dirty. He'd rather sell cars."

"The way you have talked about them to me, your father and grandfather would never have broken a promise they made. They would never have broken a man's heart, his spirit. This is on you, Jeb Axel. This, today"—the sweep of Winona's arm encompassed them all—"and everything else Erik has done. You drove him to it. How could you?"

Lily waited, they all did, for her dad to answer, but there was only the sound of the wind rifling the trees, an uneven hand.

AJ said, "Erik, give your mom the gun. Or give it to me." He hitched forward on his crutches.

Erik jerked the .45 from his head and pointed it at AJ.

Lily heard her dad yell, "No, goddamn it!"

She was aware of Shea coming around AJ as if she would shield him. It was automatic when Lily reached out to steady him and in doing so found she had her arms around them both, AJ and Shea, with her back presented to Erik, a target.

Then the awful pause.

The horrible second that dragged into forever, while she waited for the sound of the bullet ripping through the air, ripping into her spine. And a prayer filled her mind that it would not pass through her to strike AJ or Shea. Dru would be devastated to lose Shea, her daughter for whom Lily had no doubt she would lay down her life. Winona, too, would give her life for Erik, regardless of his monstrous acts. As mothers they shared in this, the undying devotion to their children. For they are always your children, no matter their age. They are your children, too, regardless of their mistakes or even the horrors they perpetrate. Lily prayed for Winona, because even if she were to give her life for Erik, it wouldn't save him from what he'd done.

"Drop the gun, Erik!"

It was her dad shouting.

AJ broke from Lily's grasp, staggering, almost falling.

And now the shot came. Finally. Cracking the air, followed by AJ's shout: "Granddad!"

Turning, Lily saw her dad crumpled on his side on the porch, Erik on his hands and knees, struggling for breath. Winona stood over them, holding the .45 in her shaking grasp. Somehow, AJ reached the porch first, and taking the gun from Winona, he ordered Erik to sit against the wall.

Lily and Shea ran up the porch steps. Shea went to AJ's side, but Lily knelt beside her dad. He rolled onto his back.

"I'm okay," he said. "Just winded." He pulled himself upright.

"Erik didn't shoot you?"

"No, he couldn't do it. At the last minute, he shot into the air. I tackled him, and Win got the gun."

"Thank God." Lily sat back on her heels, and on hearing sirens in the distance, she felt a gritty wash of relief. She glanced over her shoulder at Winona, weeping softly, and past her at Erik. But if he registered Lily's attention, it didn't show. His eyes were glassy, eerily vacant of expression.

She remembered a summer visit from years ago when he came down with strep throat. His eyes had been empty of awareness then, too, glazed with fever that at its highest had registered 104. She'd fed him ice chips with a spoon. She and Win and her dad had traded off sleeping nights in an armchair next to Erik's bed. When his fever finally broke, they'd known he was feeling better when he managed to croak out a request for ice cream. Lily's dad had driven to town for it, and without asking, he'd known to buy rocky road, Erik's favorite. Her dad had bought grape Popsicles, too, and chocolate pudding. And when AJ spiked a fever mere hours after Erik began to recover, they went through the whole routine again. After both boys were well, it had rained for several days. They'd worked puzzles and played endless games of Risk that Lily's dad had let AJ and Erik take turns winning, out on the porch.

If she closed her eyes now, she would hear the echoes of their blithe, untroubled laughter; she would see how the damp wind had ruffled their hair. She didn't close her eyes.

She helped her dad get to his feet, and a look passed between them, one that contained his acknowledgment of the secrets he had kept from her and from AJ. He would have to own them and his betrayal of her, AJ, Erik, and Winona; he would have to explain no matter what it cost him. She followed his glance when it shifted to Winona. There was such anguish in Winona's eyes; it knifed Lily's heart.

In her father's eyes, Lily saw his love for Winona. Lily saw how he wanted to go to her, to support her, and he would have, but Win's posture, the set of her shoulders, her rigid spine, warned him off. Words might have been said at that point. Raw truths might have been revealed in those initial moments following the horrific scene they'd passed through. They were all vulnerable, all at the mercy of a volatile mix of emotions, but it was then that the Wyatt police rolled up, two squad cars, five officers—nearly the entire force, and after that, all the talking that was done was to them.

23

Lily sat in an interrogation room giving Sergeant Ken Carter her account of the events that had unfolded that morning, beginning with Winona's predawn phone call. A tape recorder sat in the middle of the scarred table, and she spoke to it, reciting the details she remembered in a low voice. When she continued to shiver, Ken brought her a thin blanket, and she draped it over her shoulders. He said her shivering was the effect of the adrenaline leaving her body as much as from the AC.

Sitting down again, he read from his notes, telling her what they'd found upon executing the search warrant at Erik's apartment, which they'd done at roughly the same time Winona had dialed the ranch house landline. Among other items there had been bloody clothes and a letter written by Erik, addressed *To whom it may concern*, in which he rambled on about the perceived injustices that he felt had been perpetrated on him from birth.

Ken said, "We found a lip-liner pencil that looks to be the same color as the one used to write the notes, the one Leigh found under her windshield wiper and the one that was found with Becca. It's possible it belonged to her, or it might have been Shea's or Kate's. We'll send it to the lab, see if it's a match. We also talked to a neighbor at the complex who said that late on the night of Becca's murder, Erik asked to borrow his scooter. The neighbor saw Erik loading it into the back of a white pickup truck."

"That's how he got back to town then, after he set AJ's truck on fire. He rode the scooter," Lily said.

"Took some planning all the way around. Maybe the murders weren't premeditated, but framing AJ sure was." Ken paused, seeming to consider.

"What?" Lily asked.

"Well, you know some of what Erik did, it's like he also considered making it look like a sexual assault."

"Because of how Becca was found, partially nude," Lily said. It sounded better than saying Becca's pants had been yanked to her ankles.

"Yeah," Ken said, "but the ME found no sign of it."

A small consolation, Lily thought, that Becca hadn't suffered that further profane indignity at least. She said, "Erik is the one who called me and asked for the passport."

"Yeah, and he planted AJ's laptop and cell phone at the bus station. He talked to the pilot, too. Erik and AJ are roughly the same height and build. From a distance, wearing hoodies, they might look pretty much the same to someone who didn't see them regularly."

"He left the charm where the police would find it after he—after he—"

"Pushed Kate to her death. Yeah."

Lily tightened the blanket around her shoulders. "It takes my breath, what he's done. He was as distraught, as grief stricken, as all of us were. How does someone do that?"

"It's hard to understand, especially when you think you know somebody. Maybe he snapped, reading Jeb's will, finding out like that, that he'd been cut off."

Lily hated it, Ken knowing the contents of her dad's will, something so personal to her family. But their lives would be laid bare now, fodder for the gossip mill. That was how it worked in Wyatt. "I taught him to tie his shoes," she said softly.

Several moments passed.

Lily found Ken's gaze again. "I was so shocked when AJ showed up at Winona's. Wasn't there an officer posted at his door?"

"Well, we'd executed the warrant on Ayala's apartment by then, and we knew AJ wasn't involved, so we pulled the officer. No one saw AJ leave."

"Shea said no one could have stopped him if they'd tried. I just hope he hasn't made everything worse."

"I don't think so. He's back in his room; he's seen the doc. He's going to be okay. Shea's with him, and one of the sergeants is there, getting their statements. Don't worry."

"What about Dad? How is he holding up?"

"He's with Captain Mackie. They're about done, too." Ken shut off the recorder. "All of this, having y'all in, taking down your witness statements, it's just a formality. We've got the picture now, or most of it, anyway."

"It's not a very good one, is it?" Lily clenched her teeth, refusing to give up her tears to this man. He had already seen into the darkest chamber of her family's heart. He'd been allowed to trespass through secret-filled rooms, where it had sickened her to go. She thought of her father's betrayal and the devastation it caused that had played such a huge role in what Erik had done. She thought of Erik's dream. What he'd wanted was so simple—Kate and children in a yard in front of a house down the street from AJ and Shea. The four of them, good friends, raising their families together. The inheritance Erik had been promised—he would have counted on it to provide financial security for his family. But her father had jerked that away, and Becca and then Kate had threatened to expose him, and he'd snapped, as Ken said. If only her father had acknowledged Erik as his son; if only he'd openly recognized Erik as a blood relation, an Axel, and an equally revered heir—but, no. Her dad had chosen to keep Erik's true connection to the family secret, as if he was ashamed. And Lily was awfully afraid she knew why, that it was out of deference to her. Had he thought she couldn't handle it? Had he been afraid of her judgment?

Or was it his own judgment of himself, his own bias he couldn't face?

"Winona—is she still here?" Lily asked Ken.

He nodded. "It's a hell of a thing, you know—what her son has done, but she's holding up. She's a strong lady."

"Yes," Lily said. She and Win hadn't spoken before being brought here. She couldn't imagine the level of Win's grief and confusion. Nor could she imagine what would come of them now, how they would go on from here. "What about Erik? He's here, too?"

"Yeah, but he'll probably be transported to Dallas later in the week for arraignment; the judge will read the charges against him and set bail, or not, depending. I'd say it's likely not."

"Can I see him?" *Did she really want to?* Lily wondered.

"Well, he's asked to be left alone. He doesn't even want to see his mom."

Lily nodded, feeling relieved, as if of an onerous duty. She had no idea what she would say to him. *I forgive you?* It felt way too soon to for that.

. . .

An officer drove them back to Winona's. Lily's dad rode in front. Winona and Lily were in back, heads turned from each other, staring from the windows as if the scenery mattered. But there was too much baggage in the car with them, too many emotion-packed suitcases, taking up the space, all the air. Lily felt that. How overwhelming it was.

She was startled when her dad turned to Winona, leaning around the passenger seat. "I'll pay," he said. "For a lawyer. Erik's legal expenses. If the judge sets bail, I'll pay it."

"He won't," Winona said in a wooden voice to the window. She was hunched over; her braid was caught against the seat. Lily wanted to free it. She wanted to wind it into the coronet Winona always wore like a crown. She wanted to restore Win, her dignity, her gentle spirit.

Lily set her hand on the seat between them.

She thought her dad would turn away, but he didn't. Neither did he say anything, not for a long time. Miles passed before he spoke again. "I'm sorry," he said, including both Lily and Winona in his glance.

"I am leaving the ranch," Winona said. "I will not be back. You can do what you want with the house. I don't want it. But I will take your offer to help Erik. Yes, I will, because he is our son, we made him, we raised him, and it is only right now for us to help him the best we can. We have to try"—she faltered—"try and make—make this right."

Lily's throat closed. She felt Winona grasp her fingers, but she couldn't look. She would lose it if she looked, and Win didn't need that.

• • •

Lily drove the Jeep home. Her dad, head bent to the backrest, kept his eyes closed as if that would stop her, the interrogation that he had to know was coming, and her questions would be harder to answer by far than those the police had asked.

"How could you hide it, Dad, all these years? Never mind me. How could you do that to your own son and a woman I presume you love?"

I'll stop this car. She was on the verge of saying it, that she'd pull over until he talked to her, but then he said, "We didn't want to hurt either of you." He straightened, bent his head to his hand, pinching the bridge of his nose.

"Did you think I'd be mad? Even if I had been, it would have been on Mama's account, and I would have gotten over it. You must know that much about me, Dad. It's not as if I'm so judgmental. After Mama died, I would have been glad to know you'd found someone. Especially Winona. She was like a mother to me. You know that."

"It wasn't your judgment that concerned me, Sissy. It was everyone else's."

"Since when have you given a hoot in hell what anyone thinks of you?"

"It wasn't what they thought of me that worried me. It's what they would have thought of Win, what they would have said about her if they'd known about us. I didn't want a whiff of that to touch her or Erik after he was born."

"No one would have thought a thing of it if you'd married Win. Or even if you hadn't. No one cares about that anymore. Win was living at the xL. She's single, you're single. She's beautiful. Probably half the town suspects anyway. It's the secrecy that is so—so terrible, just unforgivable, really. It's as if you're the one who's ashamed of them."

"I built them a house so they'd be close."

"Keeping up appearances, I guess." Sarcasm edged Lily's voice.

"I was a father to that boy in every way I felt that I could be. I fed him, bought his clothes, helped him with his homework, taught him to ride and to shoot. He had chores, responsibilities, but he was lazy."

"I've heard you call AJ lazy."

"Yeah, maybe sometimes. But AJ's got heart; he's got passion for his work. Erik doesn't."

"So you cut him out of your will without even consulting his mother."

"It was stupid, a stupid move on my part. I don't know what to do about it, how to make it up. I can pay for his defense, and I will. I'll get him and Win whatever they need."

"Yes," Lily said. "But I don't know that you can ever make it up."

∙ ∙ ∙

Lily didn't explain it to Paul when she called him later, beyond saying that what had set Erik off was family related and rooted in the past. He was behind bars; AJ was free and safe, and the ordeal was over.

"I'm not family anymore, I guess."

"By your own choice."

"So, what do you want to do?"

"Nothing right now," she said. "I'm staying on here. AJ needs me."

"What will you tell him? About us, I mean."

"The truth," she said. "That you're involved with Pilar Dix."

Paul didn't like it. She knew by the impatient intake of his breath, the click his teeth made when he set them together. The truth wasn't going to enhance his image. Too bad, she thought.

"I was going to drive down this evening, but maybe I'll wait. Will you let AJ know—" Paul stopped, seeming to consider.

Lily tried to imagine what he wanted AJ to know—that he had never doubted AJ's innocence? That was a lie. That even though he'd cheated on her, he was still worthy of AJ's respect? That, too, was a lie. If she was honest, she'd cheated on Paul with Edward. Even if it was only emotionally, she wasn't proud of it. But the one thing she would never do would be to put AJ in the middle of her marital difficulties in a way that would force him to choose one of his parents over the other. AJ was an adult; he could make up his own mind about the sort of man his father was.

24

Dru went to the hospital on Sunday, the evening before AJ was to be discharged. Shea was the only other person there, and when she caught sight of Dru, her eyes widened. Dru hadn't told her she was coming. She went to AJ's bedside, steeling herself.

Unlike Shea, he met her gaze as if he'd been expecting her. She gripped the side rail. "I'm sorry," she said, and she heard the quick, astonished intake of Shea's breath. "I jumped to conclusions about you that aren't true."

"It's okay," he said. "If I had a daughter like Shea, I'd be just like you."

"It's hard for me, because of Shea's dad." Dru glanced at Shea.

AJ glanced at her, too. "She told me," he said, and then paused, taking a moment. He wiped his face, let out a gust of air. "I know I've got PTSD, that I probably need help."

It cost him, admitting it. Dru could see that it did.

Shea slid her palm over his hand.

"I haven't wanted to admit it. I'm afraid of how people will look at me, what they'll think. I figured I could—that I should, you know, tough it out, that I ought to be able to control it, my emotions, my temper. I mean, I'm a soldier, right? A marine. I should just get through it, drive on—"

"You're human, AJ." Dru's defense came unbidden out of the swift bloom of her sympathy, and she was surprised by it. But she realized she didn't regret it. She was only telling the truth. "My God, when you consider what you went through over there, what all of you soldiers go through, not to mention what's just happened. Erik could have killed you—"

"I'm scared is what I am." AJ looked at Dru, and she could see it, the fear shadowing his eyes, but there was something else in his expression, too. Something harder and more determined. "I promise you I will never harm Shea, Mrs. Gallagher."

"Dru," she corrected softly.

"He's going to get help, Mom, the way Dad did. AJ's going to go back into counseling, and he's going to work with the Wounded Warrior Project."

"I'll do whatever I have to for Shea," he said, "for our future, our children—to keep them safe. I want to come home, Mrs.—Dru—all the way home in my head."

Dru reached out to him—she couldn't help it—touching her fingertips to his cheek, letting them rest there briefly before taking her hand away and clearing her throat. "Rob wants me to go with him to couples' counseling."

"Will you?" Shea asked.

"Yes." It was only in the moment that Dru made up her mind, and she knew it was because of AJ, his honesty and his courage in the face of his vulnerability, that had decided her. She had no idea where counseling would lead her and Rob as a couple, but she knew Rob, like AJ, deserved her support, her participation—her faith.

A nurse came in, and they were quiet while she checked AJ's vitals.

After she left, Dru said, "Ken was by the house earlier. He said Erik has made a full confession. He's tried to waive his right to an attorney, too."

"He left a suicide note in the sack with his bloody clothes," Shea said. "Did Ken tell you that?"

Dru said he had. But she'd already heard about it. She didn't know how the contents of the letter had come to light—there had been little local media coverage of the story—but it had sent shock waves through Wyatt. It wasn't so much that Jeb Axel and Winona Ayala had been involved with each other for years. Most folks had figured that was the case. Some had even speculated that Erik was Jeb's son. It was what Erik had done, the pure evil of his crimes that had people reeling. They couldn't believe the boy who'd grown up near their town, who'd gone to Wyatt schools, the young man with the easy laugh who'd always been ready to help—the one who'd run the streets with their kids, for God's sake—had murdered two of their own sweet girls.

How had it happened? What clues had they missed? Even Dru wondered. She thought of meeting Erik at the feed store when she'd needed advice on caring for donkeys. He'd been so congenial and patient with Kate and Shea and their giggling adoration of him. Like everyone else, she questioned herself, how easily she'd bought into Erik's charm, been fooled by his good looks, his friendly demeanor. But as Lily had said when Dru ran into her outside in the hospital parking lot earlier, who could say what a murderer looked like?

Lily had said, too, that if anyone should have known about Erik, it was her. She'd been part of his life from the day he was born. Dru had advised Lily not to blame herself; she'd said how sorry she was for her misjudgment of AJ. Inexplicably, Lily had waved off Dru's apology, and while Lily's dismissal was a relief, Dru felt perplexed. How could Lily be so forgiving of her?

"I hope you can forgive me," she said now to AJ. The press of tears and the opposing and sudden lift of her heart surprised her.

"Of course," he said. "I hope one day you'll be able to trust me."

Dru found a tissue and wiped her eyes. "It could happen." She smiled. "Maybe sooner than you think."

Shea came to Dru's side and embraced her. "Thanks, Mom," she whispered.

. . .

Dru pushed her grocery cart up and down the aisles. She was out of almost everything. The last time she had shopped, she realized, was two weeks ago, on Tuesday, the day before Becca was found dead in AJ's apartment. Her mind did that now. It split life into before and after, and while she found it comforting, this return to her ordinary routine, it also felt strange. When she thought of Joy and Charla and how their lives would never be the same, it made her heart ache. Dru was thinking of Winona Ayala, too—that her life had also been altered irrevocably by her son's actions. Then, when turning the corner toward the deli counter, she caught sight of Win. She was behind a table, one of several food-sampling stations that were set up throughout the store. Win was giving out bite-size slices of tamales, speared on frilled wooden picks.

"You made these? I can buy them here?" a shopper, a man Dru didn't recognize, asked.

"Yes," Win said. She took a package from the cooler, offering it to him.

He took them. "Best damn tamales I ever ate," he said.

Dru would always think later that it was hearing the man's emphatic praise of Win's tamales that set the plan she didn't know she had into motion. As Dru approached Win, their eyes caught. Dru could see Win was startled; she shifted her glance toward a door behind the deli counter as if she might be pondering her escape.

"It's okay," Dru said, and it seemed laughable. It was doubtful that much in Winona's life right now was okay, but Dru wanted to reassure her.

"You would like to try a sample?" Winona asked.

"I'd love to." Dru helped herself and pronounced it delicious. "You're selling your tamales through the store?"

"I just started. I am going to sell other things, too. Barbacoa, garnachas. I make the food fresh every morning. Most of it is Oaxacan, specialties I learned to make from *mi abuela*, my grandmother."

"But you best get here before noon if you want to take any of it home." A man—Dru recognized the store manager—spoke in passing.

"He tasted many samples before hiring me." Winona's smile didn't quite lighten the shadow of grief in her eyes. Dru wanted to address it, the source of Winona's sadness. She wanted to help Winona, to reach out to her. "Is it possible for you to take a break?" she asked. "We could have coffee, my treat."

It surprised Dru, both her offer and that Win accepted it.

She needed a friend, she told Dru a bit later. They were sitting in Dru's car with their coffee. Win had suggested it. People were generally kind, but they stared, she said. They talked behind her back. It was difficult, being at the store, but she had to work. Win told Dru she was living in town now in Erik's old apartment.

"It is hard being there, but I have nowhere else. I can't be at the ranch with Jeb. Not anymore."

Dru didn't press her. "There's a small cottage on my property," she said instead. "You could live there. You could come to work with me. I've been thinking about expanding my catering business, and I'd love to be able to offer your wonderful Oaxacan cuisine to my clients."

Winona stared at Dru. "You are serious?"

"I am," Dru said, and she realized she'd never been more serious. She felt a thrill of excitement. They sat talking for a long time, making a plan, working out the details.

"I can't believe you are doing this for me," Win said. "I didn't know how I would get by." She looked down into her foam cup, empty now. "It's not only the money that I need."

No, Dru thought. It was hard to think of all that Win was facing, the terrible events that lay in her future. The Dallas prosecutor assigned to Erik's case was calling for the death penalty. According to news reports, Erik had refused Jeb Axel's offer to cover his legal expenses, and he had only accepted the help of a court-appointed attorney under duress. That lawyer, who was from Greeley, the Madrone County seat, was citing mental defect as a defense. As a mother, Dru couldn't begin to fathom how all of it would feel. Reaching out, she put her hand on Win's arm.

"I love Erik," she said softly. "He's my son, and I will always love him, but I don't know if I can forgive him." She glanced at Dru and quickly away. "I hope to. It's all I pray for. That and peace. Peace for Becca's and Kate's parents. Peace for us all."

Dru looked through the windshield. It was a good prayer, she thought. Possibly the only prayer.

• • •

Later that afternoon, Shea was at the xL with AJ, and Dru and Amy were unloading Dru's SUV, ferrying the tableware for Shea's wedding reception on Saturday into the house when a car pulled up alongside the curb. Amy was at the foot of the porch steps and saw it first. "It's Charla and Joy," she said.

"Is Gene with them?" Dru turned to look.

"No. After what he did? He wouldn't have the nerve."

Dru had known, given Wyatt's small size, that seeing them was inevitable, but she'd never imagined they would seek her out.

"Should I stay?" Amy asked.

"Yes, please. Otherwise things might get out of hand."

Dru and Shea had attended the separate funeral services last week for Becca and Kate, but they had gone late, slipped into a back pew, and left early. Even though Charla and Joy—the whole town, in fact—had known by then that AJ was completely innocent, Dru had wanted to avoid an encounter. She didn't trust herself, or her temper. While she grieved for both mothers, it rankled, the way she and Shea had been treated at Charla's house, even though in view of her own recently vanquished suspicions of AJ, she could understand it.

What she didn't understand and couldn't so far forgive was how the same feeling of suspicion had driven Joy's husband, Gene, to get behind the wheel of his pickup truck and attempt to run her and Shea off the road. In essence, he'd tried to kill them. He could have very easily. It had been such a shock last week when he'd come forward and confessed to Captain Mackie that he was responsible. He'd cited his grief over the loss of his daughter and claimed he had little recollection of the incident. He'd said he'd been driven to the edge of insanity, that he'd needed someone to blame. He'd wanted Dru and Shea to pay, however irrational his choice of a target seemed. Captain Mackie had told Dru that Gene had cried. Dru hadn't heard from Gene. Like Amy said, he hadn't had the guts to face Dru or Shea.

But Joy and Charla were here, standing at the foot of the porch steps, looking up at Dru. Two women, bonded by mutual grief. Dru's heart ached for them. Who was she to judge them? She hadn't walked in their shoes. Her fervent prayer was that she never would. Hadn't she thanked God a thousand times for sparing Shea? Hadn't she counted herself lucky?

"Would you like to come and sit?" she asked, and she felt Amy's startled glance.

Charla thanked her. "I only wanted to say I'm sorry in person for how I spoke to you and Shea. The evidence just seemed to suggest—"

"Gene and I are sorry, too." Joy interrupted Charla, as if she was anxious to get her part over. "He—he wanted to come, but he's—it was awful, what he did. There's no excuse. He'll—we'll pay for the damage to Shea's car."

"We haven't heard yet from the insurance company." Dru wished she were wealthy enough to tell Joy to forget it, but the truth was, repairing the car would put a financial strain on Shea and her.

"We want to pay," Joy said. "It's the least we can do."

Dru frowned, not taking Joy's meaning.

"Captain Mackie told us you refused to file a complaint against Gene. He thinks the district attorney won't pursue charges in light of the circumstances, because you've said you won't testify if Gene goes on trial." Joy glanced away, blinking.

Charla drew her into a one-armed embrace.

Dru's throat constricted. She sensed Amy was struggling for her composure, too.

"I pushed Kate on Erik," Charla said, and although she looked startled for having spoken, she went on. "I told her she would never find a better man, a kinder, more handsome man."

"We were all fooled." Joy broke out of Charla's grasp. "I knew there was something not right when Becca went to Dallas. She wanted to believe AJ cared for her, but it was so plain that Shea was—I let Becca go anyway. I didn't lift a finger to stop her, and even if it was the wrong man, Erik, and not AJ, who hurt her, I knew nothing good would come of it."

Dru said, "You can't blame yourselves," and when she went down the stairs to them, it was because she was shaken by their anguish. The three fumbled their arms around one another, mothers comforting mothers. Amy came, too. It was an unlikely embrace, but what else could you do in a storm but cling to one another?

The bond was broken as quickly as it was forged.

Joy said, "You know who he is—Erik."

Dru knew what was coming, and her jaw tightened.

"He's Jeb Axel's son by that Mexican woman who works for him."

"Do you know Winona Ayala?" Dru asked. "Personally, I mean?"

"No," Joy said. "But what kind of woman—"

"They're both single and over twenty-one, right?" Dru smiled.

"It's their business, isn't it?" Amy suggested.

Dru said, "What Erik did, as horrible and unforgivable as it is, his mother isn't to blame. She's struggling, too."

"I don't think I'll ever be able to forgive him," Charla said softly.

"I hope he gets the death penalty," Joy said.

"I heard he's under a suicide watch," Amy murmured.

Dru looked off, her eyes following the progress of a neighbor, a youngish man she saw regularly in the late afternoons, running along the road's shoulder. She could hear the thud of his footfalls in the soft dirt. She thought of Winona's prayer for peace, and it comforted her.

25

It was the Friday afternoon of the rehearsal dinner. They should have been getting ready for it, flinging cloths over the tables they'd set up in the pasture, stacking dishes and cutlery into the cart that would have been hitched to the four-wheeler, making the job of going to and from the ranch house easier. The air would have been redolent with the aroma of roast pork. The weather was perfect. There was a delicious breeze now as the sun was setting. It would have guttered the candlelight, carried the sound of laughter, the buzz of conversation. The scent of perfume. Music. Lily would likely have been upstairs about now, dressing in the emerald-green suede western skirt and boots to match that she'd planned to wear.

Instead, she was sitting on the front porch swing, across from AJ and Shea, who were in the rocking chairs near the front door. She and Shea had made lasagna, and it was baking in the oven. Her dad was napping. Something he did a lot of now. Maybe it was from actual need, but it might also be out of a wish to avoid dealing with his part in the mess that had been made. In Lily's mind, emotional illness was no different from physical illness. It required rest to recover.

AJ had only wakened and joined Shea and her a bit ago. They had changed his dressing earlier, and they'd both remarked how much better the wound looked. It was no longer as red and swollen as it had been. His ankle, too, while it was still discolored and sore, looked much better now.

"You may actually be able to stand long enough to marry your bride tomorrow," Lily said, teasing him.

He grinned. "I think I already said this—if I have to crawl."

"You did." Shea took his hand. "I hope we get another nice day."

While they weren't holding a rehearsal, they had decided to go ahead with the wedding. In all the chaos, nothing more had been done about canceling it. There hadn't been time to think about it, or the will to deal with how. The social protocol . . . who knew what it was in a situation like this? They would gather in Dru's garden at the hour appointed on the invitations and let matters take their course. Right or wrong, that was the decision they'd made.

What Shea and AJ wanted.

The breeze sharpened, lifting Lily's hair, slipping cool fingers beneath her collar. It ruffled the lawn that, since the rain last Thursday, was thickly patched with a wave of late-blooming bluebonnets, a sprinkling of Indian paintbrushes. Later there would be monarda, fire wheels, milkweed, and Blackfoot daisies, mixed with the grass. When Lily was small, five or six years old, she had helped her mother seed the lawn, making it into a meadow of native wildflowers. They had stood on the porch one day when the seed had begun to sprout, and her mama had held Lily's hand. "They'll come back every year," she'd said, "like hope."

Lily looked over at AJ. "I have something to tell you. It's—it's upsetting, and I've been waiting for the right time. I wanted to be sure you were okay."

AJ's gaze on Lily's was intent and gave her the odd sense that he knew, or at least suspected what she was going to say, but when she said it, "Your dad and I are getting a divorce," he looked blank.

"Should I leave?" Shea asked.

"Absolutely not," Lily said. "You're a member of the family, or you will be."

"I'm not that surprised." Now that he'd grasped her meaning, AJ seemed reconciled. "I've never thought you and Dad were very happy together."

"Really?" Lily was dismayed. She hadn't realized he'd noticed. "He's found someone else," she said, and then she looked away, because somehow it shamed her, although why she should be ashamed when it was Paul who'd been unfaithful, she didn't know.

"Who?" AJ asked.

"Jerry Dix's wife—or ex-wife, I should say—Pilar."

"Are you kidding me? Isn't she, like, thirty? Didn't she just have a kid?"

"Twins. She has three-year-old twins."

AJ snorted. "Dad doesn't even like kids."

Lily toed the porch floor again, setting the swing in motion.

"Are they getting married?"

"You'll have to ask him."

"I never felt that close to him." AJ found her gaze. "To either of you, really. It was always, like, every man for himself in our family."

For a moment, Lily felt only the sting of regret, but as it dawned on her, the depth of AJ's isolation growing up, she became furious. This was Paul's fault. He was the one who had caused their son to feel abandoned when, in the days following AJ's near-drowning, he had taken the care of her baby out of her hands.

But she had let him.

God forgive her, she had let go of her own child, let the string of nannies Paul had hired stand in for her. How could she have done that? It sickened her now to think she had been so easily convinced of her own ineptitude as a mother. Before she could reconsider, she went to AJ, and, kneeling before him, she took his hands in hers. "I know how

273

you feel, and I know why, and I have no excuse. There's nothing I can say to change it, but if you can forgive me, I'd like a chance to start over. I'd like for us to know each other, if it's not too late."

He looked away.

She couldn't see his expression. She sensed disdain, perhaps, or disgust. Certainly he would have doubts. Maybe he suspected her of attempting to manipulate his emotions, the very thing she was trying so hard to avoid. Of course it was too late. He was a grown man, not a child. She couldn't woo him with promises, cajole him with treats. She started to rise but sank back to her knees when she saw that his eyes were glazed with tears. Reaching up, tentative, gentle, she thumbed them away, unsure of what to say, how to begin. "There are things I should—that I have wanted to tell you—" She paused, thinking, No. This wasn't the right time to talk of the past—Jesse, and the ordeal at Monarch Lake—and all that those events had cost her and, ultimately, AJ as well. "I love you so much," she said instead. "From the day I knew you were conceived . . ." Her throat narrowed, closing off further speech.

He slumped toward her, balancing his forehead on her shoulder. His breath warmed the hollow beneath her chin, and when he spoke to her, when he said, "Mom?" his voice was low and broken.

She closed her eyes. "I'm right here, honey."

"I really need your help," he said. "There's a lot of stuff I have to work through, not just what happened with Erik, but you know, when I was overseas, Afghanistan—going through all of that—it kind of screwed me up."

"Oh, AJ." For a moment, her grief for him, for his pain, was so overwhelming; it was all she could say. She fumbled her arms around him. "I'm here, right here," she repeated, and she held him as best she could. He was so much bigger than the last time she'd embraced him. It was clumsy, and she was struggling, too, with the weight of her sorrow and her regret. But inexplicably now, joy came in a rush that opened her heart, and somehow it was as if the years of misunderstanding—all those years she'd kept herself apart from AJ—were falling away.

A light settling of fingertips on her shoulder caused her to look up, and she saw that Shea was touching AJ's shoulder, too, a benediction, a blessing. They smiled at each other, blinking through their tears, and Lily loved Shea instantly and without reservation in that moment.

AJ lifted his head, wiping his eyes, under his nose. He looked around at them. "What a bunch of saps," he said.

"A family of saps," Shea said, and they laughed.

• • •

It was after midnight when Lily, seeing a light on, went downstairs and found her dad sitting at the old marble-topped island. She slid onto the stool next to him.

"You can't sleep, either?"

She shook her head. "If it's all right with you, I'd like to stay on here until I can figure out what I'm going to do with myself."

"You don't need permission, Sissy."

"Dad?" Lily set her elbows on the island.

"Hmm?"

"I've been wondering—do you think I'm too old to go back to school? Veterinary school?"

He looked sidelong at her. "AJ and Shea are going to need somebody to doctor their livestock when they get their business running."

"I hadn't thought of that."

"Hasn't been a good large-animal vet in the area since old Doc Forsythe died."

"Oh, Dad."

He patted her hand. "Maybe we'll both end up working for AJ."

Lily laughed.

Her dad didn't. "I'm lucky he doesn't hate me."

Lily felt lucky in that regard, too.

"He wants to understand, wants me to explain," her dad said. "I don't know if I can. Not in a way that'll make sense."

Lily met his glance.

"I don't want it to come between us," he said.

"Then you'll have to find a way to talk to him about Winona and Erik—the same as I have to find a way to talk to him about Jesse and Phoenix."

"It's a lot to pile on the kid, especially after all the shit he's been through."

"He—we talked earlier—about Afghanistan. He kind of opened up to me." Lily looked at her dad. "I'm just so glad, you know? Not about the war. I hate it, how it's affected him, but if I can help him—if he'll only let me—" She broke off. Then, picking up after a moment, she said, "I want so badly to have a relationship with him, to have his forgiveness, his—his respect."

"Most anything worthwhile in this world takes time, Sissy."

"I told him about the divorce."

"How did he take it?"

Instead of answering, Lily spoke in a vehement rush, saying the things that were uppermost in her mind. "We need to be finished with secrets, Dad. We need to be strong enough to tell the truth and take the consequences. We need to own our mistakes. I don't want AJ's children growing up with a lot of pretty little lies that we tell them about our family because we're afraid of losing face, losing authority. We're human, fallible"—she used Edward's word—"and life is messy. Kids need to know that. They need to know we grow up; we don't grow perfect, and no matter how old we get, we never lose our need, or our capacity, for compassion and forgiveness."

"You're right," her dad said.

"I wish I'd told AJ the truth from the beginning. I wish *I'd known* the truth."

Her dad rubbed circles on her back. "I'm sorry, Sissy. I wish I'd had the guts to tell you."

She bent her forehead toward him, resting it on the ridge of his collarbone.

"You know," her dad said over her bowed head, "in spite of everything that's happened, he seems calmer and more at peace. Have you noticed?"

"It's the Shea effect," Lily said, straightening. "I love that girl. She's so good for him. So good, period. I'm even warming up to her mom."

Her dad shot her a look.

"Dru is so completely herself. She's honest about who she is—take it or leave it." Lily shifted her glance. It was how she wanted to live her life from now on, too. She didn't want to compromise herself. Not ever again. Not for anyone.

"They've transferred Erik, did you hear?" her dad said after a moment. "They'll try him in Dallas for Becca's murder first."

"Clint told me. He said Erik's on suicide watch. Win's taking it hard. He won't see her, won't see any of us." As far as Lily knew, Erik wasn't talking to anyone except the police and, possibly, his attorney. He hadn't wanted to be represented by anyone, and, in fact, before a lawyer was assigned to his case, he had made a full confession, admitting to both Kate's and Becca's murders and to the attempt to frame AJ. There was speculation that Erik had waived his right to a trial and asked for the death penalty. A court-appointed psychiatrist had certified his sanity, but Lily questioned that. Sane people didn't commit murder. The act itself must require you to become insane, if only temporarily.

"I never realized it meant that much to him—calling me Dad."

It should have, Lily thought, but what was the point of saying it now?

"I doubt Win'll forgive me," her dad said. "Not that she should, not that any of you should."

"Give it time, Dad." Lily picked up a stray napkin, running it through her fingers.

"I loved her—I still do love her. I loved your mother, too. I just—after she was gone, it felt—I don't know—somehow disloyal to remarry—"

"But it was all right, conceiving a child, I guess, one you had no intention of claiming."

"I was wrong. I'll spend whatever time I have left regretting how I handled it."

Lily folded the napkin. She would never have imagined hearing Jeb Axel say those words: *I was wrong.*

"I guess if it takes me the rest of my life to make it up to her, that's what I'll do. I'll try, anyway."

They exchanged a glance.

Lily said she would heat up some milk. "You want some? It might help you sleep." She stood up.

He caught her hand. "I'm sorry about you and Paul, Sissy. Not just the divorce." He paused, searching her eyes, perhaps searching his mind for whatever it was he wanted to say.

Lily found it hard to hold his gaze—it was so openly vulnerable, so naked in its appeal. It almost frightened her, seeing him so unmanned.

He let go of her hand, her glance. "I couldn't talk about it when your mother died. I knew you needed me to; you needed me to remember her with you, but it just hurt so much—so damn much." He looked up, blinking. "It's no excuse—"

"It's all right, Dad." Lily wasn't sure that it was, but she wanted an end to the suffering, to any further recriminations. "I caused you a lot of trouble, and I'm sorry for that."

"When all that happened—you know, in Phoenix—Paul was—he knew the right people. He knew what to do. He promised to give you a good life. I thought he would know better than me how to keep you safe."

Lily put her arms around him. "If I hadn't married Paul, we wouldn't have AJ, so how can we be sorry for it?"

"You still want to heat up some milk?" he asked, pulling free, wiping his face.

She said she did.

"I'll get the brandy," he said.

26

It wasn't ideal weather for an outdoor wedding. Fifteen minutes before the ceremony was set to begin at six o'clock, the daylong immaculate blue sky had been consumed by an imposing presence of majestic, but glowering, thunderheads. Beneath them, the light was silver, the color of tarnished coins. The tiki torches Paul and Shea's dad, Rob, had lit a while ago flickered in a capricious breeze.

"Nervous?" Lily smiled up at AJ. She and Paul, whom AJ had asked to be his best man in place of Erik, were standing with him in Dru's garden, to the right of the peaked arbor that would serve as an altar. The knotty juniper posts were buried in the lush, deep-red blooms of an old rose, and the scent perfumed the air.

"I just hope the rain holds off," AJ said. "It'll kill Shea if it rains."

"It may blow over." Paul examined AJ's shirt collar, giving it a little tug.

Thankfully, he had come without Pilar. Lily hadn't known what to expect, and asking might have given the impression that it mattered. Lily didn't want it to; she thought it mostly didn't.

"I'm surprised so many people from Dallas made the drive." Paul ran a satisfied glance over the assembling crowd. He nodded at a man and wife just taking their seats on the groom's side of the aisle and went to greet them. Lily recognized Millie and Harvey Kramer and gave them a half wave. The uncertainty of her future daunted her, but knowing that after today she might never cross paths with the Kramers and their ilk again was pure relief.

"There are Kate's parents," AJ said. "Shea and I wondered if they'd come."

Dru approached the couple and embraced them. Even from a distance, their pain was evident but also their courage, Lily thought. Kate's mother pulled tissues from her purse, one for herself, one for Dru, and they dabbed their eyes. Lily swallowed.

"I feel so bad for them, and for Becca's parents, and for Win." AJ was tight-jawed, blinking. "It seems wrong to be this happy."

Lily took his hand. "I know," she said. "I feel it, too, but—"

"No, Mom." He took his hand away, keeping her gaze. "Why didn't Erik kill me, too? Why didn't I die in Afghanistan like so many of my buddies?"

She stared at him. His sudden misery had come from nowhere seemingly, but she recognized it. She knew from researching that survivor's guilt was a natural part of the whole PTSD package. "I don't know, honey." It was hard, elbowing the words past the knot of her alarm, her concern for him—that he would feel this way today of all days—but he deserved her honesty. "I want to believe there's a purpose to everything, and if your life was spared, there's a reason, but I don't know if that's true."

He searched her gaze, and she had the sense he was hunting for meaning, an answer that would bring him a measure of peace.

She went on, haltingly. "I want to believe that given time, all wounds have the capacity to heal—if we are patient and kind to one another, if we can forgive one another and tell the truth, if we keep love in our hearts. Living in this way won't alter the past, the terrible losses, but the pain you feel, that we all feel, won't be as sharp."

He looked away at some point over her head. "Thank you," he said, bringing his gaze back to hers.

"For?"

"Not handing me platitudes, not telling me it wasn't my fault that I lived and they died. Not saying I was lucky and I should be grateful I made it."

"Well, I'm grateful you did," she said, fighting for composure.

That made him smile, and when he slipped his arm around her shoulders, her heart eased.

Paul rejoined them, and if he noticed traces of leftover emotion on Lily's face, or in the air between her and AJ, he didn't remark on it.

"Dad," AJ said, moments later, "I think it's time." He nodded toward the house, where Dru, who was filling in as Shea's matron of honor, was waiting for the best man to escort her to the altar.

Lily was scanning the crowd when she caught sight of Edward standing at the back of the seating area. He smiled when their eyes met, and she felt a wave of pleasure, even of anticipation, and then she thought she had no right to feel either one. She wondered what he was doing here, who had invited him.

AJ touched her elbow. "I asked Edward to come," he said as if he'd divined her bewilderment. "I figured the guy who made my wedding day possible ought to be present."

She looked at him, still mystified.

"If it wasn't for Edward, I'd have been sitting in a prison cell on the day I met Shea." He held her gaze. "You don't mind, do you?"

"Of course not," she answered. "It's your wedding."

"I didn't think you would." AJ's grin was teasing, as if he knew.

What? What did he know? How did he know?

Lily's face warmed. She glanced off, collecting her wits, her galloping heart. When her dad and Winona slipped into seats on AJ's side of the flower-decked aisle, she joined them. Moments later, the jazz trio that had been playing as guests arrived, stopped, and the processional music Shea and AJ had chosen began: "A Thousand Years."

Dru was delivered to the altar by Paul. Leigh and Vanessa joined her. Then Shea appeared at the head of the aisle on her father's arm, and as the lush strains of piano and cello music blended in the soft early-evening air, everyone rose. The collective murmur of their admiration was woven into the rising crescendo of the melody. Lily brought her hands together. Shea was a vision in her grandmother's wedding gown, a fitted slip topped by a lace-trimmed overdress made of the finest netting. The mermaid skirt was also trimmed in yards of delicate lace and flared from her knees. Dru had styled Shea's hair, pulling it into a French twist, and instead of a veil, she wore a comb trimmed with pale pink clematis blooms and white rosebuds, the same flowers as those she carried in her bouquet. Lily had found her mother's jewelry in the vanity drawer while tidying her dad's bathroom several days ago, and she'd given Shea one of her mother's bracelets to wear, a delicate gold chain hung with a tiny heart. It glimmered on Shea's wrist, and her eyes when they met Lily's were filled with joy.

But then her glance shifted to AJ, and they had eyes only for each other.

They had written their vows, and they repeated them now, words of love that bound them, but also freed them to be who they were— separate, yet together. After Pastor Ingalls pronounced them man and wife and gave his permission, AJ took Shea's face in his hands, and he kissed her as if she were his treasure, his gift. The two of them turned then, hands clasped, laughing out loud like children.

"Ladies and gentlemen," Pastor Ingalls called out, "may I present AJ and Shea, Mr. and Mrs. Axel Jebediah Isley."

Lily smiled even as her throat closed. It was the same for her dad and Winona. Many of the guests were similarly affected. The local folks, especially. They knew the tragic circumstances. Many of them would have known Kate and Becca personally. They would have attended their funerals, grieved with their families. The shock waves in a community as small as Wyatt would have touched everyone to some degree. But now, today, they rejoiced at this new beginning. How could they not?

• • •

Paul was right. By the time they'd finished dinner, the clouds had melted to reveal the sky's star-spangled arch. A fragile crescent moon hung in one corner. The tables, where the meal had been served, were cleared from the large platform–cum–dance floor that Shea's dad had hammered together for the occasion. A DJ set up his equipment. Dancing had always been part of the plan for the wedding, and while Shea was worried it was too much for him, AJ was determined to have the first dance with her as his wife. They'd chosen their song months ago, "Amazed," and when the opening notes sounded, he led her onto the floor. He'd traded his crutches for a cane, but passing Lily, he handed it to her. "I'm only going to get this chance once," he said.

Everyone applauded. They were moved, watching Shea and AJ, hope in motion. After a couple of minutes, the couple waved, and other guests joined them. Later in the evening, Lily danced with her dad, and with Kelvin Dermott, and once with Paul before he left to go back to Dallas. She was panicked for a moment, watching him go. She had a sudden urge to run after him and beg him to reconsider. Who was she outside her role as his wife? She'd become that person long before she could know who she might have become on her own. But something inside her was altered, and it felt immutable. She couldn't go back to the life Paul had fashioned for her. He was her past, not her future. That was up to her to find now.

"Mind if I join you?"

Her heart rose at the sound of Edward's voice. "I've been hoping for a chance to talk to you," she said.

"Oh?"

Heat flushed her cheeks at the teasing lilt in his tone. "I wanted to thank you for everything you did, looking into AJ's situation."

"It wasn't anything much, and it turned out to be a wrong turn anyway. I'm just glad you got him back."

"Yes. Thank you," she said again, and she was annoyed at herself. There was so much more she wanted to say to Edward, all of it crowding her mind, trapped in her throat.

The music seemed to swell outside the silence that contained them. Inside it, Lily was conscious of Edward's nearness, the faint scent of his aftershave, the moonlit glimmer that outlined his jaw and skimmed the muscled contours of his forearms, which were bare below the rolled sleeves of his white oxford dress shirt.

She glanced at him. "I wanted to tell you—"

"I hired a private detective," he said at the same time.

"You did?"

"Yes, but you first."

"No, you—"

"I'm going to find Charlie and try to explain, if he'll let me," Edward said. "You inspired me," he added.

"I did?" Lily doubted she had ever inspired anyone.

"Yes," he said, and they fell silent again.

They watched the dancers.

"I guess you'll be heading back to Dallas soon?" He was asking.

"No, I'm staying at the ranch for the time being, until I can figure out a more permanent home for myself."

Lily was relieved when Edward nodded and left it at that. Her decision was so fresh, unexplored in any depth even by herself. His questions would only disconcert her.

A new song began playing, one of her favorites, an old Garth Brooks standard, "The Dance." The lyrics stood out—something about life being better left to chance. She felt the warmth of Edward's gaze.

"I don't guess you'd care to dance?" She turned to him. "I have to warn you, it's a risk." He smiled at her. "I'm not very good at it."

"Well." She smiled, too. "Someone once told me life is a gamble."

"Oh?" He slid his hand under her elbow. "Do you believe them?"

Rather than answer, she looked across the makeshift dance floor at AJ holding Shea in his arms. There was no trace of his earlier apprehension, although Lily knew in all likelihood it would return. But at least they had reestablished a connection. However tenuous and fragile, they had a chance at a new beginning. She would be there for him, help him in whatever way she could. Lily was thinking of this, of the gift she'd been given, when it struck her—the horrible irony—that the very tragedy that had devastated three other families had in its way restored hers, although not as it had been. It hadn't occurred to her before, and now when it did, she felt her knees weaken slightly, enough that Edward tightened his grasp on her arm.

"Easy," he said. "Are you all right?"

She held his gaze. If she told him what had disturbed her, that she, like AJ, wondered why she had been spared the heartbreak of the other families, she suspected Edward would say she couldn't change what had happened. She couldn't give back what the other families had lost. Somehow she knew Edward would tell her all she could do was move forward. She had no real idea of how AJ would react when he learned of her past and that she had kept it secret from him the way her dad had kept Erik's true relationship to them a secret. She couldn't know either what lay ahead for her family, whether AJ would ever truly recover, or how they would manage if her dad was losing his mind. She didn't want to know, she thought. The song lyrics were right. The future was better left to chance. She looked again at AJ and Shea, and AJ, catching her at it, grinned, whirling his bride. Shea's skirt swooped, and she laughed and waved, and Lily's happiness in their joy rose, seemingly from the ground, a warm bolus of love that swelled against her ribs.

Edward said her name, prompting her, and smiling up at him, Lily slipped her hand into his. "I think we should dance," she said.

AUTHOR'S NOTE

I f you're curious about the car accident and ensuing legal fallout that shattered the town of Wyatt that Ken and Dru refer to in *The Truth We Bury*, check out *Faultlines* (Lake Union, 2016) to learn the whole story.

ACKNOWLEDGMENTS

While there is only one person named as the author of this novel, it would never have been written without the help of so many others. I owe thanks always to Barbara Poelle, because without her none of the rest of this magical journey would have ever happened. I am indebted to my editor, Kelli Martin. This is the second book we've worked on together, and both experiences have been a true collaboration of the heart. I worked with a developmental editor, Melody Guy, for the first time for this book, and am so grateful for her astute guidance and care in the shaping of this story.

A huge bouquet of gratitude to my copy editor, Sara Brady, and to my proofreaders, Jill Kramer and Elise Marton, for the fantastic job you both did in refining all the details: voice, clarity, consistency, and all the rest. Copy editing and proofreading aren't just spelling and grammar, folks! There's so much more to what Sara and Jill do! And a boatload of thanks to my cover designer, Rex Bonomelli, for his fantastic art that so completely captures in a single image the heart and spirit of this story.

Thank you to the rest of my amazing Amazon/Lake Union team, naming just a few: Dennelle, Danielle, Gabby, Michael, and Gabe. It's all of them and the countless others who work behind the scenes that give books their wings.

I want to thank Spanish-language teacher Robert Wedding, of Paschal High School in the Fort Worth ISD, for his help in the translation and usage of the Spanish terminology. Any inaccuracies in that regard are my own. I never would have met Robert without my sister's help. Thank you to Susan Harper for putting us in touch, and for a lifetime of book sharing and sister talk.

Recently, reading a Facebook post, I was brought to tears by the beautiful words of my friend, teacher, and mentor, Guida Jackson, in which she paid tribute to my writing journey. The thing is, I might never have persevered without her influence, her encouragement, and her faith. She is a brighter light on my path than she knows.

Thank you to David, as ever, for endlessly, patiently, listening to me think plots out loud, and for making me laugh. His comments are just enlightening, the very spark I need. This time, I don't think I would have found the beating heart of this book without his help. Thank you to Heather Wilson for her tireless support and encouragement, and in the case of this particular novel, her help with music choices. Garth Brooks's "The Dance" kind of says it all for this story.

And yet again, a huge and heartfelt shout-out to my readers. So many of you have been with me since the first book, or you read one and went back and picked up all the rest. You've left reviews; you've sent me notes, and there just aren't words to say how much your support over the long haul has meant and continues to mean to me. Sending love, joy, and gratitude to all of you, and to readers around the world. Thank you!

BOOK CLUB QUESTIONS

1. *The Truth We Bury* is told in alternate chapters through two points of view: a mother of the bride and a mother of the groom. Almost immediately readers learn there is friction between these two moms regarding the upcoming marriage. Neither of them believes the other one's child is a suitable mate. Do you think parents should question their son's or daughter's choice of a life partner, or should they keep their thoughts to themselves? What if they feel marriage to the prospective bride or groom will be damaging or somehow endanger the life of their daughter or son? What would you do if one or both of your parents disapproved of your choice of a life mate?

2. When Lily Isley is confronted by detectives at her home, she suspects they are there on some matter regarding her son, AJ, and determines initially not to tell them anything. Is she right in her decision to refuse to cooperate with police? If you were confronted in the same way, would you inform on a family member who was suspected of being involved in a crime? Would your decision, whether or not to cooperate, be based on the seriousness of the crime? On other extenuating circumstances? Would you harbor

a relative who was wanted for murder if you believed they were innocent? Would you assist them in an escape?

3. Lily holds on to her faith in AJ despite the evidence that appears to give overwhelming proof that her son is a murderer. In the face of such evidence against someone you love and feel you know, would you be able to keep your faith in them?

4. Lily and her husband disagree on almost every aspect of how best to help their son. It's as if the crisis exacerbates their unhappiness as a couple, driving a further wedge between them. Would you agree that a catastrophe of this proportion might bring out the worst as well as the best in a marriage? Do you feel such crises draw families closer together as a rule, or do these situations drive them farther apart?

5. What would you do if you felt very strongly that a certain action must be taken to protect your grown son or daughter, and your spouse disagreed?

6. What is your feeling about secret-keeping in families? Do you think the truth should come out regardless of the consequences, or in certain situations would you be willing to keep a secret, because the result, if you don't, might shatter the family?

7. Dru's marriage and her trust in people were destroyed as the result of an armed robbery and assault on her husband when he exhibited signs of PTSD that led him to threaten her. If you found yourself in a similar situation with a loved one, would you leave, or stay and try to work it out?

8. Dru, Jeb, and AJ are each gun owners for different reasons. What are your feelings about gun ownership? Before her husband's assault, Dru had never thought of buying a gun, much less learning to shoot it. Do you think her decision to do so was the right one, given the circumstances that led her to become a gun owner? What are your feelings about keeping weapons in the home?

9. AJ returns from Afghanistan, and while he was recognized as a hero after saving a fellow soldier, he is also diagnosed with PTSD. He's prone to nightmares and emotionally volatile. Do you feel the United States and the US military do enough to help treat our combat veterans who suffer from psychological trauma?

10. If someone you loved planned to become partners for life with an individual who had been diagnosed with PTSD, one who exhibited symptoms of violence, aggressive behavior, and depression, how would you feel about it? Would you do as Dru does and attempt to talk your loved one out of making such a commitment?

11. Some say when we marry, we're actually marrying our spouse's family, too. Do you think it's relevant to consider the family in the choice of a spouse, and how well you get along with the other family members—that is, whether you share common ground? Has friction with a spouse's family been an issue in your marriage or in the marriage of someone you know? If so, how was it handled?

12. Dru thought by leaving Houston and moving to Wyatt, she was leaving crime behind, but as Ken Carter reminds her, the current murder investigation is the second of two calamities to befall the town in a short span of time. What are your feelings regarding the relative safety of a small town or rural setting? Are these areas necessarily safer in your opinion?

ABOUT THE AUTHOR

Photo © 2013 Shannon Stroubakis

Barbara Taylor Sissel writes issue-driven women's fiction threaded with elements of suspense, which particularly explores how families respond to the tragedy of crime. She is the author of seven previous novels: *The Last Innocent Hour*, *The Ninth Step*, *The Volunteer*, *Evidence of Life*, *Safekeeping*, *Crooked Little Lies*, and *Faultlines*.

Born in Honolulu, Hawaii, Barbara was raised in various locations across the Midwest and once lived on the grounds of a first-offender prison facility, where she interacted with the inmates, their families, and the people who worked with them. The experience made a profound impression on her and provided her with a unique insight into the circumstances of the crimes that were committed and the often-surprising ways the justice system moved to deal with them.

An avid gardener, Barbara has two sons and lives on a farm in the Texas Hill Country outside Austin. You can find her online at www.barbarataylorsissel.com.